THEY DID NOT FAIL

Richard L. Cartwright

*Patricia Rogers
With appreciations*

THEY DID NOT FAIL

by

Richard L. Cartwright

Richard L. Cartwright Mar. 03

NEW MILLENNIUM
292 Kennington Road, London SE11 4LD

Copyright © 1997 R. L. Cartwright

All rights reserved. No part of this publication may be reproduced in any form, except for the purposes of review, without prior written permission from the copyright owner.

British Library Cataloguing in Publication Data.
A catalogue record for this book is available from the British Library.

Printed by Roadkings Ltd. Ruskin Road, Southall, Middx.
Issued by New Millennium*
ISBN 1 85845 174 4
*An imprint of The Professional Authors' & Publishers' Association

Acknowledgements

When writing these memoirs there were times when I became a little disappointed with my progress. It was then, that my friends and relatives came to my rescue in the form of encouragement. Such was most valuable, and I am most grateful to them all. Old comrades who served with me in Signals Intelligence during those war years, especially those from 118. S. W. Section who in recent years have shown great interest in my story. It would be almost impossible to single out individuals from these groups, as the list would take many pages.

In the early stages of my work I received good and professional advice from Nigel West. Likewise, from the start, I learnt much from Hugh Skillen. When on the subject of Intelligence, and Signals Intelligence in particular, it is always those two names that first come to my mind. I am grateful to them.

The name of Geoff. Ballard is, perhaps, better known in Australia, than in the UK. He is the author of *On Ultra Active Service*. It is the story, in great detail, of Australia's Signal Intelligence in the Far East War. Geoff. writes to me and is always pleading with me to push on, and have *They Did Not Fail* published. Thank you Geoff. Here it is.

The BBC have kindly given me permission to quote John Snagge's historic announcement that 'D' Day had arrived. The *Daily Telegraph* have also kindly given me permission to use their brief report on Spike Island.

The publication of this narrative might not have materialised without the help of New Millennium Publishers. My thanks.

To those who I have inadvertently omitted, I offer my sincere apologies.

R. L. C.

To: All Members, both present and past, of the Royal
Corps of Signals, and especially those
of the 'Y' Service.

List of Photographs

1 & 2. Inside the fort, Spike Island – 1966: One time Admin. Block and Messes and Our old Accommodation Block. Now derelict. Page 36.
3. Not taken on the Moon but on N. W. Frontier. Page 42.
4. Rocky and volcanic terrain of N. W. Frontier. Page 54.
5. On the march N. W. Frontier – early '30s – near Bazmak. Page 70.
6 & 7. N. W. Frontier, near Damdil and N. W. Frontier, British troops on the march. Page 86.
8 & 9. ENIGMA E Machine and Intercept truck interior. Page 116
10. The 118 S. W. Section. Page 148.
11 & 12. Some of the operators (all ex 118 S. W. Section) and Sgt. Vickery, author and Sgt. Pake. Page 149.
13. Enigma reunion Bedford, September 1997. Page 150.

Medals of R. L. Cartwright
(back cover)

From left to right: 1. Indian General Service Medal with clasps: North West Frontier 1936-37 and 1937-39. 2. 1939-45 Star. 3. France-Germany Star. 4. Defence Medal. 5. 1939-45 War Medal. 6. General Service Medal with clasps: Palestine 1945-48, Malaya. 7. Queen Elizabeth II Coronation Medal. 8. Regular Army Long Service and Good Conduct Medal.

Foreword

There have been few personal accounts of the 'Y' Service as such apart from Aileen Clayton's *The Enemy is Listening* which gave the WAAF oversight of RAF 'Y'. It was incomplete in that it did not cover the war in the West from Normandy onwards, and the author died before she was able to fill the gap.

It gave me great pleasure to record the memoirs of individual members of the Royal Corps of Signals in *Spies of the Airwaves* and *Knowledge Strengthens the Arm* and I have taken every opportunity to extol the skills of the ATS who were members of both sides of the 'Y' Service, Signals and Intelligence, as they had been entirely neglected by chronicles.

The biennial reunions at Bedford give further opportunities for old comrades to inform the public, and their own colleagues of other facets of the 'Y' Service quite unknown to most of us, and Richard Cartwright was one of those who shared with us his knowledge of the wartime 'Y' Service on more than one occasion.

In his book *They Did Not Fail* he expresses his continual admiration and love for the closed society that was the 'Y' Service. He is the only one who can look back over twenty-four years, in peace and in war, and bring to life many outstanding individuals who were officers of all grades, and non-commissioned officers whose combined efforts resulted in victory for the Allies and spared our nation from the horrific consequences of defeat at the hands of the Germans, Italians and Japanese.

Sadly many of our comrades did not live to rejoice in the ultimate victory, and many more did not survive long enough to see the curtain of censorship lifted on their brilliant successes. Nevertheless, there are still thousands of our wartime comrades alive in Britain and across the Commonwealth who will be able to enjoy Richard Cartwright's reminiscences.

H. Skillen Major (Rtd.)

Introduction

This is the product of a retirement occupation – writing.

It is true and accurate in as far as my memory permits. Some of the place names, and personal ones may not be spelt accurately. Did Stevenson spell his name that way, or was it with a 'ph'? I cannot remember. There are gaps in the story. Some of the routine matters are forgettable, and others would be of little interest to Mr. or Mrs. Average. Unless related to the story, I have excluded details of my personal and private life. A few, and only a few, of the gaps are for reasons of security.

At no time in my life have I kept a diary, and no research has been done.

Mostly, as a result of the war, much Army slang and terminology is known and accepted in civilian life, so explanations are few and far between.

In the early chapters there is little mention of names, and personalities. That is only because they are now hidden under the dust of ages. As the narrative progresses, so they more readily emerge.

During the Summer of 1982, I received a request from the military historian Ronald Lewin CBE; to put down on paper my recollections, and notes of my time in the 'Y' Service. He had been approached by the Oxford University Press to write a history of 'Y', and the purpose of the notes was to assist him in the early stages of his research. I met his request. Shortly after, Mr. Lewin became seriously ill and, sadly, he died. His history was never written.

In more recent years, I offered the Royal Signals Historical Research Officer a copy of the same notes to use as freely as he wished in connection with the recent Corps history 'The Vital Link' (Leo Cooper) by Philip Warner, which was then in its early days of research. Following that, I later made the same offer to Hugh Skillen in his self-published book *Spies in the Airwaves*. Both writers made extracts and use of the notes. Meanwhile, I had commenced work on this my military autobiography. Here, that material has been absorbed, adapted and attuned to take its rightful place in my story.

Those who have read either, or both, of the histories mentioned may find that some of the sentences, and paragraphs which appear in the following pages strike a familiar note. The reason being that they have been extracted from those original 1982 notes, and those two gentlemen completed their work before I completed mine.

There are many who will have no difficulty in associating themselves with the period, and the events of the time. The younger generation, with their spirit of adventure, will, I hope, share some of mine.

This is not aimed at any particular readership. With the years somebody may, in the fullness of time, regard it as an old story of former times, with a tiny historical interest. That will do.

London
January 1990   Richard L. Cartwright

Everyman's work, whether it be literature or music or pictures or architecture or anything else, is always a portrait of himself

Samuel Butler. "Way of All Flesh" Ch.14

Chapter 1

When questioned about my enlistment, the most frequent questions are: "What made you join up?" or "Why did you join the Army?". Only in recent years has the stigma reflected in those questions begun to fade. In the early thirties it was assumed by many that a young man usually joined the Army (note, not the Royal Navy or RAF) for one, or more of three basic reasons:

a) He was running away from the men with 'Big Feet'.
b) He had got a good girl into trouble.
c) He was the black sheep of a good family.

Some views went even further. All impressions of that nature were placed in the pending tray between the years 1939 – 45. Thereafter, some again saw the light of day, but with diminished ferocity. My reasons were not to be found in any of those I have mentioned. They were very personal, and mostly of a domestic and family nature. Only to some extent was I running away from anything, but rather towards something. Fifty three years later, only a handful of friends are alive who know the background to my early teens. I wish it to remain so.

It was very early in 1933 that I realised the time had come to make a firm decision on my career and future life. No pressure was put on me. As a boy, I often yearned 'To go to sea'. The Royal Navy was obviously a possibility. Without academic qualifications, the question of applying for a commission in any of the Services had to be ruled out. At that time there was a long waiting list of young men wishing to enlist in the Navy as seamen. As I had an uncle who was a commissioned officer in the Navy there was the risk of finding myself in an embarrassing position. He in the Ward Room, and I in the lower deck. An impossible situation for both of us. With that at the back of my mind, I ruled out the Navy. So it was, my mind turned towards the Army.

Recruiting literature was valuable, and answered many of my queries. It appeared that all I had to do was choose a Corps or Regiment, sign a form, and I would be 'In'. Alas, a minor obstacle arose.

On, or about, the 5th April 1933, I entered Banbury recruiting office. An interview followed then the Recruiting Sergeant made it quite clear to me that to enlist in the Army I had to be eighteen. It was possible for boys to join on reaching 14½; but only with parental consent. At sixteen, I was too young for the former, and too old for the latter. It appeared that things could be 'arranged' for me to join the Royal Artillery as a boy trumpeter. Emphatically, I said that I was not interested in blowing trumpets for the RA. I would enlist in the Royal Signals, or Royal Engineers and nothing else. The Sergeant's comments were that not only was I too young, but there were no vacancies in either Corps. I was determined, but becoming despondent. Then I noticed a change in his attitude. In a fatherly manner he said, "Look sonny, tomorrow go to Oxford Recruiting Office. Do not tell them that you have been here. They will then tell you much as I have done. Do not admit that you are 16! Say you are 18! Even if they do not believe you, stand your ground. I am sure you will get what you want". I thanked the Sergeant, and took his advice.

At Oxford, two issues dominated all else. Firstly, as expected, that of age. In appearance, I was a very young sixteen. To convince anyone that I was a day older was a difficult task. After a lengthy argument, and justifiably been called a liar, we both agreed that perhaps I would just be 18! Then came the matter of which Corps or Regiment was I to join. This Recruiting Sergeant was no push-over. Though considerably older than myself, he was no less obstinate, and was determined that I join his own local Regiment, which was the Ox. and Bucks. Light Infantry. I did not share his views, and informed him so. My comments were softened by adding that I thought he must be a very proud man to belong to such a fine and distinguished Regiment, but I would be no less proud to belong to the Royal Corps of Signals. A stormy discussion ensued. Finally, I decided to call his bluff my making for the door saying that I wished to join the Royal Signals. That, or nothing! It worked.

The following day – 10th April – I returned to the Recruiting Office for a simple basic educational test, and a very thorough medical examination. Next, I signed my attestation paper swearing my loyalty to the King (then George V.), his heirs and successors. I was handed two days pay of 4/- plus two days ration allowance of 1/6, and a Rail Warrant made out to Richmond, Yorkshire. There, I would be met by an NCO who would convey me by truck to the Royal Signals Depot, Baghdad Lines, Catterick Camp.

Deep in the vaults of my memory, I recall my feelings. They were somewhat mixed. Decisions and actions had to be bold and decisive, but at sixteen I lacked experience. Guidance, advice and help were totally absent. I was lonely – very lonely. There was always the possibility that I was making a mistake. Yet, I was optimistic and confident. The pre-war Army, in the eyes of many people, had a reputation second only to the Foreign Legion for its harsh discipline. That caused me no concern. My entire life, to that date, had been one of harsh discipline and unhappiness. The Army could be no worse.

On arriving at Catterick I was taken to the recruits barrack room, and placed under the care of a Senior Signalman. He wore at least three good conduct stripes and had served many years in the Corps. It was said that he remained a Signalman at his own request. That could be fact, it could be legend. Certainly, he was a fatherly figure to us youngsters. Already settled in the barrack room were three or four earlier arrivals. Together we were shown the Mess Hall and given a meal. It was plain but substantial. Outwardly, we were all still civilians as we wore the clothes we had on arrival. Inwardly, we all felt a little apprehensive. We soon got chatting, mostly about our new environment, and our immediate future; wondering what it held.

Henceforth, my identity would be 2323175 Recruit Cartwright. R.L. After just a few weeks my rank, but not my status, was raised to that of Signalman.

Those very early days were devoted to fatigues, fatigues and more fatigues. Our first uniform was known as fatigue dress. It was made up into a drab two piece shapeless suit, from a reddish-khaki coloured, canvas type material. In appearance we were a cross between an American convict, and a Chinese peasant. The views of our superior officers must have been the same as our own, for we were forbidden to leave the precincts of the barrack area wearing this soul destroying attire. For the first month or so, until we had undergone some basic drill and discipline, we were not allowed out at all, in fatigue dress or any other uniform.

There were educational tests, PT tests, initiative tests, adaptability tests, endurance tests and many others. There were kit inspections, barrack room inspections, medical inspections, dental inspections and umpteen others. There were lectures, mostly on VD. There were lessons on Corps and military history. We were taught the rank structures, not only of the Army but also of the other two Services. It was said that if it moved, it was to be saluted, but if it stood still, it was to be whitewashed! The days were long, but never dull. Reveille was at 5.30am and Lights Out 10.15pm. The weeks were seven days.

It could be argued that the most valuable skill a recruit should acquire was the art of 'Bullshit'. This was mostly self taught. There were no instructors on the subject, except those who taught by example. It is difficult to define the word. It can be a noun, or it can be a verb. It can describe the practice of painting a tub of coal with whitewash, or baffling your seniors, your juniors, or those around you with a long winded exuberant never-ending flow of words cumulating in verbal flatulence, and oral indigestion. Its purpose is to convince others that you are knowledgeable on a subject upon which you know sweet nothing. It must be infectious, as our civilian cousins sometimes show symptoms. Bull can be comical, and it can be serious. Its use is not confined to the lower ranks. It is known for many senior officers to unashamedly indulge in its use. In the Army, it is a way of life.

Those pre-training weeks served at least one useful purpose. We were able to feel our way into the military environment. We began to have a pride in our Unit and Corps. I was soon convinced that we were second to none in all respects of Army life. Over fifty years later, my views are unchanged.

Our Corps offered quite a variety of trades, and every man received trade training. We were able to state a preference, but not always did we get our choice. We were eager to learn our trade allocation. To my delight I was informed that I was to be trained as an Operator Signals. This was an all embracing trade in the field of wireless, visual and line communications. The ABC of that being the Morse code. Before any such training commenced, there was the small matter of fourteen weeks basic training. Most of that in the form of Square-bashing.

There were four periods to basic training. The first was for four weeks, the second for three weeks, the third four, and the final for three weeks. The time had arrived for us to start our first period. One devoted mostly to foot drill.

Recruits were formed into squads of about twenty five. The seeds of comradeship and 'mucking-in' have been well sown. I joined No. 36 Squad. Overnight, I belonged to a team. Not only was I the youngest member of that team, but also the youngest man in the Depot Regiment. That did not mean favours were bestowed. Far from it. I had to stand on my own two feet as officially, and in the eyes of the Army, I was eighteen, and I must not make the mistake of forgetting that.

Training began in deadly earnest. Discipline never let up. We were cursed at, sworn at, and castigated. Sometimes cajoled, and encouraged but not often. The instructors were junior Non Commissioned Officers. Behind their backs we called them ... well, never mind that! It must be said that they knew their job. The proof of that lay in the end product. The NCO's were never spiteful towards us. They were not brutal, only verbally. Their job was to make soldiers out of us. That, they did.

About this time I was granted my first leave. That would have been Whitsun 1933. Civilian clothes, even for leave, were forbidden. To have a leave pass endorsed with the magic words "With permission to wear plain clothes" one had to have at least two years service, and that with a clean conduct sheet. Most of us were so keen that we felt quite proud to be in uniform. On completion of that leave, a return to training.

Physical training played a large and important role in our training. Forty minutes a day were spent in the gymnasium. Furthermore, the gym was open most evenings for those sadists who were hungry for such a diet. When I had such an appetite, I would join them. The senior PT instructor was a Warrant Officer in the Army Physical Training Corps. The junior instructors were Corporals in our own Corps. I suppose my standard of PT was about average. I worked hard, and as a result felt fitter than at any other time in my life.

At school, rugby, swimming and cross country running were my main sports. Now came the opportunity to develop and expand those interests. Though rugby was my favourite, it was at cross country running that I excelled, and to my surprise found that I could win almost every race I entered providing it was not more than six miles. Another four years was to pass before I had the chance to take up hockey and tennis. Army sport is not designed to make stars out of individuals, but more to foster team spirit. Teams, at that stage, usually meant squads and Companies. Prizes for individual winners were, at times, given but they were mostly insignificant. This pooling of effort is of prime importance. We lived and breathed it.

A radio will give a poor performance if any one of the component parts is tawdry. Each, and every part must be of the best and most reliable quality. Then, when assembled, each part makes a whole, and will give the finest performance. So it is with soldiers. One day their very survival may rest on their capacity to think and act in harmony and unison with each other. Critics often say a soldier loses his individuality, and ability to think for himself. There is some justification for that in as much as he must possess a spirit of esprit de corps. Critics have also been know to say that military life kills initiative. That is nonsense. It energises and stimulates the individuals potential. Smothering of any faculty is not in the Manual of Military Training.

Someone threw a spanner in the works. There was a mild outbreak of German measles amongst the trainees, and with little warning I found myself a victim. For the first time in my life, I saw the inside of a hospital, for I was speedily moved into the isolation wing of the Catterick Military Hospital. There, I remained for the next ten days, or so. Though not feeling ill, I did feel as if my whole little world had tumbled around me, and totally cut off from my fellow men in 36 Squad. My worst symptoms were spots and frustration. Any trainee becoming sick, or entering hospital was, on recovery, automatically relegated to another squad. That, I dreaded. Those fears materialised when, returning to duty I was relegated to 38

Squad. Such setbacks often happen in our lives, and like most others, I soon got over it and settled in my new squad.

Square bashing resumed. Musketry, Arms drill, ceremonial drills and anti-gas training all formed part of the syllabus. Then, we became one of the senior squads in the Depot. Church parade on Sundays was compulsory.

We formed up every Sunday morning on the parade ground, together with D and E Companies, and a contingent from the School of Signals. This was a large ceremonial parade, and with all the trimmings. We were dressed in our 'Best'. Stiff caps, with chin straps, and side buttons. Tunics had high collars buttoned up to the neck (no shirt collars, nor ties). Leather bandoliers, with the studs on the inside highly polished. Riding breeches had leather grips on the inside of the legs, which were blancoed green. From the knee to the boot we wore long puttees. On our feet, best boots with spurs. All leather-work and brass had to be very highly polished. Spurs were burnished to a standard so high that it was possible to use them in the alternative role of a shaving mirror! The previous Saturday evening would be mostly devoted to spit and polish, preparing for the following day's parade. Our church, and I say 'our' with some affection was St. Martins-in-the-Field, Catterick Camp. It was the adopted church of the Corps. The parade was headed by the Corps Band. During the Service, music was provided not only by the organ but also our Corps Band. After the Service, there was a March Past, when the salute would be taken by a senior officer. Compulsory attendance at church was an emotive issue, and tactfully I will avoid the spiritual arguments. From the ceremonial point of view, there was much to commend it. Yes, there was swank, self-admiration, and proudness. Also, there was spit and polish by the bucketful. Our training had many sides, and complexions. Church parades were by no means the ugliest. That was my view.

Now and again we attended Padre's hour. It usually amounted to a talk. Like most others, I attend that given by the C of E Chaplain. Army chaplains hold commissions and have the status of an officer. They wear the insignia of their rank. In this case the gap between officer and man is much narrower. They gained and won enormous respect from the lower ranks. Far less importance was attached to their denomination than one would find in 'Civvy Street'. In terms of Christian unity, the Army is possibly fifty years ahead of the outside world. It was not uncommon for a Padre to walk into a barrack room, sit down on a bed and have a chat with one, or more of us. Furthermore, we could, and did, discuss any subject. Subsequently, in civil life, I have never found or made such a close relationship with a clergyman as I was able to do with most of our Army Padres. Maybe it was due to the military structure that made them "One of Us".

How can I discuss a subject when I have so little to say in praise of it? Food in the Royal Signals Depot, Catterick Camp in 1933 was both repugnant and revolting. Each of us had our own two enamel plates and china mug, and our own knife, fork and spoon. These we took with us when marched to meals. The Mess Hall held about thirty tables. Eight men sat to a table. The table tops were enamel and removable. When the cooks (?) were ready to serve the meal, a metal disc was handed to each table. That was grabbed by the two men nearest the aisle, who thereupon made a sprint for the serving hatch. Between them they collected two, or three baking dishes containing the rations for eight men, and returned to their respective tables. It was usually necessary for one of the men to divide the rations into eight equal portions. Not an easy task, and woe betide him if he miscalculated! All being well, we all, more or less had the same amount of food. At the rate we burned up calories, we would have eaten almost anything. Perhaps, at times, we did! Always we complained of being hungry. At the end of the table, we lined up our mugs and someone came round with a four gallon bucket of tea, and filled each mug in turn. Sugar was in such small quantities that it was almost impossible to detect its presence. That applied also to puddings, and sweets. A 1933 Army plate of porridge, or a military rissole would, today, be unacceptable in Wormwood Scrubs! Yet, we ate it. There was no alternative. Butter was served once a week with the Sunday afternoon tea meal. Portions were meagre, being no larger that an Oxo cube. At other times we were served margarine of a very inferior quality in mini sized portions. Breakfast was at 7.30am. Dinner (NB. Not lunch) at 1pm and a high tea meal at 5 pm. It was possible to have a supper at about 8.30pm. This late meal amounted to a hunk of dry bread, and a mug of unsweetened cocoa. As a treat, and once in a blue moon, we might be given a teaspoonful of jam. This 'supper' was not available on Fridays, Saturdays or Sundays. As Friday was pay day, it was considered we could afford to buy our own at the NAAFI or YMCA for those nights.

Adjacent to the Mess hall, was a small yard which was known as the 'Wash Up'. Here, facilities were supposed to exist to permit us to wash our eating utensils (Army jargon for plates, knives etc.). There was supposed to be an adequate supply of hot water for washing greasy plates, knives etc. In reality nearly 300 men used the same water which was most probably not even hot in the first instance. To be found with dirty utensils was unpardonable, and inexcusable, and might well result in seven days CB.

Cooking was done on large coal burning kitchen ranges. Coal and coal dust everywhere. The cookhouse floor was bare concrete. In terms of cleanliness it could not be faulted. The Army Catering Corps had not, at that time, been formed. The cookhouse was staffed entirely by Royal Signals personnel, with a Sergeant in charge. In my time it was Sgt. Cooley. We were terrified of him. Though his bark was worse than his bite.

One of the duties of the Orderly Officer was to visit all meals in our Mess. He would go to each table and ask "Any complaints?" There were many, but we were not so foolish as to mention them. For more than one man to complain would in the mind of an officer amount to almost a mutiny. Should one man complain he would run the risk of being labelled a trouble maker, or rabble rouser. So the Orderly Officer's question invariably received a negative response. Someone with the ability would have little difficulty in writing a book on this subject alone. I am not competing. On the side of the angels, it should be noted that those connected with our food ensured that cleanliness took precedence over all else. Ability at scrubbing – alone- did little towards providing an acceptable standard of food. We deserved better.

Most evenings were devoted to Shining parades. They would commence after our tea meal about 5.30pm and would continue until

8 or 9pm at the discretion of the Squad Instructor. It was not unknown for such parades to continue until 10pm. I had first hand experience of scrubbing lavatory seats after Lights Out (10.15pm). During these parades we were not allowed to leave our barrack room without permission. Sometimes a break would be granted, when and if we had the money, we could make a hurried visit to the YMCA or NAAFI. If it was a 'supper night' then we partook of our cocoa. Though this evening period was called a parade, discipline was not strictly enforced. It was possible, with permission, to visit the Gym. Some attended educational classes for about two hours on one evening a week. On Saturday afternoons we hand scrubbed the barrack room floor. On completion of that task, and to the satisfaction of the NCO instructor we were allowed out until 10.15pm.

Every coin has two sides. There was some entertainment and amusement in our lives. More often that not, Saturday evening meant a visit to the pictures. Catterick Camp boasted of two cinemas : The Garrison and The Camp. Both small, and both full to capacity for the two performances on Saturdays. The cheapest seats cost 6d. Any above that price were not within our budget. If funds permitted, we called in at Sande's Soldiers' Home for a supper, on our way back to barracks. In my case, I recall the meal consisting of a soup plate full of sweet rice pudding, and a mug of tea. Nothing more – nothing less. The pudding cost 4d. and the tea 1d. Occasionally, there was a visit to Richmond or Darlington. Such required a little more time and money. Both in short supply!

If we enjoyed the luxury of a wireless to entertain, then it has faded from my memory. Probably there was one in the canteen, but not in the barrack rooms. Necessity being the mother of invention, our entertainment was usually self-created.

Life was monastic. The only time we saw a member of the opposite sex was behind a canteen counter, or sometimes when off duty, we may catch a glimpse of a 'wife'. Married Quarters for single men were strictly 'Out of Bounds' In parallel with Monks, our existence was spartan. Our beds were made of solid heavy iron, and in two sections. When not in use as a bed, the lower half slid under the upper half making an iron frame roughly in the shape of a chair.

Running the length of each half were two, or three iron strips, which served as springs. At most the bed was 2' 6" wide. A mattress consisted of three equal sized pieces called 'Biscuits'. These were filled with coir. In the year dot, when the British soldier was given a bed to sleep on, I believe it was of this pattern. In 1933 little had changed. We were issued with four blankets, with an additional one in Winter months. They were coarse, and heavy, but warm. Sheets were issued, and pillow slips. They were made of an indestructible, unbleached calico, and a dirty greyish-white in colour. The pillows were filled with straw (?). In the height of a freezing winter, and in an unheated barrack room, I cannot recall ever being cold at nights, in bed. Furthermore, neither do I remember hearing one complaint of this kind. At the end of each day we were so tired and worn out, that perhaps we could easily have slept on the proverbial clothes' line.

Apart from the beds the other barrack room furniture consisted of a wooden six foot table, and two, six foot benches (both hand scrubbed, daily). We each had our own individual locker, but never allowed to lock it! The doors had to remain open at all times for instant inspection. These lockers were made of metal, and secured to the walls above the head of our beds. It could only be used for Army kit. The owning of any personal or private material was frowned upon. We even had to find hiding places for such matters as writing paper and envelopes. Glossy photographic plates were displayed on the wall showing the daily layout for our kit. No deviation from that was permitted.

Barrack rooms were single storey of the bungalow type. They were built in pairs; the two rooms being connected by an 'Annexe'. It served the dual purpose of providing a connecting corridor, and the location of toilets and wash basins (no baths, nor showers). I am unsure if hot water was provided. Certainly, I have memories of shaving in cold water on a dark winter's morn. But at sixteen, not a great problem!

The centre piece of every barrack room was the 'Cenotaph'. This was a brick monstrosity built in the centre of the room to provide two coal burning fireplaces. One facing each end of the room. The smoke rose into a common chimney, up and out through the roof. As we lacked sufficient coal to maintain one fire burning all evening, let alone two, the result was that only was one fireplace ever used at a time. When opportunity came, we would gather round this cenotaph for a chat. Such moments were precious, and of the happiest. They were free from the ever demanding shouts from an NCO calling upon us for some even grater Herculean effort. It was forbidden to talk or make any noise after Lights Out. That rule was frequently broken, as voices were hushed, and the soft pedal pressed, there were never any serious consequences of this. Such interludes were much enjoyed. In those early months of Army life, I learnt much about my fellow men, and what I learnt; I liked.

The Bath House was a draughty wooden structure. Inside, were about twenty showers in rows of about five, with a long wooden bench facing each row. Once a week, training would be interrupted, as we were marched back to our barrack rooms. There, towels and soap (usually Palmolive at 4d. a cake) were collected, and then a march to the Bath House. On arrival we were lined up, each man facing a shower. Nobody undressed until ordered. After the order was given, and when completely starkers, we moved under the shower. Then the NCO in charge gave the order and the water would be turned on at a master tap. There was supposed to be an adequate supply of hot water. That seldom provided to be the case. The duration of the shower was strictly timed by the NCO. When that time expired, the procedure was reversed, and we returned to our training. It was a weekly ritual. In addition to the showers there were four or so, slipper baths, but they were not for us. They were for the exclusive use of NCO's. After our daily PT session, showers were not available. Sometimes, after a big game of sport, it was possible to have an extra shower over and above the normal weekly quota. If such good fortune came one's way, then be prepared for cold water. It appeared that the system allowed one shower a week. No more – no less, and that was that! Yes, our lifestyle did have much in common with that of a monk. We found solace in the knowledge that we were not expected to take vows of celibacy!

Dare I say that civilians when evaluating a job, attach more importance to pay than soldiers do? Even by 1933 standards, the soldiers' pay was a scandal. The financial score between the proverbial small ecclesiastical rodent and ourselves was 'Love All'. Complaints there were, but not nearly so strong and assertive as would be imagined. Two shillings (10p) a day was our rate for at least the first year of our service. It was said that all was provided. In theory, yes. In practice, no. Deductions were made for haircuts (fortnightly parade), boot repairs, and laundry. Tailoring alterations were not of our own choice, but as directed by officers, and NCO's; yet we had to pay for them. The stoppage which caused the greatest irritation, and which really rankled was called barrack room damages. The amount was not large, just a few pence a week. Everyone had to pay it. It covered such items as a cracked or broken pane of glass, a damaged electrical fitting or a stain on a wall. When an electric light bulb failed, it could be exchanged for a new one, but only if the glass was intact. If broken, then someone had to pay for the replacement or it could be a charge to barrack room damages. A Quartermaster Sergeant had much power. Any item he considered unfair wear and tear, had to be paid for, and there was little the individual could do about it except pay. To recover the cost of a twopenny pair of boot laces must have involved time and paper work amounting to three or four times their value. In such a situation, it might be thought that many lies were told, and that there was much petty theft and stealing. There was not. It was 1933 not 1987.

    I opted to draw my pay at the rate of 5/- and 10/- in alternate weeks. That permitted a small sum to remain in credit. When leave came due I would have a little extra cash. Smoking was a habit that I had not acquired, and a drink of anything alcoholic was for special events, and festivals. It was all just as well. At one proud stage, I remember entering the Catterick Camp Post Office, and opening my first savings account. I deposited 6d.

    It would be difficult for the young man today to imagine the relationship that existed between our seniors, and ourselves. At no time, have I seen it accurately portrayed in a film or play, or even well defined in a book. Commissioned Officers had to be saluted at all times. If one spoke to us, we stood rigidly to attention. If a Signalman wished to speak to, or approach an Officer, then he must first do so through an NCO or Warrant Officer. All Officers and

Warrant Officers were addressed as "Sir". In most Regiments, and Corps, an Officer was expected to have a private income. He too was badly paid, but in his case it was recognised and accepted that he could not live on his Army salary alone. They were a class on their own in as much as they were almost entirely ex-Public School. Scattered thinly amongst them was the odd Quartermaster who would have risen from the ranks. Under no circumstances did we mix or socialise. The gap was far too wide for that. Had the opportunity arisen, I doubt if we would have taken it. It was better that way. It was far more important that we respected our officers, than greeted them as long lost cousins. They earned our respect, and got it.

The relationship between NCO's and Signalmen was not unlike that with the Officers. In a similar manner, we always stood to attention when speaking with them, but instead of using "Sir", we addressed them by their rank. To use a Christian name, or any attitude of familiarity would invite disciplinary disaster, with the entire contents of the Manual of Military Law being thrown at you. The culprit might well find himself being speedily and securely locked in a Guard Room cell. One who has never experience pre-war military discipline might be stunned by that. Our Army has rarely enjoyed the distinction of being the world's largest, but its standards of discipline and efficiency are unsurpassed. It was so in 1933. I believe it still is.

As that Autumn approached, so did the end of by basic fourteen weeks training. My rifle had become more than just an instrument for Arms drill. Prior to firing it on the ranges, for the first time, I had to learn how to maintain and clean it. In those days, the standard Army rifle was the .303 Lee Enfield. It weighed over 7lbs. It was, perhaps, the most efficient weapon of its kind in any Army. Range drill had many 'Do's and Don'ts', as obviously when firing live ammunition many safety precautions had to be taken. Personally, I was initially somewhat scared of the rifle, and was rather nervous of firing it. The musketry instructor was quick to spot that. He took me on one side, and gave me extra drill and instruction on the rifle. He was a first rate instructor and did much to give me confidence, and enable me to fire my passing out course on the Ranges. I cannot recall what the 'Pass' score was, but I made it.

Today's foot drill and marching is carried out in threes. That was introduced just before the outbreak of the war. Prior to that, our drill was all done in fours. It was in fours that I was trained. It was more intricate, and I believe more impressive from the ceremonial point of view. Threes were simpler, and more practical. The Corps being a mounted Corps, did not then use bayonets. We were not issued with them, and did not carry them. That too, was to change. Before the outbreak of war, we adopted their use.

A small squad of about two dozen men is numerically unimpressive, but on the day of our final 'Passing Out Parade', our turnout and drill was. It had to be. Failure to attain the high standards set would have resulted not only in two weeks additional training, but worse, the wrath of an instructor who felt that he had been let down. At this final parade a few presentations were made. The main one being the award of the Commanding Officer's whip. This 'Walking-Out' whip was awarded to the most outstanding recruit in each Squad. An excellent start to anyone's career in the Corps. Our winner certainly deserved his. It is customary for spoons to be given as rewards for highest range score. This was no exception, and a presentation was made. The last award was not the grandest. It was for the recruit who had made the most progress in the Gymnasium. I must have been on the verge of fainting when my number, rank and name was called for this minor award. If it had been the VC it could not have come as a greater surprise, and I would not have felt more proud. Oh! The enthusiasm of youth.

It was over. Just the very basic military aspects of training were completed. The foundations were laid for the next twenty three years. That training was to serve me well. No longer was I a boy. I was growing up – fast!

The next stage was technical training. For that, I was posted to 'E' Company, and there to learn the intricacies, and technicalities of a Operator Signals. But first, a few days leave.

Chapter 2

'E' Company (or 'Eddy' Company, as it was better known) of the Training Battalion was exclusively devoted to the training of Operators who made up about a half of those passing out from the Depot. My colleagues who consisted of the remainder were posted to 'D' Company for their training. The function of the company was the training of Instrument Mechanics, Electrician Signals, Despatch Riders and Clerks. The exception to that was a small minority who went to neither of those two Companies, but instead were posted to the Mounted Wing to become Drivers H.T. (Horse Transport). It should be remembered that in 1934 we, in the Royal Corps of Signals, were a mounted Corps and had not then become mechanised. Training to drive mechanical vehicles had not been introduced. Boys, aged 14 ½ - 15, on entering the Corps were all posted to 'F' Company. There, they not only did their basic training, but also their technical before entering man's service at 17½. Such boys were totally isolated from men, and 'F' Company was strictly Out of Bounds to anyone not posted to it as a trainee or member of its cadre.

On arrival in Eddy Coy. At the tail end of 1933, my training as an Operator Signals commenced. Once more, we were formed into squads. It followed, that many of the twenty or so other members of my squad had also been with me in the Depot under basic training. There was no lack of keenness, or enthusiasm when the first day of our training arrived.

The period for the training of an operator was 32 weeks. That was split into two. The first seventeen weeks were to take us up to what was known as Group 'E'. The remaining fifteen weeks were to complete the training to BIII standard, meaning, at the end, we became a Group B Class III tradesman. Providing ,of course, we made the grade.

During those early weeks we became Morse crazy. The bedrock of the training was reading, and sending Morse. It had to be mastered. A few hours each day were spent reading and sending Morse. That was done in a classroom specially wired up and equipped. Over and above, the alphabet there were figures and procedure signals to be learnt. As the days passed, so the speeds marginally increased. An instrument called a 'Sounder' was used for instruction purposes when sending and receiving. It was a low voltage/current instrument. When placed in a circuit with a Morse key and battery, it made a click when the key was pressed, but unlike a buzzer, no sound emitted when the key was held in a depressed position. Release the key and another click was heard. A most difficult instrument to read. No wonder the standard of operating in the Corps was so high. In the lecture rooms the instructor sat at his desk with a sounder and key beside him. Without any amplification, the sounder could be heard and read by all in the classroom. The instrument was, I believe, originally a Post Office Telegraph instrument and used in World War I by the Royal Engineers Signals. Most of our equipment in the thirties was 'left over' from that war. Yet, it worked.

While we were learning our trade, we were never allowed to forget that we were soldiers. We performed guard duties. There were drill parades and kit inspections. A military medley that had to blend in harmony with class-work.

Wednesday afternoons were devoted to sport. Its nature would vary, depending on the time of year, and to some extend the wishes and ability of individuals. There was an element of choice. There were no swimming baths in Catterick except a tiny pool in Sandes' Soldiers Home; so swimming was out of the question. From time to time, I played the odd game of rugby, and mostly my efforts went into cross-country running. Saturday afternoons would also present opportunities for additional sport. Saturday mornings were entirely given to cleaning and scrubbing the barrack rooms.

In Eddy Company we did enjoy somewhat more leisure time than in our Depot days. It was quite often possible on Saturday evenings to visit one of the two Catterick cinemas, though we had to be back in the barracks by 2215 hrs. (Lights Out). Occasionally, it was possible to obtain a late pass until 2359 hrs. That 'privilege' was not often taken up. Our lifestyle and late nights were not good companions. In the evenings, and at weekends, there were notes to be written up, and read. Officially a lie-in on Sunday morning was not permitted. Somehow, we usually managed an extra half hour or hour. Longer was out of the question, as normally we would be on a Church Parade. That was compulsory.

Autumn seems a short season. Soon the night frosts of winter were upon us. The barrack rooms were insufficiently heated, due to an inadequate coal ration. The lecture rooms were little better. On enlisting, I knew that life would be hard with few comforts and many discomforts. So it was.

Besides all the Morse practice, there were many lectures. Copious notes and diagrams were made. The word 'Procedure' became commonplace in our vocabulary. Under that heading came the entire mode of communications. Lectures on the subject were numerous. At school I had learnt some Physics, so lectures on electricity and magnetism were little more than a refresher course. It became a different ball game, when in the last twelve weeks of training, it all became more advanced as we delved into the depths of AC theory, AC formulae, and wireless theory. I was in deep water.

Line communications were commonplace and a knowledge of the instruments involved, and their scope had to be acquired. There was the DIII buzzer/telephone, and the Tele 110 plus the Fullerphone. Voice could be used on all three instruments. For the transmission of Morse, by line, there was the Simplex and Duplex machines. For use with the Tele 110's there was the 10 Line Cordless Field Exchange, and for the DIII the 7+3 Exchange. Not only did we have to be competent on the operating, but also be conversant with the relevant theory and circuit diagrams. The entirety were archaic.

Though there was a trade of Linesmen, we were taught how to lay a cable, and some elementary cable jointing, and connecting up.

A few hours break out of classrooms, and out onto the Yorkshire Moors was always welcome, particularly in good weather. This came about when learning the art of visual signalling. This aspect of my training I particularly enjoyed. It involved using, and communicating by flag and by daylight signalling lamp. In later years, I was never called upon to put this to any practical use, but did have to maintain and improve my standard in order to sit, and pass, by Class II, and eventually Class I.

The Army based within the Home Establishment, today employ and make use of a large number of civilian instructors for technical purposes. In pre-war years, none were used. Our instructors were no more than NCO's, but as such should not be under-rated. They had an excellent knowledge of their subject, and what is more, they had the ability to impart that knowledge to us, the trainees. For my part, I am indebted to them.

Before the 1933/34 Winter ended, I had passed my Group 'E'. With, or without, flying colours – I cannot recall. It was rewarded with five days leave. On return, there was the resumption of training. This resumed with the commencement of the 18th week.

It soon became apparent that the pressure was on, and that much hard work lay ahead in the following three months, or so.

Morse speeds were already just a little below those required for final pass off. Now came the introduction of reading through heavy interference, and reading weak signal strengths. This demand on our powers of concentration was increasing all the time. We reached the stage of passing messages (traffic) to one another. After learning the theory of Procedure, we now had to put it into practice. It was all becoming somewhat more realistic as pieces of the jig-saw began to fit into place. Procedure was not a difficult subject to learn, neither was it dull. I cannot recall any of my classmates having problems with it. Certainly, it was an important subject. Some years later, I was to learn how important it really was. Poor procedure was poor security.

Inevitably, our lectures on wireless theory became more advanced. Most of the Squad appeared to have little difficulty in absorbing it all. I was not one of them. It was not for the lack of trying; nor could I blame the instructor. If any subject tripped me up, it would be this. Some evenings, I would pore over the diagram of a simple Receiver Circuit endeavouring to understand what it was all about. Currents, condensers, resistances, transformers and even valves were, as components not too difficult to comprehend. Put them together, and I panicked.

There can only be a few of us, still alive, who were trained on the old 'A' (Ack) Set. They were already museum pieces, by the time the Second World War broke out. It was on the 'A' Set, and likewise a 'C' Set, that I gained my first experience of a set designed to both transmit and receive Morse signals. Mostly, it was on the 'A' Set that we were trained. It must have been obsolete, even in 1934. On completing my training, I did not again set my eyes on one until a Summer's day in 1986 when visiting our Corps Museum in Blandford. It should be added that we were given a brief instruction on the No. 1 Set. It was then in its infancy. This set was a gem; both for speech and Morse. It was a short range set, very robust, and very simple to operate. It could be used as a ground to ground set, or as a mobile. Later, it was fitted into small vehicles (Austin 7) and on the NW Frontier of India it was adapted to be operated from mule to mule! Like an old friend, it was reliable and would never let you down.

It might be thought that we were little different from any other body of students learning their trade, or skills. Some may think that we were little more than civilians who wore a uniform. That image would be erroneous. Military life, discipline and routine, ran parallel to technical training. It was said so often to us, by our Officers and NCO's: "You are soldiers first, and don't forget it!".

Spring Drills were a very large annual ceremonial parade held in March/April. Somewhere approaching 1,000 men would be on parade each morning at 7am. It necessitated much preparation of kit and equipment not only on the previous evening, but also on the day itself. There were three, or four of these parades each week over a period of three to four weeks. It was for a trainee, almost impossible to be exempt. The standard of turnout had to be extremely high, and it was. Riding breeches, spurs, bandoliers, peak caps; all leather and brass work highly polished. Hair cuts were very, very short. Inspections were very detailed. The Corps Band was also on parade. That was about the only cheerful aspect. Almost all Officers were present. The Senior Ranks were mounted on horses. To a spectator, it would have been a most impressive sight. Alas, there were no spectators. The parade crammed the Baghdad Square. Prior to this parade, we had a mug of 'Gunfire' (early morning tea). By 8am the parade would be over, and we proceeded to breakfast, by which time we felt that we had done a day's work. Our seniors thought otherwise. A normal day's technical training followed.

The possibility of war rarely crossed our minds. It had no place in our day to day lives, or conversation. Occasionally, we heard rumblings of what was happening in Germany. A comic, but rather odious creature called Hitler had seized power, and was making himself rather objectionable. Our concern was mostly with our final BIII tests as they loomed ever closer.

The conclusion came, and all instruction came to an abrupt end as we concluded our 31st week. The following week was devoted to tests. These were both practical and theoretical. All visual tests took place on the Moors. Practical connecting up, and operating of line were both carefully examined. Faults were deliberately created for us to detect, and so it was with the wireless equipment and sets. There were written papers on procedures, E & M and Wireless theory. That last named subject remained the only one to cause me serious concern. Morse tests in both sending and receiving were individually taken, and were in the form of messages. Too many years have passed to recall the exact speeds of those Morse tests, but a calculated guess would be about 18 words per minute (wpm.) for blocks, 22 wpm. for running hand, and 24 wpm. for figures. It was important to us that we passed each subject at the first attempt. The carrot was 10 days leave. Failure in any one subject meant possible loss of that leave, and relegation. My worst fears proved unjustified. I passed like almost all my colleagues, at the first attempt. It was interesting to note that my best subject was 'Reading Morse', That ability remained with me throughout my life in the Corps. Its impact, in the later years, was to dominate and transform my entire military career.

The pre-war qualified Operator Signals was competent, and lacked nothing that experience would not teach him. I had a feeling of satisfaction.

With the completion of my first year's service, my enthusiasm was no less than on the day of my enlistment. I had stumbled a few times, and taken a few knocks, but the bruises soon disappeared. Though still not eighteen, I was leading a very adult life. From basic, and technical training, I had benefited enormously. Without studying or reading a text book on the subject of human nature, I had learnt much about my fellow men, and how to enjoy living with them. The most valuable lesson was that learnt about myself.

CHAPTER 3

On returning to Catterick from the BIII leave, the climax came. It was the publishing of our postings. Royal Signals Units were scattered across all corners of the world. Most newly trained men were posted to a Unit somewhere in the UK – if only for a short while – before being drafted overseas. My only wish was to try to avoid Aldershot, but no particular preference. Together with two friends, Bowler and Hurst, I learnt with some excitement and satisfaction that I was posted to the South Irish Coast Defence Signal Section. On the first week in August 1934, I arrived at Spike Island at the entrance to Cork Harbour, Eire. For the next two years, or so, this was to be my military home.

The Section proved to be even smaller that I had expected. Its strength amounted to approximately thirty five men. That included a small detachment of about six men, under a junior NCO who were situated on Bere Island, Bantry Bay. Our Officer Commanding was Capt. F. I. N. McOstrich, Royal Signals.

The Unit was not totally independent, but almost. For purposes of Messing we were attached to the Royal Artillery. It was a Royal Artillery Coast Defence Brigade that made up the bulk of the Garrison. There were a few other Units of a support nature. A Company of Royal Engineers were stationed at Fort Camden. Their role was to maintain, and man the searchlights. Camden is strategically situated on the mainland, guarding the entrance to the Harbour. Spike boasted of a small military hospital, with the normal RAMC staff, plus a handful of members from the RAOC, RASC, RAEC and RAPC. The hub of the Garrison was the RA. Life revolved around the Gunners. It was their show.

The main function of our Signals Section was to provide external wireless (the word 'Radio' was little used in those days) communications between ourselves, Catterick Camp, Bere Island and the Royal Navy. Anchored in the harbour was, at most times a British Destroyer. Now and again, it would patrol the surrounding coastal waters, or make a brief visit to Bere Island.

Our wireless equipment consisted of two transmitters together with their receivers. One was a 500 watt which we used when working Catterick on a wavelength of 1600 metres. I believe we also used that transmitter and wavelength when working Bere, though my memory on this is a little uncertain. When working the Navy, we used the 120 watt transmitter, and worked on a wavelength of 600 metres. Spike was the control station. Only during emergencies did we operate 24 hours a day. Normally, we opened at 0800 hrs., and closed after our last schedule which was about 2200 hrs. Those hours were elastic, and would at times be stretched to meet particular operational requirements. W/T procedure was the standard of the day. The most used procedure signals were called 'X' numbers. Each signal comprised the letter X followed by three figures, e.g.:

X 257 ... I have nothing to communicate.

X 259 ... I have traffic for you.

Those procedure signals amounted to no more than a military equivalent to the International 'Q' and 'Z' codes.

The standard of security on the air was atrocious. Our frequencies were never changed, and our call signs were fixed. Likewise, we came on air using the same times for our schedules, day in – day out. Operators chat was common, known to all, and not seriously regarded as a security risk. Over 90% of our traffic was passed in English plain language. One had only to tune in to the BBC on 1500 metres to hear us. Listeners to that programme constantly complained about us blotting out the BBC and in turn ruining their enjoyment. On the whole, the wireless reception was acceptable. The receivers were not very selective, and we had invariably the problem of coping with interference from other stations, and from fading. The frequencies were overcrowded. Wireless operating was demanding. Fifty years later, it still is! One of our most agreeable routines was working the Destroyer. The Royal Navy standard of operating was very high, and their equipment more modern and advanced that ours. Whenever possible, I would go aboard whatever ship was on duty in the harbour, and make myself known to the 'Sparks', whereupon I would be taken to the wireless cabin, and proceed to learn how the other half work and live! I enjoyed such visits, enormously. As the crow flies, the distance between the Destroyer and our fort was about a mile only; so with their powerful transmitter we had no difficulty with their signal strength. They blew our heads off!

The aerial masts on Spike were permanently erected on the ramparts. The system was vast, or so it seemed to me. To a layman, it must have appeared as a complex labyrinth of tangled wire.

The Royal Artillery defences were 9.2" and 6" guns, of the Royal Navy type. The 6" were positioned behind the barrack block, and sunk just below the ramparts of the fort. The 9.2" guns were placed high on the top of a cliff, adjacent to Fort Camden, and looking out over St. George's Channel. Each year, in the late Summer, the RA carried out their annual shoots. One of the War Department ferry boats would be used to tow the target out to sea, say six or seven miles. This boat had a maximum speed of about twelve knots. The target was towed on a very long tow. When the order was given, the target would be wound in, by the boat, at a speed of eight knots, giving a total target speed of approximately 20 knots. Somewhat primitive, but it served the purpose. During these shoots, the role of our Section was to work with, and co-operate with, the RA Signallers in providing wireless communications between the boat and the gun sites. For that we used 'C' Sets. In their favour, it should be said that they were a slight improvement on smoke signals in a force 10 gale! A comparison could be made with the Artillery whose guns were an advancement on bows and arrows. As for the searchlights; they were little more than damp squibs.

One of our tasks, as Operator Signals, on Spike Island was the manning of the switchboard. We had not been trained on wireless alone. The exchange was a Post Office 60 line board, with a hand generator. A spell of duty on this came our way from time to time, and was a welcome break. Unlike the wireless station, it was manned twenty four hours a day. There was a night alarm, so that if a call was received during the late hours, a bell rang. The equipment was in a small room, but with sufficient space for a bed. The night duty operator, most nights, enjoyed a few hours sleep. A submarine cable connected the exchange with that of the Irish Post Office, in Cobh. In turn, trunk calls were possible to the mainland. Such calls were mostly to Western Command Headquarters, Chester, and other military establishments. Security was non-existent. There were no scrambling devices. All line communications on the Island were maintained by Royal Signals Linemen. I cannot recall one single major breakdown. British Telecom please note!

Being such a small Unit presented us with one, or two, manpower problems. This particularly when leave and sickness coincided. We could rarely boast of being 100% available for duty. On the other hand, all Garrison duties and fatigues were performed by Royal Artillery personnel. This meant that we were relieved of all duties such as: spud bashing, fire piquet, guard duties etc. The gunners bore the brunt. Bless 'em!

The verbal thrusts in Catterick that were thrown at us about being soldiers first had left their mark. Even in Spike, occasional reminders were mumbled. As a result our drill, turnout and general military duties were of a very high standard. Many Regiments specialise in Ceremonial duties, and parades. We did not. Yet, I will throw down the gauntlet and say we were second to none at performing parades of that nature. What a hornet's nest!

Church parades were not so frequent as in Catterick, but we were not exempt. On such parades there would be a small contingent from our Section. Capt. McOstrich would command, and lead us. Military music was provided by means of records (78's), on a turntable with amplifier and speakers. The parade Commander was, of course, the Lt. Colonel Commanding the RA. On special ceremonial occasions, such as King George V's Jubilee in 1935, we had a visiting Royal Artillery band. When our turn came to March Past, and the familiar Corps march "Begone Dull Care" was played, we felt that extra pride. With heads held high and well back; chins tucked in; chests out and stomachs in; arms swung high from front to rear. We would swank with pride. Proud of our Corps; proud of our Army and proud of our Country. Today, there are many who would label that old fashioned, out dated sentiment of the Kipling era. Patriotism has almost become a dirty word. It grieves me.

The topography of Spike was such that it did not lend itself to sporting activities. We had only two tennis courts, which were inside the fort. Part of the parade ground was marked out so that it could be used for hockey. There was no football or rugby ground. We did have a gymnasium, but it was little used. With the Royal Artillery, I did play in a few games of rugby. They were usually against any team the Navy could muster from their Destroyer crew. Fixtures with a local Irish team were infrequent. Our swimming pool was that which nature provided. As a keen swimmer, and quite a strong one, I was able to put the surrounding waters to good use. Alas, the tides were swift, and the currents often dangerous. So, no place for learners. From our Section PRI fund, we had purchased a good sized rowing boat. Comfortably, it could seat six oarsmen, and as many passengers. Very strict rules governed the taking out, and the use of the boat. They were mostly of a safety, and common sense nature. It was in this boat that I learnt to row, and after many blisters learnt what strenuous exercise rowing can be. Sadly, there was no female company, but with the barrack room friends, we spent many pleasant summer evenings. Fishing parties were always popular. At other times we used the boat to go swimming. Preserved in my mind is one particular incident.

Contrary to all the standing orders, on one swimming outing, I swam away from the boat and aimed for the mainland about 2,000 yards away. I did not get there. Instead, I found myself in serious difficulties. The NCO in charge of the boat was alert, and saw me in trouble. He reached me in time – just! On being revived, I instantly realised that what I had done was very foolish. Moreover, I had rendered myself liable to some serious military discipline. I was scared. Before returning to our anchorage, I had been told in no mild terms by a very angry Corporal, what he thought of me. It wasn't much! Such an action on my part might well have resulted in many restrictions being imposed on all future use of the boat, and so jeopardising the fun and pleasure others had in its use. That sickened me. This is not a fairy story, but it did have a happy ending. All in the boat, NCO included, agreed to hush-up the incident. They took an enormous risk. Had the matter later come to light, a Court of Inquiry would have been convened, and its findings may well have proved, for me, calamitous. That night I went to bed a grateful, but very subdued Signalman. I had learnt my lesson.

The ferry service to Cobh was both efficient and reliable. At high tide the boats steamed in a straight line from Spike's Jetty to Cobh Pier, taking about twenty minutes. At low tide, it had to avoid sandbanks. A detour was made adding about a further twenty minutes to the journey time. The timetable was well published, and well known. Its reliability would shame today's British Rail. The boats were roughly the size of a small coastal tug, and could carry quite a large number of passengers. As there was almost no mechanical transport on the Island, there was no car ferry. That is how it appears on the index of my memory. Being owned, and manned, by the War Department, the ferries flew the blue ensign. The crews were made up mostly from the local civilian population. Even if on duty, it was forbidden for any of us to travel on these boats in uniform.

Not until after World War II did the Army do much, or care much, about its married quarters. In Spike, the standard was little better than in Catterick. As in most Garrison Towns, they were insufficient. The few we had were built on the slopes between the fort and the sea, and on the North side of the Island. Capt. McOstrich's quarter was large and spacious, and of a standard higher than most other officers below field rank. I doubt if it had been purpose built as a WD married quarter. Among the junior ranks, only three or four were living in married quarters.

About six months after my arrival, one day, Capt. McOstrich sent for me, and asked me if I was willing to become his batman, as his present batman was being posted. The big attraction was that he offered me ten shillings (50p) a week. It was sometimes said that such a job was demeaning and servile. That was not as I viewed it. It involved little more than going to his quarters for a hour or so in the evenings, cleaning his equipment and preparing his uniform for the following day. At times I would be required to press his trousers, take his boots for repair, or uniforms for dry cleaning. He would not have trusted me with the job had he not been impressed with my own turnout. When there was a Regimental dinner in the Officers Mess, or some other formal function, his Mess kit with scarlet jacket, swan-necked spurs, miniature medals all received special attention. When preparing for some ceremonial parade his sword, scabbard, brown leather boots and leggings, would shine in the sunlight like a mirror. Capt. McOstrich's quarter was by the waters edge, large and well furnished. Inside, I had a small room allocated to me for my exclusive use. It was comfortable, and warm in the winter. At times, after completing my work, I would stay a while and read or write a letter there. Snug as the proverbial bug. Mrs McOstrich was both respected and popular. Often she would pause for a brief chat, and instructed the cook to see that I had plenty to eat. Now and again, a bottle of beer would appear. The cook, sometimes, would ask me to join her in a meal in the kitchen. There was always plenty of food, and always I ate everything that was put in front of me. There were two small children in the family, but I saw little of them. When I arrived in the evenings, they were usually in bed. Entertaining was done on quite a large scale, and then I was often asked to help out in the kitchen. Willingly, I agreed. At the end, there was a good tip. The cook was a middle aged Irish woman, with a heart of gold. Time spent in my OC's home was not part of my military duty. It was all in my 'Off' duty time, and all voluntary.

  Leave was a constant topic of conversation. Unlike those serving on the mainland of the UK; we were not able to take advantage and enjoy the odd weekend leave at home. The ferry service between Cork and Fishguard operated three times a week in each direction, and was an overnight journey. Travelling to the mainland was lengthy both in distance and time. The outcome was that our quota of twenty eight days leave a year had to be taken in one swoop, but we were given a few additional days travelling time. The cost was not a problem as we were given travel warrants. Local leave was sporadic, and subject to last minute variations and cancellations, due to our operational commitments. With one, or two, very close friends such as 'Tich' Cunningham or Jackie Walton, such leave was spent in Cork or nearby. The 'Bandon' Hotel was very small, but very popular in those days. Not a very salubrious place, but what can one expect for 3/6 (17½p) a night which included a generous, and well cooked breakfast. It was the most we could afford. It was well run and clean. Above all, there was an adequate supply of hot water. In theory, there should have been an ample supply of hot water on Spike. We all know that theory and practice do not always marry up. When visiting Generals carried out their inspections, hot water poured out of the appropriate taps by the bucketful. When they departed, so did the hot water! The reason was a well kept secret, and it is not my intention to offer an explanation. The owner of 'The Bandon' knew, beyond all doubt, that we were British soldiers from Spike Island. Though always in civilian clothes, we inadvertently advertised our identity by our haircuts, and highly polished shoes. Irrespective of Corps or Regiment, behaviour was of a high standard. Vandalism and hooliganism was not only uncommon, but I hope, out of character. We did not shout slogans, or indulge in provocative conversation with civilians. We did join them in their pubs, dances and we played them at sport. Some married Irish girls. If there was any division between Catholics and Protestants, I cannot recall it. Life was quite peaceful, and there were no experiences of disquiet, or apprehension.

Any soldier who has passed through Catterick Camp, will know of Sande's Soldiers Home. It was a haven of peace and quiet for those wishing to escape for a brief while from the atmosphere, and environment of Army life. So it was on Spike, except that here the 'Home' was situated in Cobh, near the pier. Compared to Catterick, it was very small. On disembarking from the ferry, many of us would make straight for Sande's. It was organised and run by a ladies' evangelical movement, and there was no bar. Even so, it was popular, and much used. We could always rely on a good supply of 'Char and Wads', which would be edible and cheap.

In contrast there was, in Cobh, a branch of the British Legion, which did have a bar. As serving members of the Armed Forces, we were granted honorary membership. The attraction of the Legion was that the price of beer was even cheaper than the pubs. About 7d (3p) a pint.

Canteen facilities of Spike were similar to those in most Garrison Towns on the mainland. The NAAFI was small but met most of our day to day requirements. It was situated on the ground floor of the barrack block, and thus very conveniently placed. Detached, and only about fifty yards away was the YMCA. This too, was small. Like the hospital, it was a wooden construction. Unlike the hospital, it was popular, but not allowed to serve alcoholic drinks. Both the YM and NAAFI were furnished with billiard tables (full size) and a wireless set.

  The greatest social facility, for many, was the dance hall. Dances were spasmodic, but gave much pleasure. Built into the corner of the rafters of the hall was a 'Nest'. This contained an amplifier, turntable and microphone, and for good measure, a large selection of 78 records. Only once in a blue moon were we able to enjoy the luxury of 'live' music. In the corners of the hall, speakers were installed; each backed by a baffle board. The maintaining and manning was all carried out by our Signals Section. In this I had a part, together with friends Parker and Wilmot. At the time of a dance, one of us would play the part of MC, or what today is called a Disc Jockey. The Garrison Commander (RA) took a personal interest in this, but never interfered. From PRI Funds, we were allocated a monthly budget to spend on the latest dance records, A small group would get their heads together and draw up a list of our selections. In turn we submitted it to higher authority (The Army loves 'Higher Authorities'!) for approval. In fairness, it must be said that few, if any, amendments or alterations were made to our list. The selections were naturally popular music of the day by Jack Payne, Henry Hall, Billy Cotton, Harry Roy, Roy Fox, Jack Hilton and Ambrose. Record Orders were all placed with the Gramophone Company, Hayes, Middlesex and were despatched through the post. The dances that took place were one of three types: Officers Mess. WO's and Sgts. Mess. All Ranks

  They were always formal. Uniform had to be worn and would be Mess Kit or 'Blues'. Ladies, as a rule, would be in evening dress. Though not large in numbers, the dances were quite glittering affairs. The problem was finding enough ladies for partners. The wives went out of their way to attend. Girl friends from Cobh and Cork could be invited by personal invitation. Application had to be made for a pass for her to attend. It was not all dancing. Many a girl was invited to take a stroll on the ramparts "To see the view!" Even on a dark night!

It could not be said that Saturday evenings in Cobh were exciting. There was the Tuppenny Hop. As the name implies, the admission was 2d. Alcohol was forbidden. The dance (?) was held in a small hall with a tin roof. Its aim was to supply some kind of entertainment for the local youth. That youth did not rate it any higher than we did. The resemblance between the dance floor, and a rugby scrum was that of identical twins. In the latter, I enjoyed playing hooker. In the former, I was happiest as 'Stand-Off'.

The last wireless schedule with Bere Island, at 2215hrs, was seldom a busy one. Just an exchange of call signs, and a couple of procedure signals to boot X257 and GNOM (Good Night Old Man). One such night in late January 1936, after completing the schedule, switching off, and locking up, I returned to the Barrack room. It was then, just past Lights Out (2215hrs), and the room was in darkness, except for a tiny pilot light on the wireless indicating that it was switched on. Nothing unusual about that, but no sound came from it. Walking up to the set to switch off – and thinking everyone was asleep – a voice came to me saying, "Don't switch off, the King is dying". Could it be? Quietly, I undressed, and got into bed. There was no mistaking the atmosphere in the room. Conversation was sparse and subdued. About every fifteen minutes a brief announcement came from the wireless, otherwise silence. We lay awake. Just after midnight came those moving, and historic words, "The King's life is drawing peacefully to its close". By daybreak, Edward VIII was on the throne.

A soldier's vocabulary includes, amongst other things, the wide use of slang. "Cushy" was then very fashionable. It is self explanatory. One would hear a particular officer, NCO station, or Unit described as cushy. There were those who spoke of our South Irish Coast Defence Signal Section in such terms. I disagreed violently. Life was neither soft, nor easy. In some respects it was poor. Our barrack room was dark, dingy and damp. A sketch of it would not have been out of place in any Dickensian novel. The standard of food was appalling. Working conditions in the Exchange and the Wireless station were good. The hours worked were long, and like any other military Unit there were the usual kit inspections, Arms inspections, medical inspections, barrack room inspections and so on, and so on. The OC was an officer who would accept nothing less than our best. He was not a 'soft touch' but we respected and admired him. He could be, and often was, a firm disciplinarian. Experience has taught me that young soldiers accept that. They look to their officers for leadership and fairness. Capt. McOstrich gave us both.

The camaraderie that exists in the Forces in unequalled. Nothing in civil life comes within sight of it. To explain it, is outside my compass. A very detailed and lengthy document could be written on the subject, and on completion the writer may only have scratched the surface. With clarity and detail, and without any difficulty I can picture my closest friends of those days. Pip Parker and Wilmot (the Duke) were both workshop types. Richards (on?) was a 'tiffy' who lived in married quarters. O'Sullivan was Irish and his home just a few miles away near Cobh. Without doubt, the man I spent so much time with, and from whom I learnt so much (not least how to read and understand the Admiralty Handbook on Wireless Telegraphy), was 'Tich' Cunningham. Tich was about five feet ten tall. His Christian name, William, was never used. His official Army number was 2323452. Though we had different regimental loyalties, two very close friends indeed were in the Gunners. They were Walton and Stanger. The former I knew better. 'Jackie' Walton I remember mostly. for his cheerful disposition. Before I left Spike, both he and Stanger had transferred to Royal Signals. Rarely did we come face to face with our fellow operators at Bere Island. We knew each other only across the air. Within seconds of one of them pressing a key, we could put a name to that operator. At Catterick there was quite a turnover of operators. They were selected from a group of Boys who had passed their BIII's and were waiting to reach the age of eighteen, and so pass into mans' service, and be posted. I envied them their training. Their operating was impeccable.

Each year, in the early Autumn, postings began to come in for those who were earmarked for overseas during the coming trooping season. My time in Spike was up. One day, in Orders, my number, rank and name appeared and shown against it "… Posted to 1st Indian Divisional Signals, Rawalpindi, India". I was given a provisional embarkation date for late December. Prior to departure, there would be twenty eight days leave. Following that, a couple of weeks in Catterick Camp for purposes of documentation, medicals, issuing of tropical uniforms and kit, and the inevitable inoculations.

Towards the end of October 1936, I packed by kitbag. With a heavy heart, it was time to say my farewells. Spike had been a marvellous experience. I had learnt so much. I was happy, and my time there was, perhaps, the salad days of my military life. On leaving the Island and my closest friends, I felt somewhat fragile and insecure. Such emotion was transient. A new adventurous tomorrow lay ahead.

As a result of pressure from the Government of Eire, all British Forces were withdrawn from the South Irish Cost Defences in 1938. It was a very controversial decision. The aftermath was not truly brought home to the British Government until the outbreak of war, just a year later, when the backwash was felt. Throughout the war, we were denied the use of those waters, and harbours. The subject was, and to some, still is, political dynamite. Before it explodes, I will let it rest.

After the war, I found it difficult to find out what was going on in the Island. To the best of my knowledge it became a military prison for the Irish Army, though I was never able to confirm that.

On 16th March 1985, the following paragraph appeared in the *Daily Telegraph*:

Irish Island Jail

An 18th century Irish Jail, Spike Island, off the Co. Cork Coast, is to be re-opened to accommodate young "joy riders" whose car thefts have helped to increase the Republic's prison population by 40 per cent in three years.

Not long ago, I learnt that Colonel F I N McOstrich died after a short illness at 37 (Accra) West Africa Military Hospital on the night of Monday 26 July 1948. At the time, he was Chief Signal Officer,

West Africa Command. In 1942, he had been taken prisoner at Singapore when he was commanding 18th Divisional Signals. He remained POW until the cessation of hostilities in August 1945. Such sad news.

'Tich' Cunningham followed me out to India in '38, and he was posted to 3rd Indian Divisional Signals, Meerut. During the war he was in the SAS for that elite, he was tailor made. Whatever became his lot, he would have given his best, because he knew no different. 'Tich' survived the war. In 1946 I visited him at his home in Stockton-on-Tees. We enjoyed a short post-war reunion together. With the passing of years, we had both changed, but yet that intangible bond between us was as strong as ever. Today, we have lost touch.

Prior to embarking for India, and still in Catterick, I met Jackie Walton. He was under training as an Operator Signals, and proudly wearing a Royal Signals cap badge! From that time, I have neither seen nor heard of him. The value of such friendships in inestimable, the price of their severance is one the soldier has to pay.

Inside the fort, Spike Island – 1966

One time Admin. Block and Messes

Our old Accommodation Block. Now derelict

Chapter 4

Embarkation leave was not altogether uneventful. My home, at the time, was in South East London. One evening, while visiting old family friends near the Crystal Palace, the youngest member of the household (then aged about ten) came rushing in, excitedly, and called upon us to come outside to see the big fire at the Crystal Palace. Small boys often exaggerate, and not much importance was attached to his appeal. Occasionally, even small boys can be quite truthful. After a few brief moments, we followed the lad outside. The Crystal Palace was ablaze. The night presented us with the most spectacular fire Londoners had – until then – ever seen. For days it was national news. Then, overnight, the news became dramatically international. Headlines were larger and bolder. For months, there had been rumours that the King wishes to marry a twice divorced American woman called Mrs Simpson. Now, it was splashed in all the papers and the main topic on the BBC wireless. Within days the climax came with the abdication of Edward VIII. George VI became King. Henceforth, I would be serving under my third monarch! Historic times indeed, and ones which were never to be forgotten by this young soldier.

There were over a hundred of us in the draft of Royal Signals personnel who about 10pm on New Year's Eve 1936, joined a troop train at Darlington Station bound for Southampton. There were no celebrations, and no excitement. Our mood was rather subdued. Early the following morning the train pulled into the dockside, and there, we had our first view of HMT *Dorsetshire*, which was the troopship taking us to Karachi.

The *Dorsetshire*, I imagine, was about 8,000 tons. She was one of a small number of ships owned by the Bibby Line, and designed and built as a troop carrier.

British soldiers do not expect their lives to be a bed of roses. They are trained to expect, and to endure hardship without complaint. On boarding the ship, I was unprepared for what I found. I learnt that the impossible can be done. The Army had achieved it by putting a quart into a pint pot! At first, it did not appear possible that so many men were to be crowded into a tiny hold of a ship for transportation to India. Unlike convicts transported to Australia, our ship was powered by steam and not sail. There, the dissimilarity just about ended. Had anyone attempted to ship cattle under such conditions, for a thirty five day voyage, the RSPCA would have obtained a Court Injunction to prevent it; and won their case. This was not war-time, but it was reminiscent of the Dark Ages. In my mind, I tried to picture what conditions would be like in about two weeks' time when we entered the tropics and then the Red Sea. My stomach revolted.

Before leaving the English Channel behind, it was obvious that my first impressions, and fears, were materialising. It is no great hardship to sleep in a hammock. They are not uncomfortable, even though the posture of the body becomes like the letter 'V'. Ours were so closely packed together that it was possible to reach out and touch other surrounding hammocks. Not only was there insufficient space, but also insufficient hooks for every man to "sling" his hammock. Consequently, men slept where they could which was mostly on the hard deck and on table tops. If the weather was moderate, some slept on the open decks. No mattresses were provided. Ventilation was inadequate. As we sailed out into the Bay of Biscay, seasickness increased and so did the stench!

The standard of food was little better than our living conditions. There were canteen facilities on board so we were able to purchase odd items such as sweets, biscuits and cigarettes for the smokers. For the duration of the voyage we were not allowed to draw our full pay entitlement, but an all round flat rate of 5/- a week. Why that restriction was imposed, I do not know. Beer was available in the evenings, but rationed to one pint per man, per day. That did not trouble many as the quality was so poor that it was unattractive.

In a space not exceeding more than a third of that available on the ship, were squeezed the lower ranks. There must have been almost a thousand of us; maybe more. On the other hand, there were relatively a small number of officers, their wives and families who travelled as First Class passengers. This took up almost half of the ship's space. They had cabins, proper ventilation with fans, a lounge, a bar and a spacious restaurant where they were waited on by stewards, as also in their cabins. That rankled, and was a source of bitterness. Morale was low and that was disturbing and depressing. An experience of this nature was entirely new to me, and I found it alarming. In pre-war times, the difference between the upper and lower classes was not just a gap, but a crevasse. Class distinction was the keystone to the social structure. The Army only reflected what prevailed in many other walks of life. Officers, as such, were not to blame, but rather society as it was over fifty years ago. It had to be recognised that each year, thousands of troops travelled in troop ships under conditions equally as bad as ours. They too, must have felt that their situation was explosive, but they had endured and survived. Therefore, I concluded that it would be best not to belly-ache, but to accept my circumstances and get on with it. That I did.

Sea travel was not new to me. Before reaching the age of twelve, I had crossed the Bay of Biscay and the Equator, four times on Union Castle Liners.

This time the Bay was moderate. It was a wet and misty day, and we were a week or so out from Southampton when we passed Gibraltar. Due to the poor visibility we saw no more than the outline of the Rock. It was a different story when some days later we entered Valetta Harbour. The sun blazed down on a vast array of battleships. A most impressive sight and left no one in doubt that "Britannia Rules the Waves". After just two, or three hours we were heading out to sea, and sailing for Port Said. By sunset, Malta was many miles astern, and out of sight. The sun was now making its presence felt. The days became warmer. This was very noticeable when a few days later, at daybreak, we dropped anchor at Port Said, and when all movement of the ship had ceased, the day promised to be a scorcher. Like Malta, our visit was again brief, and no shore leave was granted. Here, a mere handful of troops and families disembarked. The Army's presence in Egypt during the thirties was quite large, and in turn Royal Signals were strongly represented. Egypt was a four year station, whereas India was a five year posting.

By now, sleeping on the open deck at nights was almost out of the question. Everyone else had the same idea, and there was a nightly stampede as each man endeavoured to find himself a space. To sleep below decks, where there was no ventilation, nor cooling system was repulsive, but more often than not had to be endured.

Most of our daylight hours were devoted to cleaning. Everything had to be scrubbed. One inspection followed another. When chance permitted, I read. Books were worth their weight in gold. A Penguin Paperback only cost sixpence (2½p). Any book soon became thumb marked and grubby as it was passed from one reader to another. If I was not on any specific duty, I would spend the evenings on whatever space I could find on a open deck. Even under our austere conditions it was relaxing and refreshing to experience the coolness of a sea breeze on a tropical evening. Though it was wintertime in the Northern Hemisphere, we were now far enough South to forget the hardships of a European Winter. Troopship life failed to harm my enjoyment of the seas. A few moments – or better a few hours – on an open deck set at rest any troublesome thoughts. It was a remedy for any bitterness, and an immunisation against any sour emotions that may be festering.

Proceeding down the Suez Canal our speed seemed little more than walking pace. The Canal was narrower than I had expected, and for those who could speak Arabic, I am sure that it would have been possible to indulge in a conversation with any Arab on either bank. Its length is about a hundred miles, but it is not one long engineered canal, but rather joins up three main lakes. It is in those lakes, and only therein, that ships may pass. Suez being the most direct route to the East was in that pre-Air era, an Oceanic Piccadilly Circus.

As we discarded our serge uniforms, and donned our tropical one of khaki drill shirts and shorts, life became a little more comfortable. That the hot water showers (salt water) were always cold, was now a blessing.

Our daily ship's routine did not change as we sailed into the Red Sea. Some of the monotony was broken by the changing skyline as most of the time land was visible. The weather became humid and oppressive.

At the Southern end of the Red Sea lies the port of Aden, with its excellent anchorage. As we arrived, the scene was one of fervent activity as ships of all shapes and sizes were manoeuvring in and out of harbour. An array of vessels lay at anchor. In contrast to Malta, here, the shipping was more international, and of a commercial and merchant nature. Aden was strategically placed to make it an attractive fuelling station to the world's shipping. It offered good facilities and low oil prices. Those were Aden's prosperous and halcyon days. Its decline commenced with the advent of air travel and the simultaneous slump in shipping. It was, like Malta, a Crown Colony, and a small number of British troops were stationed there. They included a handful of Corps personnel. For climatic reasons, Aden was a three year station, but a posting that was sought after my many. Less that a year earlier, I had personally made such an application, but it was not to be.

Similar to our previous stops, our stay in Aden was just for a few hours, and again no shore leave. On leaving the port, we entered the last leg of our voyage. In less that a week's time we would be arriving in Karachi. In the meantime, we sailed into the North West Pacific, or more strictly, that part of it known as the Arabian Sea. Contrary to expectations, the temperature dropped slightly and the sea was somewhat less calm. Until that time, the elements had been kind to us and apart from a little rough water soon after leaving the UK, it had been calm waters all the way. That permitted us to get our sea legs; so the current discomfort created little seasickness. Anyway, it no longer mattered, as Karachi seemed just around the corner.

The last day at sea was the only one of the voyage that generated any excitement in me. It was a busy one, as we prepared our kit and equipment for the following day's disembarkation.

On, or about, the last day of January 1937, HMT *Dorsetshire* docked at Karachi. The most uncomfortable thirty, or so, days of my military life – so far – came to their end.

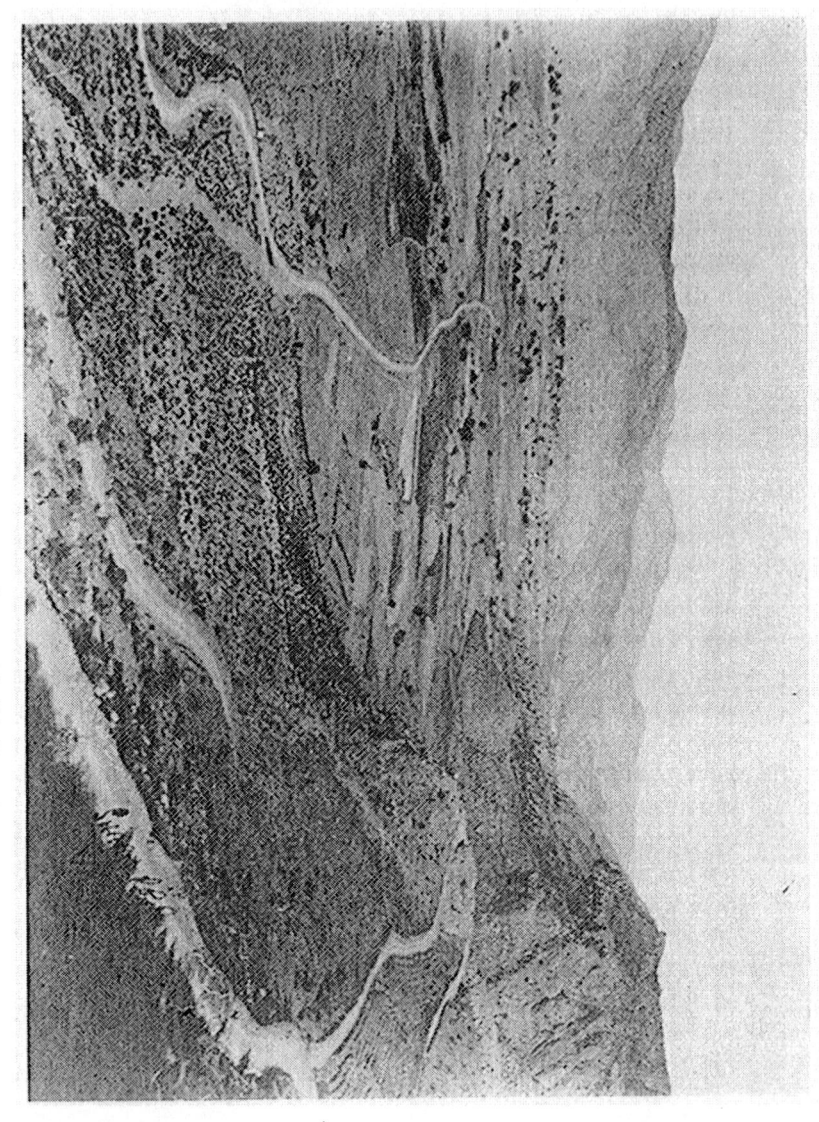

Not taken on the Moon but on N. W. Frontier

Chapter 5

This journal is a record of views and experiences of a pre-war regular soldier, including his service in India. It is apparent that most of that time was served in that part of India now known as Pakistan, but for the purposes of relating my story, I refer to it as India. Prior to 1946, the entire sub-continent was India. Partition did not come, with the birth of Pakistan, until that year.

The docks of any busy port are basically the same world-wide. Karachi was no exception, and sure as fate, the inevitable trains were waiting to convey their human cargo to the various garrison towns scattered across the Indian Empire. Together with a few hundred other troops we packed into a train whose destination was Rawalpindi. There followed a wait of at least two hours before there was any hint of movement. Fifty years later, in the UK, rail travellers are all too familiar with such an experience!

Until then, I had given little thought to the tail end of our journey other than an awareness of it involving a three day rail journey. As expected, comfort on the train was conspicuous by its absence. There were six of us in a tiny compartment. The seats were slatted and without upholstery. My companions were all Royal Signals, and like myself pleased to be on dry land, and furthermore, not unduly concerned about the obvious discomforts that would have to be endured over the following few days.

To form any kind of view, or impression of India, within a few hours of arrival, would have been as senseless as any new arrival at Liverpool judging my Country by the appearance of the docks. The forming of my views of India was to become a very gradual process that lay in the future. For the moment, uppermost in my mind was heat and flies.

While still at sea, we had been well prepared and sermonised on health and hygiene. Implanted in my mind was a formidable list of 'Do's and Don't'. Never drink untreated water. Never eat fruit that has not first been washed in a weak solution of Potash PerMag (Condys Fluid). Dairy products may only be consumed if produced by the military farms, though our milk was mostly tinned and imported. Uncovered food attracts flies. Flies bring dysentery. Uncovered human flesh attracts mosquitoes, which are particularly active during the hours of darkness. Mosquitoes carry malaria. From sunset to sunrise, shirtsleeves have to be rolled down and long trousers worn, whether in uniform or mufti. We were only allowed to enter cafés and restaurants, which displayed a military "In Bounds" sign. They were not just petty restrictions, but made sense. Anyone who contravened the rules not only paid the price for breaching military discipline, but placed his own health in peril and maybe that of his comrades. On that first day in India, a lesson was learnt in preventative medicine. The authorities regarded our health as paramount.

    It was in the late afternoon when the wheels began to turn, as our rail journey commenced. Detailed recollections of those three days of rail travel are somewhat suspect. No hot meals were served on the train. They were served at pre-arranged stops, when we left the train, and sat at tables in tents or on platforms. The coaches were divided into compartments with hard wooden seats. Above were additional wooden platforms of a shelf type which at night were lowered for sleeping purposes. To describe them as bunks would be stretching literary licence to breaking point. Though the journey was boring, hot dirty and inactive, we did not become irritable with each other. The conversation was speculative as we dabbled in discussions on our future lives in the forthcoming five years. Meanwhile, the train chugged along rarely exceeding 30mph. Our route took us across the Sind Desert. Stops were all too frequent, but in due course we reached Agra, the one time capital of the Mogul Empire, and so enabled us to enjoy an unrestricted view of this famous mausoleum. By that time our cramped conditions were having their affect on us. We became dirty, unkempt and scruffy. As representatives of the King Emperor's Army we were, in appearance, a poor advertisement. Anyone mistaking us for refugees from a small primitive country, with an undesirable political regime, might be forgiven.

    Lahore was the penultimate major stop, whereupon spirits rose as we entered the home stretch.

A glowing red sun was low in the sky when we arrived at our destination. Rawalpindi was the Aldershot of India. It seemed that half of the British Garrison was on the platforms to meet us. There were no lorries to convey our equipment to the barracks. This was all loaded onto horse drawn wagons, and taken to Cambridge Barracks. Hopefully, we thought there would be transport of some kind to convey us to the barracks. Not so, we marched. Cambridge Barracks was the home of 1st Indian Divisional Signals, and it was there that we came to a halt while there was still some daylight in the sky. Externally, the Barracks were not unattractive. The buildings were long and quite tall, comprising two floors. The ground floors consisted of offices, stores, lecture rooms and the like. The first floors were devoted entirely to barrack room accommodation. Both floors were surrounded by large spacious verandas. As a draft of about 35 men, we now ceased to exist. Henceforth, we 'belonged'. What a wonderful feeling. Here was pre-war, peacetime India in the days of the Raj. Our barrack room was large, and individually we had plenty of space. Fires were burning, as on that first evening temperatures fell. This was luxury and comfort of a standard I had not previously experienced in Army life. After taking off our equipment, and a quick wash, we were shown the Mess Room where a meal awaited us. The food was superb. We sat at tables which had been previously laid out, and with white table cloths. We were waited upon by Indian bearers. It seemed unbelievable that we, who were just about the lowest of the low in rank, could enjoy a standard so high in our catering. The NCO in charge of the cookhouse was British, but the cooks were all Indian followers. It is difficult to say if there is any significance in that. No one could be blamed for asking "Where is the catch?". In fairness, there really was none, except its duration. Due to our military obligations, little time was spent in these barracks until September 1939 when our world was turned upside down. That initial day was both tiring and exhilarating, and concluded with hot baths. The beds actually had real springs and not steel strips. The sheets were no longer of the prison calico type, but white cotton/linen. Perhaps it would be short lived, but for my part, I was determined to make the most of it.

There followed a few days 'acclimatising' period, and then I was posted to 'K' Section. This was an Infantry Brigade Signal Section and in the Field would form part of the 2nd Indian Infantry Brigade. It was apparent that I was not to enjoy the pleasure of mechanical, or even horse drawn transport. From now on, I would cover many miles – all on foot! Our Section Officer was Lt. Percy Tulloch, and our Section Sergeant was Don Ellison. Sgt. Ellison epitomised all I admire, and respected most in an NCO. In 'K' he was our leader. His ability, example and stature were of the highest order. A very find man indeed. Though we daily came into contact with Mr Tulloch, our relationship was strictly of the kind at which, in those days existed between officers and their men. I believe in the later war years, Mr Tulloch rose to very high rank; possibly Major General. He was a very distinguished officer of the Corps. Simultaneously, Don Ellison was commissioned at the outbreak of war and gained high rank.

Though life was comfortable, we soon learnt that major operations on the North West Frontier were about to take place, and in the meanwhile much intensive training. This training was aimed particularly at those of us who were fresh from the UK and had yet to learn the intricacies of mountain warfare, and our function as wireless operators with the task of maintaining communications. Route marches became a daily occurrence. Each one became longer and more arduous than its predecessor. Our wireless sets were No. 1's. When on the march, the sets were encased on a strong wooden frame, which was designed to fit on one side of a pack mule. The batteries, mast gear, spares etc.; were similarly encased to fit on the other side of the mule. Each side weighed approximately 100lbs. As we marched alongside the mule, we were fully equipped in Field Service Marching Order, complete with rifle and fifty rounds of .303 ammunition. Over our ears, and under our topis, we wore headphones. In our left hand a Morse key, leaving the right free for sending. A second operator marched alongside with a message pad and pencil (sharpened both ends), writing down whatever was called out by the receiver. When transmitting the arrangement was reversed. In that manner we worked in pairs. Being a 'new' arrival, I was appointed junior operator to a higher grade and more experienced man named Truslove. Poor chap, he was nicknamed 'Truss', but I could not have wished for a more valuable better half. In subsequent months he proved to be a really good friend. When marching, troops normally halt every hour for a ten minute rest period. For the No.1 Set Operator. This meant unloading the mule, erecting the set as a ground station, passing traffic and reloading. The word "rest" was, for us, somewhat of a misnomer.

Each mule had its own driver. He was an Indian soldier who could be either a Muslim or Hindu. They were conversant with English, and almost always got on well with their two British set operators. From those drivers, I soon learnt much about Indians and a little of their language. Our Section was made up of about 25 British ranks, plus a slightly larger number of Indian Ranks. The total strength of the entire Indian Divisional Signals must have been well over 800 men. Our Commanding Officer was Lt. Col. W R C Penny, who, during the war, became a Maj. General, and I believe the only officer in our Corps to ever command a Division. That, I understand, was at some time in Italy.

How far, how much detail, and to what depth do I probe when delineating the functions of an Indian Divisional Signals Unit, or the technicalities of wireless sets and communications? The absence of such information may cause some to think many questions are left unanswered. That is regrettable, but the only alternative would be to rewrite more than one military manual which it takes to embrace such subjects. To answer the question would be child's play if this journal was aimed at a particular readership. It is not. It is a record of experience during military service, and comprises my views, comments and emotions; albeit in retrospect.

It was fun learning Hindustani, or rather a much murdered barrack room version of it. During the first three months, my vocabulary, though still very small, was adequate to make myself understood on most occasions. Serious study of the language was available, and involved attending proper classes under a qualified instructor. They were not compulsory, but encouraged. There was a small financial reward for anyone completing the course and passing the final exam. My sense of humour did not go that far.

Strictly, sport was not compulsory, but I cannot recall anyone who did not take part in one kind or another. Within days of arriving, I had decided to take up tennis and hockey. There was plenty of good tuition at hand. Hardly a day passed that I did not spend a couple of hours on a tennis court or hockey pitch. Sporting activities, plus training and preparation for the now imminent Waziristan operations, left little time for other leisures.

Service on the North West Frontier was 'Active' service. The commencement of what became known as the 1937 Waziristan Operations brought my initiation into active service. Much has been said and written about the Frontier. Even a couple of films have been made, all portraying it as romantic, but had little in common with my life and times there. Prior to leaving 'Pindi' we listened to many tales of the Frontier from old soldiers. Some told deliberately to scare us, and others with the sole purpose of placing the teller in a good light. Such were accepted with a pinch of salt! When undisturbed, and in a tranquil mood, I tried to visualise what lay ahead, and examine my emotions. For the first time in my life I was about to encounter an enemy who was intent upon killing. Few men are brave. Fear was a subject none of us discussed, at least not openly. Would I shortly undergo the experience? A touch of nervousness was present in my mind, but also a touch of excitement. If, at times, I was to become a little frightened, it would not matter providing I was able to control it, and not outwardly show it. Training had been thorough and would see me through. I vowed to myself I would never, never, never let myself down, or worse, let down by fellow men. With such feelings I was not alone. With confidence, I can affirm they were shared by others. Not those more experienced who had "Seen It All Before", but by the new boys just out from the UK. We were barely out of our 'teens' and perhaps may be forgiven if we experienced a few butterflies when about to undergo active service for the first time.

Still in 'Pindi', our preparations became more vigorous and intense. Life was not without its 'Bull'. We polished this; we polished that. Our main tools of trade were Brasso and Kiwi!

The instrument mechanic in 'K' Section was Williams. Whenever opportunity presented itself, I sought his company. He was unquestionably the greatest amateur photographer I have ever met throughout my life, and from him I learnt many lessons. My camera was basic and old, but I soon learnt that even with such inadequate equipment, it was possible to obtain quite a presentable standard of results. There was no photographic censorship, and even on the Frontier, we would be permitted to photograph whatever we wished. My mind was made up. Never mind how heavy my pack and equipment, I would ensure that I also carried my camera and an adequate supply of film.

Mail from home arrived at least once a week. It was usually about four weeks old when we received it. As there was no air mail in those years, it was all conveyed by fast ships on the scheduled passenger routes to/from India, Australia and New Zealand When mail arrived from Home, they were happy moments and faces would light up. Sometimes an individual's expression would change to sadness or anxiousness as he received some news of an illness, or problem at home. Talk about Home and 'Blighty' was commonplace. Living in such close proximity to each other, and our existence being so communal, the consequence was that there were few secrets. Our moments of joy and happiness were shared; likewise, our moments of sorrow and sadness. If homesickness was felt at any time, it would be when mail arrived. From the day of enlistment, it was certain that at some time I would have to serve overseas. Indeed, I wished that. Finding myself in India was not a shock, and I did not find myself homesick. The knowledge that I was to be in India for five years did, at times, make me a little depressed. It seemed a long time to wait before once again seeing England. Subsequent, momentous events played havoc with even that period of time.

BBC short wave broadcasting was well established by 1937. It was by that means that we were as well informed and up to the minute on world news and events as anyone in the UK. The Nazis had, by now, complete power in Germany. A very sinister black cloud was emerging over Europe, and to a soldier in India was not all that remote. If it broke, we in the Army would get wet! As young men, we did not allow such depressing matters to overshadow our lives. Our own immediate military problems were only just "Down the Road!".

Though we were in the early months of the year, rain was sparse. Grass and vegetation was almost absent. Our surroundings were the same dull, drab, khaki colour as our uniforms. The brightest display in the environment came from the sun's glare. The most apparent feature was the soil, and ground which was parched and of a fine sandy character. When the winds rose, so did the sand. It found its way through every nook and cranny. Such amounted to dust/sand storms, reducing visibility to a mere few yards, obscuring the sun, and turning day into night. Rain did fall with a vengeance, but that came with the hot summer months and the notorious monsoons. In Southern India they arrived in the early summer, but being so far North did not reach us before July. By then, their ferociousness was slightly diminished.

Our barracks may not have been modern, but were solid and very well built. Large wide doors opened out onto the veranda, and a large wide wooden staircase led down to ground level. Until one particular day, I had never given any thought why the designer had made these exists to wide. It was early one Saturday afternoon. I had just returned to the barrack room from tiffin (light mid-day meal). After removing my boots, I made myself comfortable, and with half an hour or so to spare, stretched out on my bed. The barrack room was about half full. Some were changing into civvies to go out, others about to participate in sport and a few were about to follow my example. I lay quietly still and must have been about to dose off when I felt a sensation. The lights above me began to swing. No, I had not been drinking. Something fell out of my locker. The rifles in the rack were rattling. I was conscious of my feet rising to a level above that of my head. A voice shouted "Quake!". After getting to my feet, I rushed to the door. With all possible speed we ran down those wide stairs four or five abreast to open space, clear of the building. That barrack room and its opposite twin, had been completed evacuated within seconds. Bless the man who designed those wide stairs and doors. It was not an earthquake, but just a nasty tremor. There were no casualties, but there were a few white faces, as it was a little frightening. The by-product was dust; we were cocooned in a film of it. It was perhaps as well, as one or two were cocooned in little else! On such occasions, one does not stop to dress. If Eve had been cocooned in dust, would Adam have reacted differently?

The utmost importance was attached to headgear, particularly by the medical authorities. When out of doors, topis had to be worn by All Ranks between sunrise and sunset. They were considered an essential precaution against sunstroke. Though cumbersome, they were light and not uncomfortable. Though not subjects to military law, our civilian counterparts were always to be seen wearing topis of some kind. Our uniform was popular, and perhaps the most comfortable that I have known. Both shirts and shorts were heavily starched; likewise long trousers in the evening. Clean ones worn every day, and so too all underwear. Our laundry was done by a 'Dhobi'. He was an Indian follower who came round our barrack room late every afternoon, collected all dirty laundry, and returned it all freshly clean and starched at the same time on the following day. No such thing as a laundry list, but we always received back our own correct items. I have not got a clue how that was done! We could send as much as we liked, as often as we liked all for one Rupee (1/4d) a week! Our socks were the same heavy woollen type that we wore in the UK. Over them we wore hosetops. Short puttees covered the join where the top of the boot met the bottom of the hosetop. In the Winter months, we wore a heavy pullover over our shirts, which were always open-necked.

Ever mindful of 'the Mutiny', our rifles and a large box of ammunition were kept in the barrack rooms. They were heavily padlocked and secured. Every day one occupant of the room was detailed as a barrack room orderly. His main function was to hold the keys, and under no circumstances was he to leave the room without being properly relieved and handing over – on signature – those keys. Once every 24 hours, the Orderly Officer, on his rounds, would check those Arms and ammunition.

My confidence and experience of the No. 1 Set was increasing daily. The relationship with Truss was becoming stronger. If left on my own, and the need arose I could cope with confidence. As a Section we worked and trained together, but in the field the operators on the sets broke up into pairs with one pair at each battalion HQ and a pair at Brigade HQ. As our Brigade was not comprised of a British Battalion, it ensued that we would always be with an Indian Battalion. In these Indian Units, the only British ranks were the Kings Commissioned Officers. Apart from them, the two Signalmen manning the sets were the only British Other Rants (BOR's). Another special and unique situation.

Minor uprisings and tribal disturbances may not have been an inherent fact of Frontier life, but perhaps just endemic. To the Western world, the causes leading up to the 1937 Operations in Waziristan most probably appeared trivial. Such an explanation would be better given by a scholar in Indian religions and politics. On those matters, I am a novice. Somewhere, in official archives there are details, but I know not where. Our role was to 'Show the Flag', and restore peace. The obstacle to that was a tribal and religious leader known as the Faqir of Ipi. Before the year was out, this Faqir was to cause us many headaches. His name was constantly on our lips, and wrapped in adjectives of the unkindest nature. The impending military events, if taking place today would receive much attention by the media. In those far off days, little mention was made. If a handful of British or Indian soldiers became wounded, or killed, in the far flung outposts of the Empire – So What? Now and again, maybe, a small paragraph might appear in a newspaper and reference made to a 'Skirmish'. Perhaps we were better off without opinions, and attention of the Press and small minority pressure groups who claim to have a specialised knowledge on any subject, but whose real expertise, and motivation, lies in the field of extreme politics.

While at Catterick, and prior to embarking at Southampton, I became friendly with the Davidson brothers, Zube and Snaggle – if soldiers can label someone with a nickname they do. Whereas I had come from Southern Ireland, they had come from Northern Ireland. There they had been stationed and were also natives of the Province. Fate had thrown us together in the same draft for India. What likeable characters they were. On arriving in Pindi, Zube went to 'A'

Corps Signals, and Snaggle finished up in 'K' Section and in the bed next to mine. He was one of the few members of the Section who was not only married, but was also a 'Daddy'. Wife and baby, of course, back in Northern Ireland. His main hobby was photography, and that placed us on common ground. In post war years, I met Zube a few times, and from him learnt that his brother had emigrated to Canada where he had set himself up on a photographic business. For the time being, and the approaching couple of years, we were to be living in close proximity. During those early years in India, Snaggle was a good and loyal friend. We were compatible.

The build up in Rawalpindi reached its climax, and by the end of February we were on stand-by, followed by the final "Off". Henceforth, no more hockey, no tennis, no comfortable beds with sheets, no nights in the local bazaar, or the relaxed feeling of wearing civilian clothes. There were no leisurely strolls in the Cantonment. From now on, it would be marching, marching and marching. The luxuries would be few, and most probably confined to those I carried on my back and which amounted to a change of clothing, shaving and washing kit, a groundsheet and blanket. My pack became my pillow. Surpassing those luxuries were the necessities involving my rifle, ammunition and water bottle. As we marched out of Cambridge Barracks, the realisation came.

'Pindi Station was not unlike London Bridge during the rush hour, except that the rats in this race wore topis, or turbans and they were all dressed in khaki. The participants at both scenes appeared to be chasing their own tails. It was loading stores and mules that was our first task. Our own well being and comfort always took second place to that of our horses or mules. It was sometime later, that we were allocated seats. It goes without saying that there were no comforts, but by Indian standards the journey was short; just one night. Early the following morning, we arrived at Mari Indus, where we changed trains. The remaining part of our journey was on a narrow gauge, single track, very primitive train making a tedious crossing of a colourless, dreary dusty plain to our destination at the end of the line. It was Bannu.

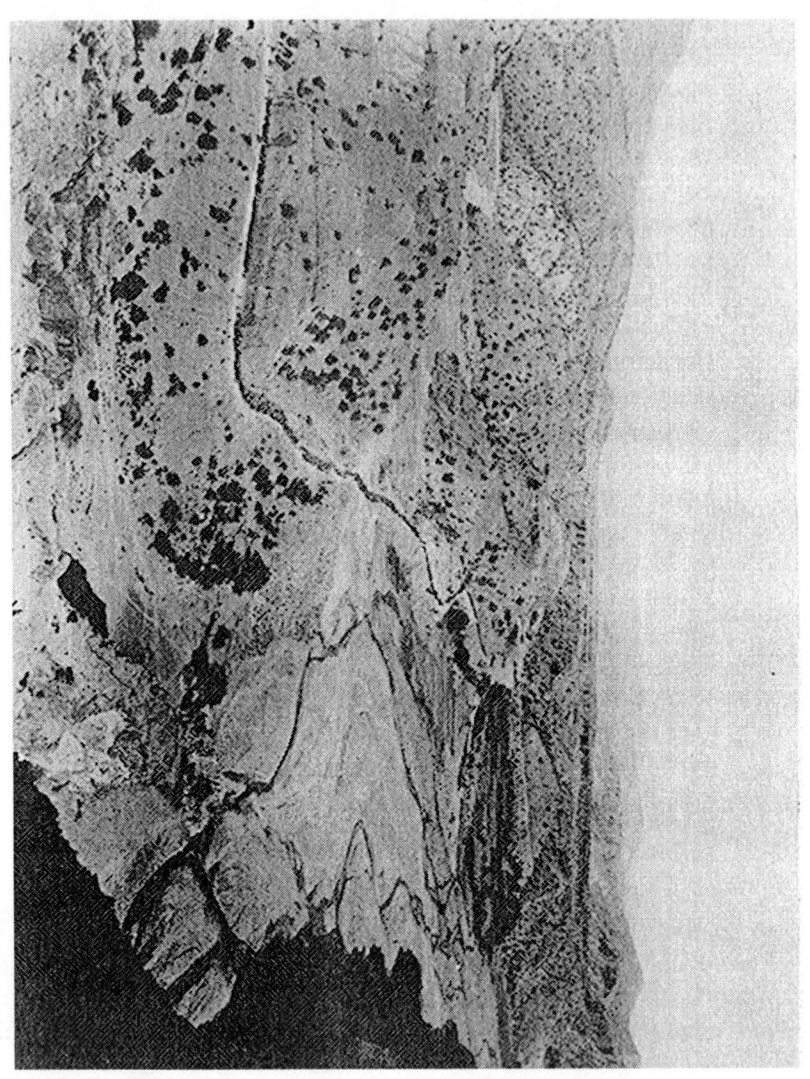

Rocky and volcanic terrain of N. W. Frontier

Chapter 6

Here was a small garrison town, which in normal peaceful times, was typical of a few others scattered across the North West Frontier Province. With the commencement of the Waziristan operations, Bannu became over-crowded, and its resources stretched almost to breaking point. It had now become within the operational zone. Notwithstanding that, there were a few military married quarters with some families, plus nursing sisters from the QA's. In addition, a small number of British civilians. It can safely be said that Bannu was the last outpost of civilisation. For 1937, at least, it was an advanced base and being at the rail head, perhaps the most important. Recapturing detail can be hazardous, but it was probably there that K Section was integrated with the other Units of the Brigade. Henceforth, we were the Signal Section of the 2nd Indian Infantry Brigade, under the command of Brigadier Noyes. After just a few days, we marched out of Bannu. Ahead, the mountainous region of Waziristan, North West Frontier.

It was a tarmac road that led out of Bannu to Mir Ali, Damdil and on to Razmak. The tarmac was narrow, and passing vehicles had to slow down and manoeuvre their near inside wheels onto the verge. To describe it as tarmac is being complimentary, nevertheless, it was of a standard higher than any other I encountered during those operations. At all other times, we would probably meet with tracks despised by – and rejected by – mountain goats. As it took us, I believe, two days to cover the distance to Mir Ali; we must have marched about fifty miles. During that time, working with Truss, our set worked well, and there were no communication hiccups. We did not encounter any hostile tribesmen, and the march was uneventful. My discomforts were confined to blistered feet and thirst.

By now, we were into the early days of March. As we were still on the Plains, daytime temperatures were beginning to rise. My only drinking water was that which my water bottle held, and it was warm. Under no circumstances would I receive any more until the end of the day's march. That really put by self-discipline to the test.

In those early days I was inexperienced, and found it very hard indeed to ration myself over a day's march under a hot sun. In the weeks to follow it would become hotter.

Truss and I were the set crew assigned to the 2/8 Punjab Regiment. It was a Regiment much experienced in mountain and Frontier warfare. Rapidly we built up a good relationship. Events in the following weeks fortified that affinity, particularly with their British officers.

Prior to the war, British Army officers found it almost impossible to live on their Army pay. Most had a second, private income, but those without faced problems. It was these embarrassments, and burdens that played a vital part in some officers applying for service in the Indian Army where pay, allowances, and often promotion prospects were better. On being accepted, they had, above all, to learn one or more Indian language and become conversant in it. That those King's commissioned officers chose the Indian Army did not denote that they were second class officers. They were not!

Throughout this story I have written of officers, and to its conclusion, these gentlemen will be mentioned both collectively and individually. That is inevitable. It will be noted that some I have singled out, and praised their qualities. On others I have made little or no comment. From that it should not be deduced that I had a poor opinion of them. My lack of comment is, more often that not, due to lack of memory, or lack of contact between us. In military, and no less civil life; I did at times award a few of my seniors very low marks indeed. Broadly, I have worked on the principle that if my opinions were low, it is better not to express them.

In less turbulent times, Mir Ali was a tiny, remote camp garrisoned by a handful of Indian troops. Accommodation in the camp was mostly tented on concrete bases. There were a few concrete buildings of a rather temporary nature, and they were of the single deck bungalow type. There was a power supply. The camp was surrounded by strong barbed wire entanglements making a formidable perimeter which was heavily guarded at night. There was no cinema, and no hospital. There was a Field Ambulance Unit. The inhabitants were entirely male. The nearest white woman was in Bannu, and the nearest tribal female in some far distant village in the back of beyond.

The stay in Mir Ali was short. Within hours of our arrival we learnt that the Brigade was preparing to march into the Tochi Valley. The Valley was notorious for its troubles, and hostility towards law and order as we understand it. This was to be no picnic.

There was just a glimmer of light in the sky as one morning we formed up to march into the Tochi Valley. The Column comprised the complete Brigade of four Indian infantry regiments, plus all the ancillary units such as Sappers and Miners, Artillery, Field Ambulance, Supplies etc.; and ourselves, K Section (Royal Signals). Truss and I were, as previously, attached to the 2/8 Punjabs. By mid-morning we were entering the Valley. We were surrounded by the typical volcanic mountains of that area. As we progressed, so the terrain became more difficult. As our driver led the mule, we marched beside it operating the set and maintaining wireless contact with Brigade HQ. For every stride we took forward, it seemed we took two backwards. Our feet were slipping from underneath us. The dusty parched ground was festooned with pebbles and small boulders of various shapes and sizes. It was difficult to find a clearance large enough to place a boot. No road, no track, but a surface without vegetation. We sweated, we cursed, we swore. Our uniforms clung to our bodies, as the temperature rose. Conversation diminished. Every ounce of energy had to be conserved. Many miles lay ahead of us before sunset. I was thirsty, very, very thirsty. Now and again I exchanged glances with Truss, and our driver, and we would try to raise a smile. I was at a low ebb.

The sun must have been at its zenith, when, in the distance, and from the head of the Column, we heard the sound of rifle fire. It was not an ambush, but certainly the firing was coming from the surrounding hills and aimed at the Column. In this kind of territory, troop formations do not just march through a valley without taking precautions to protect their head, rear and flanks. We were not novices. Within seconds of the firing, a patrol was racing in the direction of its source. In mountain warfare, the advantage is often with the attackers. They were possibly small in number, and almost impossible to locate as they camouflaged and blended themselves into the hills. The incident was short lived, and within ten to fifteen minutes, all firing had ceased. It must have been in the early afternoon, when we had halted for a ten minute rest, and once again the sound of rifle fire. This time it was uncomfortably close, and it was obvious we were being sniped at. We fell to the ground, bruising ourselves on the boulders. Not a tribesman to be seen, but the firing continued. In the magazine of my rifle, I had nine rounds, and there was one up the spout. I had only to remove the safety catch and squeeze the trigger, but at what? To open fire without orders was a serious offence, and we had received no such orders. Besides, it was not the function of Royal Signals personnel. That was the job of the Infantry; in our case the 2/8 Punjab Regt. Our field of responsibility was that of providing, and maintaining, communications with our No. 1 Set. That we did. When the mule became somewhat agitated, the driver's job was to calm the animal. That he did. This was my first experience at being at the receiving end, and not my idea of fun and games. One or two Platoons rushed off in the direction of a nearby hill, but abruptly, the shooting stopped and once more it was calm and peaceful. There were no casualties. My immediate concern was over the small amount of water left in my bottle. One of the officers shouted across to us asking if everything was OK. We were able to reassure him. So this was the Tochi Valley. What a place to be! Dust, flies, heat, sand flies, mosquitoes, no sanitation, no water supply and all in a barren countryside where the population's past-time appears to be solely that of taking pot shots at its visitors. Roll on the boat!

  In the late afternoon we halted, and made camp for the night. Goodness knows how many miles we covered on that first day. As the conditions were so cruel, the mileage was probably not so great as it seemed. The speed at which the Indian troops built a perimeter wall from surrounding boulders was amazing. Pickets were detailed off. Each piquet would be about 10 to 20 men with a NCO in charge. They were despatched to a carefully pre-selected, strategic point, outside the perimeter. Their Arms would usually include hand grenades, a Bren Gun and Verey pistol and rifles. When all troops were safely within the Camp, the set crews with their communication job done, would return to K Section. For the night we would be together as a Section. After being allocated a small plot of ground, we commenced digging. We were required to dig a large hole, just a few feet deep for over twenty of us to lie in, and hopefully enjoy a night's sleep. This dugout would also give us some protection against the sniper's bullet. After the gruelling day's march, it was not easy to raise such enthusiasm over wielding a pick axe and shovel for a couple of hours. Blisters were not confined to feet, but hands also became afflicted. Meanwhile, our Indian cook was preparing a meal. Our rations were all conveyed by mule. Likewise, pressure cookers and fuel. Meat, bacon, margarine, sausages (Soya link type), milk and many other items were all tinned. In lieu of bread, we ate hard tack biscuits which were frequently infested with weevils. Food was not a pleasure, but just a means of satisfying our insatiable appetites. Our Indian cook did the best possible under adverse, and atrocious conditions. The pressure cookers often broke down. If it rained, then so be it. Come what may, we expected our food. We expected it to be hot. We expected it regularly. That we had.

It might reasonably be thought that on completion of the 'dig', our day's work would be done. Not so, rifles and equipment had to be cleaned. At sunset there would be a 'Stand To'. A time when the camp was most vulnerable. Before that, the long awaited cooked meal. By now, my thirst had been quenched, but a mug of hot, strong, sweet tea was an epicurean delight.

At 'Stand To', together with the IOR's (Indian Other Ranks), we paraded as a Section. Lt. Tulloch, as always, was on parade. He spoke to each of us. He was not physically impressive, which was misleading. He was just as fit, and tough as the rest of us, and on the march his spirits were always high. In our Section, we were most fortunate, not only with our Section Officer, but also with our Section Sergeant. Sgt. Don Ellison was a most distinguished Royal Signals Sergeant, and his name was known and respected throughout the Corps in Northern Command. As young soldiers under his leadership, we would have followed him to the ends of the earth. In the following years, I knew more than one man who tried to emulate him. That speaks for itself.

In that part of the world, there is little twilight, and the night quickly closed in. The expected raids did not materialise. We lay in our 'Sanger'. Beneath me, just my ground-sheet. Above me, my one and only blanket and the stars. Under my head, my pack served as a very hard pillow. Around my waist, a chain which secured my rifle to my body. Whether having a meal, or going to the latrine, rifles had to be kept chained to our bodies as a precaution against sudden snatch thieves known as 'Loose Wallahs'. There was the added risk that a tribesman would try to separate a rifle from an injured, or dead body. To be separated from your rifle, and have it stolen would have automatically meant a Court Martial and a severe sentence. Our leather bandoliers had a capacity of 50 rounds, and were always full. Our morale was always high, and no less so on this particular night. We kept our voices down, but laughed and joked amongst ourselves. Not far away, on the perimeter, I could hear the muffled crunch of feet. The feet of those on guard.

Our 'chat' was short-lived as we were too worn out to extend it into the night. From that first day in Catterick Camp, I began to grasp the value and meaning of comradeship. Now, fellowship was the most precious thing in my life. Today – over fifty hears have passed – and one of my most treasured memories is that of the 'mucking-in' spirit which existed amongst us in 1937, on the North West Frontier of India. I am proud to have shared in it. Above all, I am grateful.

That routine, of our first day in the Tochi Valley, was one which formed a pattern to be repeated over and over again in the following months.

The next day (or was it for two days?), we continued further along the Valley and climbing to a slightly higher altitude. Most of us, when recalling the past, think of particular outstanding incidents which are for all time fixed firmly in the memory. Indelibly stamped in my memory is the day we made camp, and that first night at Beche Kaskai.

A small area, it seemed not much bigger than a football pitch, was chosen for the camp site. It was Hobson's choice! We reached this destination about noon, when the advance guards, rear guards and flanks scoured the encircling hills. In the afternoon, the order to withdraw was given. Withdrawals were a much practised and rehearsed manoeuvre, and in simple terms amounted to a leap frog movement so that one line of troops is facing outwards, while another line turn their backs of any potential enemy, and move towards camp. Thus, the former are able to give covering fire to the latter. All movements are carried out 'at the double'. In our case, also down a steep hill. That afternoon, our withdrawal had just got under way when we came under fire. I have come down many mountains, and at various speeds, but never before, or since, so quickly as on this occasion. Mule, the driver, Truss and I became an entangled mass as we endeavoured to retain a grip on our rifles and the set on the mule's pack. Our feet ceased to be our means of propulsion. They were replaced by our buttocks and the force of gravity. On reaching the bottom of the hill we hastily tested the set. No problems; what a robust and remarkable set was this No.1. Complying with the Battalion's withdrawal procedure, we doubled onto the plain, with Beche Kaskai just visible in the distance. Throughout we were under fire. A rifle bullet travels at such speed that it will have passed you when you hear it, but there is little reassuring about that. The Commanding Officer of the 2/8 passed a brief message to the Brigadier informing him of one, or two, casualties in the Battalion. Not too serious, and with assistance they arrived back in camp. The most horrific stories were spread around regarding what would happen to any one of us if we were captured alive by tribesmen. We would be killed. Death would be unhurried and the method would be carried out in a leisurely manner. What was left of the remaining naked body would be deposited during the night, most probably just outside, or on the perimeter barbed wire, for our comrades to discover at daybreak. Such stories were, in my opinion, not entirely fictitious. Similar atrocities were taking place on the Frontier long before the birth of Hitler, or the formation of the Gestapo.

Late afternoon, or evening, the sniping subsided, but did not cease altogether. At 'Stand To', we were very much on the alert. From either Lt. Tulloch, or Don Ellison, we were briefed and warned that a most uncomfortable night lay ahead. Once in our Sanger, we were forbidden to leave it without permission, or being ordered to do so.

All rifles were carefully inspected. Each man carried fifty rounds of ammunition, including a full magazine and one up the spout. A box of reserve ammunition was within arm's reach. Over and over again, I have in recent years, endeavoured to recall my emotions on that night, but I have failed. Most probably they were mixed. It is doubtful if there was any feeling of excitement or adventure. It was too serious for that. Probably I experienced a sense of security that I was one soldier in an entire Brigade. A Brigade whose efficiency I believed, and still do, was unequalled across the Frontier. It was inconceivable that a screaming tribal force, not more than a few hundred strong, could inflict any serious harm on us.

Since dusk there had been sporadic sniping. By now I was becoming accustomed to the sound of lead as, at high velocity, it struck nearby boulders and ricocheted in various directions. Sometime before midnight the firing intensified, and I began to feel uneasy. In response we were firing flares into the night sky, and as they slowly descended they illuminated a large part of an area. At that moment, the perimeter troops would open fire with rifles and Bren guns. By then it was known that one or two piquet's had casualties. In some places tribesmen had, under the cover of darkness, infiltrated between some piquets. For an hour or so, it seemed all hell had been let loose. To the best of my knowledge, no tribesmen reached the perimeter. Like most tribal attacks of this nature, it was a hit and run affair. Hit as hard as possible inflicting maximum damage and casualties and then run for it. That appeared to be their tactics. By dawn all was quiet, and not a soul in sight. Inside the perimeter, there had also been casualties amongst the Indian troops. In 'K' not one of us had received a scratch. One piquet with a havildar (Indian Sgt.) in charge had been badly mauled by tribesmen. Vaguely I recall just two or three of the occupants returning to the Camp who were uninjured. Most of the remainder had received wounds, and a few had been killed. The havildar was later awarded a high Indian decoration. A number of other awards were made to individuals for their conduct that night. That assault on Beche Kaskai was the heaviest made in a single attack by tribesmen, throughout the '37 operations. It is, of course, dwarfed beside subsequent situations in the Second World War; yet after the passing of half a century the impact on me was so great that I frequently recall the events of that night. They are too vivid to ever fade from my mind.

Mail from home, in spite of difficulties, continued to arrive regularly. It incurred minor delays as it was re-directed from Rawalpindi. On one of our mules we carried with us a short wave commercial wireless set. It was powered by chargeable batteries. As we carried with us a charger for the batteries of our communication sets, we had no problems in charging the battery for our receiver. That set gave us enormous pleasure, and played an important part in maintaining our morale at a high level. Not only were we able to receive up to the minute BBC news and their more light-hearted programmes, but also broadcasts from other countries. Nazi propaganda programmes were being emitted by the bucketful from Germany. We were not impressed!

Following the memorable night at Beche Kaskai, within a few days we marched out of the Tochi Valley. In contrasts to those detailed recollections, events in the following few weeks have faded into oblivion.

May 12th 1937, George VI was crowned King. We had no celebrations. In our isolated and remote world we were saddened by events that took place on the eve of that Coronation. We had set out from Damdil to a place that was no more than a map reference. It soon became apparent that our objective was a plateau on the top of some cliffs in a rather mountainous area. To reach it, an assault had to be made on some formidable cliffs, and for this a British battalion was involved. Though not certain, I believe that battalion was from the Argyll and Sutherland Highlanders. During the night they came under attack, and suffered heavy casualties, which included a number killed. On the morning of the 12th we reach our objective and I had one more Frontier address. It was Coronation Camp.

Army transport did not move about on the Bannu-Razmak road as it pleased. The road had to be 'Opened', and that only took place about three times a week. On those days, troops dispersed in Camps near to, and along the route would in the early hours of the day take up strategic positions throughout the route. Piquets were positioned in the most advantageous positions, and in so doing giving maximum protection against ambush, or raids. On 'Open' days, thousands of troops were involved in road protection duties. Nevertheless, all military vehicles travelled in large convoys. Usually, at least one a day in each direction. Occasionally, they had the added protection of an armoured car. Such cars were First World War vintage, with solid tyres. Road protection duty was by no means a scrounge. Once in a while, a few odd jokers – no doubt wearing turbans – would conceal themselves in nearby caves and hills and then amuse themselves by firing on us. They knew how to handle a rifle and were good shots, so in turn, we suffered the odd casualty. Normally, we left camp just after daybreak, and marched across rough country for a few miles, then took up a position commanding the best possible advantage to deal with whatever trouble may come our way. With our wireless set, we were always with the 2/8 Bn. Headquarters. Most days were quiet, and passed without incident.

Damdil was by no means the most uncomfortable of Frontier camps. As protection, we dug Sangers but over them we did have tents to shield us against the elements. Such luxury existed in few other unfixed abodes. Supplies of fresh food and vegetables came by road convoy, together with bread. It was not even fresh when it arrived, and after 24 hours, and longer, it was little better than biscuits. On road protection days, Truss and I would take some sandwiches out with us. We also carried a small Primus stove, some tea, sugar and tinned milk. With that, we had a banquet. On some flat ground outside the camp, the Indian troops had marked out a hockey pitch, and erected some improvised goals. On that I enjoyed a few games. When playing, we were carrying nothing more harmful than a hockey stick. To provide adequate protection a Company would be deployed in the hills about. Damdil was a few thousand feet above sea level, so the climate was bearable. It was approaching mid Summer, and with the sun, at noon, almost overhead it was hot. At the Battalion Headquarters, we were kept busy as we passed wireless traffic. When activity was low, one or two of the British officers would come and sit beside us and have a chat, even the Commanding Officer and the Adjutant. I cannot recall the Lt. Colonel's name, but I can still picture him in my mind. A man of medium height, middle aged and extremely fit. His arms heavily tattooed. One day on the march, it was extremely hot and I was thirsty. We came to a river bed, and surprisingly a small amount of water was trickling down it. That water was dirty, but I noticed that the CO knelt down and drank some of it. Excitedly, I approached him and asked "Is that drinking water, Sir?". "Well," he replied "how long have you been out here?" Sheepishly, I answered "About six months, Sir". With the full weight of experience he said "My boy, I was born in India, and have spent almost my entire life here. To me this water is drinking water. To you it is not!". He then passed his water bottle over to me and said "Have a mouthful of this". I thanked him, returned his water bottle, and saluted him. That salute was not just a physical act, but an expression of my admiration and respect for a very fine officer, and a gentleman.

Today, there will be many who know little or nothing of the No. 1 Set which I so frequently mention. Though most of the traffic passed, was by Morse, it was also used for R/T (Speech). Now and again, one of the British officers would ask to speak to a colleague at Brigade Headquarters, or vice versa. Providing the set was being used as a ground station, and the range not more than 3 or 4 miles, such speech communications presented no problems.

Tich Cunningham, my staunch and loyal friend in Spike Island days, has proved to be a most prolific letter writer. It was about this time that in one of his letters he told me that he was coming out to India in the forthcoming trooping season 1937/38, and that he had been posted to 3rd Indian Division Signals at Meerut, UP. In a less personal note he said that Spike was to be handed over to the Eire Government in the next year or so, together with all its installations.

A photograph and article on Idak Fort would not have been out of place in any pre-war boys' adventure annual. The fort was situated less than a mile from the road somewhere between Damdil and Mirali. As it was built from the surrounding clay, it blended into the locality, and was difficult to observe at any distance. It was square, and its walls did not rise to any great height, nor the ramparts above. In one corner a tower had been build which was the height of the average church tower. The centre of the fort was a courtyard. Part of the internal wall had been made into cell like rooms. A more accurate description would be one depicting them as hovels. The walls were a straw like mixture of sand and dust, and the floors were non existent. There was just the dry sand and dust of mother nature's ground. These cells could have been no more than 10ft x 5ft. There were no doors, just a space to walk through. About 200 yds. away from the fort was a small river of very muddy appearance.

It was probably in early July, that a small body of troops was sent to Idak Fort to carry out road protection duties. The formation was about one, or two, Companies plus a small number of guns with RA crews from a Mountain Battery. With our No. 1 Set, mule, driver, Truss and I were included to provide W/T communications as necessary. On arrival at Idak, we found that Truss and I were allocated the dubious luxury of a 'cell'. On the ramparts above we erected our set as a ground station. The cell we made our home, and somewhere to sleep. We soon discovered that we were not alone. Our companions were just about every variety of tropical insect in existence. The place was infested with sand fly, mosquitoes, scorpions, centipedes, praying mantis and umpteen other unidentifiables! Our illumination at night was a hurricane lamp, but the glass shade was soon blacked out by so many insects attracted to the light. For messing purposes, we ate with the small RA Unit. My imagination was incapable of picturing a more inhospitable, wretched, dirty, dingy, depressing site than this. The days were becoming hotter and hotter and the temperature went higher and higher. With so much sweating, so many insects, so many bites and heat, and dhobi rash; life became one long scratch, particularly in parts of one's anatomy not usually mentioned in decent company. It is, I believe, one of our national characteristics that when the going gets tough, our sense of humour rises to the surface and takes over. Truss was never frivolous, his humour was dry and subtle, and of the kind which I enjoy most. At a time like this he was the right man in the right place. Now and again we would laugh at our own, or each other's discomforts.

On two, or three, days of the week the road was declared 'open', and on those days we packed up our No. 1 Set, loaded the mule and went out on road protection duties with Indian troops. It usually involved quite a long march. On one such day, we had been at our destination just an hour, or more, when I felt unwell. The sun was unmerciful, there was no shade and the temperature about 110°F, yet I was conscious of a slight shiver, and I felt cold. Most odd, and then I thought the sweat was drying on my body. I did not say anything about this to Truss. When there are just two of you in a team, living and working as we were, the bond and loyalty between you is so great that never mind how low one feels, you do not throw in the sponge, and leave the other fellow to carry on alone. In the mid-afternoon we commenced the march back to Idak. I ached all over. I was hot. I was cold. I vomited. I was thirsty. It was no longer possible to conceal the truth from Truss. For some months, I had become accustomed to the weight of my pack and rifle, and they had ceased to be irksome. Now, I was aware of every ounce and the return march became a nightmare. It was a matter of pride and honour not to 'give in' when on the march. Only once did I have a colleague who had that tendency, and his fellow men thought little of him.

On return to the fort, I assisted with the unloading of the mule, and then made for our cell. I threw my groundsheet down, took off my equipment, and with my rifle securely chained to me, lay down. Truss brought me fresh water. Here, it was no longer necessary to drink sparingly, as in the fort there was a spring giving an adequate supply of water. In our first aid pack, we had some aspirin, and I took a couple thinking I would be alright in a few hours time. Not so, in a short while I was rigoring. There was no medical officer with us, but the role was filled by an Assistant Surgeon. He was a Class I Warrant Officer in either the Indian Medical Department, or Indian Medical Services. Not having the obligatory qualifications to be a surgeon or physician he was not commissioned. There is no equivalent in the British Army. During the evening, Truss asked him to come and see me. He came and stayed a while, then disappeared saying he would return shortly. When he did, I was feeling rough and that condition, plus the passing of many years, has contributed to the blurring of my memory of the detailed words he used. It was clear that he meant me to go into hospital. Also there was a mention of malaria, but such a diagnosis could only be made with certainty after blood tests. For that, there were no facilities at Idak. As the road was closed for the following day, or two, a problem arose about transporting a patient from Idak to Bannu. That was later solved by the OC Troops giving authority for use of armoured cars. Before being carried on a stretcher into one of those cars, there was the inevitable injection. It seemed that Truss was not to be left on his own. That concerned me, but no option or choice was in my hands. Unknowingly to me, at the time, he had sent a W/T message to our Section Officer informing him that I was on my way to hospital, and requesting a replacement. A relief arrived very soon afterwards. This brought to an end my team working relationship with Truss. Not until the end of the year, when as a Section we returned to Rawalpindi, did we link up again.

Perhaps it is as well that I remember nothing of that armoured car with its solid tyres, taking me to Bannu, where on arrival I was taken to the hospital. It was a combined military and civil hospital, and the first recollection I have is being in a bed – a real bed – with clean white sheets, and in a private ward. Some of the time I was aware of what was going on, but at other times it was just a blur. Within a few days it was confirmed that I had malaria (MT). I was under the care of an Indian doctor who specialised in tropical diseases. He was a tall, very heavily built man who could have passed himself off, at any time, as an all-in wrestler. That belied him, for he was one of the most gentle of men who I have ever met. No patient in my state could have wished for a better and kinder doctor. He was in and out of my ward not once, but many times a day, and an occasional visit at night. Not just an outstanding MO but a caring man. Without his dedicated professionalism, I may never have celebrated by twenty first Birthday. For one short period, I was on the DI (Dangerously Ill) list, and a cable to that effect was sent to my mother from the hospital.

In 1937 the treatment for malaria was a little primitive, but in most cases, affective. Quinine was poured down the patient's throat in what seemed large quantities. It was bitter tasting and difficult to keep down – Ugh! The symptoms were, I suppose, no different that those experienced by any other victim of the fever. Listening to a catalogue of other people's ailments can be a bore. Reading about them, I imagine, no less so.

Sitting up and feeling better, I was struggling to write a letter home to my mother, when in walked the matron. Army hospital matrons do not enjoy a reputation for the sociability. This one was the exception. We got chatting, and she took over the task of writing the letter for me. In course of our conversation it became apparent that she had been a probationer at the same time as my mother in the Western Infirmary, Glasgow. What is more, that matron remembered by mother quite well. That was during the reign of Edward VII. Who says it is not a small world?

About two, or three, weeks later, I left Bannu Hospital, and was transferred to Kohat. Another long road journey, only this time by ambulance. At Kohat, there was a stay of about five days in a small military hospital. By then, I was out of bed for a few hours each day. Lastly, came the final move back to Rawalpindi, but not to our barracks, but to the military hospital which was perhaps the largest, and best equipped in India. Now, I felt fine and fit enough to push a house over. I helped in the ward, and went for walks in the grounds. Life, and the world about me, was again interesting. Prior to our departure for the Frontier, we had left behind in our barracks a rear party, consisting of not more than say thirty men. Somehow, they soon learnt that I was less than a mile away in hospital. For the first time, since leaving Idak Fort, I had visitors, and again felt that I was among friends. Happily, after just a week stay, it was decided that I was to go to a convalescent camp.

On the march N. W. Frontier – early '30s – near Bazmak

Chapter 7

It is no more possible to be stationed in Rawalpindi, without being aware of the Murree Hills, than it is to walk around Trafalgar Square and not to be aware of Nelson's Column. The hills are about eighty miles to the North, and on a clear day are visible to the naked eye. During the Winter months they are covered in snow. During the summer, the climate is superb. Not too hot by day, and by night a log fire might be appreciated to provide a little warmth and comfort. The air is totally free from pollution, and is exhilarating. It was in the Murree Hills that the convalescent camp was situated, just below 8,000 feet above sea level.

On arrival, I was taken directly to see the Medical Officer who asked many questions, and carried out an examination even though I handed him all my medical history documents. The accommodation was of the bungalow, barrack room type, and had no atmosphere of a hospital ward. There was ample space as there were only about ten other occupants in my room. They were a mixed lot from various regiments. For no apparent reason, within an hour, I was violently sick. It turned out to be nothing worse than an altitude problem, and vanished overnight, not to return.

Life in the camp was a joy. We enjoyed many comforts and small luxuries, and the food was first rate. Now and again we were given small jobs to do, but nothing demanding or strenuous. For me, the greatest pleasure was the long walks in the surrounding woods. With sandwiches, and a few bottles of beer, a small party of us enjoyed occasional picnics. Tranquillity, and the warm sunny days made it a different world to the Frontier. Rapidly, I was being restored to my normal self.

Though it had been a happy convalescence, paradoxically I wanted to be back on the Frontier. My companions were there, and I was not. Never mind the hardships, the hazards, or the hostilities. If given the opportunity, I would have left all the comforts of the convalescent camp for a return to 'K' Section in Waziristan. It is a difficult emotion to explain, but there are many Servicemen, who will understand it. In those few months on the Frontier, I learnt of the finest qualities of men, and what brings those values to the surface.

Here, and in this recovery period, there was no shortage of time to think, and think deeply without risk of interruption. On enlisting, I had signed on for eight years as a regular, and that to be following by four years as a Reservist. Over half of those eight years had now passed, and I pondered on the future. To complete twenty one years would bring me a pension, but of only a couple of pounds a week. The pension was based not only on length of service, and not even on rank at time of discharge, but worked out on a number of years in each rank. Promotion was painfully slow. Only a few succeeded in placing a foot on the first run of the ladder before completing their first eight years, and this it would, more often than not, be unpaid. Education was not an obstacle. The only remaining subject for me to sit, and pass, for the 1st Class Certificate was English, and that standard was only required for promotion above the rank of Sergeant. Trade proficiency was essential, but to date, I still remained a Class III; not sufficient for promotion. Such qualifications were all of no avail without an above average report on one's annual Confidential Report. That, I did not have. At no time in my service had I been in any kind of trouble, but I was not considered by my seniors as NCO material. That puzzled me, but caused no worry. That I was quite happy in my career was not, in itself, any qualification for promotion. Like many young men of all generations, I had a tendency to rebel. Had I, unknowingly, on any issue, or on any occasion gone too far, and in so doing blotted by copy book? Such a possibility could not be ruled out. On all that, and associated 'ifs' and 'buts' I ruminated. The conclusion was that when I came to the end of my present engagement in April 1941, I would not sign on, but get out and take my chance in civilian life. Happy though I was, it appeared that I was in a rut, and a rather deep one at that. In the foreseeable future, there was little prospect of climbing out.

The convalescence soon passed, and after about three weeks, I was pronounced fit for normal duties and posted back to join the rear party in Rawalpindi.

With the Unit still up on the Frontier, life in Cambridge Barracks was quiet, and there was nothing to complain about. There were frequent opportunities to play tennis and hockey. After the cool of the hills, it felt, at first, uncomfortably hot on the plains. Those in the rear party all had jobs to perform. It seemed in my case that I was surplus to requirements. That brought boredom, and frustration. After a few weeks, I applied to return to the Frontier. It was granted.

To be back in 'K' Section, was like a home-coming. The faces were all familiar, but two or three were missing. One was 'Snaggle' Davidson who had been particularly ill with malaria. With no waste of time, I found myself again manning a No. 1 Set, but this time as the Senior Operator. Life was never quiet on the Frontier, but this time it was a little less turbulent than earlier in the year.

One of the first 'assignments' after returning was a night operation with the Indian Camel Corps! As the No. 1 Set operators, we were the only two British ranks involved. The Officer Commanding was a VCO (Viceroy's Commissioned Officer). Camels were used mostly for conveying stores, and supplies from point A to point B. They are silent animals. For that night, so were the troops! Boots were wrapped in sacking. Conversation had to be in a subdued voice, and kept to the minimum. The night was black, and there were no lights. Our wireless equipment was carried, as usual, by a mule. It was, perhaps, the only animal of its kind in a camel train. Operating a wireless set on a pack mule up and down mountains, and unable to see where to place one's feet, appeared me to be about the craziest, and most hazardous idea anyone could get into their head. My instructions were to keep as close as possible to the camel in front, in order that the outline of the animal would be just visible. Stand within a hundred years of a camel, and the stench is powerful. March all night within arm's reach of its rear end, and you will never forget the experience. That, I promise. The leader of the column must indeed have been a master of topography. To this day, I do not know how we arrived at our destination both accurately, and as timed at the crack of dawn.

The repetitive road protection duties once more became the routine, yet they were never dull, and seldom were two days alike.

As if to remind us of our whereabouts, on one occasion we had just settled down for the day when the sound of rifle fire came from a nearby hill, and within a split second it became obvious that the firing was meant for us. At that time, we were working with one of the Sikh regiments. The firing was neither accurate, nor heavy, but the CO was having difficulty in pin pointing its source. Turning to a young subaltern, he ordered him to take a platoon and go and investigate. Soon the firing ceased. An hour, or two, passed, then we saw the platoon returning, let by their subaltern. On makeshift stretchers, they were carrying four bodies. I was at Battalion HQ with the No. 1 Set when, almost at my feet, the bodies of four dead tribesmen were rolled onto the ground. The Sikhs had not fired a shot. Each tribesman had been bayonetted. At first, I felt a morbid curiosity, but that quickly changed to one of repulsive hideousness. Never before, had I seen a dead enemy at close quarters. It was an ugly sight.

    Waladin Camp was a few thousand feet above sea level. As we made camp there, Winter was approaching. The days were still warm, but the nights quite cold. Within a couple of weeks, there was a snowfall. Our duties in Waladin, unlike our previous Frontier ones, were mostly road construction as opposed to road protection. Early in the mornings we left camp and made our way for about a mile into the hills where the outline of a road was visible. There, armed with picks and shovels, we laboured as navvies. We regarded the work as degrading, and humiliating. Morale was at rock bottom. Most of the time our wireless sets lay in camp, unused. Soldiers, it is said, spend much of their time complaining. This was more than just 'having a grumble'. The general mood was one of discontent, and sometimes a little nasty. The situation was aggravated by an outbreak of impetigo. Like many other skin diseases, it is very contagious, and the outbreak spread rapidly. It is not a problem of pain, but more one of nuisance and embarrassment. The treatment consisted of painting the skin with gentian violet. In appearance, we then looked more like violet men than white ones. The outbreak, plus the road building work, resulted in 'K' Section's time in Waladin being a very unhappy memory. The only happy day I spent there was – the last one!

    By the end of November 1937 Waziristan operations were

winding up, and plans were in hand for our return to Rawalpindi. We had subdued most of the trouble, but failed to capture the ringleader, the Faqir of Ipi. At times, I wondered whether our efforts to capture, or kill him, were very serious ones. Many thought it politically expedient to let him slip through the net. On that point, I have no comment.

The year had been, until then, the most memorable one in my life. No one year had made a greater impact on me, nor played such an important role in the moulding of my adult character as 1937.

Throughout the year I had taken a large number of photographs. From those, I later selected the best, and compiled an album. Today, that album is held by the Corps museum, Blandford Camp. With the passing of the years, its historical value increases. It is not just a visual record of events in Waziristan, but also I hope recreates some of the atmosphere of our life style there.

By early December, 'K' Section together with the bulk of our parent Unit, 1st Indian Divisional Signals, returned to Cambridge Barracks, Rawalpindi. The immediate task was to thoroughly overhaul, and repair every item of equipment. Meanwhile, preparations were being made for Christmas. Celebrations commenced about 23rd December, and continued through to about 3rd January. Army Christmases have an element of tradition about them, and that allowed us to let our hair down. That, we did.

It was a tranquil life in 'Pindi during those early months in '38, but there was no stagnation. The political situation on the NW Frontier remained explosive and we needed to be ready, at the drop of a hat, to make a speedy return.

The years pass, and associating events with a particular period is sometimes ticklish. Having that in mind, mention must be made that in the first month, or two, of 1938, I was once more back on the Frontier, but it is doubtful if 'K' Section went in its entirety. It was probably 4th Indian Infantry Brigade, from Meerut, who were then in Damdil, and it is to that Brigade Section which I was temporarily attached. There were also a small number of Signalmen from a Signals Cavalry Troop. It was one of those who became my partner on a No. 1 Set. The relationship was excellent, if somewhat short. My attraction to Frontier life had lost none of its strength. It pulled like the unlike poles of a powerful magnet.

When writing of the previous year's Operations, I mentioned the hockey pitch at Damdil. On that pitch, I became the victim of a nasty accident. The game was between a British Ranks team against our Indian Field Ambulance Unit. No, we did not come under fire, but I was carried off the pitch. Coming towards me was the ball at some speed; with stick in hand I rushed towards it. Out of the corner of my eye, I saw a member of the opposing team also making a dash for it. Over the ball we collided, and in the excitement he brought his stick up, and it struck me across the mouth. For a few brief seconds I was 'out'. Regaining my thoughts, I was aware that my mouth was full of blood, and there on the ground, beside the ball, I caught sight of my two front teeth. They were not there when the game commenced! On arrival at the first aid post, I was seen by a WOI Assistant Surgeon. That there was no medical officer available, did not concern me. From previous experience, I had gained confidence in these Warrant Officers. Without an anaesthetic, and using tweezers, he probed inside my mouth locating and pulling out splinters of teeth. Now and again I gave a yell, and he would pause but only briefly. There followed some cleaning, some stitching and a dose of anti-tetanus by injection. The roots remained, as their extraction was a job for a dentist, who I was told would not attempt anything before my mouth healed, say in a week's time. That night I had a violent reaction to the anti-tetanus injection. All night I lay in the Sanger, and must have been quite a nuisance to my fellow men. By morning, I was better, but still with a very painful mouth, and eating was difficult. A week passed, and I was sent to Razmak to be seen by an Army dentist. It was a short visit. Just a whiff of gas, and the two front roots were extracted. Accidents of this nature result in a Court of Inquiry. The findings were that as it was an organised game of sport, I would be classed as 'on duty'; secondly I was held not to blame, and lastly I was to be given dentures at the public expense. The devotees of military bureaucracy had whale of a time. The outcome was quite satisfactory. The player in the opposing team, who was involved became upset over the incident thinking I had received some lasting injury, and that he might be held to blame. On that, I was able to reassure him. The Court did not apportion any blame on him, either. That was the last game of hockey I played on the NW Frontier. There was a sequel to the new dentures. Returning to the UK in 1943, the troopship called in at Rio de Janeiro. As we were about to drop anchor, I was seized with a bout of coughing. I leant over the ship's rail – and to my horror – out shot the false teeth, over the side, and slowly sank to the bottom of the harbour. To the best of my knowledge they are still there today. Such fame!

After a few more road protection duties, it was back to Rawalpindi.

In Europe, the amber lights of Nazi Germany were flashing, and at any moment could switch to red. BBC overseas broadcasts, and letters and newspapers from home all kept us well informed. The outlook was threatening. Yet, it is doubtful if many of us thought seriously about a European war.

One evening, a close friend and I went into the town for a meal. Goodness knows if we were celebrating, or what we ate or drank. Unforgotten is the conversation; it dwelt almost entirely on our future. Our contracts of service were due to expire at the same time. Neither of us wanted particularly to settle down to a hum drum job back home in England. Very, very seriously we discussed the French Foreign Legion. We knew little about it, except its reputation for harsh discipline. One of our major objects for our future was to avoid boredom, and to have a sense of excitement in our lives. Army service, in India, had so far served as a good apprenticeship for the Legion. The discussion was not one of two adolescents indulging in schoolboy type folly, but one of grown-up men seriously discussing their future in a mature manner. Neither of us had ever read a PC Wren book. Quite sober, we walked back to barracks, continuing the conversation. At intervals, throughout 1938, we met and renewed the discussion, but always we kept our intentions secret, and they were never to be mentioned to a soul. Had Adolf Hitler not been born, would our plans have been fulfilled, and on expiration of our military service in 1941, would we have joined the Foreign Legion? Who knows?

The monsoons had just broken in Poona, when in early May

the Sgt. Major informed me that I was to parade for Commanding Officers interview. There was no hint of its nature. It turned out that I had been selected to join the small team manning the wireless station at HQ Southern Command, Poona. Shocks, and surprises, in military life, are ten a penny, but do not often come as big as that! Poona was one of the large garrison towns in India, and like the others of its kind, was on the VV/WT Group. It was so called because of its permanent call signs which consisted of three letters, the first two being VV. The call sign for Poona was VVJ. It was on a fixed wavelength near the 31m Band. The operators were considered to be 'the cream'. The VV operators whom I had met, or knew where all Class I or II. Yet, I, who was to join them was still only a Class III. The standard of operating on the group was of the highest. Naturally, I was flattered by the news, but also puzzled and apprehensive. My departure to Poona came just a few days after the CO's interview. In that period I grew nervous, and lost confidence in my own operating ability. How on earth, I kept asking myself, could I hope to hold my own with some of the Corps' best operators, who enjoyed an undisputed reputation throughout Indian Signals? Why me, when there were many others more experienced, and better qualified to fill the vacancy? It did not add up. The Army is not the best of employers when it comes to explanations. By the time I arrived in Poona, all confidence had vanished.

The wireless station was situated in the Command HQ building. The room was small but comfortable, and cool. The equipment was simple to use, but modern. Dreading my first solo duty, I was in a cold sweat. It was impossible to understand why my seniors had placed me in a position which they must have known demanded a standard which I had not reached.

Our Royal Signals Section was small, and our day to day lives came under the control of a Corporal. Our total strength was about twelve. For messing, pay and most administrative purposes we were attached to the Somerset Light Infantry. Food was appalling, but the barrack room accommodation was good. The cantonment was attractive and clean. Had I not been so concerned about my wireless duties, I would have been very happy in Poona.

On the Frontier, I had been confident, and had experienced no difficulties when operating on the No. 1 Set. The standard was good but was governed by mobility, and local conditions, and it would be absurd to draw any comparison with operating on the VV group. The problem was of a more personal nature, and might have been retraced to early technical training when 'sending' problems first arose. In Poona, and under pressure, those problems became magnified and so a major worry.

Duty hours in the wireless station did not impose any undue strain. We opened up about 8am and worked through until all traffic was cleared in the evening. I cannot recall night time duties. There was a simple roster of shifts. In spite of much help, and guidance from our Corporal supervisor, I remained out of my depth.

After a couple of months, the inevitable happened. I was to be 'returned to Unit' which meant a return to Rawalpindi. Such action normally implies '... and with an adverse report'. In this instance not for disciplinary reasons, but for falling down on my trade as a wireless operator. Life in 'Pindi, and particularly in 'K' Section had always been a happy and contented one, and to return would cause no unease, except loss of face. There would be another interview with the Commanding Officer, which, at worst, could result in being disrated. At best, there would be an outsize rocket! When boarding the train, I felt wretched. Poona had been a fiasco.

Back in the Section, I was not treated as one who had 'let the side down'. Our Commanding Officer, Lt. Col. WRC Penny was much respected by all those under his command, but I had no desire to be at the receiving end of his wrath, when interviewed. With five years service behind me, I had learnt that on such interviews it was best to say little, or nothing. Even if one feels wronged, then stand to attention and remain silent. With those tactics in mind, I faced the Colonel. He made a comment that the report which he had received from Poona merely stated that my operating standard was not up to that required for the VV group. There was no rocket. He did not apportion blame, nor lay it at my feet; neither did he say I was a failure, but in no mild terms said I was to work harder. The climax of that interview came when the CO commented that he thought I would benefit by an upgrading course for BII. After all the events of recent months, I was not to be down graded, but given the opportunity for upgrading! Something unknown to me, it seemed, had taken place behind the scenes. What, remains a mystery. The Poona incident raised many questions in my mind. Most of them still unanswered. It was an enigma.

Preparations were being made in Europe for one of the greatest dramas ever to be staged in its history. The leading role was to be played by Adolf Hitler. Neville Chamberlain was his stooge, whose role was similar to that of a Court jester, and ran to and fro like a cat on a hot tin roof. The scenario would have been hilarious, had it not been so grave. The Army in India was no more than a back-cloth. The curtain was now rising on a production which was to have a tragic climax. As the audience share, and participate in the last night of the Proms, so here too, they eventually participate with the same patriotic fervour in their 'last night' when their freedom becomes threatened.

It was a serious international situation when I went to Upper Topa for the upgrading course in the Summer of '38. Upper Topa was the hill station for Royal Signals personnel stationed in Rawalpindi. It opened in the early Summer, and closed about the middle of September. Being much cooler than the plains, it was well suited as a location for courses. I joined the last Class II course of the season. The convalescent camp where I had spent a few weeks in the previous year was nearby. Upper Topa was marginally higher at an altitude of just over 8,000 ft. The accommodation was somewhat basic but adequate. The scenery and views on a clear day were magnificent. As far as the eye could see, to the North, East and West there were many snow capped mountains, including Nanga Parbat, and Kashmir. What an experience it was. No fogs, no pollution, but just the constant fragrance of the surrounding forests. Sometimes we were enshrouded in clouds with a not infrequent shower. The hill station for HQ Northern Command was Murree which was nearby, and within walking distance.

The course lasted six to eight weeks. At an early stage, I had forgotten Poona, and self-confidence returned. Much hard work lay ahead. Morse speeds became faster, and greater accuracy was demanded. A more detailed knowledge of visual, line and wireless procedures had to be acquired. The course was not a formality with an automatic upgrading at the end. The one subject to cause me worry was wireless and AC theory. For that, I had to give additional study. There was another side of life in Topa; there was sport. At least once a week, I played hockey, and at times a game of tennis. Because of altitude, all sport was played for shorter periods than normally. At Murree, there was quite an acceptable soccer ground, with real grass! In Upper Topa, I was as happy as a king.

The last week of the course was devoted entirely to tests, both practical, and theoretical. On all written papers the pass was 50%. Though there was a small question mark over my sending, and a larger one over wireless theory, it was gratifying, on conclusion to read my name amongst those who had passed.

Chamberlain finally visited Hitler in Munich, and on his return home waved a piece of paper in his hand declaring, 'Peace in our time'. Like millions of others, I was gullible, and believed him. Not long after that, doubts arose. A government minister, Mr Hoare-Belisha (of pedestrian beacon fame) announced a form of conscription. The young men called-up were to be known as militia men. We, in the Army of India, had different ideas, and we nicknamed them Belisha Boys. Either way, they were the forerunners of the wartime national servicemen. At home, warlike measures were being taken as slit trenches were dug in Hyde Park, and other air defence measures initiated. Did such action by the Government suggest that not even our Prime Minister had any faith in that 'piece of paper'?

Back in 'K' Section, and when Munich was fading from memory, I received word to report to the Regimental Sergeant Major. Humble soldiers tremble in awe when receiving a summons of that nature. Not being an exception, I was anxious to find out which of my many sins he had unearthed. After a gentle knock on his office door, there came the command 'Enter'. 'Sir', I said, and making sure that I was standing properly to attention, 'You wish to see me?'. It was apparent that my misdemeanours had not been uncovered, as his manner was amicable. Coming straight to the point, he informed me that I had been recommended for promotion to acting unpaid Lance

Corporal. The purpose of the interview was to sound me out, and learn my reactions, as such recommendations had to go before the CO for final approval. It was a waste of the RSM's time, and everyone else's taking the matter further, if the individual did not wish to accept. Interviews like this were not uncommon, as some men did turn down their chance. The subject of promotion was not on my mind when called before the RSM. I was thunderstruck and unprepared. Gathering my thoughts, and very politely, and respectfully, I explained that I had only three more years to serve to complete my engagement and that I could not expect to be paid for the stripe until the last year. Following that, it was not my intention to re-engage. It could be seen there was nothing to be gained by accepting promotion. The RSM I thought, accepted and understood my views. It may appear that I was now becoming a little disenchanted with my life in the Army, and that some of my earlier enthusiasm was on the wane. Such a conclusions would be erroneous. A more accurate diagnosis would have been 'itchy feet'. The prospect of joining the French Foreign Legion was never far from my thoughts, and it was still my greatest secret and was shared by no one, except a very close and trusted friend.

Christmas '38 was similar to its predecessor. 'Peace on earth, and goodwill towards all men'. The traditional Christmas message – but was it to be just a message? War, with its probability, was a favourite topic of conversation. We are not a hot headed, quick tempered race, but slow in being roused. In common with those at home, we now felt that the time had come to call a halt to Nazism. None relished the prospect of war, but its necessity was becoming increasingly obvious. Today, sadly, there are many who label anyone associated with the Armed Forces as perpetrators of war. Nothing could be further from the truth. On joining the Army, and undergoing military training the horror of war was there for us all to see. A trained soldier does not need any peace movement with all its banners and slogans to tell him what war involves. Such is an insult to his intelligence. The soldier's life will be the first at risk, and he is aware that, win or lose, the odds are against him. Because of that awareness, he is possibly the best ambassador for the peace that our Country has.

At the turn of the year, and with the prospect of war looming ever closer, I began to re-think about my future. If war did materialise, I would have no choice but to remain in the Army. That was certain, and it was rightful. In a corner of my heart, there has always been room for a touch of patriotism.

Memories can be short, and in early 1939, the Munich crisis had subsided and passed. Like the storms nature sometimes creates, long after they have passed, rumblings can be heard in the distance. Peacetime routine, and life style for a British soldier in an Indian cantonment was enjoyable, and of a standard far higher that he would enjoy if he remained in the UK. There was training, and bull in abundance, but that we took in our stride. Our social life lacked one important – if not vital – ingredient, there was no female company. Single men were not encouraged to socialise with married men. To obtain permission to visit a married quarter, was no easier than trying to gain admission to Buckingham Palace! There was a long rigmarole of applications, passes, approvals and red tape, and at the end of it all you would have to be back in barracks by 2215 hrs. Apart from 'wives' there simply were no other white females. Nursing staff were classed as officers, and who can blame them for making the most of that status? That element of monastic life was still with us.

The first draft of Belisha boys arrived. Four, or five, came to our Section. Prior to their arrival, we as regulars, did not have a very respectful attitude towards any form of conscript. We believed that they would be wide open to ridicule. On meeting them those attitudes quickly changed. They proved to be clean, smart, well trained and educated. Their attitude towards us was a good and healthy one. In no time they were fully accepted, and the position never became one of 'them' and 'us'. It was intended that their tour would be twelve to eighteen months. Hitler had different ideas. It turned out to be five years or more before some of them again saw the white cliffs of Dover. There were some who never returned. I know not their names, but they are known to God.

With the situation on the Frontier relatively quiet, and the start of the Summer season, plans were under way for a move to Upper Topa. There, once more, would be courses and opportunities for upgrading. I was cock a hoop on learning that I had been selected for a Class I Course. If I could pass that, then I would achieve the ultimate in technical qualifications. Many of the junior NCO's were only Class II. Much satisfaction would be gained by proving to myself that, as an operator, I had reached the peak. It was quite a stimulus. It would be a hard row to hoe, and in no way was I bursting with confidence. Yet, I might, just might, make the grade. Then, Poona could be forgotten once and for all.

The subjects covered in the syllabus of the Course were similar to those in the Class II upgrading. This time, Morse speeds were much faster, and had to be read with greater accuracy through greater interference. The most intense headaches came with the lectures on the W/T theory. I thought that the instructors were, at times, speaking a language other than English. It was that foreign to me. Throughout this period, I had struck up a very close friendship with Stephenson. Steve – as he was known – had the ability to soak up all this theoretical knowledge like a sponge. He wallowed in it. During the evenings he gave me hours of his time explaining in words of one syllable what the day's lectures had been about. Without his invaluable explanations, and encouragement it would have been beyond me, and still thinking of sponges; mine would have been thrown in after the first round! That friendship with Steve never faltered throughout the following years.

The course with a week devoted to tests and examinations, came to its end in the middle of August. Within days, Hitler marched into Poland. France, and Great Britain were treaty bound to go to the aid of Poland should that Country be invaded. Now what? It was inconceivable that either France or ourselves would renegade on that. We were on the brink of war.

What a kind and benevolent examiner it was who gave me 51 marks on my wireless theory paper. Just 1% above the pass mark! A team does not need to have a forty point lead over their opponents to win a game of Rugby. One point will do. All other results were less marginal, and I had my Class I. So had Steve. We celebrated.

Orders to mobilise came on, or about, the last day of August. From now on we would be on a war time footing. Hastily, preparations were made for our return to 'Pindi.

Early on the morning of Sunday 3rd September 1939 we were told that the Prime Minister, Neville Chamberlain, would be broadcasting to the nation at 10am GMT. That was 3pm local Indian time. There was little doubt what the PM would say. We sat around our wireless in our barrack room. No one spoke, except in whispers. The pent-up tension, the scene, the atmosphere was dramatic. The speech was short; his words were clear: "We are at war with Germany!"

N. W. Frontier, near Damdil

N. W. Frontier, British troops on the march

CHAPTER 8

The instantaneous reaction of most of us to the declaration of war, was one of relief. The uncertainty was over. Henceforth, we would know where we stood. Another reaction did follow, a more personal one, as thoughts switched to home, family and friends. We, in India, were to an extent cushioned by distance. Those at home would, in the early months particularly, be more involved than us. In twenty five days time I would be celebrating by twenty third birthday. At that historic moment I felt much older. As a regular soldier of a Country, now at war with Germany, which was the greatest military power in the world, I was vulnerable to risks and dangers of unimaginable magnitude. How many more birthdays might I celebrate? What were my chances? A depressing thought.

Only slowly, at first, did our life style change. Only slowly, did we drift out of our peaceful routine of life under the Raj. Morale remained high. France was thought to be a strong and faithful ally. Little did we know. In most walks of life it is not uncommon in the daily routine for matters to sometimes be bungled and botched, and not least in the Army. Then, one might well hear someone pass the tongue-in-cheek remark, "Thank God we've got a Navy!". That comment now had a different construction. The Royal Navy was the greatest, and most powerful the world had ever known. The RAF had Spitfires, and Hurricanes. The Dominions were at our side. The unity and might of our Empire had never been equalled. How dare a German Lance Corporal challenge such a formidable foe, and hope to ultimately defeat us? How naïve we were. He very nearly did!

Censorship of all mail was one of the first introductions to war. Movements of individuals became daily, and sometimes hourly, occurrences. At one moment a barrack room might be fully occupied, and later the same day, empty.

Wartime establishments were introduced, and with them promotions came thick and fast. At any moment I expected to be posted, and like my fellow men I had not the slightest idea where I may be sent. Promotion was not offered, and I did not expect it.

With the introduction of war time regulations, all discharges were suspended. Like it, or not, those who were serving on the outbreak of war were to remain so for the duration of hostilities. That was accepted. It did not demand any great intelligence to see that the war was to be a long one, so my attitude towards promotion changed. Maybe that change of heart came a little late. Now, any promotion offered would be accepted. If not offered, then I was determined not to be bitter nor belly-ache. The status of Signalman was my own choice, and it could be said of my own making.

Though in 1st Indian Divisional Signals, Steve was in a different Company, and Section to myself. Except when off duty, we did not have much contact. He too, was still a Signalman. When opportunity arose, and funds permitted we had an evening out which normally amounted to a trip into the Cantonment, and a meal in a civilian restaurant. Failing that, we met in the canteen, Conversation by now was devoted almost entirely to the war. It was on one such evening that Steve told me that he was being posted to No. 1 Wireless Company, Abbottabad. Surprise, surprise, and we went into a long discussion about the Company, well into the night. We pooled what little we knew about the Unit. It was known to have been based in Cherat NWF Province before the war, when it was known as the Wireless Experimental Station, and we also thought it was then commanded by Capt. Dagg. No one was supposed to know of its role which was clouded in secrecy, but we had little doubt that it was one of intercepting the wireless traffic of foreign powers. Like Freemasonry, it was not possible to know much without 'belonging'. To become a member was mostly by selection, and it was by that method that Steve was about to join the club. Undoubtedly, he was one of the star operators in 1st Div. His qualifications were impeccable, and I knew sufficient of his background to be confident that on matters of security he would never let anyone down. I was pleased for Steve, told him so, and wished him well. Next day he packed his kit, we shook hands, and that was it. So it seemed, at the time.

During the following few days, I was thinking more and more of the nature of the job that I believed No. 1 Wireless Coy. was doing, and its attraction became stronger, and stronger. The idea of specialising, and concentrating entirely on 'receiving' seemed tailor-made for my own skills. My sending had always been a weak link in my job as a wireless operator, and it may well have been the cause of my failure in Poona. That still hung about in the back of mind, and I was anxious to be free of it. Receiving, on the contrary had been my strongest.

My mind was made up, and there and then, wrote an application to the Commanding Officer for a posting to No. 1 Wireless Company. If anyone wished to vet my background, and look for any possible security risks, then I would be happy for them to do so. There were no skeletons in my cupboard.

Apart from Abbottabad, there was Sarafand, Palestine, where the twin Unit No. 2 Wireless Company was stationed. In the UK all such secret work was carried out by civilians. Rumour had it that there was such a civilian base in Chatham, Kent. Prior to the war there was no special recognised training for Army operators who went to either of the Wireless Companies. They just transferred from the large pool of operators within the Corps. With the rapid expansion of Signal Intelligence, and with its highly successful interception of enemy communications, it became essential that operators in this field required their own training, and the trade of Special Operator was born.

Individual applications for postings were not always looked upon favourably by Commanding Officers, particularly if they suspected that the applicant was just trying it on as a means of getting out of something, or other. Such motives were not mine. I was not very optimistic that my application would succeed. The waiting period was not too long, but it was a busy one. The war was tightening its grip. Our working days became longer, and any off duty shorter. The atmosphere was polluted with a smog of uncertainty. The future seemed to be on a razor's edge. The day came; I was ordered to report to the RSM for Commanding Officers Orders, for the purpose of an interview. The Commanding Officer was Lt. Col. Charlesworth. With much stamping of feet, and dressed in best uniform – there maybe a war, but the Army was in no hurry to surrender its peacetime bull – I faced the Colonel. His manner was surprisingly informal. He did not waste any time, but quickly came to the point, and informed me that my application for a posting had been approved. Thereupon, I expected the interview to be terminated. It was not, as he went on to say, that I had a fine record in both conduct and trade. Then, pouring over that tasty portion came the gravy. He explained that it was not too late for me to change my mind, and that if I chose to withdraw the application, I would in a matter of days be LCpl.. Such complimentary handouts were quite customary, and used by most CO's when conducting 'departure' interviews. I was sure that the Colonel was sincere, and did not doubt his word. Nevertheless, that urge to go to Abbottabad was very strong indeed, and until that moment quite unshakeable. There was no time to give it thought. A decision had to be made there on the spot. I chose to be posted to No. 1 Wireless Coy., and asked for my application to stand. The RSM marched me out. Colonel Charlesworth was as good as his word. I left 1st Indian Divisional Signals, and 'K' Section, Rawalpindi with a strong recommendation for promotion amongst my personal documents.

Emotionally, it was difficult to cope with leaving 'K' Section. Together, we had undergone some sticky experiences on the Frontier, but always, always, there was that astounding spirit of comradeship. Naturally, there was the occasional minor individual clash of personality, but when it came to the crunch and irrespective of rank, we stood by one another. Woe betide anyone who tried to divide us. Teamwork is the bedrock of a soldier's life. Those names, Sgt. Don Ellison, Cpl. Dixon, Cpl. 'Taffy' Wools, Sgmn. 'Snaggle' Davidson, Dunaway, L'homme, Truslove and many others are as fresh today, in my memory, as they were almost fifty years ago. 'K' was not the only Section in 1st Indian Div. Signals, where I enjoyed many friends. We all used the same Mess Room, the same Canteen, we played on the same sports fields; we performed duties, and drills together. We totalled over five hundred British Ranks, and maybe as many Indian. Today, when we meet at reunions, there is always one Officer's name that is mentioned. He was Capt. Gardiner, who was one of the most strict officers I ever encountered, and yet one of the most respected.

Just before the outbreak of war, Capt. Gardiner, sadly, sustained some very serious facial injuries, yet he made a wonderful recovery and returned to his duties as our Adjutant. Today, Capt. Gardiner is a retired Major General. At a reunion dinner of the Indian Signals Association in April 1988, I again met him. For twenty minutes, or so, I enjoyed his company and chat over a drink. An eavesdropper would never have guessed that over forty years previously when I was just a humble Signalman, Maj. General Gardiner had been my Captain Adjutant. Such is one of the ingredients of a gentleman.

'A' Corps Signals, too, were stationed in Rawalpindi, and their barracks were just across the road from our own. In happier, pre-war days I spent much time there as a very close friend – Alec Langley from Littlehampton – was stationed there. Goodness knows how many hours we had spent together either as partners, or opponents, on the tennis courts. His standard in all sport was much higher than mine, and on the hockey field he won his Corps Colours. Before 1939 was out, Alec was on his way back to the UK. His tour of home duty was short, and he was back in the Middle East, and took part in General Wavell's first campaign in Greece. There, he was taken prisoner-of-war by the Germans. Today, Alec and I are still in touch.

Those associations had become a way of life, not only in 'Pindi, but also on the NW Frontier. There were to be no more traditional Army Christmases for some years to come. Working a No. 1 Set, and marching for hours on end with blistered feet; those ghastly thirsts, and being a victim of malaria, were soon to assume their correct perspective as minor indisposition's in the early life of a regular soldier. A massive military conflict was to follow. Blast the war!

Departure day arrived, and with mixed feelings I left Rawalpindi, 1st Indian Divisional Signals, and 'K' Section. By choice, I was on my way to No. 1 Wireless Company, in Abbottabad. There, I was to enter the 'Y' Service, and be trusted with one of our Country's greatest, and most successful secrets.

CHAPTER 9

After serving a few years in a Corps so scattered as the Royal Signals, it can be taken for granted that whichever corner of the globe you may be posted it will follow that you will meet up again with some earlier friends and colleagues. It was no surprise, but almost planned that Steve would be one of the first to greet me. Now, he was a LCpl.

No. 1 Wireless Company was not a large one, and would have had a total strength of about two hundred and fifty All Ranks. It must have been just prior to the outbreak of war that the Unit moved from Cherat to Abbottabad. The vast majority of the personnel were Royal Signals, but there were a small number who had been seconded from a variety of other regiments, who were known as the Indian Bureau. Though their duties were of an intelligence nature, they were not then members of the Intelligence Corps. Our Company was commanded by Major R E Button. For all operational duties we came under the jurisdiction of General Staff Intelligence (Signals), which was known as GSI(s), GHQ Delhi. Shortly after, that was changed to GSI(8), and in later years to MI(8).

Abbottabad was a small garrison town in the NW Frontier Province. Nearby, and just North of the town was a small mountain range. The altitude was higher than that of Rawalpindi, and during the Winter months, maybe, a little snow. Climatically, it was very comfortable. Apart from ourselves, there were not many other British troops. It might be thought that as the town was in the NWFP there were civil disturbances, and problems. On the contrary, Abbottabad was peaceful. About half a mile up the road from our barracks, was a small military hospital. In many ways it was not unlike a small cottage hospital at home. Most of the staff were RAMC personnel, with a sprinkling of Indian Army medicals.

The barracks, including the administrative offices were encircled by a barbed wire fence. The accommodation blocks were single-decker and of bungalow design, and constructed of concrete. The rooms were small, and each accommodated about ten men. The standard was certainly high, and as good as any I had previously encountered. Some of the comforts and luxuries of pre-war days still lingered. Alas, it was plain for all to see that such a life style was speedily evaporating. That did not prevent us from, meanwhile, 'making hay while the sun shone.' The Mess Room was small, and was used by all of us below the rank of Sergeant. An unusual feature was that we paid a small amount, of just a few pence, per head, per week into a Messing Fund which enabled us to purchase a few extras to supplement the issued rations. The additions would be items such as extra sugar, and butter. In effect, we enjoyed first rate food, and plenty of it. The canteen was a detached building, and comprised the junior NCO's Mess. It was pleasant. Army canteens in the UK were all run by NAAFI whereas those in India were all contracted out to civilian firms. Their degree of comfort, cleanliness, and food was quite high, and ours in Abbottabad was well up to the mark.

Barely was my kit unpacked when I was summoned for interview by Major Button. It was just the normal 'new boy' welcome, type of interview, with a few cautionary sentences about security thrown in for good measure. There followed the reading, and inwardly digesting of the Official Secrets Act, and then my signature. From time to time, in subsequent years, that signature had to be renewed. The Sergeant in charge of the set room gave me a briefing on what the work entailed, and I was allocated a watch. There were three, or four watches which covered the 24 hour day on a roster system. The hub of the wheel was the set room. That room had a floor space about the size of the average church hall. On entering, the first thing to strike you would be a very long, strongly built, wooden bench around the three walls. At intervals, and just a few feet apart was a 'position' apparent by a wireless receiver, trays, pads of paper, and in place a chair. Thereupon sat the operator, wearing headphones, possibly turning a dial with one hand and writing something with the other; most probably concentrating to make log entries, or take down a message. In that set room, there may have been as many as twenty such positions, but unlikely all in use at one time. Today, we are all very familiar with such a scene in any Post Office! In the centre of the room, on a single table, sat the Watch Supervisor who was a junior NCO. He too, had a receiver plus a control panel which allowed him to tap in on any individual position. In that way he could advise, supervise and assist as required. Now, and again, he might have a walk round to keep in the picture of what was happening. There was little conversation or noise. Most of the sound would be that coming from headphones, and that would be of the Morse code, good, and, fast and slow. Superimposed on that came the crackling sound of atmospherics. At least once on each watch, a bucket of tea would appear from the cookhouse. That was the signal for mugs to appear, and be duly filled. Smoking was permitted. If an operator wanted a short break, it would not normally present any problem. The Supervisor would probably take over himself, for a spell. On the fourth side of the room, a door led off into the high speed room. Here, there were a couple of receivers, high speed equipment, and reels of narrow paper tape; some of it most probably falling into a waste paper basket. Not, I hasten to add, to be thrown away, but for purpose of convenience. The operator, wearing 'phones, would probably be sitting in front of a typewriter. Throughout the building there was not a transmitter, or Morse key to be found. The equipment, and layout was designed exclusively for reception purposes only; or more accurately interception. Externally, there was an intricate complex of aerials, also designed with receiving in mind. That was the scene and atmosphere as I entered the set room to commence my first watch. Some may wonder did we really throw away waste paper from a very secret source? Certainly not. Such material was destroyed meticulously, by fire.

In those early days I sat at the same position alongside a fully trained experienced operator, and wore double harness. My apprenticeship was short, and followed with an initial solo task covering Urumchi, which is the capital of the Chinese Province of Sinkiang. The Morse was pathetically slow, which was its only virtue. The standard of sending was atrocious, even far worse than my own! In retrospect, I doubt if its priority was very high.

Unlike civilians, our work did not cease when we finished a watch. Over and above, maybe, forty five to fifty hours a week in the set room, there were military duties of fatigues, fire piquets, musketry drill, parades and a variety of inspections. It was so very difficult to accept the military doctrine that first and foremost we were soldiers. The paraphernalia of military life was never permitted to pass us by. It was not unknown when finishing a night shift, and feeling utterly drained, to be told to prepare for somebody or others inspection. The small matter of a few hours sleep had to wait.

In Europe it was the 'phoney' war period. BBC news bulletins spoke mostly of the Siegfried and Maginot Lines, and reports on patrol activity by the BEF. Towards the end of '39 came the sinking of the German pocket battleship 'Admiral Graf Spee'. In the following Spring the Low Countries were invaded by the Germans, and France surrendered. With only the Empire, and Dominions, we were alone, now what? Those momentous events were the background to our relatively peaceful life in Abbottabad. We did not even endure a blackout.

Time passed and with more experience, I grew in confidence. My knowledge of enemy, and other national's, communications improved daily; both civil and military. Imagine the reactions of a Russian Army commander, or for that matter his wireless operator, if they had been told that every signal transmitted form certain stations was being intercepted and taken down by a British soldier somewhere on the other side of the Himalayas. They would have been incredulous. When visualising such a scenario it should not be forgotten that it may just as easily have occurred in other Countries.

Specially designed forms were used when writing down messages. Each one was evaluated for its accuracy by the operator as he alone could judge. For that purpose, he made an assessment 'A' if 100% accurate, 'B' if two or three possible errors, and the remainder were just 'C'. Many letters in the Morse Code when badly sent, or read through heavy interference, may be difficult to distinguish. When such doubts arose we demonstrated them by placing the possible alternative, over the doubtful letter or perhaps just a question mark. The letter 'J' in the Morse Code is .--- If the last dash is clipped it may read as .--. Which is the letter 'P'. A group with such uncertainty would be written down as follows:

```
          P                    ?
        CKTJR       or       CKTPR
```

All that took place at some considerable speed, so not only work fast, but think fast, and make quick decisions.

Apart from messages, all other signals were entered in the W/T log. This would show all call signs, Signal Strengths, frequencies and every procedure signal. Only when we reported to the set room to commence a watch did we know what group or station we would be covering, so we had to be versatile. To be told to take on 'General Search' was usually popular as it presented an opportunity to use our initiative and know-how to seek out stations out of the ordinary, or suspicious. Most stations changed their frequencies and call signs at midnight (their own local time). Sometimes it was quite easy to pick them up on their new frequencies, and disguise, and thus maintain continuity. Identification, at first, may be solely by the operator's style of sending and his idiosyncrasies. Individual operators have their own personal characteristics, which can be quickly recognised. In my own experience, I recall a colleague once saying that I had only to send the first four letters of the alphabet and he knew who was at the key the moment I sent the letter 'C'; which is -.-. He went on to explain that I never failed to slightly prolong the first dash. Of course, I strongly denied it. A little while later I made a tape recording (visual) of the way I sent the letter 'C'. There is was, and there was no arguing. He was right! His assertions were true. I ate humble pie, and apologised. Such are human frailties, and they are a give-away to the intercept operator.

Until the invasion by the Germans of the USSR in June 1941, we in Abbottabad were too distant to take much in the way of German military traffic. Hereto, our coverage included the Red Army, Air Force, Afghanistan, Southern Chinese Provinces and a wide field of International diplomatic and commercial stations. One of the tasks which I enjoyed most was covering part of the Central Asia and International Frontier Troops (Red Army). That was more commonly known as CAIFT and had quite a high priority. Their messages were varied, but to receive one in plain language was as rare as a performing cat. They were mostly in two, four and five letter codes. Now and again a five, or even ten, figure would appear. How much of that was broken by Intelligence I cannot say with any authority, but I believe quite a high percentage. The Red Army operators had a good sense of security, but their standard of operating varied enormously. Call signs were usually three letter, but at times a letter would be substituted by a figure. Their procedure signals were brief and simple and comprise two letters; such as:

PN ... I have nothing to communicate.

PR ... I have traffic for you.

PP ... Your signal strength is ... (followed by a figure)

Intercepts and logs were passed to the Indian Bureau. It was their job – not ours – to break it down, make sense of it, and put it to good use. We, in Royal Signals, were not required, and neither was it necessary for us, to have knowledge of any foreign language. That was in the realm of the linguists, whose job it was to cope with such problems. It was our task to provide them with the material that enabled them to use that skill.

Our receivers were exclusively American National HRO's. They became standard equipment, and later designated as R.106. Other makes and models did sometimes appear, and we gave them a fair trial but none seemed to match the HRO that was so ideally suited for the nature of our work.

To the best of my knowledge, at the outbreak of war, there were just two Units, No.1 and No.2 Wireless Companies, committed to this sensitive work. The latter, in Sarafand, had a detachment in Malta. With the onset of hostilities, a training battalion was set up in Trowbridge, under the command of Lt. Co. Du Cros. They were to train wireless operators specifically for the role of interception, and be called Special Operators. A concept which was new, but with the rapid expansion of signal intelligence soon justified its existence. Both the Royal Navy, and the RAF had similar training, and Units. The combined organisation became known as the 'Y' Service. Yet, I have no recollections of the term 'Y' being in our vocabulary during the early war years, in India. Outside our perimeter wire we knew little, or nothing, of the organisation as a whole. If those of more senior rank knew more, then they did not tell the deck-hands. When discussing details of our work, amongst ourselves we were most careful unless inside the set room. Even when in our barrack rooms we needed to be circumspect. Outside the barracks, such talk was taboo. On meeting other members of our Corps, it became difficult to socialise. They could, and did, talk fairly openly about their work and ask us questions about ours. Instantly, we froze or made some pointless comment about 'What do Corps wireless operators ever do'. Vague and evasive replies like that, in consequence, caused those outside 'Y' to consider us as aloof. They thought we had big ideas about ourselves, and that we looked down upon them. That hurt.

Within a few months of joining the Wireless Company, I was made a Lance Corporal. Nothing spectacular about that, except that it gave me a 9d. a day rise! It has often been said that LCpl is about the worse rank to hold throughout the British Army. I would not quarrel with that. Any unhappiness I experienced during my time in Abbottabad was never due to technical or administrative problems, but always attributable to my rank. Happily, I did not have to wait too long for my second tape, as by Autumn 1940, I was a full Corporal. With Steve, and I both now Corporals, socialising and working with each other made matters much easier. Notwithstanding, there were still a few problems as we were never on the same watch, so our off duty periods did not always coincide. If not on duty, evenings were usually spent in the Canteen. There, we listened to the latest war news on the BBC broadcasting on their short wave overseas service. It was noticeable, at news times, how voices became more subdued. If there was a Churchill speech, the canteen was packed, and we hung on to every word he said. Our morale was never low, but he always gave that extra boost. With the battle of Britain being fought, it was only natural that we worried about families at home, particularly those with homes in London, and the South East. Simultaneously, we heard of German preparations for an invasion of England. With pride and satisfaction in our work, we knew it was important and valuable. It was not until some years after the end of the war that the full extent of its value, and importance became known. Quality of life in Abbottabad was slowly deteriorating, but still totally at variance to the hardships of civilians at home. Rarely was sleep interrupted, and when it was it would not be due to bombs and air raids. Thoughts of that kind were disturbing. Was our peaceful little band, in this corner of the Globe, somewhat out of tune with the drama being played, fortissimo, on the Home Front? We had been at war for eighteen months, or so, and I had not encountered anyone more angry than an unpaid char wallah!

Any kind of local leave was out of the question. Opportunities for sport were becoming less, and less. Occasionally, I picked up my tennis racquet to join someone on the courts. My vigorous enthusiasm had gone. Within a stone's throw of the tennis courts there were a few married quarters. The occupants were mostly wives and NCO's and their children. The husbands were stationed in other theatres of war. Often they came along for a game of tennis. The chance for a single man to meet, or even say 'Hello' to a white woman, only came his way once in a blue moon. A game of hockey was less frequent than one of tennis.

My generation were brought up, and educated in an age of the British Empire. My favourite poet was, and still is, Rudyard Kipling. On leaving school, I imagined India to be a Country of large and terrifying wild animals. If it was, then by the time I arrived there they must have all emigrated. Throughout the five years in the Country I never saw a lion, tiger, or other dangerous animal; not even a poor old tamed elephant. Only in London Zoo, have I seen those creatures. Snakes, I did encounter. One evening in Abbottabad, there were about four of us in the barrack room, and it was very quiet as I sat reading. Suddenly we heard the shout 'Snake!'. The voice came from the adjoining lavatories. Seizing the nearest implement, we dashed out. There, with his trousers at half mast, stood a very white faced soldier. At his feet, and at the base of the loo was a large snake neatly coiled in a tight circle. It appeared to be asleep. Taking no chances, we attacked it. That was most probably the last time I used by hockey stick, in India. Once we were satisfied that it was dead, we promptly took its remains to the hospital, as rightly or wrongly we believed its venom may be used as a serum against snake bites. The hospital informed us that this particular snake was non-poisonous, and quite harmless. How were we to know? Snakes are still not by favourite companions.

Christmas 1940 did not come up to the heights of previous

years. C'est la guerre! Set room duties could not be cut. For us all to sit down, and have a Christmas dinner together was out of the question but we made the best of it. There was no shortage of food, but maybe a slight reluctance to enter into the spirit of festivities. It may have been due to the gravity of the war situation at home. It was about that time that the City of London was set alight by German incendiary bombs.

Touch-typing was not compulsory, but we were encouraged to learn, and master it. Thirty words per minute is not a great speed, but when we reached that standard there was a reward of 9d. a day extra. Delving into the back of my memory, I believe the money was not paid in the normal manner on the payroll, but as a separate payment, monthly from GSI(s) funds. To have this typing standard was an essential qualification before working in the high-speed room.

YAA was the call-sign of the Afghan external/internal diplomatic and commercial station. Within the group there were three or four outstations, such as Herat and Kandahar. The standard of their Morse was not so low as may be thought. On this group, plain language was not uncommon but, of course, not in English. Like most other D & C stations which we covered the bulk of the traffic was code and cipher. The outstanding feature of the Afghanistan stations was the consistently good signal strength.

The Armed Forces of all countries have, and use their own call-signs and procedure. The international wireless communication system has to be quite open, and a method used which can be understood by all wireless operators irrespective of their nationality, and without knowledge of each other's language. Berlin to Peking; Washington to Paris; London to Tokyo, and so on in its many permutations. For it to operate and run smoothly, international agreement is essential. From time to time, a directory is published called the 'Berne List'. It shows all world wide stations with their fixed call-signs and frequencies. Call-signs will be of three or four letters, with a figure sometimes thrown in. The initial letter of a call-sign will often assist in identifying its Country of origin, e.g. W = USA; D = Germany; G = Great Britain; U = USSR.

In those far off days, the old Queen Mary was GBTT, and

Portishead (Avon) was GKU. The nature of the messages passed between stations varied enormously. There was a variety of codes and ciphers. The remainder in running hand which might be in any language. That traffic was known as diplomatic and commercial, or D&C. If it was all so open then why – it may be asked – did we show so much interest in it? Any traveller is aware that when passing through a sea or airport, they have the choice at Customs between passing through the 'Green' exit or the 'Red'. It is no secret that just a handful passing through the 'Green' do, now and again, have something to declare. Messages, like travellers, are not always as innocent as they appear. Perhaps, a company in Rome may send a message to another company in Prague requesting spare parts for machinery, but is it innocent and what it seems? It might, just might, be a cover for something more sinister. As intercept operators, we harvested the crop. To sort out the wheat from the chaff was the task of the Intelligence staff, and they required accuracy. D&C stations do not normally transmit much traffic my hand, but mostly by high speed automatic. For procedure they used the international 'Q' and 'Z' codes. They can be heard in frequent use by anyone who can read Morse, and knows where to listen. Amateur radio operators will be quite familiar with both codes. Each signal is of three letters; the first one being either 'Q' or 'Z'. In many instances an operator can say the same in either code, e.g.

'Q'		'Z'
QRS	Send Slower	ZSS
QSD	Bad Sending	ZSL

When transmitting by hand their Morse was good, and the transmitters powerful; and interception not too difficult. Termez is not many miles inside the USSR border with Northern Afghanistan. We closely monitored it. One of its operators was called Nada, who always used a 'bug' key. Not every operator can handle such a key, but Nada had mastered it. She was both skilful and fast. When it, occasionally, was difficult to cope with her, we would double bank.

Very large international stations would pass messages almost non-stop at very high speeds throughout the 24 hour day. In the high speed room we did have a HRO receiver, additionally an AR88. For this specialised task it was mostly the latter which we used. An incoming signal required to be tuned vary finely, and with the highest possible pitch. Fading and interference played havoc with reception, and when the signal was recorded by an inked needle on a narrow paper tape would be totally unreadable. A five letter group say, RTWSD, would appear as follows:

Under good conditions

Under poor conditions

Sitting at his table the operator had a typewriter in front of him, with the AR88 at his side. Fitted to the top of the typewriter was a small framework. Powered by a small motor the tape was conveyed on a runner from the receiver, across the framework from which the operator "read" it, and typed the intercept onto a normal message pad; and it then fell into a wastepaper basket. Most of the time there was just one operator on duty. With his eyes he would be watching the tapes. With his hands he would be typing. With his ears he would be listening, and listening carefully to every procedure signal, knowing what it meant, and recording it in his log. He would have to react instantly to any change in frequency, and interference be it man made or atmospherical, and never fall behind with his typing. That description of the high speed intercept operators job is an over simplification. With his ability to touch-type, his value was enhanced enormously. For that extra 9d. a day our Government had very good value for money – the sale of the century!

Early Summer months, in India, are monsoon ones. When at their height a day, or night did not pass without one, or more, severe tropical storms. The rain came down like stair rods, and the monsoon drains quickly flooded and overflowed. The thunder and lightening was incessant. With volume controls set at minimum, the atmospherics were unmerciful, and obliterated all signals. It was not unknown to be forced to switch off, and temporarily close down our entire station. When man takes on nature and fights it, he often loses.

As we entered 1941 our commitments and numbers increased. I was by then a Corporal in charge of a watch, and experiencing a degree of job satisfaction that I had never previously found. It was always demanding. To have a good grumble and moan is part of a soldier's way of life. We did our fair share of that! When technical duty clashed with "bull" we often asked "What do they want of us – technicians, or boot polishers?" As always, the Army got the best of both!

Any tit-bits passed from the 'I' staff were encouraging, but they would never say which messages were broken down, nor their contents. They would give us a list of priorities. They would ask us to listen for particular call signs, or maybe particular types of traffic. Obviously, we needed to know a certain amount in order to carry out what was wanted. It is surprising the part that was played by instinct, and aptitude.

Tiredness was a common complaint. One day, I felt a bit more tired than usual, and a little washed up. I felt a little feverish, but not severe enough to suspect anything more than a cold. When seen by the Medical Officer, he just said something about 'hospital admission'. I was quite unprepared for such a comment, and it took me completely by surprise. My problem, I felt, was a minor one, and did not justify going into hospital. Why he made that decision, I cannot imagine. His reasons will appear on my medical history sheet but that document is confidential, and soldiers were not permitted to see their own histories. To this very day it remains somewhat of a mystery. The ward was small with just a handful of patients. With a day, or two, I was fine. I felt like a fraud, and said so, but that MO was stubborn and kept me there for a week. Steve, and others came to see me, and kept me updated on barrack life. The food was good, and there was nothing to complain about, except boredom.

One lunchtime, I entered the set room to commence an afternoon shift. In the corner, on the bench, there was some strange activity. There was an officer, the Foreman of Signals, and the Sergeant in charge of the set room all huddled over what appeared to be a large heavily built, wooden box with metal handles. The cover/lid had been removed. In size it was about that of two 22" television sets strapped together. From the corner of my eye, I saw a machine like an outsize typewriter, and with a similar keyboard. At first, and not taking too much notice, I carried on with the watch. An hour, or more must have passed when I was called over, and introduced to the object. It was a Type-X machine.

The machine was the latest and most sophisticated British cipher machine. It was Top Secret, and only seen and operated by a few. The first thing that struck one was the keyboard, and as first thought it was almost identical to that of a typewriter. It seemed that Steve already knew something of this, as soon he was giving me instructions.

The Type-X could be powered by either a mains supply, or batteries. Its brain cell was its 'drums', of which there were five. Each was like a metal disc roughly 3½" in diameter. The edges were serrated. By each notch was a letter. At midnight each day, a new setting came into operation. This was done by adjusting the correct letter against a fixed position on each drum. The five letters, and their sequence were obtained from a top secret setting list for the date in question. That document of settings was kept securely locked away, normally in a safe, and the key-holder would be a commissioned officer. In their correct order a spindle was inserted through the centre of the drums, which in turn was inserted into the machine. When ready, the cipher operator would have, in front of him, the message to be enciphered. He would then type it out in a manner similar to normal typing, but the Type-X would transpose it, and the message was reproduced in a five letter cipher. The first group of each message was not a dummy, but denoted a second key which was exclusive to that message. If a message was long then at about every fifty groups there would appear QQQQQ. The group following those five Q's would be a further adjustment. This would be repeated at about fifty group intervals until the end of the message. Conversely, the Type-X could, and was, a deciphering machine. The above procedure was then used in reverse. It must be realised that this description is one of memory, some forty eight years later, and therefore inadvertently, has errors and omissions. Research on this, I have not found possible. In 1987 I visited the Royal Signals museum at Blandford, and asked if they had such a machine. I was told 'yes'. In order to jog my memory, I asked if I could see it, as there was not one on display. On that I was refused. For a period of about three years I operated one almost daily, yet, over forty years later I am not allowed to look at one. Sometimes I wonder, have our Security people got their left and right hands a little mixed up. Just to rub salt in, I noticed on display, for the whole wide world to see, was a German Enigma machine. In fairness, it must be stated that I was given an explanation, but one which was to me totally inadequate. To avoid embarrassment to anyone, I am not prepared to reveal that explanation.

The Type-X machine was not just for the exclusive use of the 'Y' Service, but used by all three of the Armed Forces from the outbreak of war, onwards. Though in the early months of war, we began to crack the German enigma cipher machine codes, I do not believe the enemy ever succeeded in cracking the Type-X. Though ciphering and deciphering our own cipher, with our own machine, had little to do with enemy eaves- dropping; most NCO's soon learnt to handle our Type-X. There was no security risk as all were vetted and cleared, or we would never have been in the Wireless Company in the first place. For my part, the knowledge gained was to provide most valuable in subsequent years. Later, a trade called Cipher Operators was introduced, but in those early war years, we had not known of them. If the trade had come into being, then to the best of my knowledge none had reached India.

That Hitler made many, many mistakes is a statement that most people would agree upon. One of his gravest was in June 1941, when he invaded the USSR. Like most of our war news, we first learnt of it from a BBC news bulletin. Its impact was profound. Since the collapse of France, our Country had fought on its own. Now, one of the greatest military powers was on our side. We gave little, or no, thought how political doctrines would be reconciled. A rapid German advance soon became apparent, yet not for one moment did we think it possible that they would come within shouting distance of the gates of Moscow before their final retreat. At this stage the German Eastern front was still a considerable distance from Abbottabad. 'Y' Units in North Africa, the Mediterranean and the Middle East were in a more advantageous position than us to cover the interception of enemy wireless traffic. Now that the Russians and ourselves were at war against the same common enemy, was there any rhyme or reason to continue our coverage of the Red Army, and Air Force? From a rather humble position in the 'Y' Section, such policy matters, and decisions were not mine to make. All our Russian coverage continued as if nothing had happened. Though the two Countries were now bedfellows, they were apparently not lovers!

The impetus of the war accelerated, and the dust had not settled on the German invasion of Russia when a pro-Nazi rebellion took place in Iraq, under the leadership of Rashid Ali. To suppress the uprising a military force was hastily formed, from Indian Army Units, to be rushed to Iraq. That force was to include a small 'Y' Section. No. 1 Special Signal Section was created. It was to be commanded by Major J D Sheppard, who was originally an Indian Army Officer in one of the Sikh Regiments, but was now serving as one of the top officers in our Indian Bureau. Until now, my contacts with him had been few and far between. I had thought of him as an officer who was cool, calm, composed and unflappable. Certainly he was a man with an outstanding brain, and knew how to use it. Nothing in the following two years caused me to change my views. It puzzled me that a Section of this nature was not to be commanded by a Royal Signals Officer. Major Sheppard, I am sure, would have been the first to admit that he was no 'Admin' man. Sgt. Jim Bowen was posted as the Section Sergeant. There were to be four Corporals, Simpson, Colley, Pickford and myself. We were all pre-war regulars. LCpls. and Signalmen totalled about twenty five. Sgt. Johnson, also from the Indian Bureau was to be the Intelligence NCO. His parent regiment was the South Wales Borderers. The establishment included three Indian followers, a cook, a water carrier and a sweeper. The entire Section was formed from No. 1 Wireless Company. Had I been in a position to choose the personnel for No. 1 Special Signal Section, I could not have improved on the selection. Each member, I new personally.

The OC would be involved mostly on the operational side. Jim Bowen, as Section Sergeant, was responsible for discipline, but little of that was necessary. We were to work as a team, and there would be no room for anyone who only understood discipline. That left Jim free to spend much of his time on operational matters. Of the four

Corporals, I was the most senior, and I suspect that it was for that reason that I was briefed to be the Section's administrative NCO. At first, I was somewhat disappointed in my role, but I was assured that the job would not isolate me from operational set room matters. Over the years, I had picked up many aspects of Army administration, and understood much of its methods and paperwork. I did have an appetite for the work, and on completion of a particularly satisfying task might enjoy licking my fingers. On the Quartermastering side Cpl. Pickford would be in charge in addition to his set room duties. In pre-war years there was a famous Hollywood film star named Mary Pickford. Hence, poor Pickford was dubbed with the nickname of Mary. Before going any further, Mary's masculinity was in no doubt by those of us who had the good fortune to know him. Cpl. Simpson was better known as just 'Skim'. He was king amongst a bunch of royal operators. Cpl. Colley was known as just, Jimmy but one of the most valuable and experienced operators in the team. Over twenty three years of my Army life, I have never worked with a less selfish, or more loyal body of men.

Small Units, like 1 SSS, are seldom independent. We had to be an exception. For us to be on the back of a larger Unit would have been inadvisable, as it might have risked interference by that Unit, and raised delicate questions concerning our function. Security had to be uppermost. Independence had its disadvantages. It meant, we were burdened with the same variety of administrative duties as a large Unit with no staff to perform them. Looking in to the immediate future, I was left with no doubt about the size of my job, but I did have confidence, and felt that the challenge could be met. If the Section was a happy one, with an absence of discontent, then under Major Sheppard's command we would cope with any problems that came our way. The prognosis was good.

On Active Service, a soldier's life is very different to that of his peacetime role. Apart from the disappearance of most comforts and luxuries, decisions are made more quickly, and reactions need to be instantaneous. From the moment the Section was formed, until the day of departure, we worked long hours, spent mostly on checking and packing stores and equipment. Our workhorse – the HRO receiver

– about eight of them, were all packed with loving and tender care. The most secret item of equipment was our Type-X machine. Though the drums were removed, it was still given 'Special Attention', and would be under constant guard. All associated documents such as the top secret list of drum settings were in the care of Major Sheppard. On a more personal, and individual level our equipment was pathetic. Our rifles were 1914-18 vintage, and fit for little more than drill purposes. We took three, or four, pistols which were .45 and had a kick like a mule. Only officers received training on pistols. There were no hand grenades or automatic guns. Perhaps that was just as well, as we would not have known how to use them! The Powers that Be repeatedly reminded us that we may be highly skilled, and valuable wireless intercept operators but we were, above all, soldiers. After two years at war, it was difficult to understand why we were, in some respects, ill equipped. It was not our job to go looking for combat, or to take any form of offensive military action. The armoured, and infantry Units were trained for that. Was it unreasonable to expect good modern equipment in the form of small arms to defend ourselves if attacked? The likelihood of us encountering an enemy force, face to face was remote. In wartime, the remote can come about. Should we meet it, then our position would be little better than a troop of Boy Scouts with broomsticks. The lesson is simple. To all ye who advocate 'cuts' on defence expenditure, take heed. You are gambling with the lives of your husbands and sons.

Time in Abbottabad was running out. For me, there was more to it than that. Four and a half years had passed since I had walked down the gangplank of a troopship onto Karachi docks. In the life of a young man, that is a long time.

On completion of training in Catterick, came life in Spike Island. Then followed the voyage to India, and joining 1st Indian Divisional Signals ('K') Section. Soon after the outbreak of war, a posting to No. 1 Wireless Company, Abbottabad and into the 'Y' Service. All three had been happy Units, and now what would the future bring in 1 SSS. Prior to September 1939, I had taken it for granted that after five years service in India it would be just a small matter of boarding a homeward bound troopship. Hitler had changed all that. The ship would not be bound for Home, but for the Persian Gulf, and Iraq.

India was a fascinating Country; a Country of extremes. Extreme heat, and yet, even extreme cold. A land of palaces and pestilence. One of barren, inhospitable plains, but one of outstanding beauty. Its inhabitants were no less contrasting; Hindus, Moslems, Buddhists, Maharajas to untouchables. It has been said that within its frontiers, almost fifty different languages were spoken. A fault finding visitor would have a field day, but the vast majority of British soldiers returning from service in that Country spoke well of it, and the happy times spent there. I am one.

Saying 'Goodbye' has never been one of my strong points, specially when I leave behind good friends. Some were coming with me in 1 Special Signal Section, but some remained in the Wireless Company. Among those remaining in Abbottabad was Steve. Would we, perchance, in years to come meet, and serve together again? If we did, I sensed that our positions, and rank might well be very different. Steve's promotion prospects were far greater than mine. Of that, I was not jealous, as in almost all respect his qualifications and powers of leadership were far better than my own. Very warmly, and sincerely, I wished him well.

The train journey to Karachi was long, tedious and uneventful. On arriving at the docks, our train pulled up alongside the ship which was to take us to Basra. That ship was a pre-war Trooper, either the Nevassa, or Neuralia. Without delay, we left the train, and on the dockside proceeded to check all stores. So far, so good, but not until we had seen that Type-X machine safely aboard did we relax. Finally, we embarked.

Chapter 10

This military operation in Iraq was an Indian Army concern, under command of GHQ Delhi, and independent of events in North Africa, which was under the command of GHQ Cairo. The troops embarking for Iraq were Indian, and it was they who occupied, and filled the troop decks. All the first class accommodation was taken by their British officers. The remainder, a small number of British WO's, NCO's and men were all allotted second class accommodation, which naturally included our Section. Travelling in such luxury was a comfort and joy none of us had anticipated. Memories of that ghastly voyage out to India were still vivid, and now, in wartime to be treated in this manner was almost too much of a good thing, and caused me doubts of its reality. Two, three and four to a cabin with a bunk, and other creature comforts brought home how a convict, after a long sentence would feel when on his first night of release finds himself staying at Claridges. For the duration of the voyage it appeared at first glance that we were to travel in the laps of luxury. In a manner it was, yet the dangers and risks of war would, henceforth, be growing. In those years, few men lived closer to those dangers than those who served in the Merchant Navy.

Later in the day, and before dark, slowly, very slowly the ship began to move. At a snail's pace we left the dock, and proceeded just a mile, or so, outside the harbour. Assembling there were a number of ships of various shapes, sizes and nationalities. A convoy was being formed, and we were to be part of it. As convoys go, it was not a large one; maybe about twelve ships in all. The speed of a wartime convoy, at sea, is governed by the maximum speed of its slowest ship. It will not sail in a direct line when travelling from point 'A' to point 'B', but it will deviate and zig-zag as it endeavours to avoid attack by 'U' Boats. It was expected that our voyage to Basra would take us almost twice as long as a peacetime one. Before finally sailing as a convoy we drilled in Boat stations, Fire and Air attack emergencies. Troopship discipline was strict and rigid. It had to be, and its importance was emphasised over and over again. The troops, being

Indian were, like the British ones, very well trained with an exceptional sense of discipline. Come what may, they would give of their best. One of the many strictly enforced rules was that at all times, and in all places we carried a life jacket. We carried it everywhere, to meals, to the loo and to bed at nights.

It was Summer time, and temperatures in that part of the world were at their highest. The heat was possibly our greatest discomfort. Below decks, the nights were particularly uncomfortable. All port holes were sealed, and the blackout was total. Only in a few small selected places was smoking permitted. To strike a match, or light a cigarette on an open deck would have resulted in the offender being placed immediately behind bars, irrespective of his rank. That may seem draconian, but it should be remembered that such an act by any one individual may reveal all a 'U' Boat Commander was looking for, and risk the lives of every man on that ship. Happily, I cannot recall one such breach of discipline.

Meals in the second class dining room were superb. We were waited upon by Indian waiters. Most of the ship's crew were Indian with the officers being British. As might be expected, the standard of curries eclipsed all else. With Indian chefs, the flavour of those curries on board was, possibly, the highest I have ever tasted.

Duties on a troop ship usually fell thick and fast, but on this voyage I was not detailed for any defined job. There were no dull moments, nor time for boredom. Daily ship's routine was, in itself, a busy one. At least once a day, Major Sheppard did his rounds, and kept in close touch with the Section. It was on this trip that I first came in close contact with our OC. The more I learnt, the more respect I gained for him.

All convoys had a Naval escort, and we were no exception. When chance came my way, and during the daylight hours, I would enjoy leaning on the deck rails watching a destroyer dashing around, in and out of the convoy, and maybe chivvying one or two of its charges for some minor breach of convoy discipline. Not unlike a fussy old hen looking after her chicks. Though I had chosen an Army life, I revered the Royal Navy. Our convoy was in their care, and in their hands. In my mind, short of God, there was no greater feeling of security. To see one of our warships at sea, with the White Ensign flying at its stern, has always stirred my patriotic emotions. In wartime that was even stronger. The RAF had its work cut out at Home, and in North Africa. Aircraft carriers were in short supply, and had difficulty in meeting the requirements of the Atlantic convoys alone. We, in the Arabian Sea were not in the priority list.

The war news was depressing. German troops had reached Smolensk. They had invaded Crete. HMS Hood had been sunk. There could have been many excuses for despondency. We may not have been jubilant, but neither were we down in the mouth.

Every morning there was a ship's inspection, and we all paraded at Boat stations. The ship's Captain, with the OC troops carried out with impeccable thoroughness, their responsibilities. Such lifeboat drill was a set daily routine. There were other practices, each without warning, so when the alarm bells rang we made full speed, day or night to our allotted boat. We were so well drilled that I am not so sure that I did not, on one occasion, run to my boat station in my sleep!

There was no twilight; darkness descended quickly. After dinner, the evenings were quite enjoyable. There was a bar, and alcoholic drinks served. Mostly, it was lager, canned and always ice cold. A group comprising Jim Bowen, Skin Simpson, 'Mary' Pickford, Jimmy Colley and myself sat together at the same table. Sgt. 'Johnnie' Johnson rarely joined us. I never learnt the explanation for that. He did tend to be a 'loner', but was it just that he found difficulty in mixing, or was there a more deep seated cause? He seldom spoke of his work or function; not even a hint. Johnnie was reserved, and introvert. Not one member of the Section, then, would have believed that within a year we would be attending his funeral. In Abbottabad we had all worked together, and there was little we did now know of each other. Now, in these informal off-duty hours that bond was, day by day, becoming tighter as we learnt even more. There were other British ranks, from other Units and Regiments also using the lounge, so our popular 'shop' conversations of 'Y' duties, cover and commitments were taboo. Security was never overlooked or forgotten. Earlier brain-washing was paying dividends. No. 1 Special Signal

Section was no longer a Unit in embryo, but more a small body of men forming a closely knit team. Though each was an individual, yet each respected the other, and was prepared to sacrifice his own whims and desires for those of the whole. Each was dependent on the other. Those who have served in the Armed Forces will be familiar with, and understand the spirit that is the basis of such motivation. To others, it may assist them to understand if they concentrate on the finest of man's traits, and attributes. It was not a subject that we discussed amongst ourselves. There was no need. We knew it was there.

The ship's crew were all male. So, too, were the passengers. So many characters in these memoirs are male that some descriptions of life are more akin to those of a monastery. The absence of the opposite sex left an irreplaceable gap in our lives. The remedy was not found on a wartime troopship.

That the voyage contained an element of monotony was inevitable, but not sufficient to cause concern. It was comfortable. The sea was calm, with little rolling of the ship, and there was little sea sickness. On open decks a slight breeze could be felt which was caused by the ship's movement, but it still remained unmercifully hot. After about five days at sea we became restless, and acquired a growing appetite – not for food – but to resume our proper function as an operational 'Y' Unit.

On approaching the Persian Gulf, we were aware that Iraq was 'just around the corner'. What lay ahead? It was an Arab Country, and quite different to India. That was foremost in my mind as I looked to the near future. At this stage, the precise locality of our destination was unknown. We could be setting up business anywhere within the frontiers of Iraq. Opportunities to learn much of the Country and its people would rarely present themselves. Glancing into a mythical crystal ball can be fun, it can be frightening, but always inexact, and erroneous.

Approximately ten days after leaving Karachi, we arrived at Basra. The voyage had proved uneventful without any 'U' Boat scares, or false alarms. Not a saucer had been cracked by enemy action.

No time was lost in unloading, which was carried out by Arab dock workers. When satisfied that all stores, including the precious Type-X, were unloaded and accounted for, we then reloaded them onto lorries. Lastly, we ourselves boarded lorries, and drove off to a transit camp. My first impressions of people and places have so often proved to be unreliable, yet, that did not prevent me from forming them. Following five years in the Indian climate, the heat still seemed almost unbearable. The sun was unrelenting. The flies swarmed around in large formations like a mini replica of a thousand bomber raid. As far as the eye could see there was sand, sand, and more sand, In the built-up areas it became a fine, filthy dust. Around us was poverty and squalor, aggravated by complete lack of sanitation. Would those first impressions, once more, prove to be unreliable? They were so compelling that it would require a miracle to change them. The transit camp offered no comforts, and poor food. The duration of our stay, in Basra was dependent on Major Sheppard receiving our movement orders, which would inform us of our final destination. We did not have long to wait, just a few days.

Quite suddenly, we were ordered to proceed to Baghdad without delay. In retrospect, I imagine that Major Sheppard probably knew that before we left India, but was not in a position to tell us. One more train journey, and with less comfort than any experienced in India. After second class luxury on the troopship, we were brought down to earth with a bump! It was good to be on the last stretch, but it was a train journey remembered mostly for being hot, humid, and horrible.

ENIGMA E Machine

Intercept truck interior

Chapter 11

In our early childhood, for most of us, the first reading books were fairy stories, and early visits to a theatre were to pantomimes. All that was quite harmless, yet it did give an image of Baghdad as a city covered by a canopy of stars, with an oriental moon thrown in for good measure. As if that was not enough, there was the matter of forty thieves! If the writer of the romantic moon and stars picture had chosen those words to describe the sewers of London, he would have been no further from the truth. The statistician who quoted the figure of forty forget to add a few noughts. It is interesting to note that none of those childhood stories mentioned the smell of Baghdad. Who can blame them?

At first sight our Baghdad billet appeared as quite attractive. It was a large house built on the Western side of the Tigris. Two metres from the front door was the river which at that point was about the same width as the Thames at London Bridge. The remaining three sides of the house were surrounded by palm trees, with a short path about a hundred and fifty metres leading to the main road. The house was owned by a well-to-do Jew. On arrival, we soon learnt that we were not to be the sole occupants, as already 4 SCU were in residence. They were small in numbers, but with 1 Special Signal Section it meant that about fifty of us living in a house designed for only a large family with two, or three servants. From the accommodation viewpoint, we would be cramped, but it was bricks and mortar.

Within hours of arrival, from somewhere, there appeared a large quantity of mail. It was the first for a few weeks. Letters from home are a top priority in restoring flagging morale. The hierarchy were aware of that, and no effort was spared to ensure a constant and regular flow of mail. Complaints about mail were few and far between. Often, letters received by us, in Iraq, and under active service conditions, arrived in a shorter period than some of our UK first class mail in peacetime; almost fifty years later!

For cooking purposes we had three, or four, portable, kerosene pressure cookers. By the time Cpl. Pickford had been to a nearby

RASC depot and collected some rations, our Indian cook had the burners working well. The first evening in Baghdad, we had a hot meal. It was good. More often than not, our cook worked under rather poor conditions, not least the elements. He did his best.

The crucial issue, overriding all else was to unpack, and install all technical equipment, and have a set room in operation without delay. The erecting of masts, and aerials have been well drilled. Within a couple of days, watch-keeping had started, and we were in business.

The accommodation offered no comforts, and no furniture. In the early days we slept on concrete floors. There was no cooling system, but there was an infestation of tropical insects. In due course, we purchased, out of our own pockets, local Arab beds. There were made of a type of bamboo, so they gave a primitive form of springing. They were not so comfortable as the Indian charpoys. However we slept, we always took anti-malaria precautions by using mosquito nets. The nets had a very fine mesh in order to give added protection against sand fly fever. The health of the Section was good.

From the first day, I became so involved in my own job that I rarely showed my face in the set room. Jim Bowen, with Simpson had all that well under control, and on the admin. side, I had to stand on my own feet. That meant losing touch with the details of coverage, but I still had a broad idea what was going on, operationally. The HRO's were none the worse for the voyage, and all equipment was working satisfactorily. The sets were manned by LCpls. And Signalmen, who were by no means all regulars. Our percentage of conscripts was quite high. Their grounding in Abbottabad bore fruit, and produced a very high standard of operating. What a pity their work has never been publicised, or their contribution to the 'Y' Service acknowledged, and rewarded. That is long overdue.

Both working, and social, relationships with 4 SCU were first rate. The OC was Capt. Peter Newbold. Wherever possible, we pooled resources such as messing.

It is now no secret that it was at the Government Communications and Cipher School at Bletchley Park, that the German Enigma ciphers were broken. Great progress had been made, but by 1941 not all the Enigmas had been broken. The breaking of enemy ciphers at BP was not confined to German Enigma. Intelligence gained from Enigma was minutely examined, before distribution, or any of it passed on to the Services. It was then re-packaged, and paraphrased before being signalled to those Commanders who it may concern. All signals relating to Sigint from GC & CS to Commands, and vice versa, were made by SCU's. That was their function. They were, I suppose, not strictly 'Y' as that letter applied to Units whose task was interception. However, they were an integral part of Sigint. In as far as we were concerned in PAIFORCE (Persia and Iraq Force), it was 4 SCU who operated that exclusive channel of communication. In 1 SSS we were in daily contact with them. Therefore, the role of each had a bearing on the other. My comments are not those of one on the Intelligence staff, but those of Signals 'Y' NCO. Military Historians, after much detailed research and with a more authoritative knowledge, have written volumes on Intelligence from intercept sources. I leave it to them.

The history of our transport has faded from my mind. It was in Baghdad, I believe, that we collected the vehicles. They amounted to a 3-ton Chevrolet lorry, a Ford V8. 15-cwt. lorry, and a tiny Austin 7 open two seater, which was no more robust than a perambulator, and not dissimilar in appearance! Not being mobile, it was possible that it may meet our needs – just.

In the centre of the house was an open courtyard. There, our greatest headache soon made itself apparent. There was no public sewerage, and to compensate for that there was a pit built into the centre of the Courtyard. Into that pit poured the sewage from the loos (Arab style) within the building. That pit boasted of a removable cover. The system had been built to meet the needs of a family of five or so. It was now required to meet the needs of more than ten times that figure. Very rapidly it became full, when an Arab would arrive squatting on top of a cylindrical tank which was secured on top of a bullock cart. After removing the pit cover, the Arab with the aid of what appeared to be an out-sized ladle at the end of a long pole, proceeded to ladle the contents of the pit into the cylindrical tank. It took him best part of a day to complete his task. A more obnoxious experience, I cannot recall. That Arab returned every two, or three weeks to give a repeat performance. Not because anyone had requested an encore, but through necessity. The act was performed in tropical temperatures associated with Iraq, and deserts. During the interlude, the smell continued to linger. How we worked normally through those days, I shall never know, but we did.

Ten or fifteen minutes walk took us to El Rashid Street, the main thoroughfare of the City. When opportunity came, usually in an evening, we made visits to the City centre. There, it was possible to find restaurants offering a good meal. Meals were somewhat expensive, but there was no rationing. A bottle of beer was welcome, but it cost roughly 900 fils (about 18/-), consequently a luxury. We were paid in the local currency of Dinars (1 Dinar = £1). Beer was obtainable from the NAAFI. It was imported, and in short supply. That was rationed to one bottle per man per week. Often it worked out at one bottle a fortnight. There was little risk of any of us being eligible to join AA. The local cinemas were popular, and of quite a high standard. At least one of them was open air. That, on a hot tropical night was a good place to be. Most of the films were American. I can recall, seeing in Baghdad, Bette Davis in 'Elizabeth and Essex' and 'Dear Octopus', and many other great films of that era. Being a small Unit, it was not possible for us, the NCO's to just walk out and have an evening together off duty. Always, there had to be, at least, two on duty. The attitude of the local Iraqis was hardly anti-British, nor hostile; but neither did they rush to welcome us. I have reason to believe that there was a small clandestine pro-Nazi pocket here, and there. Off duty restrictions were few. Certain small areas were declared 'Out of Bounds', usually because they were deemed to be Red Light districts. Yet, within the 'In Bounds' area, red lights were known to shine! Providing one kept to the main streets, it was possible to walk alone, in uniform, with little personal risk. Only once, or twice did I do so when admittedly, I did not feel at ease. Outings were in small groups of two, or three, which gave a greater feeling of security, and so more enjoyable.

Sgmn. Pointer had, I recall, served in the TA before the war. He was now our instrument mechanic. On his shoulders rested the responsibility of maintaining, and repairing all technical equipment:

HRO's, D/F, Type-X, and on one occasion picked up the pieces and re-assembled our one, and only, typewriter after I had dropped it! He worked all hours, and never let us down. Very reluctantly, I have singled out this one man in the Section for special mention, but of course there were others who were no less dedicated. Pointer, like so many others in 1 Special Signal Section knew his job from A to Z. Drivers, cooks, despatch riders, clerks and storemen never saw inside the set room, yet they gave yeoman service, and the ultimate in team work. It is not uncommon in war, or peace, to hear of a body of people described as 'Unsung Heroes'. Not one of the many who I served with in 'Y' would have made claim to that! Heroes? – No! Unsung? – Yes!

As a stand-by, and in the case of a breakdown on the Type-X; Major Sheppard held two other ciphers. These were known as IC 'A' and IC 'B' (Indian cipher 'A' and 'B'). They were five figure ciphers, but not such high grade as Type-X. Once, we had cause to use the former for just a few hours. It was then Major Sheppard called me into his office, and explained a little of how it worked. It was time consuming, and I spent some hours helping him. My recollections are ones of simple adding and subtracting; nothing very complicated.

The Section was only just established in Iraq, when we learnt that we were to lose Sgt. Jim Bowen. It all happened very quickly. A message was received from GSI(s), GHQ Delhi recalling him to India, and at the same time he was to be commissioned. Great news for Jim, and we all wished him well as he departed within twenty four hours. Now, we were left without a Section Sergeant. After Jim, I was next in seniority, but that was not in itself a sufficient qualification. It did not take the OC long before he told me that I was promoted to Sergeant, and put up my third stripe. My duties would remain much as they were, but with the additional over all responsibilities of Section Sergeant. Though it meant extra work, I felt that it was not beyond me. On all set room, and operational matters, Cpl. Simpson would be in charge and responsible direct to the OC. It all made sense, but I feared a risk of drifting away from the daily bread and butter work of interception. In 'Y' that drift often came about on promotion, particularly above the rank of Corporal. In days, it seemed as if I had been the Section Sergeant since its formation. Like Jim, I was a 'Y' man, and shared all the secrets appertaining to the job. It was gratifying to find that I enjoyed the confidences of Major Sheppard. Whatever questions I put, were always answered to my satisfaction, and never evaded. From training, I had learnt not to ask too many, but only those related to the business in hand.

Army life never stays the same for long. Plans were on the drawing board for a new camp to be built. The chosen site was about ten miles South of Baghdad, on the Basra Road. It was to be a large camp, and very much in the middle of nowhere. The object of that, presumably, being that we would attract little attention to ourselves. The number of brick, single deck buildings was to be small, and just for use as stores, offices and the operational area with the set room. All accommodation was to be in tents. It was obvious that the planners had in mind for a large Unit such as a Special Wireless Group to be stationed there. The perimeter was to be built with miles of barbed wire, and guarded by Indian troops. Occupation was to take place in early 1942. That was the genesis of Habosh Camp.

Shortly after my promotion, there followed a tragedy. One night, about 3am I was woken from my sleep. With a rather alarming degree of urgency, I was called to the telephone. After identifying myself, the caller told me his story. He was the Duty Officer at one of the British Military Hospitals on the outskirts of the town. Just brought into their Casualty Department was a dead British Sergeant who they believed to be Sgt. Johnson of our Unit! I rushed to his bed; it was empty, so I roused Major Sheppard, and reported the incident to him. In a few hours, more details emerged. Johnnie had been found in a street by someone who had called the police, or ambulance. He was taken to a nearby civilian hospital, and at that moment, I believe, still alive. Within an hour, or so, they must have decided, rightly or wrongly, that he must go to a British Military Hospital. Whereupon, still alive, he was placed once more in an ambulance, and sent to a British Military Hospital. On arrival he was found to be dead. As I recall it, Johnson had sustained a knife would, opening up his arm from elbow to wrist. Its position suggested that he may have raised his arm to protect himself from an assailant. His death may well have been due to loss of blood. After the initial shock came the questions.

Why had he been attacked? What was it all about? Was he on duty, or not? Those, and a few other questions remain, for me, unanswered to this day. I was trusted with much top secret, and confidential material and correspondence, but nothing passed through my hands which threw any light on the incident. It is at the back of my mind that his next of kin was quite a distant relative, and I imagine that they were duly informed of his death in the routine military, wartime manner by telegram stating he had been killed 'While on Active Service'. That was true.

Hastily, that morning, I gathered some of the Section to act as pallbearers, and firing party and rehearsed some basic funeral drill. Sgt. Johnson was to be buried that same afternoon. It was to be an Active Service burial with a minimum of ceremony. This was my first experience of being in charge, at a military funeral. Major Sheppard would be present, but the smooth running of the ceremony was to be my responsibility. In the 3-ton, and 15-cwt. lorries, we arrived at the BMH's mortuary. The body was not in a coffin, but just stitched in canvas. We lifted him onto a stretcher, and covered him with a Union Jack. The Chaplain was a young man and little experienced. I was sorry for him. Quietly, I gave the order 'Slow March'. After just over a hundred yards, we halted, and placed the body in the 3-ton truck. We drove away slowly, to the military cemetery. Again, we slow marched, on arrival, to the graveside. The service was brief, and within minutes we were lowering Johnnie into his grave. Quietly, I gave the order to fire the salute. Before boarding the lorries to leave we, individually stood at the foot of the grave, paused, and saluted. All so simple, yet so emotional. I felt choked.

Japan attacked the US Fleet in Pearl Harbour on 6th December 1941. The news reached us in minutes. It was followed, soon after, by a statement that the USA was now at war with Japan, Germany and Italy; and that the USA were now allies of Great Britain, and the USSR. At one swoop the world was at war. Everyone was aware that there was a long hard struggle coming, but also aware that our ultimate victory was in no doubt.

Five years had passed since leaving the UK; and throughout that period I had not been granted one day's leave. For that no individual was to blame other than the most evil man on earth, Hitler. The prospects of any leave in the foreseeable future were nil. Many others were no better off, but compared to some people's war, ours was one of luxury.

Christmas 1941 was uneventful. There were no festivities, and the day was little different from any other. With the turn of the year came changes. Habosh Camp was nearing completion. We ceased to come under the command of GHQ Delhi, as PAIFORCE was transferred to Middle East Command, Cairo. The Section was no longer 1 Special Signal Section, but was re-christened as 'F' Special Wireless Section.

HMS *Prince of Wales* and HMS *Repulse* had both been sunk by the Japanese and Hong Kong had fallen. Following those disasters, came the surrender of Singapore. That all happened before the Americans could build up their forces in that theatre of war. To stem the Japanese advance in Burma and Singapore, many troops had been rushed from India. Amongst them, I feared, were friends from those days in 1st Indian Divisional Signals ('K' Section). How many, I pondered, had been killed, taken prisoner of war, or worst of all been victims of ghastly and horrific atrocities by the Japanese. It was a sickening possibility.

For some inexplicable reason, I found letter writing to friends and relatives at home difficult, so they were not very frequent. Aerographs were a wartime introduction. They were both popular and much used. The writer used a special form. A space was provided at the top of the form for the addressee, leaving the remainder for the message or brief letter. The size was slightly smaller than A4. The disadvantage was that it was open, and they were handed into the Army Post Office unfolded, and not enveloped. Their advantage was convenience, and speed. When received by the APO they were photographed. The film, only, was then sent by air to the UK where it was processed, and a print was made of each negative (aerograph), and enlarged to about a third of its original size. That was then placed in a small envelope and posted to its addressee. Many such aerographs could be photographed on one film, so saving considerable space and weight on an aircraft. If may appear as a long slow and tedious business. On the contrary, it was the quickest means of sending news home. Another wartime innovation was the 'Green Envelope'. Each man was rationed to one of these a week. Letters sent in a green envelope were not censored, and the sender was able to seal the letter. However, a Base Censor was at liberty to open such envelopes and censor if he so wishes. On the front of the envelope was a printed certificate stating that the contents were devoted to personal, family and domestic matters only. That certificate had to be signed by the sender. All other personal letters were censored within the Unit before being posted into the Army Postal system. Only a commissioned officer was permitted to read and censor personal mail. As in 'F' Spec. Wrls. we only had one officer (Maj. Sheppard), the burden was all his. Many nights he burnt the midnight oil working entirely on censorship duties. When he had read, and passed each individual letter, he would seal it, and sign the front of the envelope. If any letter contained forbidden subjects, words or comments, the offending lines were not just obliterated, but were cut out with scissors. It was strictly forbidden for military personnel to use the civilian postal service. All our mail, both in and out, was handled by the Army Post Office. We were not required to pay postage. At the top of the envelope the writer just wrote the magic words 'On Active Service'. That was sufficient.

The year was still young when we left our riverside home, and moved to Habosh Camp. 4 SCU did not come with us, but remained beside the evil smelling Tigris with the odd dead dog, and camel floating on its surface.

From a distance, Habosh looked like a film set for a Prisoner of War film, with its strong, heavy perimeter of barbed wire. In size it was large enough to hold a thousand, or more prisoners. Now, to be occupied by approximately forty men, making up 'F' Special Wireless Section. The huts were clustered together in a corner of the camp, still leaving about two thirds as an open space. The largest building was the operational area with its set room, and offices attached. It was three, or four times larger than we needed for our requirements. Work on the wiring, and aerials had been completed before our arrival, so to become operational was reasonably simple and speedy. Likewise the tentage for accommodation had been erected. Each man would have plenty of space, but live in spartan conditions. Though he would find shelter from the blistering sun, there would be no escaping the heat. At the end of the stores building there were two small rooms. Pickford and I moved into one of those, and made it our home. Our only claim to luxury was our Arab beds. Among the tents was one which was much larger than the others, and that we assigned as an All Ranks Mess Tent, Canteen, and place for any off duty communal purposes. Somehow, and somewhere we had acquired a few folding tables and benches. Just a few yards away was the cookhouse built on a concrete base, walls of straw matting, and a rather rusty, ramshackle tin roof. The Indian cook was unperturbed. At Habosh, there were no sanitation problems, as there was no sanitation. Water supply came from a water tower within the camp, and was man handled to the point of requirement. There was no main sewage system. Waste was buried, or disposed by drainage into the ground. Latrines were holes in the ground. They had been well, and deeply dug, and there was not the health hazard, or foul smells of our previous riverside billet. These were properly fly proofed making the risk of dysentery negligible. We enjoyed the luxury of showers, but these too consisted of a concrete base, with straw matting walls. Unlike the cookhouse, there was no roof, but just some bodger plumbing of pipes and sprays. During the very hot Summer days one really had only two alternatives. The cold water became so hot that to stand beneath a shower, one ran the risk of being scalded. On the other hand, standing naked waiting for the water to cool presented the risk of being fried in the hot tropical sun! In the Winter it was still a problem. The heating of the water was somewhat primitive, and was unreliable. It was often bitterly cold in the winter, and to even undress was a discomfort, but to stand in the open under a cold shower was entering the dragon's mouth!

  In a large Unit a change of command does not usually have any great impact on the lower non-commissioned ranks. In a smaller unit, like ours, it may sometimes rock the boat. Major Sheppard was recalled to India. Over the past few months, I worked very closely with him, and had learnt that his involvement in Intelligence was wider than most believed. His knowledge of the Persian language alone, must have made him a most valuable man indeed. We gave him the best send-off that circumstances permitted. Naturally, we were somewhat apprehensive about a new OC. With little notice, and no ceremony he arrived. Lt. R P Hughes, Royal Signals was our new man, and took command. He soon won us over, and any early doubts, and fears rapidly vanished. Rather like Major Sheppard, he rightly concentrated his time and effort on the set room. That left my duties, and responsibilities unchanged.

In the 'Y' Service there were 'A' type Sections, 'B' types, 'G' types, 'R' types, and probably a few other types unknown to me; though I was aware that we were the only 'F' type in existence. On the grape vine, we had heard hints of an increase in our establishment, and that it would bring promotions. Our vine did not let us down, and we were not kept waiting long. Cpls. Simpson, Pickford and Colley were made up to Sergeant. That really was good news, and at the same time I was promoted to Warrant Officer Class II (SSM). Like all war time promotions, they were acting ranks, but at least we received the pay and privileges that accompanied the ranks. It was congratulations, and celebrations, all round.

On 1st April we received guests. They were 106 Special Wireless Section. They arrived direct from the UK, and after disembarking at Basra, drove in convoy direct to Habosh Camp. They were a 'B' type Section with a total strength, including Intelligence staff of about a hundred and twenty. Capt. 'Jake' Lambert Royal Signals was the Officer Commanding. After their formation, they came out to the Middle East with little, or no experience. Their purpose in Habosh was to polish off their training, and gain set room interception experience. 106 and 'F' did not work together as one Unit, but that was never intended. We mixed well, and at all levels there was co-operation and harmony between the two Units. Their technical equipment, such as HRO's, was much the same as ours, but we did envy them their transport which was newer than ours, and well equipped. Often in the evenings we got together in the Canteen, and if we had any beer we enjoyed a drink. Having left the UK quite recently, 106 SWS were in a position to bring us up to date on wartime news and events at Home. Their stories, and news always cheered us up, particularly when they spoke of the morale, and high spirits of the civilians in the bombed cities. The time came, all too soon, for 106 to leave. About late May, they moved on to Sarafand, en route for North Africa, and later Italy. We missed them. They were the only 'Y' Unit, in post war years, to organise and have an annual reunion dinner in London. For many years now, it has been my privilege, and my enormous pleasure to attend those dinners. May it continue for many more years to come.

    The GI at GSI(8) GHQ MELF was Brigadier W Scott. He was the No. 1 'Y' man in the entire Middle East Command. One of my daily responsibilities was to seal, and dispatch the previous day's intercepts. Those, I placed in large envelopes, carefully sealing each one with wax. They were then individually marked 'Top Secret' and 'To Be Opened Personally By Brig. W Scott'. The complete consignment was placed in one large outer wrapper, and addressed to GSI(8) GHQ MELF. When satisfied that all was in order, I placed the package in a weighted bag, and tied on a label with the same address on it. The last act was when the bag was taken to the Airport at Baghdad, and handed personally to a RAF officer, who of course always gave a receipt. Forty years later, at a 106 SW Section Reunion Dinner, we invited Brigadier Walter Scott to be our Guest of Honour. Like myself, few had previously met him. He was then retired, and living in Kent. He was in great form, and we all enjoyed his company. Regrettably, about two years later, we learnt of his death.

    Where there is desert there will be sandstorms. Usually, they built up in the afternoons. The first indications were an uncanny stillness, and a considerable rise in temperature. The sun would become diffused, and the sky would lose its blueness and turn into a steel grey. On the distant horizon, there would be a build-up of cumulus clouds. It may be an hour or so later before the storm struck. That it was called a 'Sand' storm, is rather like calling some objectionable smell 'A Delicate, Delightful Perfume!'. The ingredients of the storm were not just sand, but minute particles of dust and refuse from many miles around. Visibility was often reduced to a few feet, and the wind rose almost to gale force. Closed doors and windows offered little protection, and tents none. Those storms were a curse.

Late one night, Pickford and I left our Canteen tent, and walked about a hundred yards to our room, looking forward to a night's sleep. In that extremely dry, hot, Summer climate, blankets were put aside. The most comfortable way to sleep was totally nude, with a minimum of covering. On our wicker beds, we each had an old sheet which we used as a loose cover to throw over ourselves in bed. That night, we undressed as usual, and without a stitch on, I placed one leg beneath the so-called sheet when, to my horror, out jumped at me, a rat! That creature was the largest desert rat I had ever seen. It was the size of a cat. I screamed with fright. Pickford's reaction was instantaneous. We cornered it down a hole in the corner of the concrete floor. Not knowing how to get it out, we seized from the stores a drum of cresol, and slowly poured some of the thick liquid down the escape route. Very slowly, and half dead, the enemy emerged. Within seconds, we put it out of its misery. Never again did either of us get into bed before conducting a search for rats. I am an animal lover, but today, if I see a rat I relive that night in Habosh Camp. Perhaps soldiers are not quite so tough, and hard bitten as some like to believe. Underneath that uniform is a normal human who is just as likely to be frightened of rats, as his civilian cousins. As a young schoolboy, I believed all soldiers, sailors and airmen to very brave men. As a young soldier, I soon learnt that they were no braver than anyone else. Personally, I have been scared more times that I care to remember. The military way of life, the team spirit and training all assist the soldier to cope with fear when he experiences it.

Every so often I took a turn and did a spell on the Type-X machine, which was installed in the set room. If not for that purpose, a day seldom passed when I was not in the set room for a while, yet my memory fails on the matter of our coverage, and commitments at that period in 1942. The Germans were pushing the Russians back, and advancing down into the Caucasus, so it is safe to say that there was a strong emphasis on the interception of the German Army and Air Force wireless traffic, and much of that would have been Enigma. As the Sergeant Major, and with my many other administrative duties, time was on short ration, but it was still possible to keep in touch with the operational side. With a back-up team of outstanding, and experienced NCO's plus a fine OC all contributed to a happy and efficient Unit. No history of the 'Y' Service would be complete without a generous mention of the contribution made by 'F' Special Wireless Section.

About fifty miles South of Habosh was Babylon. There, the YMCA had set up a small leave centre. Both vacancies, and leave were difficult to obtain, but we did manage to arrange both for just a handful of our Section. They had no more than a week each. One day, Skim Simpson was taking the Ford V8 to go to Babylon and bring back a couple of fellows on such a leave. It was one of those days when I had an urge to just get away from it all for a few hours, and go somewhere beyond that barbed wire. It was agreed that I would go with Skim just for the ride, and that he would do the driving. For the outward journey we would be on our own, and the occasion gave us the opportunity to have a chat on many matters. We were always the best of friends, and shared many secrets so it was great to have Skim's company. The journey had another complexion which was of an uncomfortable nature. At times there was no tarmac, and we drove on a track suitable for a camel train. It was unmercifully hot. We had an adequate supply of drinking water, but after travelling ten miles, or so, it became almost hot enough to make a brew of tea! On arriving at Babylon, it was our intention to stay a while, and see something of this old biblical town. It was not to be. Time was running out, as we wished to be back in Camp before sunset. We had a meal and drinks (soft) at the YMCA, and then after meeting our colleagues, commenced our return journey. As for Hanging Gardens, I did not see any. Had it not been for Skim, it would have proved a rather miserable day.

Shortly after the USSR entered the war, they released thousands of Polish prisoners who they had been holding. Many of those men were handed over to us in Persia and Iraq. They had been held in captivity under atrocious conditions, and were half starved. They were physically in poor state, and much of that could be attributed to lack of proper medical care. Their most common ailments were malaria, and dysentery, and their predicament was not unlike that suffered by our own men when in Japanese hands. When those Poles came to us we cared for them and rehabilitated them; most went on to join the Free Polish Army. They were not a rabble of illiterate, unruly peasants, but often educated men with degrees, and who had been in the professions. In their wisdom, someone had decided that here was some valuable, potential material for Sigint. After some rather intensive vetting, and investigation, a small number – I imagine less than two hundred – were selected.

With little notice, I received warning from the OC to expect about a hundred and forty Poles. In Habosh, we had the space and facilities to cope with that number. Tents were hastily erected, and a large number of rations drawn from the RASC Depot. At that time the GII at GSI(8), PAIFORCE was Major Austerfield, Intelligence Corps. His must have been one of the prime roles in the entire Polish operation. Now and again, I went to Baghdad, and sometimes had cause to visit the Major's office. More frequently, he came to our Camp, and often he would pause, and have a chat. If, while in 'F' Special Wireless Section, I had been given the chance for one wish to become reality, it would have been that as long as I remained in the Army, my officers would continue to be of the same high standard that I had so far encountered. Time was to prove that reality, and wishful thinking are not quite the same thing.

The Poles arrived, clean, smart and well turned out in British battle dress, and kit. It is difficult to say who won over who. They greeted us as if they had known us all their lives, and made quite plain their joy at being free, and their admiration for all things British. That was a little embarrassing. Language, at first, proved to be our only difficulty. Very few of them spoke any English, and the knowledge of those who did was not great. The Poles lost no time in organising themselves. They came to us to be trained as intercept operators, or what was later to be known as Special Operators. For our only three Sergeants to undertake the required instructional duties, on top of their existing tasks, was out of the question. So it was that Sgt. Jock McKay joined us. On his shoulders rested the responsibility of training and instructing the Poles. For my part, I found that I had much of their paper work thrown at me, but that was only in the early weeks until such time as they learnt the British Army way of administration.

It came about that no one in 'F' Section had any idea, or training in First Aid, except myself, and that knowledge was meagre. We had no resident Medical Officer, and only on request would we see one. The nearest British Military Hospital was about thirteen miles away. I had a telephone number to use in case of emergency, or wanting advice. Until now, that had been little used. The Poles did not enjoy our standard of fitness, and good health. Before long a mild outbreak of dysentery hit them, whereupon I made use of the 'phone number. To my amazement, I was asked if we had any Angustura bitters. My reply was in the affirmative. I was then instructed how to administer it in very small doses. That I did, and the foul tasting treatment worked; what a strange remedy! Sometimes individuals ran a fever and high temperature. In such cases, we sent them to the nearest military hospital without delay. More often than not, it turned out that they had a malaria relapse. After the passing of just two, or three months their health improved considerably.

The Polish Section remained in Habosh until April, or May, 1943 when fully trained, and equipped they pulled out for North Africa. They were in Torbruk during the siege, and later went on to serve in Italy. By name, I can recall only two. One was Major Joseph Minski, who was their Intelligence Officer, and the other was a chap called Berka who was much younger. The Major I knew only by sight. In 1987 I visited him in his home in Ealing where he is now retired. From him, I learnt that after the war most of the Polish Section settled in the UK including Berka. Berka spoke a little English so I was able to converse with him without the use of an interpreter. It was from him that I found out some of the details of the suffering of the Poles during the Russian invasion, and later their ordeals in Russian prison camps.

Turkey remained neutral throughout the war. With, or without, their consent – I cannot say – but a small 'Y' Unit was formed to be sent to that Country. As a belligerent Country ourselves, we could not send a military Unit, so understandably they were sent as civilians. From our Section, we contributed three, or four, operators. It was my wish to be one of them, and I did try to pull strings but my rank was a barrier. They had to be Signalmen, or junior NCO's. Those selected were some of our most experienced, and valuable men. To the best of my knowledge, they were absorbed into the staff of GCHQ, and set up business in Istanbul. After the war it was Jim Bennett who was sent to Istanbul to arrange the withdrawal of that Unit to the UK. In the early war days, Jim was conscripted into Royal Signals, and was trained at Trowbridge as a Special Operator. He served in Malta, and later Heliopolis, Egypt with 2 Special Wireless Group. He transferred to the Intelligence Corps, and then on to MI6. In his MI6 role, he went to Istanbul. Bennett went, later, to Canada, where he worked as a top security man for the RCMP (on the Russian desk). It was there his career came to a premature end. The official reason for this retirement was 'Sickness'.

Towards the end of 1942, the Battle of Stalingrad was being fought with ferocity. It has already been recorded in military history as one of the most fierce, and bloody battles of World War II.

About that time, we received a very interesting document. It concerned regular soldiers who had served overseas for a period in excess of their normal peacetime tour. The scheme was devised with the object of repatriating those eligible. It started off with men who had about eight years, or more, overseas. They may now apply to be sent home. Those with seven years may apply for repatriation in about two months time, and those with six years in about four months. Not only did I come within that category, so also did my three colleagues Sgts. Simpson, Colley and Pickford. The scheme was not compulsory. Senior Commanders may reject applications and of course all was subject to the exigencies of the war. Furthermore, no guarantees, or promises were made regarding the individual's future after arrival in the UK. Within days, or weeks, one may be returned to the Middle East, or posted to any other theatre of war, such as Burma. The scheme was attractive, but also something of a gamble. The alternative was to remain in 'F' Special Wireless Section. As my rank was not substantive, I would have to revert to that of Sergeant. With my three Sergeants, we talked it over for hours on end. Eventually, we all made up our minds, and reached the same decision. We would apply.

Desert Winters are cold, bitterly cold at nights. One morning, I received a telephone call from a Welfare Officer in Baghdad. He had just received a consignment of welfare goods, and he offered us some woollens. Quickly, I arranged transport, and a couple of hours later a large crate arrived. Together with a couple of Sergeants, we opened it. There, inside, was a large quantity of woollen garments; socks, scarves, pullovers, balaclavas etc.; all conforming to Army specifications. Then we spotted something. On each garment was a tag showing the name, age and school of some small child who had knitted the item. Some of those ages were very young indeed. Each school was in the Edmonton, or Winnipeg area, in Canada. By sea convoy they had come across the Atlantic, round South Africa, through thousands of miles of ocean infested by enemy 'U' Boats. The woollens, and the labels said it all. It was an emotional moment, and for a short while we did not speak a word. Each of us knew how the other two felt. My generation, neither Canadian or British, did not fail those kids.

The 8th Army in North Africa was advancing, and the Germans there were in full retreat. The situation at Stalingrad was, for the Germans, no less serious. They were about to surrender, with enormous losses, to the Red Army. We in 'F' Section continued to wage our war through wireless waves. For us, it was a battle of wits, and dots and dashes. That was the over simplified, and condensed scenario in early 1943.

As my time in 'F' Special Wireless Section began to run out, so my feelings about the departure became more, and more confused. Leaving was not going to be easy. I regarded 'F' almost as if it was my own Section. Never before, had I enjoyed such an immense feeling of 'belonging'. My experiences had been those of job satisfaction, and happiness. How can happiness and war be reconciled? I do not know the answer.

In March came orders to stand-by for embarkation. All troop and shipping movements were classified as a secret in wartime. When, in early April, the order came to report to the Embarkation Staff Officer, Basra, my three colleagues and I, packed our kit, and said our farewells. As we travelled by train to Basra, we had no idea of our actual sailing date, or on what ship. Without doubt, the voyage would be long, and hazardous, and what would follow in the UK? It was like entering a long dark tunnel, with a very unpredictable future. Repeatedly, I asked myself, had I made one of the greatest mistakes of my life when applying for repatriation? Perhaps I was just undergoing a bout of depression. Later that year, in his Christmas broadcast, the King (George VI) used a quotation:

> "I said to the man standing at the gate of the year, 'Give me a light, that I might find my way into the unknown'. He said to me 'Put your trust into the hand of God. That will be better for you than a light, and safer than a known way'."

CHAPTER 12

Prior to leaving 'F' Special Wireless Section, authority was given for me to retain my acting rank of WOII for the duration of the voyage home. That was an advantage, or should have been, as WO's enjoyed the advantage of second class travel when it was available.

Tied up at Basra docks, and in full war paint, was the *City of Canterbury*. She was to convey us as far as Bombay. Not a large ship; I would guess about 12,000 tons. In peacetime, she had been a one class ship on schedule runs to the Far East. My three colleagues were allocated their accommodation. With a small bunch of other Warrant Officers, all from different Corps and Regiments, I was waiting to embark when word came that the ship was full. If, however, we so wished we would be permitted to travel as deck passengers, which amounted to nothing more than sleeping rough on a hard, open, wooden deck. Meals and facilities would be as second class passengers. If we declined the offer, it meant hanging around in a transit camp in Basra waiting the next boat. Without hesitation we opted to travel. Once more it would be a voyage in convoy, taking about ten days.

My feet had hardly touched the deck when, without warning, I felt giddy. The deck was crowded, but I sat down. Within moments, I was cold and shivering. That, in a temperature of well over 100°F. It was ludicrous. Then came sweating, and rigoring. Picking myself up, I searched for, and found, a bathroom. A bath did not help, and by then I realised it was a fever, and like it, or not, medical help was the only answer. With difficulty, I got dressed, and made my way to the ship's sick bay.

The sick bay, or tiny hospital was high up on the ship's stern. It contained about sixteen beds, or cots as they were called. Like a ship's compass, each was suspended on gimbals. My first recollection is one of finding myself in one of those cots, with a medical officer alongside who was speaking to a male nurse. About an hour had passed since we had left the dockside. Sometime later that MO returned. This time he inserted a needle into the base of my spine and commenced to withdraw fluid. A lumbar puncture was not a major operation, but neither was it amusing when performed on a moving and vibrating ship. Not until the following day, when still feeling very ill, did the MO sit down and have a chat. He explained that his first fear was that I had meningitis, but tests had proved negative, and his diagnosis was now heat-stroke, which is mostly caused through lack of salt in the body. Consequently, from then on I was drinking salt water by the bucketful ... Ugh! Mercifully, I was too ill to care. Very quickly, a good relationship built up between that MO and myself. He was from the Royal Canadian Army Medical Corps, and his home was in the Winnipeg area. Not only was he an excellent doctor, but a very caring man. To him, my debt is unrepayable. A few years later, I heard that the 'City of Canterbury' had been sunk by enemy action. If that was true, I do hope that my Canadian MO survived, and ultimately returned safely to his home.

Before I moved out of the cot, a week must have passed, by which time most of the strength in my legs had vanished. Sitting by the hospital porthole, I scanned the surrounding ocean. Densely dotted on the sea was a host of shipping. Our convoy was a large one. Slowly, we sailed on, unmolested, and on tranquil waters. The enemy failed to raise even a clenched fist.

Immediately we docked at Bombay, disembarkation commenced. Also docked, were two large pre-war liners. The *Strathmore* and the *Strathaird* were both well know passenger ships, in their day, on the Far East run. Simpson, Colley, Pickford and myself were all transferred to the former. Once aboard, I had to report to the Sick Bay, and there I was detained. This was much larger that the 'Canterbury's' and more spacious. Though feeling better, heat-stroke was still causing me problems.

Troops, some with wives and children, arrived from various parts of India, and together with those from the *City of Canterbury* soon filled the *Strathaird* and *Strathmore*. For three, or four days we remained docked. The Suez Canal was closed, and our route would necessitate sailing around the Cape of Good Hope. It was no secret that troop ships taking that route called in at Durban. Indications appeared that we were about to sail. No official mention came of our destination, or ports of call. Maybe we were off to the North Pole! But our grapevine had it right, as always.

After a few days, I was discharged from the Sick Bay, and rejoined my three Sergeants. Soldiers, when in hospital, tend to feel isolated, and are happiest when with their own Unit, or Corps. Though still a little weak about the knees, life from now on should resume some normality.

What a wonderful ship was the *Strathmore*. Ships, like homes, have atmosphere. This had one of peace and happiness. For a while, I was excused all duties, so much of my time was spent on the open decks. The routine was much of one of war at sea. That was not a new experience. Emergency station boat drill, and inspections took place daily. During the hours of darkness, the blackout was absolute. The temperature rose higher, and higher, as we sailed deeper into the tropics. On this voyage, we were not part of a convoy. The *Strathaird* and our *Strathmore* became partners with a single escort of a destroyer from the Royal South African Navy. That escort seemed to be continuously circling around us. Both ships were fast, and we sped along at about 28 knots. That speed being far greater than the possible maximum of a 'U' Boat. On our stern there was a 6" gun, and some anti-aircraft rockets. The ship's Asdic would provide warning of any 'U' Boat activity within range, but with our speed we were quite capable of out-distancing an enemy, very rapidly. That would leave the destroyer to fulfil its purpose of seeking out, and destroying enemy 'U' Boats.

In peacetime, it could have been the voyage of a lifetime. The ocean was smooth, the food was good, and for a lover of the sea it would have been bliss. Alas, we were at war. At no time was it possible to completely ignore the risks, and hazards. Day, and night we carried our life jackets. Practice alarms were ten a penny. Within a week, I was feeling fine, and completely recovered from heat-stroke.

It had to happen, and it happened the day before we were due to arrive at Durban. The alarm bells rang; the ship heeled over, and the engine vibrations became more noticeable as we increased speed, and altered course. Within seconds, so it seemed, we were at our boat stations. For a while, we stayed there with no further orders or announcements on the speakers. It was all calm, and orderly, and not even the sound of a crying child. Instinct told us this was not another practice drill. The order came to 'Stand Down', and the ship resumed its normal course, and speed. Only later, did we learn that the alarm had been raised by either the destroyer, or the *Strathaird* who had picked up a 'Ping' on their Asdic. It was a very re-assuring incident in as much as it left no doubt that if put to the test, the drill and discipline would stand up to the test; including the women and children.

Together, the following morning, both ships entered Durban harbour, and docked. In September 1939, the largest ship afloat was our own *Queen Mary*. She was the No.1 transatlantic liner. The original *Queen Elizabeth* did not come into service under after the outbreak of war, and then not as a passenger liner but into direct service as a trooper. The French crack liner was their *Ile de France*. It may have been No.3 in the world's rating. On arrival at Durban, we saw, what to most of us, was the largest ship we had ever seen. It too, was docked. That ship was the *Ile de France*.

The dockers had only just secured our ship's ropes when orders came for us to prepare to disembark. Now, one more transfer of ships, which was little more than a re-run of the one in Bombay. The human cargoes disgorged themselves from the *Strathaird* and *Strathmore*, and were funnelled into the depths of that huge ship *Ile de France*.

If proof were needed that "All that glitters is not Gold", then the *Ile de France* would provide the evidence. Externally, she appeared magnificent, and splendid. Internally, she left me totally unimpressed. Every nook and cranny had been converted into over crowded accommodation. The four of us remained together, and were allocated bunks in what had, one time, been the ship's cinema. The bunks were made of wood and built in rows, and tiers one above the other to a height of eight levels. Mine was on the top. Then sitting up one knocked their head on the bunk above, or in my case on the ceiling. To go to bed at night, I climbed up, and over the seven lower bunks. Tough on the occupants! The atmosphere was one of sweat, and unwashed feet. Need I say more? Some rather odious blankets were provided, but due to the atmosphere is was unlikely that blankets would be necessary even if we finished up at the South Pole! Some of the accommodation I saw was even worse. We were well down in the ship's bowels, so portholes were permanently sealed. Meals were served around the 24 hours. It was possible to be given a breakfast ticket for 3am! The food was served on the cafeteria system. It was plentiful, but the standard was grim. If was often said that the *Queen Mary* carried about 16,000 American troops on each of its transatlantic crossings. If that was so, then a fair estimate of the number on the *Ile de France* was about 15,000. That figure would include women and children who were also passengers. Men from the Royal Navy, the RAF, Dominion Forces, Free French, Free Poles, Canadians, Australians, South Africans were all represented on this ship. Our own Army were in the majority.

When France collapsed, the *Ile de France* joined the Free French Forces forming in the UK. The ship, I believe, came under control of the P&O Line, and was captained by one of its officers. Most of the ship's crew were French.

Soon after boarding, we learnt that we were not about to sail, but would be remaining in Durban for a few days. It turned out to be a week. After ship's daily inspection, at about 12 noon, all those not required for any duty on board were to be granted shore leave until 2359 hrs.

During those war years there were thousands upon thousands of British servicemen who passed through Durban. Ask any one of them, what is their most vivid memory of their visit. The overwhelming majority will all give the same answer as myself. It is one of a wonderful, white-haired, loveable lady who each, and every morning came to the docks. There looking up at thousands of troops on their ships, she stood with great dignity, and began to sing, quite unaccompanied. Without a microphone, and without amplification she sang into a megaphone. They were not pop songs, nor folk songs, nor songs from the shows. The lady sang opera!!! Yes, opera, from a busy dusty dockside to might troopships, packed to capacity with ex-Desert Rats, and the like. It was incredible. No opera singer ever enjoyed a more enthusiastic, and appreciative audience. She was no sexy Miss World clad in a swimsuit, but the troops loved her. She offered her talent, and God given gift to us in the Forces, and asked for nothing in return. It is doubtful if any of us knew her name. Shortly after the war, I heard that she had been honoured by the King with either an OBE or MBE. If true, that would have delighted us. Some years later, probably in the early sixties, I read her obituary in one of our national newspapers. It caused me sorrow.

The people of Durban were renowned, in those years, for their kindness, and unstinted hospitality to the British. At noon, when we left the ship, and docks for our day's leave we poured out in our thousands onto a main road. It was full with parked private, cars, and standing by each was the owner, both sexes, and all ages. They approached us with a smile, and an extended hand. My friends, and I were overwhelmed. There was a lump in my throat. They invited us to their homes. Would we like to have a meal? Would we like a bath? (Had they not been so tactful they may have added 'You seem to need one' with a finger to their nose!). What about a cinema show? Or a drive out into the Country for a picnic? So the offers, and suggestions came thick and fast. Our little group of four were approached by a middle aged Jewish couple. Very simply, they asked us to go home with them, and join them for lunch. Without hesitation, we accepted. Their house was on the outskirts of Durban. Their car was large and luxurious. Their home was also large, but simply furnished, and very colonial in style. The garden was huge, and included a swimming pool, and tennis court. Like all 'White' homes, they employed coloured African servants. Before placing our hosts in an embarrassing position by suggesting we had a bath, we took the matter into our own hands, and requested one. I had never seen such a sumptuous bathroom. A touch on the tap, and out poured gallons of boiling water. A servant appeared with clean warm towels. How I wallowed in the extravagance of that bath. Sick Bays, Boat Drill, nasty smells and overcrowding all seemed light years away in a dim and dismal past. In reality, they were just a few miles down the road! An hour later, we were all sitting together at a table which groaned with the weight of food. We joked, and we laughed and chatted. Those good folk treated us as if we were all that mattered to them. I was relieved that the subject of Jews, and Germany was not raised. To have discussed such horrors would have cast a cloud over the occasion, and it was good to forget war for just a few hours.

The afternoon was spent out of doors. We enjoyed drinking tea from real cups. To round off the day, we were taken to a cinema. The film may have been fact or fiction, good or bad. I do not know. For the first time in my life, I was inside an air conditioned building. It was cool and comfortable. The evening promised to be an enjoyable one. It was. I fell asleep!

At about 11pm our hosts drove us back to the docks. We expressed our appreciation, and thanks, but most probably quite inadequately. Lastly, we bid each other 'Good Night'. One glance at the ship, and I heard a voice say, "After the Lord Mayor's Show, comes the proverbial ...!"

That was just one day of our lives in Durban. Six more followed. Each with different hosts, and families. Each with varied forms of hospitality. All with the same goodwill, and generosity which demonstrated the admirable goodness that existed in their hearts. To repay them was way beyond our means. They gave us so much happiness, and we left with memories which will be treasured for all time. Today, South Africa is tearing itself apart. That distresses their friends.

On the day that short leave was cancelled, we knew that our departure was imminent. It was now May, and the South African winter had arrived. Ahead of us was a long, and miserable voyage which would last for six weeks, or more.

With the aid of tugs, this misbegotten, floating, hulk slowly eased away from the docks. Simultaneously, the alarm bells rang for our first boat drill. At our boat station about sixty men mustered, including two officers. Being the only Warrant Officer, I was appointed the boat's Sgt. Major. In front, there was the greatest variety of cap badges I had every seen in such a small space. Basic military discipline is the same throughout the Army. Degree, and emphasis, may vary slightly in different branches, but it seemed unlikely that in this situation I would encounter any additional problems. An hour later, and the outline of land was disappearing over the distant horizon.

On this, the last and longest leg of the homeward bound voyage, we were not in convoy. Like the *Queen Mary* and *Queen Elizabeth*, the *Ile de France* always sailed as a loner, without even a naval escort. The ship was fast, with a speed of about thirty knots. That alone, provided a good defence against attack except from the air. The gun on the stern was a modern 6". Anti-Aircraft defence was mostly rockets, and there was Asdic to give warning against 'U' Boats. If attacked, this ship would give a good account of itself. As I saw it there might possibly be a problem in an emergency in that it could be difficult to get out of that overcrowded accommodation below to the open decks above, and the boat station.

The first day at sea brought rougher, and more wintry weather. Large, low black clouds brought heavy rain, and the seas rose. The ship, large as she was, began to pitch and toss. We were never informed of our position, but it was a calculated guess that we were keeping well out from the African coast and sailing almost due South. The days became colder, and colder. It was not long before we heard claims that ice floes had been sighted. After a few days, we changed course to a Westerly direction. Clearly, we were many miles away from any of the recognised shipping routes, but that would be an anti-'U' Boat precaution. A few more days, and there was another change in direction, as we sailed North Westerly. Since leaving Durban there had not been a single sighting of another ship. The weather continued cold, and wet. One afternoon, on the starboard bow, land was sighted. We steamed towards it, and within a few miles of its shores. This was Tristan da Cunha. How desolate, and depressing it looked with an umbrella of low clouds, and a drizzling rain.

Tristan brought back to me many childhood memories. About 1,500 miles North is the Island of St. Helena, where I spent four years of my boyhood. In terms of square miles, the Bishop of St. Helena most probably has the largest diocese in the world as it extends from Tristan in the South to Ascension in the North. The Governor of St. Helena is also Governor of those two Islands. We often spoke of Tristan with its tiny population of under three hundred, and their lonely life, and fight for survival. In the mid-twenties, a ship called at Tristan da Cunha about once a year. What an isolated and remote place to live. To relive those days, when Tristan was our neighbour, was easy.

Without slowing down, we exchanged ship to shore visual signals, and greetings. Through the mist, we sailed on into the Atlantic. That most reliable grape vine informed us that our next port of call was Rio de Janeiro.

Time passed, but conditions on board did not improve. Morale was low, and grumbling prevalent. Our routine, and life style was, I suppose, no worse than that on many other wartime troop ships.

The current news from North Africa could not have been better. The German Army there, was surrendering in large numbers.

With so much foul air below decks, it was refreshing to get up in the mornings onto an open deck. Most days, I did so before reveille. The morning we arrived at Rio was no exception. Soon after 5am, high up on the decks, the Brazilian coastline was clearly visible, as the sun rose over the horizon. A small number of WO's and Sgts.; were also about, but outwardly the ship appeared deserted. There was not a ship in sight. Without warning, we suddenly listed over to one side, and tilting to an alarming angle. At the same time, we realised that without decreasing speed we were making a complete 180 degree turn, and heading back out to sea. For such a huge ship to carry out that manoeuvre requires a large expanse of water, which we had. Walking on deck, at that angle, was not easy but I made my way towards the boat station, expecting the alarm bells to ring at any moment. They did not. No explanation was given why we were indulging in such nautical antics. About half an hour passed, when a destroyer appeared. We again did an about turn; this time more slowly headed for the mainland. The destroyer escorted us.

The entrance to the harbour of Rio de Janeiro is renowned for its beauty. Slowly, we steamed through a gorge with stately mountains on either side rising out of the seas and reaching up to the blue skies overhead. It was a not-to-be-forgotten sight of magnificence, and majesty.

Shore leave was not granted, and our stay was only about five hours, during which time we refuelled, and took aboard fresh water supplies. By sunset we were, once more, well out to sea, and land no longer in sight.

Still unescorted, we sailed almost due East towards the African Coast, and running almost on the Equator. Every possible moment was spent up on deck, as it had become very hot and humid. Conditions below decks were revolting.

My knowledge of astronomy is not good, but at various times I had learnt where to look, and find the Great Bear, and the Southern Cross. Neither presented any difficulty on a clear night, providing one was in the correct hemisphere, but to see both constellations at the same time, was not an every night occurrence. That experience came to me from an upper deck of the *Ile de France* in June 1943.

Crossing the Atlantic had its risks, but we were fortunate. Our boat, and emergency drills were all practices, with no hint of a 'U' Boat, or enemy surface raider. Late one morning we entered Lagos. The harbour was full with shipping. Again, there was no shore leave, and our visit was just a few hours. On departure, we sailed almost due North towards the British Isles, and home.

For some days, it had been known that there was an outbreak of measles on board. Under such cramped, and crowded conditions, an infectious fever would spread rapidly. Only a day back at sea, and I developed the symptoms. On reporting sick, the MO admitted me to the ship's emergency isolation ward, hurriedly introduced to meet the outbreak. My fever was mild, and did not cause me much discomfort.

Sailing towards home, while still in isolation, I heard that for most the daylight hours we now had air cover. That was reassuring.

On a wet, and depressing early July day, we dropped anchor at Clydebank. All my friends were immediately given fourteen days disembarkation leave. I was not permitted to join them. The MO said that I was still unclean and together with about thirty others transferred to an isolation hospital somewhere in the Clydebank area. The first day of the voyage, in the Persian Gulf, was in a ship's hospital. The last day of the same voyage was also in a ship's hospital. In between there had been some coming, and going. What next? I asked myself. My first seven days in the UK were spent in that isolation hospital. The hospital staff were kind, and we were spoilt. It might be thought that I was thrilled, and excited to be back home, but not so. My feelings were a little impassive. Almost seven years had passed since sailing from Southampton, and during that time, I had not been on a single day's leave. Now, everything was so strange. It was a strange homeland to the one I had left behind in 1936. The environment was one of war. The thought of readjustment, and what it involved was frightening. Perhaps, I may apply for an immediate posting, and return to somewhere overseas. If only I could run away from it all, and back to India, and Iraq and the war which I knew, and understood. That war waged by Signals Intelligence.

    The day came, when after an examination by a civilian doctor, I was pronounced a fit person to rejoin society. Next day, I drew some pay, a rail warrant to London, emergency ration cards, and a leave pass for fourteen days. Topographically, I was fully aware of my surroundings, but philosophically, confused. I went home.

The 118 S. W. Section

Some of the operators (all ex 118 S. W. Section)

Left to Right: Sgt. Vickery, author and Sgt. Pake

Enigma reunion Bedford, September 1997. Author third from right

Chapter 13

A home-coming leave like this should have been the most enjoyable, and exciting leave of my entire Army career. It was not.

At Euston station, my Mother was there to meet me. Within a few minutes she told me of the death of Jack Lane. I first met Jack in February 1925, when only eight years old, on the Island of St. Helena. As boys, we spent much of our time together playing, and in each other's homes. In the following years we had kept in touch, as he became a trusted, and most valuable friend. He had completed his training as a Sergeant pilot in the RAF in Canada. Only a few weeks previously, when pilot of a Lancaster Bomber, and returning from his sixth operation mission on a raid over Germany, he had been brought down over Holland, and killed. To be greeted with that unhappy news left me dejected. During that leave, I visited the Lane family; what a sad time. I also met other families who had lost relatives, and friends. It was commonplace.

Leave enabled me to visit a couple of West End shows. To spend an hour, or two in a colourful world of music, romance, and often make-believe was an exhilarating way of re-charging batteries. The Summer of 1943 was almost free of enemy air raids, so there were no unpleasant interruptions. Always, I wore uniform. I did not own any civilian clothes, and even if I had they would have been more of a hindrance that a help. London was crammed full of servicemen from all the freedom loving countries of the world, not least the American GI's. It was impossible to be alone, but I was often lonely.

For some inexplicable reason, I had the notion that it would be easy to call on, and see old friends. Without thinking, I believed that to pick up the threads, and renew old acquaintances where I had left off seven years earlier would follow with ease. Not so; the changes had been too big. The culprit was not the war itself, but that long gap in time. To sit down, pick up the pieces, and put them together again, in the matter of a few days was out of the question.

It was quite natural to find myself comparing the England of 1943 with that I had left behind in 1936. In the earlier year the soldier was looked upon as a course, vulgar, uneducated youth rejected by most of society. 'Nice' people did not associate with them. Now, on return, the lines of Kipling came to mind:

> Oh, it's Tommy this, and Tommy that,
> and Tommy go away!
> But it's 'Thank You, Mr Atkins' when the
> Band begins to play.

That I was not peeved by that about turn in the public's attitude was probably due to the admiration, and respect which I had quickly gained for the civilians. Their unstinted dedication to the war effort, their belief in the cause, and their undivided loyalty to the Country. The courage and morale, were not mere propaganda stories, but fact. Food rationing was strict, and meagre. Hardship followed hardship. Air raid followed air raid; yet they did not complain. Our civilian population won the admiration of the world, and rightly deserved it. It was a time of feeling very proud of being British. Later generations have not had the good fortune of experiencing such pride, and emotions. When finally the war was won that indomitable spirit vanished, never to return. It might be that since 1945 our greatest enemy has been ourselves.

Fourteen days leave opened by eyes on many matters. Not all the time was spent in London, so my views were not just of the capital city at war. There were moments of great pleasure, but also some of sadness. The times were not conducive to holidays. To completely escape from, and forget, the war was impossible. The fortnight did not live up to my expectations, and before the leave was through I felt restless, ill at ease, and itching to once more be back in the 'Y' Service doing what I was best qualified to do. My orders were on the expiration of leave to report to Catterick Camp. That I did.

In August 1943, Catterick Camp was a nightmare. Not only was it the depot and training centre for the Royal Corps of Signals, but also a gigantic assembly point for all Royal Signals personnel arriving, and departing from and to, all corners of the world. Due mostly to over crowding, conditions and food were both appalling.

Rank made little difference. Perhaps a few officers had more jam on their bread, but even that is questionable. That I was a member of the 'Y' Service caused my seniors to have little interest in me, which meant that I was left alone. Moreover, it had the advantage of reducing my stay in the Camp to just a few days. It was 99% certain that my next move would be to the UK Army 'Y' Training Centre, which was the Special Operators Training Battalion in Douglas, Isle of Man. Confirmation came with the posting.

The War Department had taken over most of the hotels and boarding houses on the Douglas sea front. One such large terraced block was completely occupied by the SOTB. Other sections of the sea front were taken over by the Royal Navy, and Royal Marines. There were no barracks.

The Battalion strength was about three hundred men, and possibly over seven hundred ATS. On arrival, as expected, I reverted to the rank of Sergeant. It was a great job to be back amongst old friends. Due to my hospital stay on Clydebank, I was the last to arrive from the *Ile de France*. Simpson, Colley and Pickford had arrived about ten days before me. Accommodation was somewhat cramped, but by wartime standards had a few comforts. There was nothing wrong with the food, that a good cook could not have rectified.

Though it was a large Unit, it was in a manner one more example of Chiefs and Indians. There was an abundance of both. The senior NCO's were much experienced providing a large reservoir overflowing with knowledge of enemy communications, and the art of intercepting. Unbelievably, a number of them were under employed, and just kicking their heels. A few were instructing. I often felt that the presence of many of us was an embarrassment to the authorities. A solution, of a kind, was found. It was decided to run a classification course of about four weeks. That, I joined. The official object was not so much to upgrade us, but to confirm the ratings we already held. Anyway, many of us were already Class I and could not go any higher. The real purpose was more likely to have been just to keep us on the ball with something to do. Christians are sometimes accused of preaching to the converted. Likewise, so it could be said, that Special Operators sometimes tried to teach those who were already taught. On completion of the Course, each of us were confirmed in our grading. How could it have been otherwise?

Italy had surrendered. It was September 1943. The cease fire did not come as any great surprise, but it was nevertheless welcome, and cause for a small celebration.

Until arriving in Douglas, I had not worked with the Women's Services, or lived in a mixed WO's and Sergeants' Mess. At first it was all a little alien. The social side was no problem, and what could be more welcome, and enjoyable than some female company? At work, it was a different story. To adapt myself to accept women as soldiers was most difficult. Not, I hasten to add, through reasons of prejudice, but rather for reasons deeply rooted in my previous military life style.

Any person who is good at their trade or profession, normally requires certain basic qualifications. That is no less true of an instructor, or teacher. Firstly, they require a natural aptitude. They need the ability to 'Put it Over', and also 'Win Over' their class. It is taken for granted that they are well experienced in, and have an excellent knowledge of, the subject. Personality also plays a role. My only qualification to be an instructor was my knowledge of my subject. In all other respects, I fell down and was aware of the fact. When told to take over a class of ATS, and instruct, I protested. That protest fell on deaf ears. There was no shortage of senior NCO's who were well qualified, without choosing one who was not. One officer said to me, 'Anyone can instruct'. My reply was in military jargon 'Improper', as I said something about one of the weaknesses in Douglas was that maybe there was the odd 'Anyone' instructing! Such a comment could have led me into disciplinary hot water. Discretion being the better part ...! I shut up! That I was a square peg in a round hole was, to me, obvious, if not to others. It followed that I was miserable, and unhappy, and just longed to get away from Douglas.

At weekends, and sometimes in the evenings it was possible to spend a little time in the town. Compared to the mainland it was a little more peaceful as they did not experience any enemy air raids. The relationship between the civilians and ourselves could not have been better. For the duration of the war, Douglas had ceased to be a holiday resort.

The training syllabus provided instruction on just about all a trainee special operator would be required to know. The theory of electricity and magnetism was included, but the greatest importance was attached to the training in reading Morse. A few hours a day was devoted to that subject alone. At the end of their training, trainees had to reach speeds of about 18 words per minute for block letters; with higher speeds in plain language, and figures. The tests were carried out over much longer periods than a normal wireless operator did, and read through stronger interference. Above all a high degree of accuracy was demanded. Sending was taught, but with a lower degree of accuracy and speed. Few were ever called upon to put their sending to practical use. Foreign procedures were the foundation, and scaffolding of training. He/She would be called upon to gently turn the dial of the receiver, and just be listening to a particular station be able to identify it by the nature of the procedure it was using, and the type of traffic it was passing. Very quickly, the operator should be able to identify the nationality, and break down its recognition into greater detail e.g. is it German Air Force, Italian Navy, International Diplomatic and Commercial, USSR Navy or Red Army, or just a neutral Country? There are many more possibilities. Operators had to acquire a good working knowledge of Direction Finding, and the nature of the equipment used. The HRO was the standard receiver throughout 'Y'. Those subjects were the main body of the syllabus; there were a few others. At the end of their training, and passing all subjects, the trainee was classified and graded as a Group B Class III Special Operator. Prior to their arrival in the SOTB all personnel underwent basic military training in drill, use of weapons and other fundamentals. Few could argue that their true value was not recognised, and to this day is still not. They deserved better treatment than they often got.

In field units, complaints were often heard about the low standard of training in the SOTB. They were more about the quality of the training rather than of the programme. Certainly, they were never of the individuals whose standard could not have been bettered.

From my own experience, those complaints were usually justified. Through compulsion, and not of my own fault, I admit that during my few weeks as an instructor I contributed towards that low standard. My love of Army life was, in Douglas, put to the test. There were early symptoms of military madness in the form of a furious, frenzied feeling, culminating in feeble-mindedness. Treatment was at hand!

    Somewhere behind the scenes, amongst the officers, unknowingly I had a friend. I was ordered to appear before the Commanding Officer for an interview. Previously, I had known him only by sight, and even now his name escapes me. The summons suggested that the proverbial rocket was on its way. Happily, someone forgot to light the fuse. The CO came straight to the point saying that it had been brought to his notice that I was very unhappy, and discontented in the Battalion, and he asked me was that so, and if so, why? In reply, I said 'Yes', and considered the reason to be mostly due to my awareness of my own inability to instruct, also adding that I wished to be more involved in the operational side of 'Y' rather than in the training. More than anything, I wanted to take part in the Second Front, as and when it arrived. The Colonel was a good listener, and a sympathetic one. Nothing pleased me more than when he said something like, 'There is a 'B' type Section – 118 Special wireless Section – now being formed in Castletown, IOM. The vacancy for a Section Sergeant has not yet been filled, would you like the job? If so, you can pack your kit, and go tomorrow'. I was over the moon. Next day, I reported to the Officer Commanding 118 Special Wireless Section at the Links Hotel, Castletown.

Chapter 14

The Section was the last of the 'B' types to be formed. Somewhere, scattered across the war torn world, were seventeen others. My immediate concern was this, 118 Special Wireless Section.

We were commanded by Capt. H Napper, Royal Signals. The only other officer was Lt. D J Hann. There was no establishment for a Warrant Officer. The three senior NCO's were Sgt. W F Vickery, R McPake and myself. Of those, I was the senior, and therefore the Section Sergeant. My role would not be unlike that of a Sergeant Major. As a Class I Special Operator and with a number of years 'Y' experience, my value was more than just a discipline and admin. man. In charge of the set room, and operational matters was Vickery. McPake's responsibilities were stores, supplies, rations and associated matters. From the very start a good relationship built up between us, which was to last until our day of disbandment. Below the rank of Sergeant were about a hundred other ranks. Many of them were great characters who did so much to build the Unit into a happy team.

Our home in the Links hotel was spartan, but tolerable. Castletown was about two miles away, but just down the road were a few cottages, a church and a pub. The building which was to give us mush pleasure was a small hall. The Section was in its infancy, and much hard training lay ahead. The programme was intensive, and it would be a while before we would become fully mobilised, and operational. Not until that stage would an Intelligence Corps detachment join us. In due course, we would become one of the Army 'Y' Units deployed in the Second Front. At that time (Autumn 1943) none of us had the faintest doubt in our minds that it would be in the following summer. We did not give much thought on the location. That was anyone's guess.

When in Douglas, I had often wished for the kind of position I now held. This Section, its work and its future was a reality of that wish. My future would rest mostly in my own hands. There would be headaches, there would be problems, and at times a clash of opinions with my seniors. All that was inevitable, but I felt happy and comfortable with the way things were moving.

Sporting facilities were virtually non-existent. Now, and again we rustled up a football team. In a modest way we were fit. As in any other 'Y' Unit, if only indirectly, we were all in it for the end product of intercepted enemy wireless traffic. At the Links it was training, but soon intercepted material would be live, and a valuable contribution to military intelligence.

It was in this formative stage of the Section's life that the foundations of its unity, compatibility and discipline were built. It is my proud belief that efforts in that field bore fruit as succeeding months provided the evidence. The rare visits I made to the set room were purely to show my interest in the operational side. Its responsibility was Vickery's, and he was on the ball.

Recreational, and spare time was devoted in the greatest degree to our concert party. For such a small Unit as ours – only about one hundred men – we were gifted with much amateur talent, enriched by boundless enthusiasm. Jack Warner possessed a fine trained tenor voice, and was our key man on all musical matters. Assisting him was Ken Barrett who played as a cinema organist in civil life, but also more than justified himself as a pianist. Taffy Down was a ventriloquist. In contrast we could boast of a handful of comedians. Without difficulty, we could rely on abut twenty five in the party. Many doubled-up and sang in our small choir of about eighteen voices. Sadly, it had for reasons beyond our control to be all male. Due to shift duties, it was very difficult to arrange a full attendance at rehearsals. From its early days, I became not just interested, but absorbed in the concert party. Soon, I was landed with a triad of tasks; comprising producer, bass singer in the choir, and make-up man. The scripts and parodies were the work of my colleague, Sgt. McPake. Very occasionally I made a small contribution to his efforts. We christened our show "Loud and Clear", and our aim was to give our first public performance in the small local hall, it was decided to charge a small admittance fee in aid of charity. That required military blessing, and approval which was obtained without difficulty. Always, one eye had to be kept on the calendar, as our stay in the

Links would only be for about two months. In November the curtain went up on that first night, and all proceeds were donated to the Red Cross Prisoner of War Fund. "Loud and Clear" was born. The audience appeared to enjoy themselves, and we certainly did. We gave about three performances over a period of about two weeks. That made great demands on our meagre spare time, but it was rewarding. At one performance, the local paper sent a critic, although at the time we were unaware of his presence. The resulting write-up in the local paper was generous, and kind. Jack Warner's widow recently sent me the original cutting of the write-up in that Isle of Man paper. In turn, I passed it on to the Curator of the Corps museum in Blandford, where it can be seen today.

By the 1st December we had moved to the vicinity of the Pt. of Ayre, in the Northern tip of the Island. Here, we just continued our training, and life was really a case of 'The Mixture as Before'. For our stay there of a few weeks, we were able to keep the Concert Party alive, and gave two or three more public performances in Ramsey. Our contribution to the Prisoner of War Fund was now in three figures. How we managed to make the time is somewhat of a mystery. The organising of any leisure was becoming increasingly difficult as pressure was running out, and orders for a move to Hampstead had been received. The endeavour, and commitment was by no means wasted, as it had served to build up that all important team spirit. By the middle of December we had given our last performance of "Loud and Clear". Down came the 'Final Curtain'.

The night was dark, wet and depressing when in the early days of 1944 we arrived at Euston station. The blackout was total. Our feet had just touched the platform when the sirens sounded an air raid warning. Not withstanding, we loaded the waiting vehicles, and moved towards Fitzjohns Avenue, Hampstead. We pulled up outside three large houses which had been taken over by the War Department for the duration of the war. For a while, they were to be our home. After a hot meal, it was good to get our heads down for the night.

London has many, many faults, yet always I have had an affection for it. In 1944 there were no bright lights. The whole place was in need of a coat of paint. Rubble from buildings, demolished by air raids, was strewn North, South, East and West. What I saw from the roof of one of those houses saddened me, but that emotion was outweighed by a sense of pride, and admiration for the Londoners. No 'Heil Hitler', goose-stepping, strutting German would ever conquer these people. So often in our history others have underestimated us; not least Philip II of Spain, Bismarck, and Napoleon. Now Hitler was making the same mistake. Some people never learn!

As we were admitted into 1944, so we were conscious of entering an area where the most critical battle of the war would be fought. We in 118 SW Section would be involved with our task of intercepting enemy wireless communications. The Country was bursting at the seams with Soldiers, Sailors and Airmen from all the Allied Powers. One day in this year would be 'D' Day, and one hour would be 'H' hour as we landed somewhere in Europe to put paid, once and for all, to the horror of Nazism. The landings may be anywhere on the thousands of miles on the European coastline. It was anyone's guess. The war on the Eastern front was going well. In Italy, there was heavy fighting at Casino. One February day, I received news that my cousin Robin had been killed whilst on active service in that Country. He was about the same age as myself.

After the fall of Singapore, the war in the Far East had received little attention from the media. Our 14th Army in Burma had pre-fixed their nomenclature with the word 'Forgotten'. The 'Forgotten Fourteenth' had now become their recognised title. Their war was hard and cruel in the jungles of Burma. The atrocities of the Japanese were already known to the world. As we prepared for 'D' Day, so the forgotten Army were on the brink of defeating the Japanese at Imphal (the gateway to India).

Back on the mainland, hopes had risen that there may be some leave. That was, as I recall, no such luck. Sometimes we had tickets for West End shows. More often than not, they were complimentary. While in Hampstead I saw Ivor Novello, for the first time, in 'The Dancing Years'. On some evenings it became possible to cross over to South East London, and visit relatives for an hour or so. More than once the return journey to Hampstead was eventful, as I made my way back in an air raid. When the 'Alert' was sounded, that part of the

Underground which goes under the Thames, was closed. The watertight doors on either side of the river were shut. Travelling from the South, we had on arrival at London Bridge to leave the Underground and come to the surface. To complete the journey it was then necessary for me to walk across London Bridge, and return to the Underground at Bank Station. That crossing of the river, over the Bridge could be a little hair raising. My fear was not so much from enemy bombs, but more of shrapnel raining down from above. Lumps of metal falling down, from a dizzy height, onto the surrounding road, and pavement, in a complete blackout on a dark night is just not my idea of fun and games. Whether, or not, my steel helmet gave any protection, I do not know, but it certainly provided a little 'Dutch' courage. Not far from Hampstead, in Kilburn was Jack Warner's home, where he had lived in pre-war days. Some very enjoyable evenings were spent there listening to some of his records on a wind-up gramophone. He possessed a fine selection of the classics; all 78's. It was also with Jack, that one Sunday evening we had obtained tickets for a classical concert at the Golders Green Hippodrome, where we heard the pianist Solomon, play the solo on Tchaikovsky's Piano Concerto No.1.

Throughout those few months in Hampstead, the general well being of the Section was good. The overall, health, discipline and efficiency was well up to standard, if not above. Hampstead was not to be our last habitat in the UK. There were two more stepping stones to cross before our arrival on the Second Front. We packed our equipment, changed our address and placed our feet on the next stone. It was in Eastbourne.

The environment in a wartime South Coast holiday resort was very different to that of today's. Eastbourne was no quiet, peaceful, retirement home for pensioners. It was noisy. The distinctive sound of bombers, with fighter escorts flying overhead in the direction of Germany was a far cry of a pre-war Wall's ice-cream man crying, 'Stop me and Buy One'. To have been at the receiving end of one of those raids must have been a terrifying experience, and on a scale which none of our own people had endured. Today, there are those who are all too eager to judge the war in retrospect, and often without considering what was justifiable at the time. They will label such raids as inhuman, brutal and as Angle-American terrorism aimed at innocent civilians. They will preach that we should have felt pity towards the Germans, and wept bucketful's of tears. I did not.

Eastbourne had no vacant hotel rooms. Each were full to capacity as they housed American, and British troops. Like any other South Coast town, it was virtually sealed off to civilians. They could move neither in, nor out. The beaches were mined, closed and fenced with barbed wire. The Devonshire theatre was devoted mostly to entertainment for the troops, which was provided by ENSA. It was not easy for a civilian to gain admission.

At the foot of Beachy Head, and standing in its own grounds, was a very large and well built modern house. Most probably built in the early thirties. It boasted not only of large gardens, but also of its own tennis court. The owner must have glowed with the Midas touch. This was our billet. Therein we accommodated over one hundred men, plus offices, set room and stores, and yet we were not unduly squeezed.

Day by day, the pressure stepped up, as 118 SW Section began to fully mobilise, and prepare for its function in the now almost imminent invasion, and second front. We received deliveries of live ammunition, hand grenades, and a PIAT gun. We had received no training on the PIAT (an anti-tank gun), nor on hand grenades. As the Section Sergeant, I did not even know how to prime the latter! During the battle of the Ardennes there arose a sequel to that. We did learn how to use the PIAT but happily never had cause to use our somewhat imperfect knowledge. Like other 'B' type Sections, 118 was mobile. That became a reality as we collected our full quota of transport. Any Army Mobile Unit without vehicles is as useful as a Navy without ships.

Signals Intelligence was not a Royal Signals prerogative. The actual interception, by the Army, was exclusively a Royal Signals responsibility, but once received all intercepted material was passed to the Intelligence Corps. It was for them to make what they could of it. All 'B' Types had an Intelligence Corps Staff as part of their establishment. They consisted of about three officers, and a dozen NCO's. It was at this time in Eastbourne that our 'I' Staff joined up with us. Though we wore different cap badges, we worked well together. Had we not, life would have been difficult indeed, and the outcome disastrous, particularly from the operational viewpoint. To all intents, and purposes we were one team. Any friction on the administrative side, might well have had a knock-on affect on the operational side. Throughout the Army's history there has always been inter-Regimental rivalry, and it is usually quite harmless and amounts to nothing more than leg-pulling, or letting off steam on a sports field.

In the few weeks preceding 'D' Day, the contribution by the 'Y' Service to military intelligence must have been enormous. Anyone having doubts about that has only to read Prof. Hinsley's "British Intelligence in the Second World War" which is an official history on the subject. Page follows page, and chapter follows chapter recording the contributions from Sigint, and 'Y'. It was on the evening of 5th June, in Eastbourne, that I was shown a map. It was no ordinary map. It was a wall map, and on a large scale showing the coastline of Northern France and the Low Countries. The central area was the Pas de Calais where a variety of small coloured, paper flags on pins had been inserted. Each bore the name of a major German Army formation, and in some cases the rank and name of its Commander. To our own military Commanders, that must have been valuable information. My personal position was not such that I was told the detailed source of that Intelligence; neither was I informed which Units, or individuals had provided it. Nevertheless, it made no demands on my brains to put two, and two together. To be in 118 SW Section, and in the 'Y' Service at this historic time was exhilarating. I was proud.

That same evening, the atmosphere became very tense. The drone of aircraft engines grew louder, and louder as the day closed. It had been a long and busy day, and I was tired, yet there was little sleep. There was no heated, excited conversation or chatter. Off and on, we asked each other 'What is going on?' This was not just one more thousand bomber raid on Germany. Something far greater than that was taking place. Just after daybreak I looked out of a window towards the Channel. Never had I seen anything like it. The sea was packed tight with shipping. Ships of all shapes and sizes, sailing down the Channel in the same direction. Overhead, were hundreds and hundreds of aircraft and the never ending sound of their engines. It was the 6th June 1944. Someone switched on a wireless, and this is what I heard:

"This is London calling, in the Home, Overseas, and European Services of the BBC; and this is John Snagge speaking.
Supreme Headquarters Allied Expeditionary Force have just issued a communiqué:
'Under the Command of General Eisenhower, Allied Naval Forces, supported by strong Air Forces began landing Allied Armies this morning, on the Northern Coast of France'.
That ends the reading of Communiqué Number One from the Supreme Headquarters, Allied Expeditionary Force."

That is how I, and many millions of people across the world learnt that 'D' Day had arrived. The events of that day have been well recorded, and told by film, radio, the Press and historians. Graphically, have they depicted the battle. Few mention the reactions and emotions of individuals. That may be due to the different manner in which we received the news. Some shouted with joy. Others just calmly and quietly went about their normal day's work. Empty Churches began to fill, as many went to pray. To pray for final victory, and above all for the safe return of the soldiers, sailors and airmen involved. No military operation, on such a massive scale had ever before been attempted. After listening to that BBC announcement, I was stunned. For a long, long time, we had all been working, and waiting for 'D' Day. Here it was. Unashamedly, I felt an overwhelming sense of pride, and patriotism. It was my belief that at no time had my Country held its head higher, or made a greater contribution to freedom than on this day. Forty five years later those views are unchanged. My greatest fear was that the price would be high, and that within days the casualties would be astronomical. Like many others, I prayed: "Please God ..." Our worst fears did not materialise, as our casualties though heavy were well below the lowest forecasted figure. Events were too prodigious, and following too rapidly one upon another to absorb. My mind was in turmoil. I cannot recall how long I remained by that window. It seemed a long time, but was probably not. On leaving the room, I went in search of something I needed. It was a cup of tea.

Some hours passed before we learnt where the landings had taken place. News was scant. Work was not. Time in Eastbourne was running out, and preparations were in had to move to Littlehampton. A few days later we made that move.

Littlehampton was to be the last stepping stone, and jumping off point. A year earlier I had acquainted myself with this small resort. It was the home of my pre-war friend in Rawalpindi, Alec Langley who was now a prisoner of war in Germany. That previous visit was to call on his family, and make myself known to them.

Carpenters's Home, on the sea front was externally quite an attractive building. Internally, the horrors emerged when we settled in, to make it our short term home the sewers were not connected to the mains, but the building boasted of its own sewage farm in the grounds. More often than not, it failed to operate. Blocked lavatories were the order of the day. We had, in that 'Home', about one hundred and twenty men which was about twice the number it was planned to accommodate. No wonder the system could not cope. The smell was offensive, but not from the roses. They flourished!

Understandably, we were now working round the clock. Our last major task was water-proofing all vehicle engines. They had to be sealed in order to keep out water. That was vital. Water-proofing imposed certain restrictions on the engines, and once safely ashore on the other side it would have to be quickly removed. On leaving the landing craft, the vehicles would have to be driven into a few feet of the sea, and then forward for some yards onto a dry beach. A breakdown of any one vehicle would most probably lead to it being abandoned with the added risk of the total loss of its vital load. Loading tables had been prepared, so it was known where any one item of equipment was packed, and on which vehicle. The bulk, and load weight were other important factors. Nothing could be left to chance.

During our brief stay – of about a week – it was possible to spend a few hours in the evenings away from that ghastly Convalescent Home. My first social act was to look up the Langley family. It was in their home that we spent some very happy musical evenings. Alec's mother was indeed a very charming lady. His sister, Peggy, was a local school teacher. Peggy's friend, Dorothy Arthur, also joined the party. I was asked to take two, or three friends along and one was Jack Warner. In a very tiny sitting room, we laughed and sang. We made our own fun, and it could not have been bettered by any soap opera emanating from a 'Goggle Box'. Unknown to us, at the time, the seeds were being sown for a very happy love story. As Shakespeare wrote: 'Thus bud of love by Summer's ripening breath may prove a beauteous flower'. Before the war was over; it did!

'Careless Talk Costs Lives' was a very famous, and successful war-time slogan. It caught on, not only with the Armed Forces, but equally with the civilians. Throughout our close associations with the Langley, and Arthur families, they never questioned us about our work, or movements. Amongst ourselves, it was no secret that we were about to pull out of Littlehampton for the other side of the Channel. Once outside Carpenters' the subject of movement was not discussed. Our friends no doubt made an intelligent guess, but kept such thoughts to themselves. They were fully aware that one morning they would wake up, and find that we had vanished. There would be neither 'Farewells', nor 'Good-Byes'. Wives, families and sweethearts received no better treatment. Troop movements were secret. That was never questioned.

On, or about, the 19th June, and in the late evening we formed our vehicles up, in convoy, within the grounds of Carpenters'. 118 Special Wireless Section paraded, and as their Section Sergeant, I called the roll, and conducted a preliminary inspection. After calling the Section to attention, I reported to the OC 'All Present and Correct, Sir.' Every man was fully armed, and equipped. On completion of the OC's inspection, they boarded their respective vehicles. There was then a short wait for darkness to fall. Time came, engines were switched on, wheels began to turn, and then slowly, and in convoy we set off for a Greyhound Stadium in East London, which turned out to be a large assembly area for troops proceeding to Normandy. Through the blackout, and with only the faint convoy light of the vehicle in front visible, driving was difficult although our speed was slow. From now on, my driver was Wilson. He was slightly older than myself, and a man with an excellent sense of responsibility. In his skill I had complete confidence, and trust. In the ensuing months, we spent many hours together in the cab, driving across Europe as the advance took us from Normandy to the Rhine. In the meantime, and in darkness, we crawled through the side roads, and lanes of Sussex arriving on the outskirts of London just after daybreak. There, we were met by a small Police escort on motor cycles whose job it was to lead us through Central London to our destination.

At the Greyhound Racing Stadium there was little to do but sit, and wait. With the passing of the years, and as we grow older, we find that nature is kind in that many of the miseries of earlier years are readily forgotten. That day or so in East London was a misery, but details have become somewhat obliterated by mother nature. Buzz bombs (VI's) flew just above our heads, and often fell nearby. It was not a comfortable night.

Without regret, on the following afternoon, our Section once more boarded the vehicles, and now drove to Tilbury docks. No time was wasted. Immediately, our transport was loaded onto an American 'Liberty' boat which was tied up at the dockside. A few hundred troops had previously embarked, and we now climbed up the gangway to join them. About 6pm we got under way, and steamed down river. A couple of hours later, we dropped anchor off Southend Pier, and waited for darkness to fall, when we up-anchored, and sailed in convoy through the Straits of Dover at about midnight. At Calais the Germans had installed large calibre guns capable of firing into Dover. Not to be outdone, we had similar guns on the cliffs of Dover which were no less powerful and damaging. They fired into Calais. From time to time they took pot shots at each other, or the Germans at our shipping. This night was quiet as we sailed, with a Royal Navy escort, through the darkness, and were unmolested.

The morning was cloudy, and overcast as we passed into what should have been the sheltered waters of Mulberry Harbour. The pre-fabricated harbour had been badly mauled by storms just a short while after 'D' Day, and now gave little protection. We anchored about a mile or two off the beach at Arromanches which was the British sector of the Allied landings. We were not under enemy fire and not bothered by their aircraft. The sound of gunfire was almost continuous as just a mile or two inshore heavy fighting was taking place. By now, the Allies had quite a strong foothold in Normandy, but had not broken completely clear of the beach heads. Since my days in Douglas, nine months earlier, I had wanted to take part in this Second Front. Not for reasons of schoolboy adventure, or stupid heroics, but for the desire to participate in what was obviously going to be the greatest military operation of all time.

The impressive, noisy panorama stretched, without interruption, for the full 180 degrees of my vision. A military spectacle of men, and machinery on a scale far beyond any preconceived scene in my mind. A camera man, or commentator may record the scene, but to depict it with its infinite organisation, co-ordination, discipline, joint effort and fellow-feeling is not in the same book. In post war years it has been fashionable to throw figures around telling us how many 'Compo' rations were consumed; how many gallons of petrol were used; how many ships were involved; how many rounds of ammunition fired, and so on, ad infinitum. Statistics are often a bore, and miserably fail to answer most questions. Few, if any, of those taking part in this military operation will, in later life, have a more dominant memory than the one of the day they landed on the beach at Arromanches. I have not.

By mid-morning a landing craft had tied up alongside our ship. It was flat-bottomed, and floated just a couple of feet above the water. At first glance it looked not unlike an out-sized steel raft with an outboard motor at the stern to propel it. Its purpose was, primarily, to covey transport to the shore. From the ship, our transport was loaded by crane onto the landing craft, and each vehicle secured to the deck. It remained for just our personnel to transfer. To enable us to do that we had to climb over the ship's side and down a huge rope-net-type ladder. The ship, unlike the craft was high out of the water, so there was a considerable drop to be negotiated. Why, in our training we had never rehearsed, or practised such a manoeuvre I will never know. As a boy, in St. Helena, I had learnt at a very early age how to climb up, and down the sides of ships on similar ladders, and could do it with confidence so the experience was not new to me. For some of our men it was new, and there were those who were nervous. That could so easily have been avoided with a couple of hours training and instruction in the UK prior to departure. Someone, somewhere along the line must have known how we would be expected to get from ship to shore. Each man carried his rifle, or sten gun, ammunition, full equipment and accoutrements including a ground sheet, greatcoat and blanket. Any slip on that ladder would have been fatal. The mere weight of equipment would have dragged a man to the bottom of the sea; swimmer or not. More likely he would have been crushed to death between the ship's side, and the landing craft, as the latter gently swayed to and fro with the swell of the sea. Watching each man descent caused me a few anxious moments. Happily, all went well.

The crew of the landing craft amounted to no more than a couple of junior ranks from the RE's. On leaving the mother ship, we moved in towards the shore but after just a short distance we stopped. Somewhere on the beach there was a slight hiccup, and we understood that it may be an hour, or longer before we would be called forward. Someone made the suggestion that we had a brew of tea; three cheers for that! Each man had been issued with a 'Tommy' cooker, and compo tea. The tea was a few leaves, together with powdered milk, and a minute quantity of sugar all compressed into a cube about the size of an Oxo cube. The idea was to place the cube into a mug, and pour on boiling water. 'Hey Presto!' and the result would be a mug of tea. How misleading instructions, and descriptions can be. The taste was revolting. Beggars cannot be choosers, but it was that or nothing else. To make our brew we required water but we possessed only what was in our bottles, and at this early stage that was not to be consumed. It was suggested that our Sapper friends might help out as they probably had gallons of the stuff, furthermore they would be more likely to oblige if the approach was made by a Sergeant! I got the message. Seeing the crew sitting by their engine in the stern, I made the approach. Above the engine, and rudder was a small wooden framework, and on that sat two, five gallon drums of oil. As I opened my mouth to speak, a freak wave hit the craft. I reeled, and simultaneously one of the oil drums broke loose, and crashed down in front of me and landed on top of my right foot mostly on the base of the right toe. The pain was excruciating. The Sapper called his colleague, and gently they lifted the oil drum off my foot. Within minutes, Jack Warner who was our first aid man – in addition to his Special Operator duties – appeared on the scene. Blood soon began to seep through the sock, and boot. Taking his knife out of his equipment, Jack cut away the boot and sock. It was not a pretty sight due to blood, and swelling. Next, I heard him say something about putting the foot over the side of the craft, and into the sea, which I did. Good sound instruction, as it is known that salt water can be a good anti-septic. It did clean up the wound, but showed a deep and angry gash. Jack placed a dressing of acriflavine emulsion on the wound, and tied up with a bandage. Wearing a boot was now out of the question, besides it had been cut to ribbons. By the time we closed in towards the beach, I had hobbled back into the seat in the cab, and received a cheerful grin from Wilson. I swallowed a couple of pain killers, but they gave little relief. What a time for this to happen. Before we had even landed, the Section Sergeant was the first, and only casualty, and that not due to enemy action. Jack said that I should see a medical officer. Poor Jack, I gave him a rude answer. Only slowly would I be able to move, and that would be a hobble on one foot. Providing no serious problems arose, that would see me through. Cautiously, we approached the beach, and came to a halt. The ramp in the bows was lowered. One by one, and in single file we drove down the ramp into the sea, and up onto the dry sand. Je suis arrivé en France.

The landings were still in the early stages. Mines on the beaches had not been swept, and many anti-tank obstacles were clearly visible. To reach the roadway at the back of the beach there was one route, and one route only. That was marked out by white tape, and if you valued your life then you drove the vehicle within the limits of the tapes, which only allowed a margin of a foot, or so, on either side. Deviate, and you would probably finish up sitting on a cloud, in the nude, twanging a harp! That beach was no place for careless, or reckless driving. Just to add to the driver's problems, he had to keep his foot down in order to maintain a minimum speed and not become bogged down in the sand. Whoever selected the drivers for posting to our Section, served us well. They may not have been special operators, but their contribution to the team was no less valuable. Sitting in that cab I felt that the best help I could give Wilson was to keep quiet, and let him get on with it. Besides, my mind was preoccupied by pain. To traverse the beach, and reach the road took just a few minutes. Our destination was little more than a map reference. It proved to be a field about ten miles SW of Bayeux, and about one mile NW of Balleroy. The area is known as Foret de Cerisy. We arrived there in the evening, having stopped en route to de-waterproof all vehicles. It was cold, damp and misty.

All transport, and stores were properly scattered, and camouflaged. The Luftwaffe, by now, was reduced to only a handful of planes, and rather reluctant to appear in the skies, but no chances could be taken. With pain, I did what I had to do, and that was my job. In normal circumstances, sleeping in a field in June, is no great hardship. This night was for me, far from normal. Throughout the night, I lay awake on a damp field with nothing more than a damp blanket to cover myself. If, someone had offered to cut off my right foot, I think I might well have accepted. The following morning Jack cleaned up my foot, and put on a fresh dressing. That he did twice a day for the following ten days, or more. It must have been about the third day before the pain eased off, but a couple of weeks followed before I could again wear a pair of boots. During the remainder of my Army service, that injury gave me no problems. Thirty years later, by which time I was established in 'Civvy Street', problems re-appeared. They necessitated ten days in hospital for an operation when pieces of bone had to be chiselled out of my foot. It speedily healed up, and today it is fine.

On the day following our landing, all masts had been erected, and our two wireless vans were fully operational. The Germans who we were monitoring were now little more than shouting distance away. Our operators were on shift duties covering the full 24 hours of the day. They were trained, and now experienced on shift duties. I think their greatest problem in Normandy was getting sufficient sleep, and rest when off duty. Green pastures do not offer many human comforts or amenities. Ideal though it was, for cattle!

For our first couple of weeks, we lived on a diet of 'compo' rations. With no fresh vegetables, nor bread, it was monotonous. 'Hard Tack' biscuits replaced the bread, and in lieu of fresh vegetables we had only tinned, and dehydrated. At least, there was no shortage.

Like most walks in life, there were some things which we tended to take for granted. One was our mail. Very soon we were receiving letters from home, and often they took less than forty eight hours to reach us, in a remote field in Normandy. That was achieved by overcoming enormous difficulties. The morale value cannot be overstated. Full marks to the wartime civilian, and Army postal authorities. Nearly half a century later I received a first class letter, posted in Derby, three days earlier. Many Christmas cards posted in mid-December 1988 were not delivered to me until mid-January 1989! Whatever happened to progress?

I was once asked, how did we keep clean? Apart from what we wore, we carried in our pack spare underwear, shirt and socks. Close to our site there was a clean, cold river. There we were able to wash out our 'smalls' and bathe. Our life style was hardly that of gracious living and good taste. Without alternative, when bathing or swimming we wore little more than a smile. Giggling was heard at times, but such mirth came from some of the local girls who sat on the nearby banks watching us, and waving. After the initial ritual, both sides grew accustomed to the ablutions, and we reciprocated by waving back.

118 SW Section was one of the 'Y' Units of the 2nd Army in 21 Army Group. General Montgomery's No. 1 Intelligence Officer was a very distinguished soldier called Brigadier 'Bill' Williams. Like Monty, Bill was the type of officer who liked to make himself known

to those who worked for him. One evening, soon after our arrival, we assembled in that field when he came to address us. I was enthralled. Not often did Brigadiers assemble a small body of troops around them, and speak to them as intelligent adults. He confided in us, passing on some of the intelligence gained, and saying what kind of information he wanted us to produce. From him, we learnt of the forthcoming second landing which was to be made in Southern France, and what its objectives were, and the approximate dates. He paid a tribute to our work, and what we had, so far, produced. Praise from Brig. Williams was praise indeed, as he was not the type to throw it around indiscriminately. On Sigint, any recognition of our work was extremely rare. The Brigadier knew the value of 'Y' and said so. He had been on General Montgomery's staff since early days in North Africa. That speaks for itself.

Caen was liberated in early July. Our strength on the Bridgehead was rapidly building up, and we were capturing large numbers of Germans as POW's; but they were far from being a defeated Army. As Section Sergeant my time was fully occupied from dawn to dusk, and at times from dusk to dawn. Any prospects of relaxation were out of the question. Whenever the opportunity came for Vickery, McPake and myself to be together and as Sergeants we could freely talk them over with each other. Before the month was out, the famous bomb attack was made on Hitler's life.

The break-out in Normandy came, following the Battle of Falaise. Automatically, we too advanced into Northern France during the third week in August. On pulling out of 'Our' Normandy field morale was at its highest. As our convoy drove through – or rather around – Caen, I saw for the first time devastation that previously I would never have imagined man could inflict. It was terrifying just to look at it, but a foretaste of what to expect when we came to cross the frontier into the industrial cities of the Ruhr. Driving that day, we progressed Easterly; eventually turning off the main road we drove up a long straight drive with a very impressive Chateau at the far end. It was quite close to the border of Calvados, and Eure and perhaps North of Brieane. We were now in open countryside which was untouched by the ravages of war. At the Chateau, we found that No.

1 Special Wireless Group were already in occupation. This was our first contact with them. 1 SWG was quite a large unit of six hundred men, or more, and was commanded by Lt. Col. 'Sammy' Barton, Royal Signals. This was a brief halt by 118 SW Section, being no more than a couple of nights. The 2nd Army was now advancing rapidly across Northern France. Before we could say "Amiens", we were there, or to be precise just a couple of miles on the outskirts. A Seminary became our adopted billet. Nor exactly the comfort of Claridges, but better than an open field.

Operational matters were becoming more, and more outside my domain. Details of our commitments, and cover were not given to me, so I did not ask. Of course, it was German but it was not until years later that I was given to understand that the traffic was 'Double Playfair', which was broken down on the spot by the 'I' Corps detachment. Had that not been the case, much of its value would have been lost. That I was not kept in the picture was not some kind of fend off, but just that I did not need to know. I had been long enough in the game to have learnt that one of the rules was to never tell anyone anything they do not need to know.

While at Amiens, it was my wish to see the Cathedral. It did become possible to make a short trip into the town, but time was all too short. My wish was not fulfilled; all I had was a glancing view, externally, but then our presence was not that of a party of tourists. Within a week, we were once again on the move.

It was on 3rd September 1944 that our advance troops crossed the border into Belgium. We followed close behind them. On the following morning the Guards Armoured Division entered Brussels, without firing a short. 118 SW Section followed in the same afternoon. The streets were lined with thousands of jubilant, and excited people eager to demonstrate their freedom, and show their welcome to the British Forces. They regarded us as gallant liberators. I have never felt gallant in my life, and never liberated anything greater than a bird from the jaws of a cat! As the Germans pulled out of Brussels, so our 2nd Army moved in, and the City never became a battle ground. Our Section occupied :'Hospice de la St. Jean, in the NW suburbs. It was a large clean building, and gave us ample space, both inside and out. We had broken out of Normandy, sped across France, and into Brussels in a period of about ten days. That was a rapid advance, and we felt that victory was not far away.

No. 1 Special Wireless Group joined us, and for our stay in Brussels we harnessed up with them. It was soon apparent that life was going to be more comfortable, and enjoyable than anything we had experienced since leaving the UK. Rations had greatly improved, as fresh vegetables and real bread appeared. Better food, reasonable accommodation, reliable mail, and the benefits of being on the fringe of a large city; all contributed to high morale.

With a few friends, it was possible on some evenings to take a tram into the City Centre. There we would usually spend a couple of hours in a café, or restaurant. Such places were always full to capacity. The local wartime beer was nothing to write home about, but it was the only available brew. Seldom we were asked to pay for it. Mostly it was freely offered by civilians at nearby tables. Their ecstatic welcome was not a one day wonder, but more of a long running serial. Many of the restaurants boasted of an electric organ. Much of the music was British/American made famous by the much loved Vera Lynn, when we all joined in and sang our hearts out. Though the civilians had undergone grim hardship, with their rations reduced to little more than necessary to sustain life, they were always offering us little gifts. The warmth of their welcome, their kindness, and their hospitality knew no bounds.

The purpose of our presence was to learn, from interception, what the enemy was doing, or about to do, and not to concern ourselves with Allied intentions. The Airborne landing, that month, at Arnhem came as much as a surprise to myself as to any civilian back in the UK. Its objectives, method and tactics have been researched over, and over again by professional military historians. It has become a competition which I am not entering. Within a short while, it was known that all was not going well, and that our casualties were high. One evening, sitting in a restaurant with a few of my friends, the doors opened and there stood a small party of bedraggled British soldiers. They were unshaven. Their uniform was dirty, and in tatters. Some wore blood stained bandages. All wore the Red beret.

We rose from our seats. The atmosphere was emotive, and then the applause started culminating in an effusiveness which I had never previously experienced. Spontaneously, from a nearby table a voice was heard above all others. It came from a Belgian civilian with a rich baritone voice who, in English, began to sing. The tune, and the words were familiar, and we instantly joined him. It was "God Save the King".

As might be expected, the stories and descriptions of the operation which the survivors related were of hopelessness, sacrifice and suffering, and of their comrades who had not returned. They did not speak of their own courage. There were those who will say Arnhem was a victory; others say it was a defeat. All will agree that it was one of the greatest epics in our military history. No other battle in World War II stirs my emotions more vehemently than Arnhem. It does not take a movie to moisten my eyes.

By the early days of October, the Allied advance had slowed down, and the Germans had withdrawn from most of Holland into the Fatherland. Keeping pace with the general advance, we left Brussels, and moved into Southern Holland.

About 12km south of Eindoven lies the small village of Leende. Like most of Holland, the countryside is flat but not uninteresting. When our convoy drove into Leende there were no great crowds to welcome us. Many of the inhabitants had left, leaving a thinly populated village. Though they were undemonstrative, their welcome was no less sincere than the one in Brussels. Before seeing our billet we could smell it! There are foul smells, and ultra foul smells. This came in the latter category. For the time being our home was to be in a tannery! My first reaction was one of revulsion, and my initial attitude towards the Dutch was not very friendly. How wrong first impressions can be. The smell persisted, but my feelings towards the people swiftly changed.

Leende, at that time, was a sad little community, and their lives under German occupation had been humiliating, and wretched. Always, they had been hungry. The absence of children was noticeable, and only now and again did I meet one. Like their parents, they were so polite, and very grateful for any small kindness we were able to show them. How their faces would light up when we offered them some chocolate. It is difficult to say who had most pleasure out of such an act. Was it the donor, or the recipient? It is anyone's guess.

    A tired operator is a poor one. Our accommodation was so bad that many of our men were weary through lack of sleep before they even commenced a shift duty. After just a few weeks in that dirty smelly tannery we were re-housed, and we moved just a few hundred yards away to somewhere far more acceptable. The occupants squeezed up to make room for us, and extended a friendly, and genuine welcome. They were Nuns! They had given up a couple of rooms in their convent for us, plus the infants school in the compound. All our transport including the operational vans, we were able to park within the grounds. Cooking, and eating was in a lean-to shed. Though our work load was no easier, it was easier to perform. Most of the Nuns spoke a little English, and we were able to enjoy a small chat with them.

    Nearby, was a small electrical corner shop which was owned by the Staals family. We three Sergeants slept in a small room above the shop. The family did not speak English, but it proved to be no obstacle in our good and happy relationship with them. Sgt. McPake spoke German, and so did they; so through McPake as interpreter we were able to converse. Sometimes, at the end of the day, our hosts would invite us to join them in their small sitting room. There, they had a combustion type stove, and providing sufficient fuel could be 'obtained' we enjoyed its warmth, and that of our Dutch friends. As Autumn arrived the days became shorter, and the nights colder. Winter was approaching. In many ways, the Dutch are very like ourselves. More so, in my opinion, than any of the other European people. That helped considerably toward mutual understanding. Throughout our time in Leende there was not one minor incident between the local civilians and ourselves. I was falling in love with tiny Leende, and its big-hearted people.

    Our closest British neighbours were about 10km down the road, just outside Valkenswaard. They were 10 Special Wireless Section, who were another 'Y' Unit, but being an 'A' type they were slightly larger. Their Commanding Officer was Major Peter Newbold,

Royal Signals, who I had previously met when as a Captain he was commanding 4 SCU in Baghdad. The Section Sergeant was Sgt. McQuade who I had also previously met, and knew quite well.

Following the liberation of Holland, one of the Allies' major problems was to feed the civilian population. Food supplies were urgently needed. We only had to walk a few yards from 'our' Convent, and glance at the first civilian we met, to see how desperate they were. Their faith in our ability to produce the food never drooped. Supplies were soon forthcoming. It was illegal for us to hand over any of our rations, but it was done. I knew a number of times when tins of food exchanged hands. As a Sergeant, it was my duty to have stepped in, stopped it, and taken disciplinary action against the offender. Instead, I turned my back, and pretended I had seen nothing. For that neglect of duty, I make no apology.

Though still only twenty eight years of age, I had travelled many thousands of miles across the world, and experienced many varied climates, but I was quite unprepared for the severity of the impending Winter.

The temperatures dropped, and snow began to fall quite heavily on, or about 14th December. The big freeze-up had started. Two days later, the German Army made their last desperate offensive in the Ardennes, as they attempted to break through to Antwerp. Instantly we doubled guards, and tightened security, and also making sure that if necessary we could move out at a moments notice. It was the first few days of the battle, that the OC ordered me to ensure that the PIAT gun was handy, and ready for instant use. Furthermore, I was to prime the hand grenades. I had forgotten about those grenades tucked away in the stores van, somewhere. Together with McPake, we unpacked them and sat at a table in the infants' school and took a close look at them. Never before had I seen a hand grenade at such close quarters, let alone primed one! Repeatedly, I asked myself 'Why was I not given some instruction and training in the priming, and use of these grenades, before leaving the UK?' It was too late now. Carefully, we read the enclosed instructions, and step by step tackled our first grenade. Prospects of ever celebrating my twenty ninth birthday receded rapidly. After priming the first one I was conscious of my pulse rate returning to its normal rate. With a little confidence we completed the task, and indulged in mutual congratulations on each others efficiency, and calm(?). My description will provoke a chuckle by many self-respecting infantrymen. From the experience, I learnt to appreciate the feelings of a turkey with the approach of Christmas!

One of the scourges of trench life in the First World War, was filth, and body lice. In our war, much was done to eradicate, and combat such disagreeable tribulations. Mobile laundry and bath Units were introduced. They could, and did, operate in quite forward areas. Often, they were set up in disused factories and warehouses, and occasionally in an open field. They carried with them large stocks of clean – sometimes new – clothing. Early one Arctic morning I rustled up about forty men. We filled two, 3 ton lorries, and skidded our way to Bourg Leopold, where such a Unit was operating. Horror, upon horror, it was in an unheated marquee tent. There were rows of showers, and plenty of hot water which was heated by oil fired pressure burners. After undressing, we handed over all our shirts, socks and underwear. There followed a restricted period under the shower, but it was adequate. Drying ourselves with a clean, dry towel was a luxury which we had not enjoyed for many weeks. Proceeding to another counter we were re-issued with clean clothing to replace that which we had handed in at the onset. The entire system was on the conveyor belt type, but satisfactory and unquestionably fulfilled its purpose to keep ourselves, and our clothing as clean as possible. Later, we had three or more visits to a similar Unit in Eindhoven, where conditions were a little less primitive.

Just before Christmas a large carol concert for British troops was held in the Philips factory in Eindhoven. We were able to send a number of our men. Two of our members; Jack Warner (tenor), and Arthur Langford (baritone) were selected to sing solos. The former I have previously mentioned; the latter was a Sergeant in our Intelligence Corps attachment. Before the war, Arthur was associated with the BBC when he sang and accompanied himself in children's' programmes. That concert was, I believe, relayed home, and transmitted on what was then the Light programme. Another BBC personality was also in our Intelligence Corps team. He was Capt.

Trevor Harvey. In the early seventies, I heard that Trevor had just conducted one of our well known Symphony orchestras in the Royal Festival Hall concert. I was unable to confirm that, but imagine it was true.

Christmas did not permit any celebrations, or relaxation. With the battle of the Ardennes on our doorstep, it was essential to remain vigilant, and alert. Greetings and a few gifts were exchanged with local friends, particularly with the Nuns. The Hallé orchestra, under Sir John Barbirolli gave a few concerts in Eindhoven. Every time I tried to attend one something materialised and prevented me, but many of our Section were able to go.

Throughout the campaign we had seen little of the German Air Force, and had not been troubled by it. Now, we had learnt that they had a new type of aircraft which was jet propelled, and was considerably faster than any of their earlier aircraft.

About 200 yards from the infants' school we had a small trailer which was equipped as a Direction Finding unit. At about 9am on New Year's Day, I had reason to visit that trailer where two of our operators were working. The morning was cloudless and bright, but bitterly cold. To reach them, I had to cross a field which at some time had been ploughed, but was now frozen solid giving clusters of soil which had sharp icy edges. When about half way, I heard a new and strange sound rushing towards, and at a low height above. It was a German jet fighter. As it opened fire, I was aware of small cannon shells smacking the ground aside, and ahead of me. The gunner was aiming for the trailer, and I was far too close for comfort. Instantaneously, I fell flat on my face as I hit the ground. In seconds it was all over. I was unharmed except for cuts, and grazes caused by falling hard on the sharp frozen ground. Rushing for the trailer, and fearing the worst I opened its door. There, to my relief were two fellows brewing tea on a Primus stove! Thereafter, I never saw another German aircraft, but I did enjoy the mug of tea which I was offered.

Captain Napper, our OC, was recalled to London to attend a conference. He was to proceed to Ostend, and from there travel on by sea. The night before his departure, in mid-January, he asked me if I would like to keep him company on the road trip as far as Ostend and there, after spending a night in a transit camp, the driver and myself may spend two days leave in Brussels before returning to Leende. Early the following morning, in the staff car, we set off on a miserable journey. The snow was falling, and the roads were icy. With such poor visibility we proceeded at a slow speed, but by the end of the day we had reached our destination. Leave in Brussels was a non-event. The city was overcrowded with servicemen from many Countries in addition to the normal civilian population. I reported to what was called a WO's and Sgts. Mess for meals. It was a large warehouse with rows of what appeared to be hundreds of trestle tables. My first impression was one of a Victorian workhouse. The food did not improve that impression! For sleeping purposes, I was given a ticket, and a civilian address to go to where I would be offered a room. It was clean, and comfortable. I saw little of the family. They spoke no English, but with my schoolboy French we managed. As there was no one around me who I knew, I was lonely, and bored. When the time came, I was pleased to return to Leende.

From the time the Germans invaded Poland in August 1939, we heard stories of Underground movements, both there, and later in other European Countries as they too were overrun. One of the strongest and most effective movements was the Dutch. In the course of our day to day lives, it came about that we met those who had, during the German occupation been involved. It was never easy to get them to talk of their experiences. Neither subtlety nor guile would encourage them.

One Winter evening when in the sitting room with Mr and Mrs Staals, I noticed some RAF caps in the drawer of a cabinet. As there were no RAF units for miles around, I was curious, and asked how they had collected them. Their reply was perfunctory. Forty one years later, I reminded Mrs Staals of that incident, but laughingly she 'Could not remember'. Yet, on all other matters, her memory was remarkably good! I was not – and still am not – convinced. It is a historical fact that the Dutch Underground had a very efficient, and well organised escape route for RAF crews brought down over their Country. Did the Staals play a part in that? They deny it, and there is no real evidence that I have. There is a lot more that I would like to know. Today, it is my belief that they have an untold story to tell.

The deeds, the courage, and bravery of the Dutch during their long years of German occupation, have been well recorded. Their contribution to the freedom of Western Europe is beyond measure. No story of mine would be complete without expressing my admiration, and respect. I salute them.

The severe Winter continued until the end of February, when slowly the ice began to thaw. As the days became a little warmer, it became clear that the end of the war was in sight, certainly as far as Germany was concerned. Their push in the Ardennes had failed, and they had now withdrawn to, roughly, their national boundaries. Our plans for the crossing of the Rhine were well advanced.

Capt. Napper, one morning, informed me that we were soon to return to the UK. The purpose, I understood, was to reform and retrain. He did not say what for, but an intelligent guess told me that the object was for us to be sent to the Far East. As the enemy withdrew inside Germany, so they began to use their postal, and civil lines for communications, more and more. That resulted in less wireless traffic, so our daily takings of intercepts began to fall. Without our Section, there would remain sufficient 'Y' units to cope with diminishing commitments.

After dismantling our equipment, we said our 'Good-byes' to the Nuns, and many local friends. It was an uneventful journey, by road to one of the coastal ports. The next day, we disembarked at Tilbury and drove direct to Harpenden, Herts.

Within a few days, 118 Special Wireless Section no longer existed. We were disbanded.

CHAPTER 15

The disbandment of 118 Special Wireless Section was a little sad. The greater majority of us remained together, but only as part of a larger 'Y' melting pot.

At Harpenden, we lived and worked in a beautiful old house (almost a stately home), near the town centre. It had many acres of its own grounds. I have heard it said that it later became the home of Eric Morecombe.

George Dunn was a fellow Sergeant, and one of the 'Y' characters. During my brief stay in Harpenden he was the instructor on Japanese Morse, and interception. Soon, I commenced a course on Japanese Morse, and procedure. This was not easy to master. Their alphabet consisted of seventy six symbols. So, over and above our usual twenty six, we had to create, and learn many more. For that purpose, we used many varied signs. The standard of Japanese Morse, and operating was mostly very high. I soon learnt that intercepting, and taking it down was a very formidable task. I cannot recall that we picked up much in Harpenden. It must only have been their high powered transmitters, and then only at night. Instead of writing from left to right across our message pads, we took down our intercepts in symbols, in columns, down the page. The text of an intercepted message, as taken down by us, would appear something like this:

We gave the name 'Khana' to Japanese Morse. There are other languages which have more symbols in the alphabet then we use. Earlier, I mentioned Red Army intercepts. Just now and again, there would be one in plain language, and then we used barred letters, e.g.: C̄.

Events in Germany were daily becoming more dramatic, and as our troops pushed further Eastwards, we were becoming more excited. The Russians were on the outskirts of Berlin where, by the hour, the scene was becoming more Wagnerian. The inevitable link-up with the Russian and American troops came about. When the German Army surrendered on 4th May we went wild with joy. At Home, the blackout was lifted and the lights went up. Every town and village across the Country rejoiced, and celebrated. The joy, and happiness of the people was something which I could never have imagined, had I not been here at the time. Our hero of the hour was Churchill, who was acclaimed and extolled as the one person who had led the nation, if not the free world, to victory. He was quick to remind us that the war in Europe may be over, but not so in the Far East. There, a strong foe was still undefeated.

When relating my brief stay in Littlehampton, prior to the crossing to Normandy, I wrote of 'The seed being sown of a very happy love story'. These seeds were now about to bear fruit. VE Day was still in our minds, when Jack Warner told me that he was going to marry Dorothy Arthur. As I had been instrumental in their initial meeting, and introduction I received Jack's news with great delight, and enthusiasm. After being granted a special licence, a few weeks later, they were married at St. Mary's Parish Church Littlehampton, and I was their Best Man. Theirs proved to be one of the happiest of marriages that any man and woman could desire. I know, because it has been my privilege to enjoy their close friendship throughout the ensuing years. Jack died in Autumn of 1985. There are few sorrows greater than the loss of a loyal friend whose value had been second to none. One of my many pleasures, today, is making one of my regular visits to Littlehampton, when I call on Dorothy and enjoy a cup of tea and a chat with her.

My work in Harpenden brought me once more back into the

operational side. For the time being, there would be no more administrative duties. Now, I was a Sergeant in charge of a Set Room Watch. In the aftermath of the European war, some of the aura, and reward became a little cloudy, but perhaps only temporarily while the entire 'Y' Service was being geared up to concentrate on the Japanese war.

Spring turned into Summer, and I was posted to Bishop's Stortford. Once more, we inhabited a large house, but this time a more modern one, built in this century. It was situated in a farming area only a few miles outside the town. We lived in reasonable comfort. Our commitments were similar to those in Harpenden, and here I was also a Set Room Sergeant. The total strength of the Unit was about a hundred and fifty.

Public transport was poor, with just a couple of buses a day into Bishop's Stortford. The use of Army transport for recreational use was not then permitted. What little social life we had was self-made. Well almost; there was a Woman's Land Army Unit nearby. The problems of partners in organising a dance did not arise. With little delay one was arranged. Next day, we were swamped by volunteers eager to "Help the local farmers!"

That Unit, at Bishop's Stortford, appeared on the surface to be something of a dog's dinner, which was misleading. On looking at the individual components in detail, it could be seen that here was a nucleus of either an 'A' or 'B' type Section. Selecting an OC and a couple of Subalterns from among the officers would have been simple. If anything, we were a little top heavy with good experienced senior NCO's. In the lower ranks the potential was no less strong. The possibility that before too long, I might well be that Unit's Section Sergeant was never far from my mind. Following that, would be the certainty of embarking on a troopship for a landing on, or near, the Japanese coast. Then came 6th August 1945.

One – just one – bomb was dropped on Hiroshima, and it was laid waste. The world quickly learnt what devastation that first atomic bomb created. Three days later, on Nagasaki the second atomic bomb was dropped. The Japanese reacted quickly, and rumours were flying around at supersonic speed that they were about to surrender. On 14th August, they did. VJ Day had arrived, and the Second World War had come to an end with total victory for the Allies. Our enemies had now all surrendered, unconditionally.

War had become so much a way of life that its abrupt end was, at first, difficult to accept and believe. I had forgotten what it was like to live the life of a peacetime soldier, in a Country which was no longer fighting for its survival. The first, and most natural reaction was one of relief and joy. One thing, above all else was manifest. The post war peace would be a very different one to that we had put aside almost six years earlier. When the celebrations ceased, and the party was over I would have to consider very seriously about my future career.

For a while, our routine was little changed. All thoughts of forming a new Unit for the Far East were abandoned. The word was now becoming 'Disbandment'. Into our daily vocabulary came the word 'Demob'.

Many of my Regular colleagues were due for discharge, or if they so wished could sign on for a pension. It came as a surprise that so many were choosing to be discharged even though, in most cases, they had only a few more years to serve for that pension. Personally, I had about ten more years to serve. Was I to soldier on, or join the Civvy Street stampede? The authorities did not appear to care, or give a lead. The Army was to be run down, rapidly. 'Y' in particular would be slashed. New commitments would emerge, but it appeared that a small peacetime Service would meet the demands. Those Regulars who accepted their discharge may opt to return within six months. Those that did, would be able to re-enlist in their previous rank, and all service to count towards pension. Very few seemed attracted, and those that left did not appear enthusiastic about re-enlisting. I was undecided, and wavering, but finally decided to give civilian life a try. It was a brief, and not very happy time. I failed, in heart and mind, to become a civilian.

Well before the six months had expired, I re-engaged, and signed on to complete twenty two years, thus qualifying for a pension. Without loss of rank, I returned to the only life I knew, and loved. Retracing my steps back into the 'Y' Service was both painless, and satisfying. If it had been a mistake to join the mad rush out of the Army; it was no mistake to do an about turn. On doing so, I was ordered to report to the War Office Wireless Station, Hildebrand Barracks, Pennypot Lane, Harrogate.

The Commanding Officer was Lt. Col. Du Cros, Royal Signals. Within hours, it was apparent that the accommodation, and messing were good. The operational centre was at Forest Moor, about ten miles away on the Yorkshire Moors.

There were among the Warrant Officers and Sergeants many who I knew as we had, at some time previously, served together. Among the offices was one face which was far more familiar than all others. Not since those early days in Abbottabad had we met. Then we were both junior NCO's. It was Steve. He had, meantime, been given a War Emergency Commission and was a Captain. There was little change in him. Within an hour of meeting, the gap of the war years had melted away. He was now married, and living in Harrogate. One evening, when we were having a great time in a celebrative, and reminiscent mood our conversation switched more to the present, and our future. I was totally unprepared for the bombshell that Steve suddenly presented to me. On the first opportunity he was going to take his demobilisation, and go into civilian life. I was dumbfounded. That such an experienced and valuable man to the 'Y' Service should be even thinking about such action was, to me, incomprehensible. Besides, he had just a few more years to serve for an officer's pension. Like myself, he knew little or nothing of civil life. Using every trick in the book, I tried to persuade him to change his mind, and to think again. To throw so much away, seemed such a waste. Steve did not tell me what was behind his decision, but there must have been a very good reason for it. To this day, I do not know. Soon after he joined the ranks of civilian life. Between us, the mutual understanding and friendship was of that intensity known only to those who have served together in HM Forces. His departure left me dejected. Since those Harrogate days of 1946, we have sadly both failed to keep in touch.

Without delay, I returned to the role of Sergeant in charge of a Watch. The intercept station at Forest Moor was very well equipped, and quite large. Each Watch consisted of about sixty operators.

During the war years the ATS Special Operators worked here in large numbers. Their standard was extremely high, and their service had been invaluable. It has often puzzled me why, after the war, they ceased to train women as Special Operators, and into the 'Y' Service. Such thinking still persists, but I believe that, today, there are some in High Places who are having second thoughts on this matter.

With each watch there was a Duty Officer. Mine was a young Captain with an emergency commission. I had respect for him, and we got on very well together. On duty, one night, at about 4am my 'phone rang. It was the Duty Officer calling. He said something about having a mug of tea, and if I was not too busy, would I care to join him, in his office? Nothing unusual, or strange about that, so a few minutes later I knocked on his door, entered and saluted. Over our tea, the conversation was quite informal until unheralded he asked me if I had ever considered applying for a commission, and if given the opportunity what would be my reaction? That caught me unprepared, but fumbling for words I replied to the effect that I would be delighted. Thereupon, this young officer summed-up by saying that he was going to recommend me to the Colonel. Naturally, I looked upon it as a pat on the back, but was not optimistic.

Some weeks passed, then came a summons to attend a local War Office Selection Board, together with two other candidates. When called, I was invited to sit down, and the questioning commenced. Most of the questions were difficult, but that was to be expected. As is often the case, it was the simple question that I believe was my undoing. It seemed quite easy : 'Why do you want a Commission?'. I hesitated, then replied truthfully, and politely that my ambition was not so much to have a Commission, but rather the officer's pension that would follow. The Commission was just a means to that end. That reply later caused regrets. There is a distinct possibility that in place of the truth, the answer should have been what the questioner wanted to hear; then the outcome of that interview might have been very different. Before decisions were made known – officially, there was to be an interval.

It was now over a year since the end of the war, though many of its legacies were still with us, and they were ones which mainly concerned civilians. Clothes, bread and all rationing continued. Many military changes were already evident. In 'Y' and throughout the Corps, our ranks were top heavy. Once more, the classic example of too many chiefs, and not enough Indians. Promotion was at a standstill, with little prospect of any improvement in the foreseeable future. Regular recruiting fell to almost zero. It would be unjust to lay all the blame for that on the Army. The people, generally, were understandably war weary, and possibly felt that the less they had to do with the military machine, the happier their lives would be. After their mammoth war effort, it could never be said that they lacked patriotism, or loyalty. Nowadays, Regular recruiting is often damaged by the narrow minded doctrine of those with tiny minds in many of the small, rowdy, extreme pressure groups which have become fashionable. There was the disturbing possibility that the public may return to their pre-war contemptuous attitude towards soldiers. Certainly, they were already losing interest, but that attitude of looking down their noses at us, happily, did not recur. It was difficult to imagine what life in the new peacetime Army was going to offer. Not being psychic, I had no means of telling.

It was late Autumn when I was interviewed by the Commanding Officer and informed of my failure to pass the WOSB for a Commission. That was no surprise. No explanation was given, and I did not request one. My only question was directed towards myself: 'Does it not sometimes pay to be untruthful?' Before being dismissed by the CO he told me that No 2 Wireless Regiment were to leave Sarafand, Palestine, and make their new peacetime base at Famagusta, Cyprus. Continuing, he said that I was to be promoted to Squadron Quarter Master Sergeant, and posted to join that Regiment at Famagusta. My application for a Commission may have failed, but this was a good consolation prize, and one which brought me satisfaction.

Within days, I was on disembarkation leave. On returning, there was a short period at Catterick Camp, for the purpose of inoculations and medicals plus all the paraphernalia preceding an overseas posting. One of the severest Winters for many years was, by now, making its presence felt.

It was snowing when, in mid-December, and with a draft of about fifty men under my care, we commenced our journey on what was then called the MEDLOC route. Very soon, I was giving it other names. We embarked at Dover.

CHAPTER 16

At Calais we disembarked. Only a few yards away stood a rather dilapidated 1920 vintage, French train, with all its windows, and doors iced up. With a tiny engine it looked incapable of towing anything greater than a two wheel trailer. Our worst fears were soon substantiated. Following an issue of sandwiches, we boarded that rundown, ramshackle of an ice box. Soon we were on our way to Toulon. The journey was a nightmare. Not one compartment had any heating, and the toilets could not be used as they were frozen solid. The lighting was no better than that given by a couple of candles. As darkness fell, so did the temperature; lower and lower. There was no question of sleep. The seats were wooden struts without upholstery. Wearing full heavy, winter serge with greatcoats, we all shivered with the cold. We each carried a spare blanket around our packs, which we unfolded and brought into use. It made no difference. The night became one of survival. The train's maximum speed was no more than 30mph. When in India, I often travelled by rail, and usually cursed their discomforts. That night I would have paid a high price for an Indian train, which by comparison would have been luxurious travel. About noon the following day, and at snail's pace we reached the docks at Toulon. There, to greet us was a 1930's Union Castle liner looking clean, and smart in her freshly painted superstructure, and hull. With the appearance of the sun, the horror of the night evaporated, and morale rose. Once on board the ship soon got under way, bound for Port Said. No misfortune, or trouble marred the short voyage of less than a week. For the time of year, both the weather and the sea treated us kindly. It was a cloudless sky on the morning we arrived.

Most soldiers regard transit camps as abhorrent, particularly the one at Port Said. Troops in transit to, and from, the Middle East passed through that Camp, usually staying at least a few nights. It was Army 'Bull' of the worst kind. Here, our draft disbanded with small groups moving on to various Middle East, Royal Signals Units. As an individual, I now set out to complete my journey by rail, and road to Haifa, Palestine. No time was wasted there, and I boarded a ferry boat taking me to Famagusta, Cyprus. The trip was nothing more than an overnight one.

Leaving the docks, we drove through the town of Famagusta, onto the Nicosia Road when four miles out, we arrived at my final destination. For want of a better name, the Camp was known as 'Four Mile Point'. At that early stage, it was more of a building site than a Camp. At first glance, its appearance was a little hostile. It had been raining, and the ground was a quagmire of reddish-brown mud. The perimeter, was of high barbed wire. Inside, and under construction, were three or more brick buildings and about twenty Nissen huts, plus another twenty, or more concrete bases for tents. One of the brick buildings was to be the Set Room and operational area, and others were to be office blocks one of which would be the Regimental Headquarters. If that first impression of the Camp was unwelcoming, then that could not have described the human one which was both warm, and hospitable. The outlook for the next three years was good. My mind was peaceful.

The only occupants of the Camp were a small advance party who had come from Sarafand, direct. The main body of the Unit was still there. There was much preparation to be done before their arrival. Our work would be cut out as we fought the clock to receive them in a few weeks time. I was assigned as SQMS in charge of clothing, barrack stores, bedding, armoury, RE fixtures and almost everything else except technical stores, which was in itself a big responsibility held by another SQMS. Of the two divisions, mine was the one I would have chosen, given the opportunity. That left me satisfied. The work, and the rank were both new to me.

It was common practice for those on promotion above Sergeant to be transferred out of 'Y' into normal Royal Signals duties. Throughout the Corps Warrant Officers, and senior NCO's were more often, then not employed in administrative and instructional duties. Only a few remained employed in their trades, and on live operational work. So transfers out of 'Y' caused few problems. That personally I remained in 'Y' was my good fortune. No reason was given, but it may well have been due to being a Class I Special Operator. If needs be, I could at a moments notice be switched to set room duties, and take over with ease and confidence. There was now little chance of that happening in the rank of SQMS. Oddly, many of the WO's and Sergeants in the post war 'Y' Service were posted in from non 'Y' units, and knew little or nothing of what went on in a set room. They could not possibly have carried out the simplest of intercepting work as they were untrained, and not special operators. That is no reflection on their ability as soldiers, or administrative men. A good administrator is good either in, or out, of 'Y'.

Settling in at my new work was not difficult though, at times, it had the similarity of being thrown in at the deep end. The working relationship between the QM (Capt. E Jordan) and the rest of the department could not have been better. Coinciding with the move, came instructions to reintroduce peacetime accounting for all stores. From now on even a ball of darning wool was an accountable item. The 'Vocabulary of the Army Ordnance Stores' became the fundamentalism of my daily life. 'In' trays, 'Out' trays, 'Pending' trays, and even 'Laugh and Tear Up' trays, all overflowed with ever increasing paper work. Many long hours were spent at my office desk. In a singular manner, I was happy.

Cyprus, during the early part of 1947, was a very peaceful station. Only once in a blue moon did we hear a whisper of political unrest amongst the Greek Cypriots.

Many of the local people were of Turkish origins, and now and again I would meander into the old part of the town and chat-up some of the locals, and always carrying my camera. From there, I would stroll on into the dock area. The port was a busy one, though small. Famagusta's main attraction was its beach. There were miles of undeveloped, uncommercialised clean sands washed by a blue, tideless sea. As a holiday resort, the Island was undiscovered. From the very beginning, I knew that as much of my spare time as possible would be spent on that beach, and swimming. The sea never became too cold for that, but from November to March it became infested with seaweed, there would be quite a lot of rain, and the air temperature fell dramatically. While that was taking place, the Troodos mountain area became the recreational attraction, as heavy snow would fall and skiing was possible for a short season. The leave camp there was open for a short spell of about six weeks.

    Alas, there was no leave and not much recreation for any of us as the arrival date of the Regiment from Palestine came ever closer, then in the middle of February they arrived. The Officers' Mess, and the WO's and Sergeants' Mess was complete, but like most of the accommodation it was in Nissen huts. About half the junior ranks were in huts, and the remainder in tents.

    No. 2 Wireless Regiment was the heir of the pre-war No 2 Wireless Company which was also stationed in Sarafand. The Unit was now commanded by Ltd. Col. H Winterbotham OBE Royal Signals. Here at Four Mile Point I was part of, and witness, to the establishing of the Unit on the Island.

    The QM's department was quickly in full effect, led by Capt. Jordon. WOII Jack Hastings was the RQMS. He was one of the most likeable, and popular member of our Mess. Many times he caused me to rock with laughter as he indulged in his party-piece which was to sing – but he sang his songs backwards! The other SQMS who was on tech. stores was a good working colleague, but for the life of me, I cannot recall his name. His task was a big one as our range of very sophisticated equipment was huge, and many of the items were on the list of War Office Controlled Stores. Each of us had a storeman, with an additional one in the armoury. A tiny department, but a close knit and efficient one. I was frequently at my desk for an hour, or more before breakfast, and again for a couple of hours or so in the evenings. Whenever possible, I would make a couple of hours in the afternoon swimming, and on the beach.

    On the operational side, the set room came under Sgt. Pooley who was later awarded the BEM. There was also a Sgt. In charge of each Watch. It was not my concern what tasks were being covered, or the nature of interception taking place. Using my experience, and know-how it was not difficult, with a little clear thinking, to arrive at some fairly accurate, if not spot on, conclusions. Sporadically, I had a touch of envy that I was still not in on the act, but usually that was offset by satisfaction in my new rank, and learning the 'Ins' and 'Outs' of 'Q' work.

    Life in the WO's and Sgts.' Mess was little different than in any other Mess in the Corps. Local brandy, and wines were good, and very cheap. As might be expected that resulted in the urge to over indulge! Our entertainment was self made, and on a DIY basis. Television was non-existent. Even back home it was a black and white fledgling. We held games nights, dances, and formal functions such as Dinners. On most of those occasions it was customary to invite the officers, and sometimes their ladies, plus an invitation to the Padre. One dance, which was to be held on a Saturday night, the usual invitations were all sent out. The Padre replied with his formal acceptance, but also he enclosed a short note. In that, he made it clear that whilst he was pleased to accept, we would appreciate that as the following day was the Sabbath he would have to leave, rather like Cinderella, before the clock struck the midnight hour. He went on to say, however, that we was holding his usual party on the following morning at 11am in the Chapel, and that all WO's and Sgts. Were cordially invited to attend. He called it Divine Service. That is typical Service sense of humour, and we much appreciated the Padre's wit. Surprisingly, the attendance at that Service was well above average. Compulsory Church Parades had by now been abolished.

Army Chaplains were – in the denominational sense – often 'shared'. There was no guarantee that a Chaplain posted to a particular garrison would automatically be Church of England. Ours was, I believe, a Methodist and was the Chaplain to all of us of Protestant Faith. It would have been out of character for him to have discriminated against anyone who was, say, Baptist or Anglo-Catholic. The Services were non-denominational. His responsibilities were not confined to those of us living in the Camp, but also those living out in married quarters in Famagusta. He was a member of the RAChD. Running counter to that was the Roman Catholic Padre. The Catholics always had their own priest. Ours was not a member of the RAChD, but was a civilian, and classed as an officiating Chaplain to the Armed Forces. We gave little attention to denominations. Both were respected, much liked, and great fun.

The position of our Medical Officer was similar to that of the RC Padre. He too, was a civilian but a retired doctor living in Famagusta. Each day he held a sick parade, when anyone wishing to see him was conveyed to, and from, his surgery in military transport. He came to the Camp when requested. The nearest RAMC Medical Officer was some forty miles away stationed at the British Military Hospital in Nicosia. All urgent cases, and emergencies were sent direct there. One graphic incident is indelibly stamped on my memory.

About half a mile outside the perimeter fencing, there was a remote controlled transmitter. It was un-manned, and in a small brick building which was very securely locked and visited at irregular intervals by an armed guard. Each morning, one of our radio mechanics made a visit to carry out any maintenance that was necessary. The transmitter was a powerful one. It had to be, to fulfil its purpose, so required a high voltage. It was Summer, and our uniform was shorts, open neck shirt with rolled up sleeves, and Army boots with steel studs. That morning, I was in the clothing store checking stock when in came one of our radio mechanics who I recognised, instantly. He looked pale, and was shivering. Quickly, I grasped his story. Some previous visitor to that transmitter must have dropped a pencil. As this chap put one of his feet on the pencil, so it rolled from under him causing him to fall forward, and across the transmitter. On his bare arms he received burns, and was badly shocked. With help from a storeman we made him comfortable. I 'phoned the Sgt. In charge of the Cookhouse, who immediately produced a mug of hot strong sweet tea. Next, I rang the MO. He said that I was to keep the patient warm, and that he would be on his way with an ambulance in minutes. He was. Wasting no time, he was soon on his way, the MO and the patient to the BMH at Nicosia. It was a close run thing, and that pencil might well have been the cause of a fatal tragedy. Some weeks later, our radio mechanic was back in his job after making a good and lasting recovery. Now, whenever I see a pencil on the floor or ground, I have no option but to pick it up. For a few brief moments I experience an evocative emotion.

Photography was a popular hobby, and enthusiasm was on the increase. Cameras, and films were not expensive. Not before long, a few of us decided to start up a Camera Club. We sought out a small room, which we considered suitable for converting into a dark room, and then applied for permission for its exclusive use. No obstacles were put in our way, instead we received encouragement with a grant from Regimental PRI Funds to help us on our way. Each member paid a small subscription of a few pence a month. In next to no time, we had sufficient funds to enable us to purchase the necessary equipment, and chemicals to carry out our own processing. Colour, in those days, was too expensive, but we were quite happy to plod on with black and white. Soon after that, we purchased our own enlarger. Countless nights were spent burning the midnight oil in that dark room. When going to bed, I was often very tired, but always with a feeling of satisfaction, and achievement; never mind how small.

Though we worked hard through that Summer, and into Autumn, we also enjoyed our leisure. Suddenly, I was faced with a family, and domestic problems at home. It was sufficiently serious to be granted a month's compassionate leave, albeit a low category one which meant that I would travel by sea, via Port Said. This time, my stay in the transit camp was of only a few hours duration before boarding the *Georgic*. At one time in the war she had been bombed by the Germans, and sunk in shallow waters just South of the Suez Canal. She was then re-floated and towed home. Much of the ship was rebuilt, and all of it refurbished. She was one of the fastest, and nicest ships which I ever travelled on. The leave served its purpose, but I was not sorry when the time came to return to Cyprus, and No. 2 Wireless Regiment. The voyage back went well until reaching the last sector by road, from Port Said to Haifa.

Britain's mandate for Palestine was speedily coming to an end, when we set out in a convoy of Army vehicles for Haifa. It was a cold and very wet day. The road was splashed with mud, and very greasy. Fighting between Jews and Arabs was at its height, and both regarded us as their enemy. One side, or the other, was quite happy to snipe at, and open fire on, our convoys. With about fifteen other senior NCO's and Warrant Officers, we were told to travel in the back of a 3 ton lorry. It had no canopy, so we were exposed to the elements. To keep warm, and as dry as possible, we all wore greatcoats. So that we were not easy prey for snipers, the convoy speed was not the usual maximum, but rather a minimum one. Our vehicle was the last but one in the convoy. The one behind us was a small 15 cwt. truck with just three, or four NAAFI girls in the rear. When about half way, our speed increased. We were not aware of the reason, but perhaps the convoy commander had received word of trouble ahead. If there was any firing, I cannot recall it. Slowly, then more quickly we were swaying from one side of the road to the other. The driver, a young RASC man, did what he could to get out of the skid, but we were travelling too fast. A sudden lurch, then we rolled over, and down an embankment. Later, with lucid descriptions from my colleagues, also involved, and my own few salient recollections, it was undemanding to sketch in my mind's eye what followed.

Two important features most probably saved a few lives, including my own, and prevented the casualties from being worse. As there was no canopy over us, we were not thrown together in a confined space, but all were thrown out of the lorry, and clear of it. Moreover, we landed in a sea of mud, which cushioned our fall. About six or seven of us received injuries, the others picked themselves up. Among the injured, I had the dubious distinction of coming out of it worst of all. Though very dazed, I recollect smelling petrol. Not surprising, as nearby where I lay was a 'jerrycan' which had burst open. If that had ignited, no one would be reading this story. Off, and on, I was conscious, but could not move. Standing over me was a Warrant Officer from the South Wales Borderers. After calling a couple of his colleagues, they then carried me back onto the roadside verge. All the convoy vehicles in front of us not knowing what had happened had driven on, and were now out of sight. The small truck with the NAAFI girls had stopped. Those girls ripped their skirts, and underwear for use as bandages. Someone must have summoned help as very soon ambulances, with an MO, were on the scene. They were cutting my greatcoat and uniform. Faintly, I heard a voice mumble something about 'Morphine'. Minutes later my pains eased, and I became drowsy but still aware of being in an ambulance with a couple of other stretcher cases, speeding along a road towards … goodness knows where. Throughout the incident, no Arab or Jewish snipers had opened fire on us. Our major hazard was the adverse weather. In that ambulance, there was one, if not two male nurses. The journey was long, and took us over an hour before we arrived at the British Military

Hospital, Haifa. Still in great pain I lay on a stretcher in the casualty department, and pleaded for a pain killer. The answer was a firm, and emphatic 'No'. Then a voice spoke 'You've already had morphine, and you're not having any more, but soon you will be going into the operating theatre'. In my bewildered mind, I reasoned the conundrum of how they knew. An attendant unknown to me, had with a coloured marker written the letter 'M' on my forehead. Glancing, from a stretcher, at my own forehead has never been one of my successful undertakings!

Recollections of entering the operating theatre, or of coming out of it are non-existent. About 3am the following morning I returned to life, and found myself in a large ward. The light by my bedside was switched on, and dimly I saw the night Sister. With an appalling thirst, I asked her for something to drink. She produced a glass of milk. I dozed.

By degrees, during the subsequent few days, and with the reassurance of the surgeon, I began to realise that my condition was no great cause for concern. My right arm (upper humerus) was fractured, and the shoulder was dislocated. It was bandaged, and secured to a large heavy, iron frame splint which encompassed my right ribs and that half of my body. Over my left eye was a nasty cut which had about eight stitches in it, but my eye was safe. As a result of the blow on the head, I had been concussed, and now the victim of rather severe headaches. I had got off lightly, and none of the injuries were likely to cause lasting damage, but I was soon warned that recovery would be at the speed of a tortoise.

The total withdrawal of British troops from Palestine was now only days away, and the hospital was about to close down. All patients were to be moved. As I was stationed in Cyprus, within a week it was decided to transfer me to the BMH at Nicosia. That was good news. Now my friends would be able to visit me regularly. Among the first was the Warrant Officer from the SWB's who with such genuine concern, and who had acted so promptly at the time of the accident was stationed just outside Nicosia. The hospital was small but of a high standard. The atmosphere was a very military one. In the vanguard of that regimentation was the matron whose bosom was festooned with a blaze of colours as she wore the ribbons of First World War medals. By us, the patients, she was regarded as a 'Battle Axe', and as a young man I thought she was old enough to be my Grandmother. Alas, my grannie had died twenty five years beforehand!

The weeks dragged on at funeral pace. When now feeling fit, I was longing to return to my 'Q' work. Did someone in that hospital have a grudge against me? Like an octopus, with its tentacles, they clung to me, and were pathetically slow with my discharge. When the day came, it was thirteen weeks since the lorry had skidded off a road in Palestine. When returning to 2 Wireless Regiment, at Four Mile Point, there was no happier soldier in Cyprus. It was bliss.

About six months had passed since leaving my 'Q' work, with the outcome now being that I had lost the job to another SQMS. My pride was damaged. Did the CO or Capt. Jordan think that I was still too shaken to resume the responsibilities of my rank, or worse, was it over sensitiveness on my part imagining that I was being rejected? When told to take sick leave, I was left with the impression that maybe there were one, or two problems unsolved, and such leave might offer time to ponder.

It was mid-Summer 1948, and the Famagusta plain was dry, and very hot. The leave camp at Mt. Troodos was open. A telephone call, and arrangements were soon in hand for a seven day leave there. It was about 7,500 feet above sea level, and the climate was superb. At night the temperature dropped sufficiently to warrant fires. Sometimes they were in the open, and other times, indoors. Always, they were log fires. The accommodation was mostly in tents, supplemented by a few wooden huts built in a small clearing between countless upright pine trees. A Medical Officer visited the Camp daily, but I had no cause to make use of his services. The standard of food, and cooking was some of the best that I experienced throughout my service. Credit for that went to NAAFI who ran the Leave Camp. Those staying there came from various parts of the Middle East Command, and from all three of the Armed Services, but the Camp's capacity was not more than three hundred.

During the first evening, I met a NCO in the RAF of my own

age, and soon learnt that our views, and tastes were very much in common. He too, was on sick leave. After that, we just kept together, and proceeded to enjoy ourselves.

Rose was not only a WRVS worker, but also the Camp's No. 1 personality. Everyone knew, and liked her. She was middle aged, and tough. She organised, and took part in all that was taking place; on long mountain climbs, and on goat track paths Rose led the way. There may still be many ex-servicemen who will recall her walks to Platres, and particularly the overnight climb to the top of Mount Olympus (approx. 8,000ft), and there at daybreak enjoy the breathtaking views of the Island as the sun rose over the distant Eastern coastline. It was one of those never-to-be-forgotten experiences. Some twelve, or more years, later we were still writing to each other, by which time she had emigrated, and was living in Canada. Pity about that age gap!

If I missed anything at Troodos, it was swimming. It offered no facilities. After a week, my new found RAF friend and I decided to rectify matters. With a week's leave sill unexpired we dashed off to Kyrenia.

On leaving Nicosia by car, we climbed a small range of mountains. Once over the summit, we saw one of the most picturesque places imaginable. It was small with a tiny horse shoe shaped harbour. The coast was rocky, but the sea calm, blue and inviting. There we found a little Turkish owned hotel with only four, or five rooms. We were the only non-Cypriot occupants. We liked it. The only meal we had there was breakfast. Everything was fried, but acceptable. Neither of us had much money, but here we could manage on our budget. The place was modest, but clean. During the week we toured the adjacent coast, and daily swim. There were no sandy beaches like Famagusta, but we managed. Usually, we stopped any old where on the coast road, paused, swam in the sea, ate, had a drink, paused, and then we went swimming once more. It was all very carefree, but time began to run out. Before reporting back to my Unit, we said our farewells. From that day, we have never been in touch. Such is Service life.

What job would I be given, how was I going to be employed?

That was uppermost in my mind as I returned. A few miles outside Nicosia, and close to the SWB Camp we had a small detachment of about fifty men, commanded by a National Service Officer. The senior non-commissioned man was WOII Smith. He was about to be sent home, I think on retirement, and a replacement was required. Such a small Unit did not justify a WOII or even a SQMS but we were still surplus in those ranks, so I was sent as a replacement. The Troop ran itself. Much of the administration was carried out by RHQ at Four Mile Point. Time was on the fringe of boredom.

One cold wet night, and just before midnight, I was woken by our duty Driver who informed that there had been a serious road accident about four miles away, and he felt that he ought to turn out and see if assistance was needed. I told him to inform the Troop Commander, and that he would sign the Works ticket, not I. He replied by saying that he had been to the OC but the officer was 'Not Available', or words to that effect. Soon after, I confirmed his report. That left the ball in my court. I signed the document, and furthermore hurriedly got dressed, and accompanied the driver. When about half way there, we too became involved in an accident. Without any warning, I saw a civilian in our headlight and just a few feet away. We struck him. It was unavoidable. After stopping, we picked up the man and took him to the civilian hospital in Nicosia, nearby. Before daybreak, he was dead. It had now become a major incident, and all the machinery of a full military inquiry began to turn. In addition the civilian police became involved making it a very large kettle of fish. Not only was I the key witness but being very senior to the Driver, there was the risk that someone may try to pin some of the blame on me. In the days that followed, I made many statements, and answered a thousand and one questions, but nothing to incriminate the Driver, who I believed was blameless. A Court of Inquiry was convened, but while waiting for that to take place a different crisis arose.

Due to a family death, domestic issues and worries were once more dominating my mind and that was reflecting on my work. Again, I was sent home on compassionate leave. This time with a top priority, so I travelled by Air. At daybreak, I flew by Cyprus Airways, on a Dakota to Athens. We bumped along as if being driven in a car over a ploughed field. On arrival we were transferred to a British European Airways flight on a Viking aircraft for Northolt. It did offer a few more comforts than Cyprus Airways, but not many. That I was nervous of flying, would be an understatement. More truthfully it was fear. That was in the years of long ago, but was overcome with the arrival of the jet age.

The leave solved some problems, but others still remained. That road death had badly shaken me, and I was worried. When returning to No. 2 Wireless Regiment I learnt that the Court of Inquiry had been held in my absence. My written evidence had been accepted. The Driver had not been held to blame, and having now completed his National Service was back in the UK for discharge. For him, I was delighted; for myself I was also pleased. Pleased to forget the whole incident.

Through no ones fault, one crisis in my personal, or military life had been followed by another.

In spite of two eventful years in Cyprus, I still loved the Island and No. 2 Wireless Regiment, and longed for nothing more than an uninterrupted settled period over the last year of my tour. With that in mind I had a long chat with Capt. Jordan. His comments and news were both good. Not only did he want me to rejoin his 'Q' Staff, but to do so forthwith. Might it have been that he was just wanting me to show an interest, and make some initiative? Unlikely, but just possible. It was a happy beginning to the end.

On learning that there was to be a change of Command of the Regiment, our faces dropped. Lt. Col. Winterbotham's departure was to be a sad occasion. I had first heard his name in the early war years, when I entered the 'Y' Service. After serving under his command, it was child's play to understand why he enjoyed such a high reputation, and was both popular, and respected. That respect was mutual, and it is placed on record by Philip Warner in his story of Royal Signals 1945 – 85, "The Vital Link" (Leo Cooper) in which he quotes some of the Colonel's recollections. They are a fine tribute to the contribution made by the Special Operators in 'Y' to Sigint. As the words emanate from such a notable senior officer in the Corps, they must carry enormous weight. I am proud to quote:

"For me, the background is always the Set Room. It might be a comfortable building; it might be a dugout, a room cut from desert gravel. At each set a subdued light picks out the left hand of the operator on the tuning dial. His head is bent towards his message pad; his right hand dances across the red lined page. Sometimes he stops writing; his left hand turns this way and that. Ah! He has the reply. The air is full of subdued cheepings and chirpings. As I walk down the row I can hear who it is; busy tonight, I think.

"All Sigint effort stands or falls by that one solitary man. For many hours at a time he waits, searches, listens, writes. What comes from under his hand is mostly gibberish, strings of five-letter groups. No one can check his work now or ever. If for a moment his attention fails, the group is lost. Maybe a battle is lost. Only his hunter's instinct keeps him to his task as he tracks his quarry down the echoing whistling corridors of space; only his tracker's ear recognises the old friend, the little tricks of his fist as good as a signature.

"One is inclined to forget that without that man the whole super structure of traffic analysis (as we later learned to call it – I used to call it drawing circles), code breaking and the Ultra world, that whole structure would have vanished; with what consequences, who knows?"

    Our new Commanding Officer was to be Lt. Col. Du Cros who had been my Commanding Officer when I was with the War Office Wireless Station in Harrogate.

    One lunchtime in the Mess, I was having a chat with Mac. Mac was WOII McClennan, one of our Squadron Sgt. Majors. In the course of the conversation I mentioned our Concert Party in the Isle of Man, 1943, and the fun we all had out of it. The subject obviously aroused his interest, and within moments he invited me to join his wife, and himself for dinner that evening in his married quarter at Famagusta. Over a good meal, and an ice cold lager we were soon onto the subject which we both had in mind. What on earth was stopping us from building up our own concert party, here, in 2. Wireless Regiment? Though we were working long hours, we agreed it could be done, and together we would devote as much as possible of our spare time to that end. The concert party was born. Mac had a good knowledge, and background of music with a pleasing tenor voice as a bonus. The entire musical responsibility would be his. All remaining responsibilities were to be mine. Such a division could work as there was a complete understanding and team work between us. We sought, and obtained the assistance and blessing of others. The CO gave the 'Go Ahead'. The Entertainment's Officer became involved. Our first obstacle was quite a large one. We had no theatre, and nowhere to perform. The largest building in the Camp was the OR's dining room which was nothing more than an extended, and outsize Nissen hut, but without a stage. Unofficial contacts, and string pulling were vital, and the RE's came to our aid, magnificently. The stage they erected was everything we asked. Spot lights; foot lights, and all the necessary wiring were installed in a matter of days.

 In the interim we made an appeal to All Ranks for volunteers to become 'Stars'. The response was excellent. Not less than thirty five turned up at our initial meeting to discuss our aims, and listen to views and suggestions. Being an all male Unit was a handicap, but also a challenge. With more ambition than talent it was agreed that we would tackle a pantomime; one duly written and adapted to appeal to a military audience, and of course, its wives and families. With considerable help from others, I commenced work on the script of "Ali Baba and the Forty Thieves". It was not too difficult. Our comedians had their own lines, and there was to be lots of music. Mac started work on a choir of about twenty six voices. Mostly, they could not read music by sight, but their zeal was abundant. Mac tackled the problem by placing the bass, baritone, alto and tenor voices in each of the four corners of a room. There each group, in parrot fashion, learnt their own musical voice lines, and then when they knew it thoroughly, they were brought together, and blended in harmony. With an inexhaustible supply of patience, a sympathetic pianist, and many laughs, the end product was remarkably acceptable.

Eric Vernon, one of our National Servicemen, was the No. 1 vocalist. His was a trained baritone voice, and had previously sung with D'Oyly Carte. Mac's voice was untrained, but he sang well. His tenor solos were always well received. Though I sang bass in the choir, my voice was not of a standard to attempt solo work in the same show as Eric, and Mac. The entire show was more ambitious than 'Loud and Clear' in Isle of Man days. The first two, or three performances were within the Camp. We followed those with about five weeks when we gave about one performance a week to other military camps on the Island. The culmination came when we (the choir) were invited by the OC of the Cyprus Forces Broadcasting Station to give an hour's excerpts at the peak listening time of 8 to 9pm on a Sunday evening. The choir again came into prominence during the following Christmas festivities. A piano was loaded onto a five ton lorry, with some of the choir members. The remainder boarded a second lorry. Both vehicles were decorated with coloured lights and a Christmas tree. We then set out for the Famagusta area where we toured the families, and married quarters to sing carols. The stops were frequent, and at each one drinks were proffered. By the end of the evening our harmonies went haywire.

Troodos was not the only leave camp in Cyprus. Five miles, or so, from our Camp at Four Mile Point, and on the outskirts of Famagusta, was another. This too, was run by NAAFI and like Troodos was a Middle East Leave Camp for all non-commissioned ranks of all three Armed Services. The centre enjoyed a good reputation, so when the opportunity of ten days leave came my way during that last Summer in Cyprus (1949), I decided to spend it at this nearby Leave Camp. Its situation was ideal for those like myself who loved the sea, and swimming. It was a small camp, and built beside the clean sands and warm waters of the Famagusta coast. Temperatures at that time of year were in the nineties, and occasionally above. Little attention was paid to comfort. The accommodation was in tents, on concrete bases. There were four beds in each tent, though most had no more than two occupants. The town was a short walk away, so anyone wishing to visit the local restaurants, or shops, had no problems.

Sailing in these waters was popular, and not too demanding on skill. My experience in this sport did not match up to my enthusiasm. At the time, there were three of us lying on the beach enjoying the sun; the other two being senior NCO's in the Royal Artillery. Someone suggested that we went for a sail. The Camp sailing boat was lying idle just a couple of hundred yards further down the beach. It was a small craft, owned by NAAFI and for the free use of anyone who cared to use it. The senior person – this case myself – just filled in a small form, signed it, and away we went. There was a breeze, which we underestimated, and it was becoming stronger as we sailed further from the shore. Sailing faster and faster it became exhilarating. Knowing no better, we were carrying too much sail and we should have reduced it. Too late; one short gust of wind, stronger than the rest, and over we went! Efforts to right the boat failed. There was no panic. Our position was about a mile off shore, and about half a mile East of the Camp. Sitting on the water-filled hull, we talked the matter over, and decided to 'Abandon Ship', and swim to the shore. A swim of a mile in these good conditions was well within the ability of all three of us. The sea was warm, and there were no dangerous currents. In due course we made it, and on reaching the beach we walked along the sands to the Camp to report the mishap. We were met by a very irate Commandant. As the senior of the three, I was blamed, and had to accept responsibility and received a well delivered rocket with enormous velocity! Among the many sins which it appeared I had committed was leaving the boat while it was still afloat, and that we should have stayed with it until help arrived. Someone on the shore had seen us capsize, and raised the alarm. A rescue boat was despatched but on arrival reported no sign of life, and thought that we had all been drowned; a reasonable deduction. On completing his tirade, the Commandant soon showed his relief that we were all very much alive, if somewhat subdued and calmed down. When departing from his presence, I had the impression that all was forgiven, and the matter closed. It was.

Returning to routine was not difficult. There was no shortage of work, and when off duty I tried to get away from Camp. The WO's and Sgts. Mess offered few comforts. It was just two Nissen huts connected by a short passage. The furnishings were basic; the bar was ample and the drink prices cheap (some would say 'too' cheap). Food was not exciting, but passable. All those material matters may reflect on morale, and make a happy Unit, but in the long run it is the spirit, and character of the Unit which brings contentedness, and well-being. No. 2 Wireless Regiment was rich in those invisible, and inestimable qualities.

Cyprus was a three year station, and in the Summer of '49 I gave serious though about applying to extend my present tour by a further three years. Eventually, I decided to let events take their course, and accept repatriation. Whether, or not, I took the right decision will never be known. My time in No. 2 Wireless Regiment hit one, or two black spots, but they were not the making of the Unit. With the approach of departure, my feelings were certainly not mixed, but totally wretched. The *Empire Windrust* called in January 1950, and I climbed up the gangway, and became homeward bound. This ship had been purpose built as one of Hitler's "Strength – Through – Joy" ships, aimed at the Nazi youth market. She survived the war, together with remnants of German shipping, and was used by us to replenish our own depleted Merchant Navy. Since then, she was taken into service as a troopship. In those days, when overseas travel was still mostly by sea, the Bay of Biscay was top of the notoriety list of high seas. I had crossed the Bay no less than ten times, but on none of those crossings did the seas compete with those we encountered on that homeward bound voyage in the Mediterranean. Though a good sailor, and had never been sea sick, this time I came dangerously close to it. Air travel does have advantages.

We called at Malta, and arrived at Southampton about ten days after leaving Cyprus. Immediately, I went on leave. With some weeks leave accumulated over the past three years, plus disembarkation leave I was eligible for the maximum permissible of about fifty six days. Enjoyable, but towards the end a bit of a bore.

CHAPTER 17

Leicestershire is one of England's well-favoured Counties. Before the Spring of 1950, I had failed to appreciate that.

When approaching the end of that protracted leave, a posting order came, one day, instructing me to report to 10 Wireless Training Squadron, Garats Hay, Woodhouse Eaves, just a few miles outside Loughborough, and not far from Quorn. The large wartime training establishment for special operators in Douglas, IoM had been closed for some years. 10 Wireless Training Squadron was its successor. Though only of Squadron strength it was adequate to meet the needs of the post-war Army 'Y' Service.

The Unit's centre piece was the old vicarage belonging to the tiny village church of St. Paul's. In the spacious surrounding grounds were a number of Nissen huts which provided accommodation for non-commissioned officers and men, and also training rooms. The officer accommodation, and Mess, plus the WO's and Sgts.' Mess were all within the old vicarage. Across the forecourt, in the old stables the QM's stores were accommodated. It can be seen that none of this was purpose built for its present use, but rather the military, yet again, "Making-Do". At that we were experts. Compensation lay in the beautiful countryside, which was quite unspoilt. 10 WTS was commanded by Major Galbraith Royal Signals, and the Adjutant was Capt. Bremner. I had not met, nor served with any of the Unit's officers previously, and only a few of the Sergeants.

Within hours of arriving I learnt that, once more, I was surplus to establishment, or more bluntly there was no real job for me, so one was created. The Squadron already had its SQMS and there was not work for two of us. The Chief Instructor was Capt. Salisbury so it was directed that I was to be made his assistant.

There were roughly two hundred men under instruction, and they were divided into about ten squads. Each squad has its own instructor for the basic cornerstone subject of receiving Morse. Others specialised in such matters as foreign procedures, Wireless theory and AC. The instructional staff were Sergeants and Corporals. The system was little more than a scaled down version of that which existed in Douglas during the war years. Six years after that war this, the very heart of the 'Y' Service, was receiving some rather shabby treatment. Both the accommodation, and lecture rooms leaked badly when it rained heavily. No new equipment was available, just the leftovers from the war. The majority of the trainees were National Servicemen, and it is not surprising that when approached, and asked to consider making this a career, gave a very emphatic 'No'. It may be deemed that such conditions reflected adversely on the standard of training. That, it did not; thanks due mostly to the high standard of instruction, and careful selection and vetting of the trainees before joining 10 WTS.

Much of my job was office paperwork, and ensuring that those concerned kept to the timetable, and syllabus. Now and again, I stood in for an instructor who may have been sick, or on leave. In my military life, it was the closest I ever came to a nine to five job. The main problem with my daily task was its insufficiency. Often, I was bored.

There was little social life, and no facilities existed for one. The only transport to, and from, Loughborough was an erratic, and unreliable country bus service. At weekends, my destination was either London, or Nottingham.

Negating that grey side to life was a happy unit. Throughout my stay there were never any serious problems relating to discipline, or morale. From the CO down to the newest trainee there was a good spirit, and team work. It was rewarding to, once more, be involved in the 'Live' side of 'Y' as opposed to the administrative; albeit half a loaf.

About half a mile from our Camp was Beaumanor. The present manor is about a hundred and fifty years old, and is within its own park, where two previous mansions stood. For over three hundred years, it was owned by the Merrick family. At the outbreak of World War II, it was purchased by the War Department, and became, possibly, the most vital 'Y' centre during those critical years. It was manned by civilians, many of whom had previously served in military 'Y'. Their standard was unequalled, and their value to Sigint was worth its weight in gold. Beaumanor was probably our prime source of German Enigma intercepts. Being no great distance from Bletchley Park, intercepted enigma traffic could be in the hands of the BP 'Boffins' almost as quickly – and in some cases sooner – than received by the German addressee. At its peak there must have been a few hundred operators at Beaumanor, yet the utmost secrecy was maintained, and the nature of their work completely unknown to the local inhabitants. They had not the remotest idea that the Nation's most precious source of intelligence was in their own back gardens! Set rooms were mostly in huts built within a few yards of, and surrounding, the Manor. In 1943, when in Douglas, a small group of us including my old friends Simpson, Colley and Pickford visited Beaumanor on a short Course. It was that visit which brought home to me the enormous value of their work. Amongst ourselves we often discussed the secrecy of our work, and whether our efforts, and loyalty would be made known to the outside world. Security, and secrecy were so much part of our lives that we invariably came to the conclusion that most of what we knew and did, would remain secret for the remainder of our lifetime. The Official Secrets Act took care of that.

After the war, over thirty years passed before even a whisper of Ultra, and 'Y' emerged from under the dark cloak of secrecy, and began to make itself known to the general public. At first it was a mere trickle, then slowly, very slowly, more came out into the open. For that we must be grateful to military historians of the calibre of Ronald Lewin, and more recently Hugh Skillen with his book "Spies of the Airwaves". They fought hard against many 'security' obstacles. In spite of their efforts, there remain many gaps in the story of Sigint, which even now, as we approach the end of the twentieth century, are considered 'Too Sensitive' to be revealed. Why are some war-time 'Y' records not to be released to the public until the year 2045? Such questions have answers which come under the heading of National Security. Perhaps, one day, someone will undertake the writing of a detailed history of the work carried our at Beaumanor in the years 1939 – 45. Such would reveal hitherto unknown names, and brains, and how they organised, and operated a large, intricate and successful interception of enemy communications. That is just one of the many 'Gaps'. Will we have to wait until 2045 for that? I wonder.

In a letter dated 9th November 1978, which I received from Ronald Lewin, he wrote:

> "My own feeling is that we shall never be able to write approximately truthful accounts of the battles of the last war until we have a very detailed picture of the contribution of 'Y' Service. All the senior Intelligence Officers whom I know constantly emphasise this point ..."

Later, in another letter of 20th January 1982, Lewin wrote to me as follows:

> "... I have now made a further contract with the OUP to spend the years 1984 to 1987 in writing as definitive a history as I can manage of the 'Y' Service.
>
> "I want to do this for the obvious reason that the actual conduct of operations during the war will never be fully understood without such a history while the members of 'Y' Service deserve such credit, just as much as those who worked in other secret fields which have been more publicised".

Ronald Lewin was awarded the Chesney Gold Medal, by the Royal United Services Institute. In 1983 he was appointed CBE for his services to military history. He had done little more than research of his history of 'Y' when sadly he died.

My 'created' job came to an end in the early Summer of 1951, when the regular SQMS was on leave for a while, and I took over his stores, which were small and well organised. Though the job did give me responsibility for a short while, in reality it ran itself. My stay was now drawing to a close, as in August a posting order came through. This time, I was going to No. 1 Wireless Regiment, BAOR. The Unit was located in Munster. Of the Unit, I knew little, but it was a relief that for the time being I was to remain in the 'Y' Service, as I had almost taken it for granted that my next move would be a reversion to a normal Royal Signals Unit. So soon after the war, news of events in Germany were frequently reported in the Press. To be unaware of what was going on in that Country would have been an admission of ignorance on current affairs. Germany was not a station I would have chosen, but it could have been worse; say Siberia!

That was not the last I saw of Woodhouse Eaves. At home, and sitting back enjoying a cup of tea during a November afternoon in 1988, when my telephone rang. A voice the other end identified himself as the Commanding Officer of one of my old units. Immediately, I wondered why, after all these years should anyone there now wish to contact me, least of all the Commanding Officer. The Colonel soon explained the purpose of his call. It appeared that he had visited his Corps museum and while there had picked up some notes which I had made about the 'Y' Service (about a year earlier, I had sent the curator a copy as I thought they would be of interest to him). The CO then went on to invite me a visit to his Unit, and in his words to 'Sing for my Supper'. That involved giving a talk, for about an hour. I was to be the Colonel's guest, and stay overnight in the Officers' Mess. It was a wonderful invitation to receive, and there was no hesitation on my part in accepting. A date was agreed for early December. Both the talk, and the visit went well. As the audience – officers and NCO's of the Intelligence Corps, and Royal Signals, were all security vetted, and serving in 'Y', I was free to talk frankly, and uninhibited on my subject which was a broad outline of my years in 'Y'. Paradoxically, that freedom was an encumbrance. For the past forty years, when discussing this subject, I had to be very guarded in what I said. Each word would be taken out of my mouth, and closely examined before uttered, for fear of contravening the Official Secrets Act. Now, if only for an hour, when that restriction was lifted, I was free to recount, in tiny morsels of detail, the interception cover we gave to Foreign Powers, and which ones. I was addressing today's young generation in the Service, who had the know-how of the latest technology at their finger tips. To them, much of what I said would have sounded a little primitive. To their credit they had heard about Units, and places such as Cyprus, Abbottabad, Sarafand, 2 SWG Malta, 1 SWG, 'A' Types, 'B' Types and so on. In retrospect, I believe that I may have failed to take advantage of the freedom of speech which was given me. It is not difficult, now, for me to understand how an inmate of Dartmoor may feel if released for an hour, or so from his imprisonment, but with the knowledge that when his time was up he would have to return to his captivity. Hence, the talk was a generalisation, but was well received. That return visit, with its social associations was one of my highlights of 1988.

Although under-employed in 10 Wireless Training Squadron, I had been happy there, and enjoyed the relationship with old, and new friends. When moving its members around, the Army gives no consideration to personal relationships, or emotions. My imminent new life in Munster would be different; that was certain. Having no prophetic powers had advantages. Cards, crystals, and tea leaves, I scorn. There was no indication what tomorrow was about to bring. I was unprepared.

Chapter 18

Hitler cared for his own. For his Army, he built barracks of a standard far higher than any government in this Country had ever built for our Army. Munster was a classical example. On arriving at No. 1 Wireless Regiment, the first impression I had was of the excellent accommodation which had been built, by the Germans during the Nazi era.

No time was wasted. As contemplated, my job was to be in the QM's department performing the normal duties of a SQMS. Not unlike the set-up in Cyprus, my responsibilities were for most stores other than technical. Given the choice, I would have preferred a technical job relating to my trade as a Special Operator, and in the Set Room, but now my rank was becoming a barrier to that. Munster was a new location, but there was nothing new about the 'Q' duties, and responsibilities. In those early days in the Regiment, as I embarked on this new life, no alarm bells rang.

The WO's and Sgts. Mess was comfortable, and the standard of food, and cooking was high. The membership was large. As in any 'Y' Unit, there was a mixture of Royal Signals, and Intelligence Corps personnel. Not unexpectedly, there were a few who I had served with previously. Within days my sixth sense told me that all was not well. The camaraderie, which was normally so evident in Messes, was in shortfall. To a lesser extent that link was also missing outside the Mess. It did not take long to form the impression that here, were a few hundred individuals who had failed to become a single Unit. The closest they came to a team, was in the formation of numerous small cliques each with their own axe to grind. From the outset it was manifest that my presence was not particularly welcome. That sensitiveness was strong. By this time I had served in many corners of the globe, and in many types of Units, but at no time had I previously encountered such unpleasantness. It was, spasmodically, directed at me, personally. It was not always in the directly spoken words, but more by inference. The reason was quite unknown to me, and almost forty years later, still is. Many hours I spent worrying, and pondering over it. I was confused.

In the midst of that uneasiness came an antidote, if only of short duration. Each week I was submitting an entry on a football pools coupon. It amounted to no more than a small block permutation on the penny points, costing 6/9d. When marking my entry one Saturday evening, it was obvious that one line was a correct forecast. A few days later, Vernons Pools credited my bank account in London with £1,045. From that date, I gave up doing the pools. Such good fortune could not occur twice in a lifetime. As a greetings telegram had come to me through military channels, it would have been impossible to have kept the win secret. For a celebration, I gave a party in the WO's and Sgts. Mess, for all members, and wives. Drinks were duty-free, and at a give-away price. My bill for the entire evening was little over £50. When arranging the party, I had a few qualms knowing that the atmosphere contained a little poison. Some would think, at best, that I was being ostentatious. My fears proved groundless. The evening went well.

Most of my fellow men considered Germany to be a good posting. Particularly that was true of the married ones who lived in married quarters. Their standard of living was far above that which they would have at home. Such views were not mine. When out of barracks and in the town of Munster, the locals made it quite clear that they disliked British Soldiers, and were just coldly polite towards us. My reaction was instantaneous as I made it equally clear that I disliked Germans, and would be equally cold in my attitude towards them. The German language was not mine. I neither spoke it, nor wished to do so. The war had only been over six years, and memories were still too vivid. I would fraternise with them no more than was necessary in the course of my duties. In late 1951 that was how I felt, and those were my views. For that, many will today condemn me; particularly those who are too young to remember the war years, and the early aftermath. They will judge my attitude in the light of today's world of NATO and EEC and the necessity of Anglo-German co-operation, and friendship. With hindsight, I should have adopted a more Christian tone, and extended the hand of forgiveness, and friendship. Life in the German community would, for me, have been more comfortable had I done so. He who never made a mistake, never made anything.

The German economy was still struggling to stand on its own feet. We were not paid in Marks, but in British Armed Forces Vouchers (BAFV's). It was still paper money, and in appearance not unlike Monopoly money. Notes were printed in denominations of Pounds, and Shillings. Through military channels, it was possible to exchange a limited sum into Marks. The exchange rate was fixed, and there was a ceiling on the amount we were allowed to exchange over a fixed period. The system was not a howling success, as there were too many loopholes. The easiest way to obtain Marks was by means of the 'Black Market'. The currency was in coffee. Tons of the stuff was brought over from the UK; mostly by individuals returning from leave. Officially, it was against all orders. As those who scorned were often participants, nothing was done to eradicate the practice. Often it was a case of, 'Do as I say, not do as I do'. Throughout those years in post-war Germany, I neither encountered, nor heard of, disciplinary action being taken against any soldier for indulging in the coffee racket.

That Germany was not yet out of a period of near starvation was indisputable. He would have had no soul who did not, at times, feel pity towards them. The shelves in food shops lay bare. In some which dealt in luxury items, it was a different story, but you cannot feed a hungry child on a pair of Nylons. In the UK, Nylon stockings were in very short supply, and sometimes unobtainable. Buying those ladies' stockings was about the only shopping I did in local shops. When coming home on leave, they made wonderful gifts, and always much appreciated by the recipients. When observing some of the appalling conditions which still existed in Germany, we felt compassion towards them, but it was not unnatural – at that time – to feel another nagging emotion. "Who's fault was it, anyway?". Certainly not mine, nor my Country's. It was not the Allies who had invaded Poland in August 1939, and neither had we been responsible for the holocaust. Now, what little food we could spare was being sent to aid these people, and the whole world knew that the Americans were sending in food on a gigantic scale. As that was taking place, our own folk at home were still strictly rationed. Almost a further three years were to pass before those controls were lifted. How short memories can be; and not just British ones.

That feeling of insecurity, and unease continued unabated. Attempts on my part to locate the roots failed. Daily, in my stores, I carried out a spot check on different items. Soon, I began to notice a small number of discrepancies. Checking, and re-checking the paper work offered no explanation. Not unexpectedly, matters came to a climax. I found a serious deficiency in the stock of sheets and pillowcases. Unhesitantly, I reported the matter to the QM. His reaction was quick, and instantly pointed his finger of blame at me. With abnormal haste he told me that a Court of Inquiry would be convened. Meantime, I sought an explanation. There was no obvious one. Such items were almost unobtainable on the open market, but they were on the black one. There, I suspected, the linen would soon find its way, but who was responsible, and where was my proof? It is one thing to have strong suspicions, and another to provide evidence. As a senior NCO who was responsible for the stores, it was my head that would roll.

Though always interested in military law, being a barrack room lawyer was not my line. From the onset there was much about that Court of Inquiry which perturbed me, and before its completion I found much to question. My faith in 'Y' Units, and my loyalty to them was not impaired by that. The operational side of the Regiment was apart from the administrative side of which I was now a member. From the early days of my arrival, my impressions of No. 1 Wireless Regiment had not been good. Subsequently, nothing had occurred to improve them. Matters had only worsened the pollution.

A few days after that Court of Inquiry I was summoned for an interview by the Commanding Officer. By then, he would have known the Court's conclusion, and almost automatically rubber stamped it before passing on the proceedings to the District Commander. No mention was made of the Inquiry. It appeared that the sole purpose of the interview was to inform me that I was being posted to Northern Army Group Signal Regiment at Herford. That meant out of 'Y'. He offered no explanation, and I cannot recall asking for one. I was so utterly fed up with the shabby way I had been treated that the news was not unwelcome. It was never implied that I was leaving under a cloud. To this day, I remain uncertain whether, or not, there was such a cloud. If so, then it was found to have a silver lining! It was not suggested that I would leave with any kind of adverse report. Before departure, I was told that the findings of the Court of Inquiry would be forwarded to my new Commanding Officer.

Too much of my life in Munster had been floating on a surface with an unsavoury undercurrent for it to be labelled as either coincidence, or a chapter of accidents. The source of the effluent, I failed to locate, but its ingredients were probably a mixture of bed linen; a large Pools win; envy and venom.

My short spell in 1 Wireless Regiment, Munster is my happiest memory of it.

It had been a long innings. Longer than most others in the team. When taking up the game in 1939, I was a novice. Twelve years later, I could claim professional status. There had been times when I had batted on a sticky wicket, and other times when I knocked every ball for six. For a split second I must have taken my eyes off the ball, for someone yelled "Owzat?". The umpire answered, "Out!".

What I gave to the 'Y' Service was no more, and I trust no less, than others in the organisation. We were never led to believe that there would be any rewards. It might have been hazardous to have drawn attention to ourselves. The outside world was unaware of our existence until thirty years later. That, in itself, demonstrates the dedication, and loyalty of those in the Service to respect their obligations under the Official Secrets Act.

Much in recent years, has been made known about the German Enigma cipher machine, Ultra and Bletchley Park. Yet the success, or failure of all that surely rested on the material it was handed. It had to be fed. It was a glutton, and its appetite was never satisfied. It demanded both quantity, and quality. The intercept operator's job was to feed it, and ensure that it did not die of malnutrition. They did not fail.

CHAPTER 19

Twelve years earlier, when leaving the normal duties and life in the Corps to join the 'Y' Service; flags, lamps, horses and mules were all commonplace. Line communications were more used than wireless, and line instruments were hand-me-downs from our fathers in the 1914-18 war. Since then, much had taken place, not least a major war. My approaching return would be to a very different Corps life. Understandably, I experienced butterflies.

Northern Army Group Signal Regiment was a large Unit of about nine hundred All Ranks. The Barracks were similar to those in Munster. There was little else in common. My new Commanding Officer was Lt. Col. JDL Morrison. Without delay, I found myself in No. 3 Squadron, commanded by Major PES Mansergh OBE. All my previous 'Q' work had been in centralised system. Here, each Squadron ran their own department, but under the watchful eye of the Major Quartermaster. In most aspects of my work I was answerable to Major Mansergh.

Christmas 1951 was just a few weeks away, but before that came the finalé of the Munster drama. The findings of the Court of Inquiry had been received by Col. Morrison. They directed that I be charged with neglect, which was not a very serious offence in military law. My new CO had no alternative but to obey. No one goes through Army life without making mistakes, but I knew very well that I had not been neglectful, and this was no mistake or misdemeanour. That I was to be someone's scapegoat, was nearer the truth. From out of the blue came a helping hand. I was still a new arrival, and sufficient time had not passed for me to become well known in the Regiment. Such trust and loyalty from a particular officer, caught me unawares, but very grateful. In time that respect proved mutual. Calling me into his office, he spoke of 'An unofficial chat ...' then continuing, his words were in the following vein:

> "Do not get upset about this. The CO knows full well what has taken place, and what is not mentioned in the

Inquiry. His views are his own, and do not necessarily concur with the official findings. He probably knows far more about the incident than you think. The best advice which I can offer you is to accept the findings, even though you may feel you are in no way to blame. That way the Colonel will do no more than he has to do, but he cannot just dismiss the case. The matter would then be closed, and forgotten. The alternative might well be that in the long run you might have all the hassle of a Summary of Evidence".

Those words gave me much food for thought as the source was one which I so greatly respected. To say: "Yes, I was neglectful" knowing full well that to be false amounted to being untrue to myself. The Unit, and the surroundings were still new to me but first indications pointed towards a period of harmony, and well being. It took just a few hours to reach my decision. The advice was sound, and I would accept it.

When brought before my Commanding Officer, I haltingly just said 'Guilty'. No more, and no less. He did not lecture me, but simply said 'To pay £7 towards the cost'. It was all over. For peace of mind, it was good value for money. There would be no stain, and no entry on my conduct sheet. My informant had known a thing, or two. All he said came true, and I had no regrets in taking his advice. Admittedly, a nasty taste lingered in my mouth; not a bitter one, but one of nausea. On life's voyage we do not always sail in fair weather. The sea at times can be quite stormy. That is true in both military, and civilian life. My loyalty to the system, and my trust in the execution of military law governing Courts of Inquiry, had been weakened. In the days that followed, those around me never mentioned the subject. From them, I took my lead, and also remained silent. No more being said, the matter was closed. I was relieved.

The children of All Ranks opened the Christmas festivities with their own party in our mess. The decorations were colourful, the tree sparkled with tinsel and coloured lights. From an amplifier, and speakers came the sound of Carols. There were sickly cakes, and lashings of ice cream, and above all Father Christmas. This loveable old gentlemen was none other than the writer. The costume had been taken out of mothballs, and smelt like it! No climbing dirty chimneys for this Santa. With an escort of despatch riders on motorcycles, I arrived with great ceremony standing in a Jeep which had been well decorated. Beside me were a couple of sacks of toys, and presents. The kids loved it. Come to think of it, so did I!

As far as duties permitted, Christmas through to New Year was a holiday. It is an Army tradition that Christmas day is devoted to the junior NCO's and men. Those of us living in Barracks, and in the Mess, rose early. Soon after 6am I was in the cookhouse assisting in the preparation of 'Gunfire'. No, we were not loading guns, but preparing gallons of coffee in four gallon buckets. In each bucket, with the coffee, we emptied a bottle of rum. Carrying our precious load with great care, we made for the Barrack Rooms making as much noise as possible upon entry. No man was allowed to sleep on. Sleepily, they proffered their mugs for filling. The experience of seeing their Sergeant Major, and Sergeants bringing them 'Gunfire' on Christmas morning provoked much banter, but enjoyed by all. Christmas dinner was the highlight of the day. In accordance with tradition, the menu was the same as last year, and hopefully the same next year, and no different to that enjoyed by their families, and friends at home. There was to be no cafeteria service on this day. Each man was waited upon. That chore was carried out with great enthusiasm, and merry-making by the Commanding Officer, officers and senior NCO's. Like the men, we wore uniform. On arrival at their Mess hall we were greeted with great shouts of excitement. Drinks, mostly beer, were plentiful. With the exception of wartime, and other active service operations, a military Christmas is an extraordinary event. No one attempts, in barrack life, to recreate that inseparable family life, and atmosphere. The inseparable bonds of Corps, and Unit comradeship are expressing themselves in party mood; there for all to see. After the dinner, the junior ranks were left alone to continue the day's celebrations in their own manner. For my part, the remaining day was quiet. On Boxing Day, tradition again took charge, when we had our celebrations in the WO's and Sgts. Mess. The RSM presided at the dinner which was formal, but fun. Like the previous day, the meal, and the cooking was superb. Many soldiers, many times, have cursed many Army cooks, and mostly with good reason. On this occasion it was nothing but praise. The holiday wound up with a fancy dress ball on New Year's Eve in the Mess. When the Army entertains – whether it is themselves or outsiders – they do it well. Always efficiently, and often lavishly, and this had been no exception. It was good to be back in a happy, unsullied environment.

"There is no such thing as a bad Unit, only bad Officers". That quotation was, at times, frequently banded about in military circles, and was, I believe attributed to General Wavell. Inversely, it may be said "There is no such thing as a good Unit, only good Officers". Northern Army Group Signal Regiment, and my own Squadron came under the heading of 'Good'. It was a happy, and efficient Unit. To have one without the other is no more value than a camera without a film.

One of Major Mansergh's customs was to walk alone around the Troops and Departments of the Squadron, and unexpectedly drop in, not with the purpose of catching people out, but to seek and search out for himself what was taking place at the grass roots. Such a visit came my way in early January. Initially, the OC asked some detailed questions about the stores, and accounting. Then, sitting on the opposite side of my desk, he switched the conversation to a more informal, and personal nature. He wanted to know if I was now quite settled, and happy in his Squadron, and did I have any worries. The questions presented no problems, and in answering I was able to assure him that all was well. The opportunity presented itself for me to comment that as a result of spending so many years in 'Y'; there were times when I felt a little out of touch on matters unrelated to 'Q' duties. On that point he was most sympathetic, and understanding, and offered his help and advice should I wish to seek it. We discussed the Squadron generally including the sporting life, and social activities. That chat must have lasted a couple of hours, but had been worth every second. Nor for some years had a Squadron Commander so genuinely, and generally participated with me in such a true and trusting conversation. One, which was most refreshing.

On rising in the mornings, one of my first acts was to switch on my wireless, and listen to the BBC early morning news relayed by the British Forces Network. On a dark February morning, came the stunning announcement of the King's death, during the night. One of my first reactions was to associate it with that night when as a teenage soldier, in a Spike Island barrack room I listened to the BBC announcement of his father's death, George V. What momentous events had taken place spanning those years, and what history I had witnessed. The ancient proclamation was made "The King is dead, long live the Queen". Henceforth, I would be soldiering under my fourth monarch. The passing of George VI was to have little effect on our day to day lives. He had been a much loved King who had reigned through troublesome years, and not without any personal difficulties, and ill health. Our new Queen returned hastily from Kenya, and arrived at London Airport dressed in black.

Though the last nineteen years had been in the Army, at no time had I previously participated in military exercises, or manoeuvres. That was about to change. In the Spring the Regiment commenced training at Unit level. That built up to a climax when in September NATO exercises were held. All manoeuvres of that kind involved temporarily vacating the comfort of our Herford barracks, living rough and working as a mobile unit in a manner meant to simulate that of potential conditions in a war; possibly atomic. That side of Army life was one which I never learnt to enjoy; neither was I ever convinced that if the balloon did go up it would do so in the way the war planners envisaged. War games were the quintessence of our military presence in Germany.

The king pin in any squadron must be its Sergeant Major. In a Squadron of over two hundred and fifty men, he was the only Warrant Officer, and I was the only SQMS. It was in the interests of both the Squadron, and ourselves that we worked well together. That we did. SSM Jones was a first rate Sgt. Maj. His standards were high, and he served as a model to those younger soldiers under his wing. From them, he got their best; not by bullying; not by ranting, and never by raving; but by leadership.

During the following Summer SSM Jones went back to the UK;

and until his return I was called upon to act as the Squadron Sgt. Maj. Those duties were not altogether unknown to me, but not before in peacetime. It bore little resemblance to those days in Iraq, when I held the wartime rank of SSM in a 'Y' Unit. Now, my responsibility was for almost ten times as many men. That tour of office lasted just a few weeks, but long enough to gain some valuable experience. Certainly, I enjoyed it. If further promotion was to come my way, that would be my rank, and role. On the Corps promotion roster my position was now quite high, but that alone guaranteed nothing.

Friends in Northern Army Group Signal Regiment were not in short supply. My closest was Sgt. Harry Fox. We shared, and enjoyed many attitudes and views; not just on matters military. During our working day we saw little of each other. He was a Troop Sergeant and spent most of his time with them. At weekends, he often asked me to his home. There, with his wife and two sons, I spent many enjoyable hours.

Daily, a ration lorry visited the married quarters delivering fresh bread, meat, vegetables and the like. On one of those routine visits, an appalling tragedy occurred. It was a large 3 ton lorry, and one of those where the cab sat over the front wheels. On stopping, and delivering to one family the driver failed to notice a small child playing on the road in front of his parked vehicle. On returning to his lorry, he started-up, and commenced to drive away. In his absence, that small child had crept under his front wheels to play. The accident was fatal. The findings of the Court of Inquiry, I cannot recall, only the horror.

Our relationship with the local Germans in Herford was marginally better than that in Munster, but it was by no means close. Civilians were not invited into the Barracks, and Messes for social events. We did have a small civilian staff who were employed mostly as drivers and cleaners. Only once in a blue moon did I enter a local shop. More frequently, a small number of us would spend an evening in a restaurant, or bar. The most popular ones were those which offered entertainment of some kind. Mostly, off duty time was spent in the WO's and Sgts. Mess.

The coronation of our new Queen in Westminster Abbey on

the 2nd June 1953 was shown on German TV. Earlier on that day, we held an impressive ceremonial parade to celebrate the event. The remainder of the day was a holiday, but taken up with an All Ranks' children's party in the afternoon, and a formal dance in the evening in the Mess. As in London, so in Herford it rained most of the day.

If the past did not have a bearing on the present then history would be irrelevant. In the twenties, and early thirties when I was still a boy, it was not uncommon to see veterans of the 1914-18 war standing on the kerbside selling matches, or bootlaces. On their miserable and tattered clothing was a small splash of colour. It came from their medal ribbons. They all looked old, but they were not. Most of them had been born within this century, but they were hungry. There was no welfare state. There was no DHSS, and no NHS. Any night in London, on the Embankment, they could be seen forming a queue outside a tiny trailer. It was a mobile canteen run by a charitable lady known as the 'Silver- haired Lady'. There, together with the unemployed, and down-and-outs, they waited their turn for a free bowl of soup, or a cup of tea and a hot pie. Such men were worthy of better treatment from their Country. That page is written in our social history to our everlasting shame. On this small boy, the image left its mark. Coming out of it was the determination that such an existence did not become mine. My paramount aim for later life was security. In 1953 I was on target.

In two years time I would complete twenty two years service, thus making myself eligible for pension. Now, I must once more consider my future. For the present, I was happy and enjoying life. There was no reason to believe that over the next few years there would be any major upsets. The option of signing on for a further three years to complete twenty five was there. If I seized it, my pension would be increased, and still only forty one years old. Not too old to make a start in civilian life, and hopefully from that earn another pension. That was how it appeared. Making up my mind was not protracted reasoning. My application to extend my service was approved.

For some time, my QM duties had been running very smoothly, and none of the Munster problems re-emerged. I snatched at every opportunity to join in other aspects of the Squadron life. Apart from a few games of hockey, I was no longer taking a very active part in team games. By no means was I desk bound, and my work frequently took me out, and about in the Barracks. Opportunities cropped up to visit Troop offices, and learn what was going on. Contacts of that nature were invaluable, and if in the process a mug of tea appeared beside me, I made known my appreciation. The Sgt. Maj.'s office was a most reliable venue for such a beverage.

Daily, I visited the OC's office usually for the purpose of obtaining his signature on documents, and explaining what I had done, and not done. On one of those visits, I was about to salute, and depart when he asked me to stay a little longer as he had some news for me. It caught me off balance. Firstly, I was to be posted to 2 L of C Signal Regiment, at Dusseldorf, and secondly with my move was promotion to Warrant Officer II (SSM). He congratulated me. Very shaken, and with mixed feelings, I then saluted Major Mansergh, and departed. The climb to Warrant Officer rank is, perhaps, the most difficult, and most sought after promotion in the entire structure of non-commissioned ranks. To leave the Squadron, and Northern Army Group Signal Regiment was not going to be easy. Here, my confidence in the Corps and Army together with my self-respect had been quickly restored. Much of that due to my Colonel, and Major Mansergh.

The process of stocktaking, and handing over the stores took no longer than a week. The final act was a social one. In the Mess, I had a combined promotion and departure party. On the following day, for the first time wearing the Crown of a Sergeant Major on my sleeve, I departed for Dusseldorf.

Chapter 20

There are those who attach importance, and high value on first impressions. To form them may be natural, but in my life I have usually found them to be unsound, and that it is better to play the game of 'Wait and See'.

2 L of C (Lines of Communications) Regiment was a piecemeal unit. Here, the accommodation was cramped, and not of the usual BAOR standard. Quickly, I learnt that new barracks were under construction, and almost ready for occupation. As the Regiment had one of its Squadrons in Hamburg, and another in Hanover, there remained in Dusseldorf just Regimental HQ and one Squadron; so large barracks were not required. It was in No. 1 Squadron (Dusseldorf) that the vacancy existed for an SSM, and that was now to be my province.

While in Rawalpindi, in the early days of 1937, I encountered a Sergeant Rough Rider named F A Young. Sgt. Young's work kept him fully employed in the stables, so I had little contact with him. He enjoyed the reputation of being very knowledgeable on horses, and was considered to be a good riding instructor. With the advent of mechanisation, and the demise of horse transport the term 'Rough Rider' faded into obscurity. My position then was that of a young Signalman, newly arrived from the UK and still had white knees. Twenty years later I was a newly promoted Sergeant Major, and my new Commanding officer was none other than Lt. Col. F A Young! Mention of our common past was for some time not made. It was some weeks later, at a social occasion when having a drink with the Colonel I raised the subject. It was not well received, and proved to be a regrettable mistake on my part.

With our SSM 'Badgey' Thirkell, there was no previous, mutual common ground which proved to be of no hindrance. We shared many opinions both on, and off duty. In the early days, when settling in my new rank I found him extremely helpful, and often picked from his greater experience. He was a good friend to have.

No more than a few weeks passed before we moved into the

new barracks, and what a let-down they were. Apart from the administrative buildings, there were three, or four accommodation buildings of the single deck, bungalow type. Even the external walls were only built of a thin, flimsy concrete. Bang a door, just slightly, and concrete from the surround fell away. Rooms were inadequately furnished, and those close to a nearby public road had no curtains. The WC's had been designed, and built for giants, and as they had no seats it was virtually impossible to use them in the recognised manner. A cold porcelain bowl which is many times too large is a poor substitute. Carrying out the natural functions of the human body was both laborious, and embarrassing; particularly as some of the loos had no doors! These were not active service conditions, but new barracks built for a peacetime Army. It may have been incredible, but it was also the source of much amusement, and many witticisms. Plumbing problems were not confined to the toilets. The heating, and hot water supply could be relied upon to break down; usually when most needed. German Winters, generally, are a little colder than those in the UK. Concrete paths were still under construction, and insufficient. The buildings in Winter time became concrete islands in a sea of mud. The only messing facilities within the perimeter were for the junior ranks of Corporal and below. The Officers' Mess was a mile, or two down the road. The WO's and Sgts. were swallowed up in the District HQ Mess in the Rhine Centre, which was about four hundred yards away. It was in that environment, and under those conditions that roughly two hundred men lived in what was new, purpose-built, peacetime barracks. Nine years had passed since the cessation of hostilities. If the shoe had been on the other foot, and we had lost the war, the German Army would have been very comfortably established in the UK and lived in a luxurious manner. Humiliating their soldiers was not their *modus operandi*. Deriving from that, I found myself with a Squadron which had low morale. Not surprisingly, I felt ill at ease.

   The discipline, and turnout of the Unit was no cause for concern, but underneath there lay an unhealthy resentment. I mentioned my fears to the Squadron Commander, Major Hewitt, and the RSM but they already had the same awareness. In common with the Army as a whole, the percentage of National Servicemen was then very high. Nothing wrong with that except in our case among those young men, the Army was damaging its own reputation. The problem was deep seated, and was mostly an accommodation one. Sgt. Major's can do little in such circumstances.

A District Headquarters draws its staff from a wide range of Regiments. Each man has his own cap badge, and regimental loyalties. The Rhine Centre WO's and Sgts.'s Mess was in that situation, and to weld its members into a single social life style, and promote a spirit of togetherness was not easy. Somehow, it was achieved. From 2 L of C we contributed about a dozen members. The Garrison Sergeant Major was the Mess President. Married members made good use of the facilities, and many enjoyable social events took place. That complexion on the face of life was rosier than the barrack one, and somewhat compensated for the latter's discomforts.

Dusseldorf was one of the many German cities which had been heavily bombed in the war. Much of the rubble, and damage was, in 1954 still there for all to see. The Town Centre was a short tram ride from the Barracks. The hassle of currency exchange, and restrictions still existed, and did nothing to encourage shopping in the town. Also at the Rhine Centre was a very good NAAFI shop which had excellent facilities, and of course accepted BAFV's.

My new rank with its different responsibilities, and obligations, brought with it a sense of loneliness. A married Sgt. Maj. Living out in married quarters would not have encountered that. Being single, I did. To some extent, a Sergeant Major has to build a wall around himself, and always on his guard against being too familiar with his juniors. There were many, particularly of the old school, who believed that familiarity bred contempt. His position is often one of isolation. Outside normal working hours, I was often the most senior living-in member. All Ranks, and not least the officers, took advantage of that. Often, I was called upon at night to deal with a matter which did not justify my presence. Such a call would never have been made had I been married and living out. Each day there was an Orderly Officer, but he was normally commissioned and so kept to himself. Warrant Officers were called upon to do that duty so I was aware of what it involved. In a small area with two hundred men around you, it may appear ludicrous that any one individual could be lonely. From now on, in my present rank, I would have to learn to live that way, as there was no solution. A couple of aspirin would offer no relief.

The RSM was a man with a happy disposition, and always bright and cheerful. On one visit, I entered his office, and he appeared even more bright and breezy. Good news was written all over his face. In seconds I shared it. He was commissioned in the rank of Lieutenant (QM). Later that day, the Coat of Arms disappeared from his sleeve, to be replaced by two 'pips' on his shoulder. He was now entitled to a salute, and from me he would get it with a very personal respect. My RSM had been awarded an Oscar.

That same day, the Adjutant informed me that as no replacement for the RSM was expected in the immediate future, I was to take over those duties in addition to my existing ones. There was no question of being promoted to RSM. My position as SSM was still far too junior to be given the slightest consideration. I was to act as the RSM but without the rank, and pay. The extra responsibilities were not arduous, and became short lived.

On enlistment, I had knowingly given a false date of birth, but thereafter had given the subject little, or no, further thought. Now the matter reared its ugly head, at first in the form of an intellectual exercise. Whether by chance, or decree, it came to my knowledge that there was an age limit of forty in order to qualify for the rank of WO1 (RSM). Now in 1954, I had by Army age reached that exclusion barrier. Counter to that, my birth certificate allowed me a further two years, but the authorities were unaware of that. Over the years, stories had floated around of cases like mine, when individuals had declared their true age, but not in one instance was it possible to find out the outcome of their declaration. If matters rested a they were, I would remain a WOII for the remainder of my service. That would be a rut. The alternative was to officially declare my true date of birth. To do so would be nothing less that an admission of making a false statement at the time of enlistment. That, in military law, was an offence. It was a dilemma. The matter was uppermost in my mind for some days. While still acting as RSM one afternoon, I knocked on the door of the Adjutants office. Without giving a reason, I asked him if he could arrange for me to have a personal, and off the record chat with the Commanding Officer. "Of course", he replied. Within an hour, the Adjutant called me on the 'phone and said that the CO would see me there, and then. In a matter of seconds, I was sitting relaxed in front of the Colonel. After telling my story, and explaining the problem as I saw it, I asked for his unofficial advice. Giving a re-assuring smile, he gave it, and added that if I cared to make an official declaration he would forward it with his strong recommendations in my favour. Being a Warrant Officer he also said that the matter would have to go to the War Office. The Colonel's advice made sense. I took it.

Some weeks passed before I was once more called to see the CO. Saying that he had received a reply from the War Office, he picked up a letter, and began to read it to me. Briefly, the contents said that for all military purposes my age would remain as declared at time of enlistment. For all remaining purposes (e.g. legal, civil, etc.) my date of birth would be as shown on the Birth Certificate. The letter concluded with a small paragraph adding that no disciplinary action need be taken against me. I thanked the CO for all that he had done on my behalf; after saluting, I returned to my office. The picture was now quite clear. My recommendations for promotion were good, and so too the qualifications with the exception of age. On that limit, I was powerless. That was the rule, and no one would bend it. There was no evading the fact that recommendations in respect of promotion were for 'Military Purposes'. For as long as I chose to remain in the Army, there would be no question of climbing another rung in that promotion ladder. It all provided me with much food for thought. Whatever conclusions I came to; they did not have to be made known to anyone unless I so desired. Notwithstanding, within a matter of days, I decided on a two fold plan. In the first place, to continue as if nothing had happened, and see through my present engagement to complete twenty five years. Without question it would be in a rut position, but at least it was not a deep one. Life was comfortable – if not physically in those jerry-built barracks – and all in all I was quite happy. Events had stirred in me an urge to get away from Dusseldorf, and that was the remaining part of my plan. By co-incidence, a vacancy arose for a Sgt. Major in our Hamburg Squadron. One more interview with the Commanding Officer, and I was on my way to Hamburg.

Just a few of the Hamburg features were similar to those in Dusseldorf. The Squadron lived, and worked in the same Camp as the District Headquarters; situation in the suburbs at Blankenese which was about four miles from the Town Centre, and on the river Elbe. Unusual for military camps, it was semi-rural, and in a delightful setting with plenty of trees both in, and around the Camp. Any well-to-do stockbroker would have been happy to have owned a home in the locality. Possibly some did.

As in Dusseldorf, we shared in the District WO's and Sgts.' Mess, and very comfortable it was. The food was superb. Our officers too messed in the District HQ Mess and so did the Other Ranks. The Squadron, in theory, was a component of 2 L of C, but in practice we operated almost as an independent unit. Major Murray was the OC and Second In Command was Capt. George Homer.

My predecessor had done a good job, and had bequeathed me a rattling good, and smooth running Squadron. As the accommodation had been built during the Nazi era, it had none of the Dusseldorf headaches. My personal quarters were most comfortable and warm, and the plumbing worked!

The relationship between both officers, and myself got off to a good start, and remained that way. George Homer had a strong personality, and much liked. At any party he was the star attraction. The Major was also a good mixer, and the right type to participate in the social life. Neither were frivolous, but took their work, and position seriously. Quickly a strong rapport grew between the three of us. Being a 'Yes' man was not my line; yet I cannot remember ever being in dispute with their policies, and mode of leadership. The effect of that team work penetrated down to the most junior soldier. Finding myself in a Squadron of this nature, and character was not new to me, but this was a first in as much as, now I was in a position to influence events. If when the day came for me to depart, standards had fallen, then I might well be answerable. I became determined that, at all costs, that did not happen.

In common with my fellow men, the work of the Royal Signals Association was of great interest, and many of us were life members. The Corps monthly magazine 'The Wire' was greatly sought after, and well read. The Benevolent Fund was recognised as worthy of our support. Soon after my arrival, Major Murray asked me to take over as Secretary, and run our Branch of the Association, which was then No. 1 Unit Branch. It was a voluntary, off-duty job, but a rewarding one. In the Winter of 1954/55 we raised, and forwarded to the Fund, some quite large sums of money, particularly having in mind our relatively small numbers.

It was a cold Winter's Saturday afternoon, and I was to play in a game of hockey; my first serious sporting activity for some time. The game had only just got under way, when I noticed that as soon as I started to run, I felt a pain in my chest. To leave the field complaining of feeling unwell was possible, but ran the risk of investigative questions being asked. Anyway, it could not be anything serious. So I thought at the time. Somehow, I put on a brave face, and struggled through the game. A few days later, while walking through the Lines with the OC; he turned to me and said: "Lets have a fire practice, sound the alarm!" On the sound of a fire alarm, everything is done at the double. In that way I went about, with the Major, ensuring that everyone knew what to do. The pain returned. Once more, I stuck it out.

The turn of the year brought a change in command. We lost Major Murray who was replaced by Major John Waller. Immediately, the old, old fear arose 'Here comes another new broom'. That proved to be unfounded as Major Waller did not approach his new command by making clean sweeps. The change sent no more than a ripple through the Squadron. With an artificial leg, he was physically handicapped but he possessed the ability to laugh at himself. He did not permit the disability to master him, but he had mastered the disability. Accompanying the Major was Mrs. Waller. She came to be well known amongst us, and never failed to help with social and sporting events.

The trio of OC, Capt. Homer and myself continued with the same degree of harmony, under Major Waller's command.

Winter frosts became less severe, and daffodils about to bloom. About that Springtime, I realised that my health was below par. Skin problems began to erupt, with swelling and itching on hands, and feet. The time had come when, like it or not, to see the MO. Throughout my service I had considered that the Medial Officers of the RAMC had served me well. That confidence was to be shaken, if not lost. Our MO was a young, National Service doctor, and therefore not greatly experienced. That was no fault of his. After explaining my problems to him, it was obvious that he was unconvinced. He did not say that. He did not need to; he just showed it. It is doubtful if he believed a word I said. Making no mention of chest pains, I spoke only of the skin complaint. As the symptoms arose unpredictably, and mostly at the latter part of the day, I had nothing visible to show him which served to be a weakness in support of my verbal statement. I left that MO with a strong impression that he considered the whole thing was a sham on my part. A week, or two, later I again visited that MO, and retold my story. This time he sent me to see a dermatologist at the Hamburg Military Hospital. No tests were made, and the consultation was short. By now I had concluded that nothing I could say, or do, was going to convince anyone. Admitting defeat, I surrendered. Intentions to see the medical authorities on the matter of chest pains, were now discarded. Such pains were totally invisible, and my ability to convince anyone of them was now so remote as not to be worth further consideration. Perhaps, I thought, it would be wiser to lie low, and as far as possible that my physical condition was not 100%. If, during the remaining period of my service, any MO questioned me then I would answer truthfully. That was below the horizon.

There was no failure on the part of any MO to investigate, and diagnose my chest pains. How could they? At no time had I told an MO of them. That had been my decision, and mine alone, and was rooted in my loss of faith and confidence in the Hamburg Medical Service. This medical anecdote did not end there.

Within weeks of entering Civvy Street, the attacks of pain returned, so I consulted my GP. Without delay, I was sent to see a Consultant Cardiologist at Guy's Hospital, London, who diagnosed

Angina. When open-heart surgery was still in its infancy, in 1978 I underwent a 3-way coronary bye-pass operation at that hospital. A rather traumatic experience, but worthwhile as it was successful. I was given a new lease of life. The lesson learnt was not to allow a misunderstanding with a doctor to ever again prevent me from approaching him/her on other matters. The consequences might be serious, and not always, as in this case, end happily.

With its high proportion of National Servicemen, the Hamburg Squadron was representative of the Royal Corps of Signals in 1955. To maintain the strength of our Armed Forces at that time it was, I am sure necessary, but much of that necessity was due to the inability of Governments in making the Services attractive to young men as a career. The media were beginning to ask questions, and quoted many cases of individuals, and units where under-employment, and mis-employment were rampant. All performed the same duties whether they were National Servicemen or Regulars, but not all were on the same rates of pay. The conscripted man was on a much lower rate. There was no serious attempt on the part of the authorities to make Service life more attractive, and so encourage more Regulars. All too often, what the conscripted men saw of Army life he found deterring. Poor food, poor accommodation, and frequently after being trained as a tradesman was used as cheap labour to carry out menial tasks such as potato peeling, sweeping floors, whitewashing stones, and highly polishing everything within sight. That early post-war youth were worth something better. To their credit, and to the best of my knowledge, they never allowed their discontent to surface, and boil over into anything more serious than grumbling. They earned, and won my respect.

In today's sick society of hooliganism, violence and crime, we often hear the demands: "Put 'em in the Army", "Bring back conscription", "They need Army discipline", "A Sergeant Major would soon sort them out"; and so on. There is no place for those kind of young men in the highly technical Army of today. They are neither wanted, nor needed. Self discipline is. It is not the job a Sergeant Major, or NCO to make good citizens out of the Country's riffraff. Why should it be their job to put right that which schools, and parents have failed to do? Do what you like with lager louts, but please keep them out of the Army. I cannot think of any Corps, or Regiment that would welcome them. Those views are personal, and very strongly held, but I believe shared by many.

Thanks to a good friend, Sgt. Rosenstein of the RAEC I received in Hamburg, my introduction to live opera. A performance in the Opera House of Weber's "Der Freischutz", was being well acclaimed; so that was it. From Rosenstein, I learnt my first lessons on the magic of opera. They proved to be the foundation for many hours of pleasure received by me in the years that followed.

The Summer of 1955 was nothing to write home about. Weather, and commitments permitting, picnics on the Elbe were popular. We hired a boat, with a small local crew and departed about 11am and would return about 5pm. Refreshments, food and drink were loaded aboard, and children joined us. We wore informal civilian clothes, with shorts and sandals being quite acceptable. The river was a busy one, with much shipping, and barge activity. Added to that were some dicey currents, so swimming was ruled out.

Hamburg could make claim to the dubious honour of being one of Germany's most heavily bombed cities. The Great Fire Raid now has its place in the history of bombing in the Second World War. Though not completely obliterated, Hamburg came perilously close to that. Ten years later, there was still visual evidence of the devastation. Building, and reconstruction had commenced, and was progressing at a rapid rate. The survivors of that air raid spoke unhesitantly of their horrendous ordeal. So too, I imagine, did the survivors of Coventry.

Leave entitlement had been good throughout my time in BAOR; and was on the same scale as that for those based in the UK. Leave travel was not then by Air, but by ground and sea. Homeward bound, we travelled on a troop train, by day, to the Hook of Holland, then by night ferry to Harwich. Another troop train, and we arrived in London soon after 9am. There was a bonus of a few additional days travelling time.

On posting to Germany, it was the practice to remain there for four years. My time there was now coming to an end. With twenty two years service behind me, I had just the three years supplementary service ahead. Some of the units had been of the best, it had been the region which I found disagreeable. By the end of the Summer, there was a strong desire for a move to the Middle or Far East. That would be a more apt conclusion. In submitting the application, in the full knowledge that preferential requests usually went unheeded, I nevertheless made them. They included, Aden, Malta, East or West Africa, Singapore, Hong Kong and most places East of Suez. My request was granted, and fate was kind. In early October, I was on my way back to the UK for embarkation leave prior to a posting to Singapore District Signal Regiment.

CHAPTER 21

A draft of about eighty newly trained Signalmen were also bound for the Far East. Again, I found myself responsible for delivering them, trouble free, to their destination. Like myself, they would be disembarking at Singapore.

Like so many November days, it was cold, wet and miserable as we climbed the gangway of HMT *Devonshire*. A guide then led us to a troop-deck which was to be the accommodation for those Signalmen throughout the voyage. The ship had been modernised, and re-furbished. There were built-in tier bunk beds, and adequate ventilation, toilets, and showers. It was a far cry from my own early experience of lower rank facilities, or rather lack of them, in 1936. Our men only took up about half the space available. When pondering on who was to occupy the other half, I was called to the ship's RSM's office. There, the RSM informed me that a party from the 11th Hussars (Prince Albert's own) were on their way to fill that troop-deck gap. He added that for the duration of the voyage, I was to be the Troop-deck Sergeant Major, with responsibility for a total of about one hundred and sixty men. The officer in charge was to be a Royal Signals Captain. The Hussars were better known throughout the Army as 'The Cherry Pickers'. They were immensely proud of their nickname. They are the only Regiment in the British Army who do not wear a cap badge. The explanation lies in their Regimental history, and I leave others to tell it.

Once every man was on board, I checked to see that there was a place for each individual soldier. Calling them together, I gave a brief talk on what life on a troopship was like, and what to expect; then closing by saying that those members of my own Corps need not expect any favours, and that as far as I was concerned we were all in 'The Same Boat' in more senses than one! To the 'Cherry Pickers', I made some comment that they were to regard me as just one more Sgt. Maj., and not concern themselves with my Corps.

Dusk fell, and a couple of tugs towed the ship away from the dockside. Once more, I was outward bound.

On a peacetime troopship, and being a Warrant Officer, I enjoyed the privilege of second class travel. My cabin was shared with another WO from the RAOC. It was cramped, but comfortable. Nineteen years earlier, when travelling as a Signalman on a pre-war trooper, it never occurred to me that the day would come when I would travel in relative comfort, only bettered by commissioned officers.

The ship's officers were British, but we had no contact with them. The remainder of the crew were lascars, including the catering staff. They, particularly, are worthy of mention as they cooked and served superb curries. Possibly, some of the finest I have ever eaten.

It was going to be a long voyage, with an expected duration of approximately thirty three days. The days of conveying troops across the world, by sea, was rapidly phasing out; to be replaced by air travel. This was, I believe, the last performance of HMT *Devonshire* as a troopship; and may even have been the final voyage of any troopship to the Far East.

By the time we left the Bay of Biscay, my daily routine was well established. After breakfast, I went to the troop-deck, and supervised the cleaning, and preparation for the daily rounds of the ship's Captain. Accompanied by the OC Troops, the Captain carried out this inspection meticulously. Woe betide anyone responsible for the microscopic speck of dust, or dirt that was found. The blast was felt from bow to stern. Simultaneously, life boat drill was held on the open deck. It would be almost noon before we were 'Stood Down'. For the remainder of the day, my time was, more or less, my own. About 7.30 pm; after dinner, I often made it my business to make an informal visit to the troop-deck. Those visits proved to me most valuable, and from them I was able to get the 'feel' of the men, and their standards and morale. It was a satisfying way of ending the day, and enabled me to go to bed with ease of mind.

The 'Cherry Pickers' caused no problems. They were well disciplined, and behaved. Very soon, I formed the impression that the 11th Hussars (even without a cap badge) must be a very fine Regiment. Then there was the other half consisting of my own Corps. If I had been permitted to personally select eighty men from a Training Regiment to accompany me, then I could not have chosen better. In the best of troopships, conditions are crowded, and difficult. The more junior the rank, the more difficult, and irksome daily life became. On a long sea voyage, such as this, they feel under constant pressure. Those young signalmen – many of them National Servicemen – were a credit to our Corps. Men from both Regiments blended together as a team. That made my task, not only much easier, but also quite enjoyable. Each morning our Deck Officer was present when preparing for 'Rounds', he would state what he wanted done, and then left me along to do it; my way. I liked that.

Ships, like people, have their own character, and no two have the same. The *Devonshire* was a happy ship. By the time we arrived in the Eastern Mediterranean, and changed into tropical uniform, I was thoroughly enjoying the voyage. If it took a year to reach Singapore, it would not have bothered me. On board there were wives, and children. They all contributed towards the ship's entertainment and social life. Keeping fit on a long voyage is a problem, especially where there is little space for physical activities. We made the effort, but it was a losing battle. A pain in the chest was only sporadic.

After leaving Port Said, came my last view of the Suez Canal. As always, the Red Sea was hot and humid. At Aden we anchored for a few hours, and I managed a short trip ashore. Aden was a cheap place to shop, and the purpose of going ashore was to buy a new camera, which I did. On, across the Indian Ocean to Colombo.

The 'Cherry Pickers', and my own Royal Signals draft were both receiving their baptism of a tropical climate, but they were coping well. A close watch was kept for signs of any health problems. No serious ones arose, but there were minor cases of prickly heat, and dhobi rash. Clean socks, and underwear had great emphasis. Foot powder was issued, and used liberally. The value of salt, and risks of dehydration were always mentioned in health talks. Small matters, but they played a large part in the health education of young men entering tropical climates for the first time. In the First World War, in Iraq, more British troops died of fevers, and tropical diseases than were killed by enemy action! This time, we had been quick to learn the lesson.

As troopship voyages came to their end, it was customary for an award to be made to the best troop-deck over the period. That took the form of the Captain's cake. It was made by the ship's chief chef. On the day before our arrival at Singapore it was announced that the award had been made to our troop-deck. Our Royal Signals, and 'Cherry Pickers' had completely integrated, and worked as one unit, and in so doing had brought home the bacon. What more could I ask?

This last sea voyage on possibly the last troopship to operate, had been a memorable one. Had it been the *Queen Elizabeth*, or any other of the world's great luxury liners, and I a wealthy civilian, it would have lacked one important factor. The military background, which was now so much a part of my life, would have been absent. The materialism of luxurious living, without the compatible company of all the same piece, is worthless.

Throughout my military life, I had met, and known many who served in Singapore. From them, I had gained a fairly accurate picture of the base, so on arrival little was unexpected and there were no shocks. The ship's engines rather lazily came to a halt, and our thirty three day voyage was over. In the same breath, in the still air the sweltering, humid heat was exhausting. Movement was not necessary to bring about sweating. Stand still for just a few moments, and one's uniform began to cling like the damp rag which it quickly became. The sky was cloudless, but not blue. Overhead was an expanse of steel grey space. That was my initiation into the climate of Singapore, and different to any I had previously encountered. A couple of senior NCO's from Singapore District Signal Regiment were at the dockside to meet me. After a few formalities, I was soon on my way to Princess Mary Barracks which was to be my new home. In four days time, it would we Christmas day 1955.

The WO's and Sgts. Mess was not very large. On the ground floor there was a lounge, bar and dining room. Above, were the quarters for single WO's and Sgts. Both floors had a generous veranda surrounding them. My room was comfortable, and adequate. Apart from bed linen, there was just one blanket which was never used, plus the indispensable sand fly net. There was no air conditioning, but a large fan hung from the ceiling. That was rarely switched off.

The first instructions I received were not to concern myself with any duties for the next week, but just to join in the Christmas festivities, and settle in. I did. It rained almost daily, and came down in torrents typical of monsoons. The downpour would last an hour, or two when the monsoon ditches spilled to overflowing. When the rain ceased the steam rose, and rapidly normality was resumed. In our wardrobes (metal), we fitted electric light bulbs. They would emit sufficient heat to counter the humidity, which otherwise could bring about blue mould on polished leather-work and clothing.

The number of Christmas days, which I had spent in tropical climates had, by now, almost equalled those in more moderate climates. To sit down to a Christmas dinner in shorts, and open neck shirt was not new, but rather the 'Mixture as Before'. Peacetime garrison life in a British Colony had returned, but as we all knew not for long. For all formal social events we had to wear tropical mess kit, similar to that worn by our officers. The jackets were of the 'Bumfreezer' pattern, white, and unbuttoned. The trousers were tight, with a broad four inch scarlet stripe down the outside seam of the legs against a midnight blue material. The cloth was all light weight. Around the waist, was a cummerbund. A black bow tie was worn on a white shirt. Miniature medals added a splash of colour. It was one of the smartest uniforms which I ever wore. Though mandatory we were given no allowance towards the cost which came out of our own pockets; and the cost of such a uniform in Singapore was extremely high. On learning that, my enthusiasm was somewhat dampened.

The Unit was rapidly becoming Malayanised; the British element was already reduced to a mere handful of All Ranks. In early January, I took over the role of Squadron Sergeant Major, but with a difference. The work was done most efficiently by a very likeable Malayan WOII named Yahiya. Malayan Signals were working alongside their British counterparts in Royal Signals, who were really preparing them for the day of independence which was now appearing on the horizon. There was an abundance of goodwill on both sides; which augmented the tranquil life.

I liked the Unit, my job, and enjoyed the high standard of living which was part of the package. It was rare to hear criticisms, or grumbles. The local people were fun. They would laugh a lot, and they gave me the impression of being a happy community who enjoyed life. During those first few weeks, I would not envisage anything that might prevent me from spending the remainder of my Army life, happily, here on this Island.

One of the most agreeable pleasures was with friends, or maybe sometimes alone, to spend an evening in the City, and invariably concluding the evening with a Chinese curry. The best, and often the cheapest, were to be found in the 'Out of Bounds' district. On more than one occasion I saw an officer whom I recognised. We both pretended not to see each other. Neither my financial, nor my social status permitted a visit to the world renowned Raffles Hotel.

By chance, one time, I made a hurried visit to Changi, notorious for its gaol. The war time Japanese atrocities committed there have been recorded in many books, but can never be overstated. My thoughts on that day were, and still are, too powerful to be expressed. Some of my old close friends from those far off days on the NW Frontier had been sent to join the Burma campaign. Not all returned. Silence and sickness overtook me. There was little comparison with my relatively comfortable war, and their suffering. Nowhere is an epitaph on a war memorial, in my opinion, more moving than that on the 14th Army one at Kohima:

"When you go home,
Tell them of us, and say
For your tomorrow,
We gave our today."

An undeniable truth.

Chinese culture, and their festivals are subjects upon which I have little knowledge, but when our Malayan Signals invited me to their Chinese New Year Party, without hesitating, I accepted. The only regret was that prior to the event, I did not seek out some instruction in the use of chopsticks. We ate from bowls, which proved impossible to empty. More, and more food appeared. It all tasted good and enjoyable, but much of it was a first time experience. Was it chicken, pork, fish? I could not distinguish as it was all mixed with so many other spicy, and unverifiable ingredients. The drinks were not less plentiful as the food, and no less bewildering. The bottle labels were written in Chinese, but if translated may well have read: "Fire Water". Our hosts knew their job, and entertained well. Each year, now, when I hear of their New Year celebrations in London's China Town, I am reminded of that happy, and wonderful evening in Singapore during early 1956.

By this time, the climate was an element in the way of life. Of the two extremes, I have always leaned in favour of heat in preference to that of cold. Living in a land of flies, mosquitoes and sand flies was no undue hardship. At night, when going to bed, it was of vital importance to ensure that the sand fly net was securely tucked-in around the mattress. In my room I could never be alone. My companions were all from the insect world. The electric light attracted them in their thousands, and not least any uncovered part of my own flesh. Praying Mantis fascinated me, as they sped across the wall looking for a meal, which consisted mostly of sand flies. I owed them a debt of gratitude.

A letter from home brought dramatic, and distressing news. There was just a change – but a rather remote one – that the situation was not so serious as at first appeared. A fortnight later, came further news confirming my worst fears, and added that a relative was about to contact the Soldiers, Sailors and Families Association (SSAFA) in an attempt to have me sent home on compassionate leave. My first duty was to inform my OC and tell him the full story. He was kind, and sympathetic but it was not within his powers to do much from that great distance, and advised me to leave everything in the hands of SSAFA and the home authorities, which I did.

My posting to Singapore District Signal Regiment had got off to a brilliant start, and I was quite contented with the way things were going, and had no desire to return to the UK. Now, I had adverse circumstances creating turbulence in my mind. My anxieties took over command of all thoughts, and dominated my thinking. Loyalty to my Unit, and Corps was being contested by that towards my nearest, and dearest. Giving my job even the minimum of attention was becoming increasingly difficult. This, after only four months in the station. That pain in my chest had returned, but I did not associate it with anything.

A 'phone call from the Adjutant, summoned me to his office. There he passed me a message to read. It was from the War Office, giving authority for me to be sent home forthwith on twenty eight days compassionate leave, priority 'A'. The following hours were taken up with hurried explanations, and farewells. At the following dawn, I was at Singapore Airport boarding a QANTAS Constellation aircraft bound for London.

Through the day, we flew to Calcutta, and then on to Karachi where we stopped for about three hours. We were taken off the 'plane, offered showers, and given an excellent meal at the Airport. At 9pm local time, we took off for Beirut, Lebanon. The night gave me a most hair-raising experience as we flew through heavy monsoon weather. Like a thousand pancakes on Shrove Tuesday, we were tossed up, down, and sideways. The following day was calm, and we touched down at 4 pm at London Airport.

Chapter 22

When returning to duty in mid-May, I reported to 4 Training Regiment, Gaza Lines, Catterick Camp. The Unit's establishment of Warrant Officers was filled. Once more, there was no vacancy for me. As a tentative measure, I was posted to HQ Squadron under the command of Major Tucker.

I had made no application, on compassionate grounds, for a home posting, so the possibility existed of a return to Singapore. The leave did little to lessen my anxieties. The cause persisted, but might well terminate abruptly, and at any moment. With my length of service it was permissible to obtain my discharge by simply giving three months notice. Due to that Army age barrier, there was no prospect of further promotion. By entering civil life my real age, still under forty might prove to be to my advantage. To complete my contract of twenty five years, when I would be forty two, may well be to my disadvantage. Without mentioning any reason, I made a formal application to be discharged. This was not the way I had imagined that my service would terminate, and certainly would not have wished it. Non-military events over the past few months had become too complex. Leaving the Army would not unravel the tangle, but just make life easier to live.

Before the three months expired, the Suez crises came to the boil. All discharges for Regular soldiers were suspended, but those with compassionate grounds may apply for exemption. I did.

On 25th August 1956, I received a telephone call with news, though sad, signified that the bubble had burst. My depression, and worries ceased to exist.

The following day was my last as a Soldier in the Royal Corps of Signals. A career had come to its end. The whistle blew; I left the team, and walked away from the ground, disconsolate. They had been stupendous years. Today, they are my greatest source of happy memories.